A NOVEL

Rainy Days And Sundays

by Brewster Milton Robertson

HARBOR
HOUSE

This is a work of fiction. I have exercised the novelist's prerogative and created landscapes of both Wrightsville Beach and Myrtle Beach which in certain aspects reflect a much earlier era. In the case of Wrightsville Beach, I gave them a lighthouse which of course exists only in this writer's mind. Readers who think they see themselves or someone else in this book are mistaken.

RAINY DAYS AND SUNDAYS
BY BREWSTER MILTON ROBERTSON
A Harbor House Book / May 2000

Copyright 2000 by Brewster Milton Robertson

For information address:
Harbor House
3010 Stratford Drive
Augusta, Georgia 30909
harborbook@aol.com

Jacket Painting by Wendell Minor
Author Photo by Kenton Robertson
Book Design by Lydia Inglett

Library of Congress Cataloging-in-Publication Data

Robertson, Brewster Milton,
    Rainy Days and Sundays : a novel / by Brewster Milton Robertson.
        p. cm.
    ISBN: 1-891799-12-6
    1. Presidents--United States--Fiction. 2. Pro-life movement--Fiction. 3. Abortion--Fiction. I. Title.

PS3568.02479 R3 2000
813'.54--dc21

                                                                00-026801

Printed in the United States of America
10 9 8 7 6 5 4 3 2 1

Dedication

For my parents, Lida Brewster and Harry Milton Robertson
My aunt, Blanche Brewster Pedneau
My sons: Kerry, Kevin, Kenton, and Kelly
And, most especially to the bright new generation:
Latham, Benjamin, Kaila, and Rachel

Acknowledgements

Cheryl Smith Lopanik, who makes me better
than I know how to be.

My cousin, Pat Saunders, the midwife at the
birth of Buchanan Forbes.

Appreciation

Geroge Garrett, Les Standiford, John Miller, Dan Cloud, M.D.,
Alan Brown, Wendell Minor, the Michelangelo of book illustrators,
publishers E. Randall Floyd and Anne Shelander, Lydia Inglett…
my brother James Robertson, the old doc, Dan Zeluff…
and Sherrill, Joyce…and the gang,
you know who you are.

"All men should strive to learn before they die
What they are running from, and to, and why." –James Thurber

"Rainy Days and Mondays
always
get me down." –Bert Bacharach

"Someday the man I used to be
will come along and call on me
and then because I'm just a man
You'll find my feet are made of sand
But 'til that day I'll be your man
and love away
your troubles if I can." –Rod McKuen

Prologue

THWACK!

The sharp clatter roused Buchanan Forbes instantly awake from a fitful, uneasy sleep. In the inky darkness, the distress call letters SOS were blazing fiery red, inches from the tip of his nose.

Save Our Souls! Save Our Ship? Blinking hard, Buchanan struggled to clear his sleep-fogged brain. Magically, the shimmering, ethereal SOS was transformed into the laser-sharp ruby numerals 5:05 on the bedside digital clock radio.

Thwump!

The noise again. Somewhat muted now.

Listening intently, Buchanan lay still, tracking the long-familiar, slowly fading tattoo of dull thuds as the roguish paper boy moved steadily up the hill, tossing the morning paper with an unerring vengeance against every front door in the neighborhood.

Finally, taking great pains not to disturb Alma, he slipped out of bed. Fumbling in the dark, he gathered his cutoff jeans and his *Gamecocks Are Chicken* T-shirt and padded quietly into the hall to the large bathroom. Mistrusting his aim in the dim reflections from the street lamps, he sat on the toilet seat to urinate. After he flushed, still clad only in his bikini briefs, he paused just for an instant in the hallway by the adjoining doors of the two bedrooms of the youngest three of his four sons. Their sleeping faces bathed in lemony moonlight filled his throat with a tight, aching sweetness as he moved silently down the hall.

In the kitchen, Buchanan squinted hard against the ghoulish flare of the florescent night light under the range hood as he wriggled his slender, athletic hips into the cutoffs and shrugged the T-shirt over his crewcut head. He found his SUPERDAD mug, slopped it full of yesterday's coffee, slipped it in the microwave and punched the "zap" button twice. Then, with a practiced hand he dumped yesterday's grounds, replaced the filter and—pausing to sniff the bouquet—measured out fresh coffee. Efficiently, he rinsed the carafe and refilled the well on the Krups coffeemaker. He had just pushed the switch to start the fresh pot brewing when the buzzer on the microwave went off.

Alma's swanky space-age coffeemaker was gurgling flatulently as, steaming SUPERDAD mug firmly in hand, Buchanan gingerly made his way down the half-dozen steps to the slate-paved landing of the high-vaulted split entry foyer. Opening the front door, he deftly retrieved the paper and pulled the door closed behind him. He tiptoed down the remaining six steps to the lower level, and eased by Granger's—his first-born's—bedroom. Taking care to avoid the disaster area of toy cars, building blocks and enough other innocent little-boy death traps to give his insurance underwriter a nervous breakdown, he felt his way across the large family room to the door to his tiny office. Safely inside his hideaway, he shut the door before he turned on the light and sat at his desk.

He risked a cautious sip of the scalding coffee and distractedly unfolded *The News and Observer.*

The jarring headline fairly jumped off the page.

Five Die in Miami, NY, and LA
Abortion Bombings

President Closes Abortion Clinics
Under Force of National Guard

Then, just below the fold of the front page there was a second jarring headline.

Surgeon General Announces Promising
AIDS Breakthrough

Abortion and AIDS. So what else was new? Sales of Virecta, his company's new improved male erection pill, were soaring. Idly, Buchanan blew across the mug to cool the coffee. *Bad news? Good news?* Fleetingly contemplating the nightmare of a sexually unrestricted population of human rabbits suddenly without the recourse of abortion on demand, he shuddered. *Shades of flower children and the carnal sixties!*

He shrugged, took another sip of coffee and put aside the paper. Leaning across, he picked up the badly-rumpled envelope from the keyboard of his laptop. Extracting the wrinkled, dog-eared corporate memo sheet, he reread the unsettling message for perhaps the hundredth time—he hadn't had a good night's sleep since the note arrived three days ago.

Call me at 540/259-9521 from a pay phone at exactly 11:00 Saturday morning. No credit cards. Be sure
and buy at least a 30-minute phone card. This is
~~important~~ very serious.

Findlay Hanks

Findlay, a fellow pharmaceutical salesman from Buchanan's days in Roanoke, Virginia, had run a lucrative but flagrantly illegal moonlighting operation bootlegging high-priced prescription drug samples he bought for pennies on the dollar from the sample closets of private doctors and clinics. Over the past four years since Buchanan had been promoted down here to Raleigh, he hadn't seen or heard from the man.

Recalling his last misadventure with Findlay Hanks, Buchanan had-n't had an easy moment since Hank's cryptic note arrived. Now he nervously checked his watch.

Five long hours until 11:00.

He retrieved the paper and turned to the sports. For the moment at least, a cure for AIDS and medically safe abortion were the farthest things from Buchanan Forbes' mind.

@

WHEN SHE SAW THE FRONT PAGE OF *The Palm Beach Post,* Zoni Corbett caught her breath.

Abortion Bombings in Miami, NY, and LA Kill Five

Abortion Pill Outlawed as White House Closes Abortion Clinics

Panic-stricken, Zoni picked up the TV remote, punched up CNN, and focused her attention to the screen. Across the bottom of the screen, the familiar graphic CNN...BREAKING NEWS pulsed in red.

Switching to a panoramic view of the floor of the U.S. Senate with a superimposed split-screen showing a reporter outside the entrance to the main chamber, the camera pulled back to reveal a dignified silver-haired man standing with the reporter ready for the interview.

"This is Daryl Lopanik for CNN," the reporter began. "It's been twenty-nine years and one month and one day since January 22, 1973, the historic date when the Supreme Court opened up the right to abortion with *Roe vs. Wade.* Dating back to a clinic bombing death of a Tampa physician in the late nineties, over the past several years a radical faction of pro-life terrorists has become increasingly combative in its actions. Yesterday's bombings of abortion clinics in Miami, New York and LA resulted in the deaths of five. The twelfth bombing since New Year's…the fifth in less than a week. This raises the death toll since he took office to thirty-one, forcing pro-life President Aaron Claiborne Powers to live up to his promise to take protective action. In a drastic move last night, President Powers ordered Federal marshals to temporarily shut down all of the nation's licensed abortion facilities, including private practitioners and hospitals. From Maine to Alaska, Hawaii and Puerto Rico, the Justice Department and the Pentagon responded with lightning speed…"

The screen switched to a rapid montage of National Guard troops stationed in front of abortion clinics and hospitals across the nation before the reporter came back live.

"With us today is Charles Fearington Graham, the senior senator from North Carolina. Senator Graham is chairman of the committee that has been in an all-night emergency session to consider the White House's decision. Senator Graham, you're openly critical of the administration. Is President Powers using this as an excuse? The first step in overthrowing the right to abortion?"

As the camera came in tight on the regal, self-assured senator, Zoni pushed the mute button and turned off the sound.

"Oh, please, God…" she whispered under her breath as she anxiously dialed the phone.

The clock showed 7:05 A.M.

"Hello?" Her party picked up before the second ring. The woman's voice sounded guarded, but wide awake.

"Mary? This is me, Zoni, Zoni Corbett. Did you see the morning paper? Or TV?…"

"Yeah, Zoni, I wanted to warn you, but I was afraid they'd tapped this phone…"

"But, Mary, you're in private practice. You can still 'do' me today, can't you?"

"Sorry, babe. You should see out my window. Federal marshals are skulking behind every freaking fireplug and lamppost. Would you believe at midnight Feds were taking an inventory of my abortion pills? Left me a receipt. Everybody's scared shitless. All bets are off. Gotta go."

[12]

"Oh God, Mary, NO!"

"Sorry, shoog. I'm heading out. First bombers, now Feds. It's not healthy around here."

"But Mary, my husband will be stateside in a few days. I can't wait. If he finds out I'm pregnant…oh, God, what'll I do?"

"Maybe this will blow over. Give me a few days. Maybe I'll get back to you…"

The line went dead.

Zoni redialed.

No answer.

Fighting to clear her head, Zoni pushed disconnect and dialed another number.

"Oh, Maggie, thank God."

The party on the other end listened quietly as Zoni started in, sobbing out her tale of woe.

As she finished, Zoni wailed, "God, Maggie, what'll I do?"

"Well, you know I'm moving back to North Carolina tomorrow. It's been awhile, but I might have the number of a doc who used to moonlight in a clinic near Wrightsville Beach."

"Oh, Maggie, could you? Please? My daddy's old beach cottage is just south of there, near Southport. It's empty this time of year."

"You told me, Zoni, remember? Calm down and hold on a sec." Zoni could hear Maggie rattling paper. "OK…here's a name and number…get a pencil…take it down…"

Zoni grabbed a pencil and read back the numbers as she copied them down. "Oh, Maggie, thank you…"

"Just pray it works. No guarantees, you understand? And Zoni, no way can you mention my name."

Part 1
Alma

Chapter One

LEAN AND ATHLETIC in faded jeans and a frayed GO TARHEELS sweatshirt, Buchanan Forbes looked more like a well-scrubbed captain of the America's Cup sailing yacht than the serious-minded devoted father and undisputed skateboard champ of his highly respectable Northmoor neighborhood. Now, squatting on the sidewalk, he dipped a paper napkin in a cup of water and did his best to scrub the thick smudges of chocolate ice cream from four-year-old Garrett's face.

Across the way an electronic bank sign scrolled: 10:56 A.M....SAT...FEB...23...2002....

Finally, Buchanan gave up and tucked a fresh napkin under his youngest son's chin. Under the table, a fat mongrel puppy licked drippings from his four sons' ice cream cones. Contemplating the seriousness of fatherhood, Buchanan struggled to hide his amusement.

"Can we take him home, Dad?" little Garrett begged.

"Don't start that. You know we can't, Garrett." He stood erect and wiped his hands.

"Is Mom ever gonna let us get a dog, Dad?" Garrett's saucer eyes pleaded up at him.

"Well, your mother has her hands full taking care of you guys, son, and I'm gone a lot." Resolutely, he always stood up for Alma, but sometimes his heart wasn't in it. "Now, you guys just sit here and finish your ice cream. I've got to use the phone before the movie starts...OK?"

They all nodded solemnly as—not so innocently—Garrett dripped more ice cream for the pup.

Still scrubbing his own hands, he took three deep breaths and looked casually around the large Cameron Village Shopping Center, trying to calm the vague uneasiness in his stomach. Slightly apart from the department stores, arty boutiques, ethnic restaurants and supermarkets, across the street, a scraggly line of kids—a few with parents—was beginning to form in front of the movie house. The marquee advertised the regular Saturday kid's double feature: SPACE DOGS ON MARS and GODZILLA, a 1998 rerun.

Buchanan's smile slowly faded as he walked across to the empty phone booth. All morning, he had felt like a spy in some spooky old Hitchcock film. Driving away from home with a car full of giggling little boys, he'd struggled sheepishly to reconcile this unsettling, overly-melodramatic sense of secrecy with the smug seclusion of his upscale Northmoor neighborhood.

Now, extracting the wrinkled envelope from his pants pocket, he anxiously reread the note, reconfirming the time Hanks specified. Carefully folding the sheet of stationery so he could read the phone number, he saw the ominous wording of the final sentence. It gave him just the beginning of a stomach cramp.

```
...This is important very serious.
                              Findlay Hanks
```

It was precisely 10:58 when Buchanan reluctantly moved into the old-fashioned booth. The faint stink of last week's vomit wrinkled his nostrils and he frowned disgustedly at a dried yellowing condom stuck on the floor of the badly littered cubicle before he brushed an accumulation of dirt and dead insects off the seat and wrestled the squeaky folding door closed. Methodically, he took out the thirty-minute phone card. As an extra precaution, he nervously stacked a handful of quarters, dimes and nickels into neat rows on the metal shelf beneath the phone.

Holding the note so he could read the number, he mustered a heroic effort to control his shaky fingers as he punched in the numbers and followed the recorded instruction to insert the card.

"Buck?" Hanks answered on the first ring.

"Findlay? What the hell's going on?"

"A small problem, man...FDA raided my main outlet in Richmond. Would you believe they estimate fifty or sixty million?"

Buchanan gasped. For a number of years Hanks had lived high on the hog bootlegging competitors' drug samples he picked up for pennies on the dollar from doctors' sample closets.

"Shit, Findlay! Did any of it come back to you?" Buchanan's heart sank. He really liked Findlay. The old pirate had had more than a few close calls in the past.

"Oh, shit, all right!" Findlay's laugh had a hollow ring. "You might know. The bastards nailed me walking right in the front door. My dick's really in the ringer now."

"What if Vitamerica finds out? Think they'll make a stink?" Findlay had been a top rep for the reputable old line Philadelphia Vitamerica pharmaceutical company for over fifteen years.

"Be serious. I'm history, man. Fucking Food and Drug made damn sure of that. My so-called asshole buddies at Vita-A flew down from Philly with the FDA and graciously accepted my resignation."

"Jeez...I'm really sorry, Findlay. So? What can I do?" He hoped Hanks wasn't looking to ask for money. With a PC wife and four young sons, he was always short on cash.

"Oh, this call isn't about me, Buck. I just wanted to warn you. You best cover your ass."

"Me? You're kidding, right?" Buchanan felt a sudden tightening in his gut as his thoughts flashed back. Four years ago, in a moment of weakness, he had given Findlay some Lhamda-Alpine samples to convert into quick cash. "Aw, come on, Findlay! Christ, that's ancient history."

"Ancient history or not, Buck, Feds found a Lhamda-A carton with your shipping label..."

"Bullshit! You know that carton didn't come from me." Buchanan caught his breath, fighting back his panic. "What did you tell 'em, man?"

"Hold on, now. Don't go blaming me. I swear, Buck, I didn't breathe a word. But Food and Drug squeezed me pretty good. Worse than that...frigging IRS got my bank records...came across that old check for thirty-five grand made out to you, April, 1998. But don't sweat it, man. I stuck to our little story about when you were promoted to Raleigh, Louise wanted to buy your house here in Roanoke but our loan fell through. Swear to God, Buck, they got nothing on you there." Findlay sounded sincere enough.

IRS? Buchanan swallowed hard. Those three little initials had a chilling ring.

"Judas, Findlay, you didn't mention the IRS. Are we talking litigation...a...l-legal problem?" He couldn't bring himself to say the word "criminal."

"I don't think so. Not really. All Food and Drug wanted was to close my operation down."

"Yeah, but what about Internal Revenue?" Buchanan held his breath, afraid to hear the answer.

"I doubt it. I gave IRS over a hundred names of very upstanding docs and druggists. One former vice-president of the AMA, not to mention a prominent member of the state board of pharmacy. When they saw that, they backed off. It's too political."

Made sense.

Maybe. You could never really trust the goddamn Infernal Revenue. Even with all the congressional heat the IRS took back in 1998, it was always a mistake to trust any branch of the frigging Feds.

"I still don't understand about that carton with my label. Something stinks..."

"Oh, something stinks, all right. Of all people, we both know that carton didn't come from you. When I handled that stuff of yours back in ninety-eight, your paranoia almost drove me nuts. Remember how you went to the supermarket for all those Great Northern toilet paper and Kotex shipping cartons to repack your stuff? Hurt my feelings. You knew damn well I always checked everything twice. Never once left anything incriminating."

"OK, OK." Cringing at the word 'incriminating,' Buchanan struggled to make sense out of what Findlay was saying. "So, you think the FDA will take this to Lhamda-A?"

"That's what I'm trying to tell you, man. The Feds already had me talk to your corporate people Monday. Your buddies really pumped me hard, but that shipping label and my check is all they got. If you stand up for yourself, good chance you might keep your job."

"Yeah, right. You don't know Lhamda-A. My ass is probably dead meat already."

"Well, maybe not. Look on the bright side; it's been a week."

"Judas priest, Findlay, how can I tell Alma? I'll never hear the end of this..." Looking at his sons playing with the pup, Buchanan's knees went weak as the chilling consequences hit him.

"Alma? What do you mean? She's got no bitch coming. The entire deal was her idea in the first place. Remember the Medical Society Valentine's Day dance at Hotel Roanoke?"

Remember?

How could he forget?

Watching his kids, his heart sank as he listened numbly while Findlay's voice droned on, pulling up the memory of that awful evening.

At the Medical Society dance, they had been celebrating his promotion and transfer to Raleigh. He and Alma had just gotten back from house hunting in Raleigh and Chapel Hill.

"I've found the greatest house. Perfect for the boys...still under construction... the contractor can add Buck an office..." Alma kept drinking Merlot like it was cherry Kool-Aid and chattering on about choosing kitchen and bathroom fixtures and wallpaper...and how the house was only walking distance from shopping and the snobby St. Timothy's Episcopal School.

Finding that house had been Alma's first real show of enthusiasm for leaving Virginia.

The main problem had been that Joe Acton had reneged on his promise that Lhamda-A would buy out the equity on their house in Roanoke, which would have given them the necessary cash for a down payment. A question had been raised by some jerk at Corporate in New Jersey that Buchanan's new duties as research liaison didn't officially qualify him as management. Secretly, Buchanan knew Acton could have stood up for him if he had really wanted to. The SOB was too invested in kissing Harvey Kearn's ass to care that Lhamda-

A had left him with the house in Roanoke to sell and no cash to bind the $200,000 contract on a new one in Raleigh.

At the dance, Findlay's wife, Louise, had had a few too many herself and told Alma, "Don't sweat it honey...forget Joe Acton. More ways than one to skin a cat. Buck can just slip Findlay a few sample cartons of that new high-priced instant hard-on pill he peddles...Findlay will get you the hard cash in a New York minute."

Buchanan tried to ignore it all but Alma was obnoxious. She kept getting louder and louder about how the doctors all sold or traded their samples. Finally she'd almost screamed, "Even Joe Acton does it. For a Mensa candidate, Buck Forbes, you're such a simple shit."

So, he'd given in. The miraculous new Virecta 25 mg. was $20 a pill— $1000 for a bottle of fifty wholesale. At fifty cents on the dollar on the black market, a mere seventy bottles had netted him $35,000 cash.

"Alma really got on your case that night, remember?" Findlay's voice brought him back to the moment.

He remembered right enough.

Those memories were popping inside his skull like a string of fire-crackers.

For four years the goddamn guilt haunted him every time he drove home through that yuppie neighborhood and walked into Alma's dream house.

But, truth was, not Alma...nor anyone else, had held a knife to his throat.

"So, what did you tell the Feds about the check?" Buchanan tried to clear his head.

"Told 'em when our deal to buy your house fell through, you gave us back our 35K with a check on a bank in Raleigh. Look, we've been through this. You still got that check?"

"Oh, yeah." Buchanan silently thanked his middle-class-Baptist father for saddling him with a terminal case of pack-rat paranoia, giving him the wisdom to keep a safety deposit box.

"Good. So, just dummy up...let 'em take their best shot. If the Feds do try to come at you, stick to our little story about the check and deny everything. My guess is that now the FDA is out of it, you may never hear from the Feds. Still, watch out. You can bet somebody in Washington's got their eye on you."

"Findlay, there's just no frigging way they could've gotten a carton with my label. I hope they do come at me. I'm clean. I think they faked the whole thing." He couldn't let his anger go.

"Buck, don't you get it?"

"Huh? Get what?"

"You're making this tough for me, pal. Jeezus, man, you can't let on any of this came from me. If IRS knew I was telling you this, they'd audit my ass for the next hundred years."

"C'mon, Findlay, what's going on? Tell me plain. I'd never give you away."

Across the sidewalk, Garrett was letting the pup lick his cone. Buchanan picked up a quarter and rapped sharply on the phone booth glass to get his attention.

"Do I have to draw you a fucking picture? Alma was dead right about Acton. Joe's been dumping truckloads of Lhamda-Alpine samples in Richmond for years—probably other outlets, too. I told you that a long time ago. Acton set you up to take the heat off him."

"What?" It was all coming too fast. As research coordinator for the medical schools at Duke, Chapel Hill, and Winston-Salem, Buchanan received huge quantities of samples for large clinical studies. Generally, he was supplied with regular trade packages of fifty or one hundred tablets or capsules. Most of the follow-up phases of formal clinical trials in the large outpatient clinics were in the hands of residents and interns. It was really just a thinly disguised method of getting all these soon-to-be doctors used to prescribing his company's drugs. Compared to the volumes of samples he got, the regular field reps, with their stingy little promotional packages of two or four pills, didn't handle a lot of samples at all—and they were strictly accountable. His own accountability factor was a joke. Joe Acton was forever begging extra samples from him to *"...help out the other reps..."* Several years back, Joe's wife Greta had had too much wine and confided to Alma that Joe routinely used samples to run a regular charge account at their local supermarket pharmacy.

But, then, what the hell? So did half the reps he knew.

But that was nickel-and-dime stuff, not wholesale lots...

He knocked louder on the window and shook his head "no" at Garrett.

"I know you told me." Buchanan conceded grudgingly. "It's still unbelievable."

"Listen to me. Not just believable, Buck...it's a goddamn fact."

"You think Joe planted that carton with my label on purpose?"

The pup had Garrett's cone in his mouth. Garrett shrugged, grinning an impish grin.

"Figure it out. Stanley Herbert, the FDA guy, was Joe's classmate at Maryland School of Pharmacy."

"That bastard! Do you have any idea how much I have on Joe Acton, him and his boozy girlfriends? I'll hang him good. I'll hand his ass to Harvey Kearns at Corporate in Teaneck."

"Won't work, Buck. Kearns was with Acton and Herbert at College Park. Herbert pitched in and helped his frat buddies throw you to the Feds to keep themselves clear with Lhamda-Alpine."

"Is this some kind of a sick joke?" Buchanan's heart sank. Now that he thought about it, he did remember that Acton and Kearns had been classmates at Maryland.

"Acton and Kearns have already been officially deposed by their sticky-fingered old FDA school chum. By the way, Kearns' wife drives a Mercedes and they take vacations at Herbert's condo on Hilton Head. That's no goddamn joke..."

"Well, screw 'em. I'll call Acton and have it out. That rectal orifice's not going to get away with it. I got my sons to think about. I'll fix the Baptist preacher's boy's ass. I'll have his job. When I tell Greta, she'll have the fat bastard's balls..."

"Cool it, man. You can't win. Just sit tight. Trust me, Buck, Food and Drug's really got nothing concrete. Certainly not from me. Why go begging for trouble? Play dumb, man. Feds'll probably let the whole thing drop. Lhamda-A may just decide to look the other way."

Buchanan fell silent. His head was fuzzy and his heart was coming right out of his throat.

"OK, thanks for the warning, Findlay. I'll stay in touch."

"No, absolutely *no* calls, Buck. Lay low. Watch your step. I'll get back to you in a few days to find out what happens. And for God's sake don't tell anybody about this conversation. *No-fucking-body*. Least of all Alma. Remember, no calls. I'm serious. I'll be in touch." The line went dead.

Numbly, Buchanan removed his phone card and picked up the stacked coins.

The frigging IRS! Christ! He gave the parking lot a furtive look.

Nothing...at least nothing he could see.

He thought of Alma and the enormity of it all blew over him like an icy wind.

With four young sons and a wife who loved fancy schools and clothes from the Gap and preppy neighborhoods...his savings in Lhamda-A's credit union were under ten grand.

What would happen if he had to miss a single paycheck? If he lost his job, he was up the well-known creek.

No medical insurance.

No company car.

All he had to show for the thirty-five years of his still-young life was Alma's four-year-old Chevy Tahoe and the pitiful equity he had in that fancy house.

Should he go straight home and tell Alma he was putting the house on the market?

Screw that!

Not yet, anyway.

Findlay was right. Alma certainly couldn't be counted on for loyalty, or anything else.

Certainly not sanity.

Involving her now would be begging for disaster.

Besides, things hadn't been good in the marriage for several years.

After Garrett's birth, her desire for intimacy had lapsed into the motions of ritual duty.

"You expect me to be romantic? You're just like my father. You leave me here all week cleaning up after your little rug rats while you're out wining and dining some stuffy doctor or research fellow in a fancy restaurant. Don't expect candlelight, wine and music from me."

Desperately, he had gone to great lengths to offer her romantic get-aways. But no matter how hard he tried, he never seemed to please her.

"Since you got so holy about trading a few lousy samples, we can't afford such foolishness," she'd nagged and pouted.

What was the use? He'd accepted his fate. Still, he could be thankful that she had remained a caring mother for their sons. That made up for damn near everything.

Wistfully, he watched a slender, long-legged young woman about Alma's age, wearing a thin cotton shirtwaist frock as she bounced happily along window-shopping. With this new breakthrough in AIDS control, in his hedonistic world of medical academia, he had almost daily chances to stray. No matter. Glancing fondly at his sons waiting for him to take them to the movies, he took great comfort that he'd never betrayed his boys that way.

With a wayward pang of sadness, his attention wandered across the parking lot to a raggedy-looking black man about his own age with a young boy wearing tattered hand-me-down jeans two sizes too big for him. The father and son were painstakingly sifting through the busy shopping center's overflowing trash receptacles, scavenging for soft drink bottles and cans, which they were loading into a rusted-out old pickup truck.

The poor devil had obviously fallen on hard times. Still reeling with shock over Findlay's call, all at once Buchanan was overcome with a great sense of failure.

Thoughtfully, he watched the man and his son. No father should ever have to feel such pain.

Buchanan looked at his own sons. Could it be that because of Acton and Kearns, his boys would have to suffer that kind of humiliation?

The sudden overwhelming sense of betrayal soured in his gut like the aftermath of a frozen Mexican dinner. With a burst of rage, he kicked at the balky door of the foul-smelling booth as the full consequence of Acton and Kearns' cold-blooded treachery descended over him. This was more than merely his job at stake.

More than likely the arrogant bastards had rendered him totally unemployable!

Those back-stabbing bastards had coldly conspired to destroy his credibility as a man.

Who did those twin blobs of dog shit think they were, to rob his sons of their birthright?

Didn't they know that Buchanan Forbes wasn't about to take this lying down?

On sudden impulse, he strode purposefully across the parking lot until he got within hailing distance of the man and the boy.

"Hey, man, I been looking all over for you. I want to pay you back the loan." Buchanan greeted him warmly and walked over and clasped his shoulder.

"Huh?" The man stood openmouthed as Buchanan put two crisp $20 bills in his palm.

"Son..." —Buchanan patted the small boy on his frayed Braves baseball cap and stuck a dollar bill in his hand— "...you'll never know what a good man your daddy really is."

"Oh, I can't take this, sir. You got me mixed up with..." The man stood flabbergasted.

"Just take it...pass it on someday." Buchanan smiled. Without another word, he turned and retraced his steps.

"God bless you, sir." The man's protest of gratitude followed Buchanan across the parking lot.

"C'mon guys, Godzilla's waiting..." For the moment, there were important things at hand. The biggest kid in the neighborhood, Lieutenant Buchanan Forbes, had promised his troops he would take them to the picture show.

Walking with his sons to the movie house, Buchanan's mind raced ahead.

He had survived a nightmare of bloody hell in the Persian Gulf. Those chicken-shit bastards Joe Acton and Harvey Kearns were about to find out they'd fucked with the wrong man.

Ex-Silver Star hero Lieutenant Buchanan Forbes had the beginnings of a plan.

Chapter Two

IN A RUNDOWN MOTEL ROOM on U.S. 17 a few miles north of Wilmington at the edge of a dispirited little village called Hampstead—a wide place in the highway distinguished only by a faded sign: HOME OF THE VENUS FLYTRAP—Zoni Corbett sat on the edge of the sagging bed, idly thumbing the pages of *Seventeen* and nervously eyed her watch.

Outside on the highway, the whooshing sound of an occasional passing car or truck broke the silence of the late night.

"*...In Washington, President Powers proclaimed, 'A return to Godliness' in defense of reports the National Guard fired into marchers protesting the closing of a Tampa abortion clinic. Rumors are rampant that with the four new justices on the court, the Christian Coalition White House is considering avenues to do away with state-run lotteries and legalized gambling in general. Tomorrow's forecast for the beaches indicates a chance of rain...*"

The picture on the tired old TV was pulled in from the bottom and top. The announcer's head looked squeezed up, like one of those alien sci-fi movies on the cable channel.

Zoni changed to TCM channel before she moved to the window and peeked anxiously through the blinds. After a moment she turned, sighed and went into the bathroom without closing the door. When she'd wiped and flushed, the late show was coming on.

"*Do not forsake me, o' my darlin'...*" Tex Ritter's twangy voice drifted into the room as the wavy title and credit scroll of the old black-and-white Gary Cooper classic *High Noon* ran a jagged course across the messed-up television set.

Before she could sit back down, there was a light rapping at the door.

"W-who is it?" Her voice cracked a little. Still clutching the magazine, she tiptoed to the door.

"Corbett in there?"

"Doctor Smith?"

"Who the hell you think? Open up, I'm not going to stand out here all night. "

She took the security chain off as a man in a raincoat stepped quickly inside, closed the door, and refastened the chain. He was carrying a worn black doctor's satchel and a heavy green plastic garbage bag tightly wrapped around something bulky.

The man put both bags on the chair and shed his raincoat, revealing a much-laundered white clinic coat underneath. "Where's the cash?"

"I have it," she said nervously.

"Well?" The man picked up the doctor's bag and stood waiting.

"Well? Do you have some I.D? How do I know you're Dr. Smith?" She flared back at him.

"I'm not in the Yellow Pages. Now give me the money and let's get this over with."

Zoni tried to stare him down, but after a moment she slumped a bit in the shoulders and looked away. Finally, she sighed, went to the bed and opened her purse and extracted a large fold of bills.

"A thousand? Fifty twenties, right?"

"Right."

The man watched carefully as she counted.

Impatiently, he took the money without counting it again.

When he'd stuffed the bulky wad of bills in the pocket of his khaki wash pants, he opened the plastic garbage bag and took out a package of two discount-brand bed sheets and unfolded one halfway and placed it across the middle of the bed.

"Take off your panties and lie down across the bed this way."

He showed her how he wanted her to be.

"I'll only be a minute." He took his bag and went in the bathroom and started washing his hands. When he returned he opened a package and began donning surgical gloves.

"Will this hurt much? I'm a sissy. Really." She tried to laugh and couldn't.

Lying on the bed with her dress gathered up below her breasts, the cheap flowered frock only heightened her sense of innocence.

"Did you take the Valium?"

"An hour ago...and I had a little drink. I probably shouldn't have, but the woman, Jaynie, said..." Her voice trailed off without finishing the thought. Cruelly exposed to him, she was trembling now.

The man's voice softened a bit as he took a closer look. "How old are you? I mean, really?"

She hesitated. "Eighteen...in two months..." Her voice trailed off again.

"It's OK...I won't hurt much...maybe not at all." He took a headband with a light attached out of his bag and adjusted it on his forehead. Testing the light on the palm of his hand, he grunted mild approval when he had it focused to suit him. Then he removed a small package and began opening it as he instructed her quietly, "Feet on the edge of the bed...there now...knees wide apart..."

Fascinated, she watched his hands. She couldn't bear to look him in the eye.

Methodically, he placed a series of items on the bedside table within easy reach then unwrapped an instrument and held it up for her to see.

"Ever seen one of these?"

"Oh? Oh, yes...my doctor uses one when he takes my PAP smear."

"It's called a speculum. I'll be using it to widen the vaginal canal so I can see what I'm doing. It's stainless steel so it's going to feel a bit cold."

All the time he was talking he was busy. Zoni flinched as she first felt the cold instrument touch her down there, but he had an easy touch and she hardly felt the intrusion as he gently worked the instrument inside her.

"Ah...just a little...a little wider...there now..."

She felt the pressure increase but there was no real pain.

"Cervix's clean as a pin...a bit vascular...how long since your last period?"

"Two months, give or take a...oh...wow!" She flinched. "...a week...or two."

"Uhmmm...now, I'm going to insert a squiggly little plastic thing inside your uterus. It's called an IUD...that stands for intrauterine device...you've probably read about 'em..." She could smell his cologne and feel his breath on the inside of her thighs. "Doctors been using them since the sixties. It's really supposed to be a contraceptive...I mean to prevent pregnancy...you know...instead of a diaphragm? Or the pill... The way it really works is that it prevents the fertilized egg from implanting on the wall of the uterus and the uterus expels it, same as in the normal menstrual cycle."

His voice droned in a low, uninterrupted monotone as he worked. "Not many people realize...no one writes about it...the Planned Parenthood people are afraid of the Catholics and adverse publicity...but if it's inserted into an already pregnant uterus, all hell breaks loose...it causes a spontaneous abortion. The truth is that it's just a modern-day version of the oldest abortion trick known to man, a foreign body in the uterus. I understand that way back before abortion was legalized, a lot of abortionists used to use a urinary catheter...a Foley..."

He looked up and wiped his brow with the back of his sleeve before he went back to work. "Anyway these IUDs are much simpler. OK, easy now. Just hold still. Of course, you shouldn't use either one after the first trimester; after three months is risky. In a few days you're going to get the cramps just like your normal period, maybe a trifle more severe, maybe not, but you'll come around. There's a chance that you may expel this device as part of your period, so don't use a tampon…most likely though…"

"OH…WOW! You're hurting. OOOH, AH!" She gasped and raised her hips, gripping the sheets with her hands.

"Be still! I'm sorry. Hold on! OK? Don't move…easy does it, now…There! Better?"

"Oh…oh yeah. Whew. Are you…"

"Just a little longer. Now…after you've had your period most likely this little gadget will remain in place. Then you'll have your own built-in birth control. Wait maybe a month then go to your doctor and have a checkup after your next period. There! That didn't hurt much, did it?"

"Huh? Are you? I mean, you're not done, are you?"

"Yep. All done. See?" He held up a long thin plastic cylinder that looked something like the insertion tube for a menstrual tampon. "Neat, huh?"

Carefully wiping the speculum with a handful of tissues, he began replacing his things in the bag he'd brought along.

"Here, get dressed." He reached across and handed her panties to her from off the chair.

She sat up and slipped on the tiny undergarment. Then she wriggled side-to-side to help him remove the extra sheet he'd placed beneath her. She folded it and held it out to him.

"If your doctor asks where you got the IUD, just tell him you went to Duke, maybe, or anywhere out of town. Now that they've closed down all the legal abortion clinics, all hell is going to break loose. But it won't be long before some of the more enterprising doctors around here are going to be doing the same thing I am. This is the latest hi-tech version of the IUD, brand new. Around medical circles, they call it the T3…made by Graham/unLimited Technologies up in Richmond. The local medical community is a little slow. If you run into a problem, Richmond might be the right place to say you got it." He reached across and took the folded sheet from her and wrapped the speculum in it.

"If these IUDs are legal, I mean, why then…"

"Oh…no, no, no. Legal to use in the non-pregnant patient… as a prophylactic device. If there's any suspicion that the patient's pregnant then no doctor would touch it. The president closed all the clinics. Abortion is against the law now. Why do you think I'm doing this under these circumstances?"

"Oh, well, what you said confused me…"

"It is complicated. I guess I shouldn't have run off my mouth so much…"

"Oh…no, I understand now, I really do. It's clever, sort of. Are you the only doctor who knows this trick?"

"No, not really. But the only one I know who's seen the opportunity to take advantage…"

He examined the little tube under the light and held it out for her to see. It had a trace of blood on the end.

"Did you bring a sanitary pad?"

"Uh-huh." She nodded. Wide-eyed, she gasped, "Is it starting already?"

"No, not really, but you're going to spot some blood, maybe quite a bit. We just violated the barrier of a very pregnant uterus…rammed a weird-looking piece of plastic right in the middle of the whole thing. You can't imagine what a complex little network of blood vessels has been building up in there for the past two months. Now it's going to all come crashing down. I'd put on a pad right now. But the big event won't be tonight."

The man in the clinic coat turned and placed the crumpled cellophane of the IUD wrapper and the package for the gloves in the plastic garbage bag. Then he looked around carefully to make sure he wasn't leaving anything.

"When then? Did you say two or three days?"

"Maybe longer, but it could be tomorrow. Don't worry. If it goes longer, then go to your doctor and complain of cramps or spotting, anything. Tell him you have an IUD and ask him to remove it. If all else fails, that'll do the trick."

"Oh, God. Do you think I'll have to…"

"No, quit worrying. So far I've never had a failure, slick as a whistle. This is the twenty-first century, no more rusty coat hangers. Give a cheer for modern medicine."

He'd finished packing now.

"Empirin with Codeine…these will help, just in case the cramps are severe." Reaching in the pocket of his clinic coat, he handed her a little sample package of pills.

She noticed now that underneath his clinic coat the cuff of his shirt was frayed but it bore a fancy monogram.

There was an "E" and something else…an "I" or "L"…but not an "S."
Well, so much for Dr. Smith.

"This isn't the end of the world. I can't help but point out that you have your whole life ahead of you." He touched her hand.

She cringed at the idea of a young doctor who did abortions in cheap motels passing out fatherly advice.

"Is this all?"

"Yep. All done." He retrieved his raincoat and moved to the door.

"How will I get in touch…"

"You don't. I've done my job. Don't worry."

"Well, ah, thanks," she murmured. *I think!* The afterthought remained unspoken.

"Well, good luck." He opened the door and was gone.

"…*In Washington, President Powers proclaimed, 'A Return to Godliness' in defense of reports the National Guard fired into marchers protesting the closing of a Tampa abortion clinic. Rumors are rampant that with the four new justices on the court, the Christian Coalition White House is considering avenues to do away with state-run lotteries and legalized gambling in general. Tomorrow's forecast for the beaches indicates a chance of rain. Now back to the movie…*"

The picture was still messed up and the TV announcer was in a rut.

In the bathroom, when she pulled down her panties there was already a tiny spot of blood. She quickly put on her sanitary pad.

Straightening her dress, Zoni noticed she hadn't even taken off her shoes.

She gathered up the magazine, put the liquor bottle and the discarded IUD tube in her oversize canvas bag. In the bottom of the bag she located her car keys.

Good luck? Was that all?

Twin tears slid slowly down her cheeks.

She glanced at her watch. Only twenty minutes had elapsed.

If she hurried she'd make it back to Caswell Beach before it started to rain.

Chapter Three

BUCHANAN FORBES FINISHED STACKING the last of the boxes in the muted shadows of the rented mini-warehouse and took a final look. The storage cubicle was nearly overflowing with large brown shipping cartons emblazoned with Scott toilet tissue, Kleenex, Kotex and Bounty paper towel logos. Over the past week it had taken him a half-dozen pre-dawn trips in Alma's Tahoe wagon to complete the transfer. All identifying Lhamda-Alpine Pharmaceutical labels had been carefully removed. Behind him the radio droned through the car's open door. "*Good morning. It's Monday, March Four. Current temperature at RDU is forty-two degrees with the promise of clear skies. In Washington, Congress is at an impasse regarding legislative avenues to overturn the President's preemptory move to set aside* Roe vs. Wade. *While reports of violent outbreaks at abortion clinics across the country continue…"*

Buchanan retrieved a yellow legal pad from the front seat of the car and removed the carbon paper from beneath the top sheet and put it carefully in the back of the tablet. Then he tore out the carbon copy and held it so it caught the reflected lights of the car's headlights. In the bad light, he ran down the meticulously recorded inventory of each drug in the cartons and the precise values he'd penciled neatly in a column.

The total read: $508,500.

Any way you looked at it, that was a lot of very expensive miracle drugs. Lhamda-Alpine was at the top of the industry.

At fifty cents on the dollar, on the black market that equaled $254,250, just over a cool quarter-million. That translated to more than five years' hard-earned pay at his current salary.

On the concrete floor at his feet, the headline on a wrinkled sheet from yesterday's *News and Observer* announced:

Annual College Tuition Averages
Nearly $13,000 Nationally

Duke Near Top At $38,500. UNC and NC State $12,500

It comforted him to think this lucrative little cache would buy his sons four years at Chapel Hill at the current cost of living. He was sorry it had come down to this, but his sons came first. Those low-life bastards, Acton and Kearns, owed him that.

Reluctantly, Buchanan folded the yellow sheet and wedged it in a crevice between the nearest two boxes. He turned, stepped outside, pulled down the overhead door and locked it tight.

Driving back out between the ordered rows of garage-sized storage buildings, he made a right on Six Forks Road and headed east in the predawn darkness. Just at the rim of the horizon, the sky was showing a thin pencil-tracing of the palest orange with a luminous blush of lavender-blue pushing against the breathtaking indigo-black upper gradients of the star-filled night.

It filled him with momentary awe.

The dawn of creation? Or doomsday, perhaps?

In his gut he couldn't help but feel a wayward tug of anxiety and a pang of regret.

He shivered and tried to shake his guilt.

Past St. Timothy's School, he turned onto Rowan and went down the hill. In the second block he pulled into his drive and left Alma's station wagon. Driving his company Chevy now, he drove back up the hill to the Northmoor shopping center and stopped at the pay phone across from the Winn-Dixie near the liquor store.

The luminescent digital clock on the car dash indicated 6:45.

"Plantation Inn, good morning…"

"Ring Joe Acton, please…" Feathery traces of his breath evaporated in the chilly early March morning air as he listened while the hotel operator made the connection.

"Hello?"

"I'm on my way, Joe. What room you in?"

Chapter Four

THE RAMBLING OLD BEACH HOUSE had something of a Victorian air.

At Youpon Beach, south across the Intracoastal Waterway from Southport, it was still misting slightly from a pre-dawn shower. Warmed by the ever-present Gulf Stream, a balmy breeze wafted primordial marsh smells as the wind pushed the clouds seaward toward Bald Head Island. Just past seven, the broken sky was already fracturing into a kaleidoscopic profusion of rose-tinged shards, promising a lovely early-March morning.

For the minority of year-around residents, neatly-rolled copies of *The Wilmington Morning Star* rested snugly inside a scattering of the yellow-plastic delivery boxes fronting the closely-spaced cottages along the lonely beach road.

Monday's headline proclaimed:

Jerry Falwell Nobel Nominee

"Rotten way to begin a week…" the stocky plainspoken middle-aged man with a bushy salt-and-pepper mustache observed with candor as he sidled to the railing of the cottage's rear deck. The others standing there understood Mack Jones' remark had nothing to do with Falwell's Nobel nomination. The sheriff was referring to the bloody mess inside the cottage.

A trifle bowlegged, wearing slightly rumpled khakis, the bulldog sheriff was a Vietnam veteran who, fresh out of East Carolina University in 1965, had enjoyed three seasons as an All-Pro middle linebacker for the Redskins before Vietnam caught up to him. He always paid close attention to his dress but even against the morning chill, keeping a sharp crease in his uniform was a losing battle in the seaside humidity.

Beside him, the prematurely white-haired Brunswick County Coroner, Amos Lyon, was attired in a hard-used but neatly pressed gray business suit. Old as the suit was, it had obviously been cut by an expensive tailor. The gentlemanly doctor suffered in silent disgust as his otherwise estimable associate leaned over the wooden railing and launched a jet of oily brown tobacco juice into the thick carpet of dark-red and yellow beach daisies growing at the foot of the ponderous sea-oated dunes.

Standing on the deck beside them was a distraught young woman dabbing her eyes with a Kleenex. Between her snufflings, she gave both strangers a wary look.

Seen from this height, the dunes stretched to near infinity in both directions like a drowsing row of overweight porcupines. Northward in the middle-distance, the stark coastal landscape was dominated by the gray-banded, cigarette-shaped Caswell Lighthouse thrusting against the spectacular morning sky like an obscene finger. The curiously plain structure stood as a homely sentinel at the end of the narrow beach road at the entrance to the large church-owned summer camp. The camp occupied that point of coast where the historic ruins of old Fort Caswell overlooked the south bank of the mouth of the storied Cape Fear River shipping channel.

Toward the street, parked half-on, half-off the badly-broken tarmac drive, was a mismatched assemblage of two police cars, a hard-used weather-faded red Ford pickup truck of uncertain vintage, and an equally aged hearse from a funeral home in nearby Supply. The collection bracketed a sleek new tan Cadillac convertible with a Florida plate with an up-to-date decal for the current year, '02. Beneath the deck, parked between the sturdy creosoted wooden pilings which supported the rambling but well-cared-for old beach cottage was a faded blue 1998 Ford Explorer wagon. Though the license plate bracket bore the logo of a nearby Boliva, North Carolina, dealer, like the Cadillac, it too displayed an '02 Florida plate.

Doc Lyon watched, disapproving, while the earthy sheriff stepped away from the rail and wiped tobacco juice from his mustache with a neatly folded red bandanna.

"Here's her license, Mack." The gentlemanly physician gave the driver's license a perfunctory glance before he returned it to the sheriff, who accepted the plastic-encased rectangle and tugged a dog-eared little spiral notebook from his hip pocket.

He glanced up at the woman, looked back at the photo and made a face.

"Never will understand why the DVM can't take a decent snapshot." He glanced back at the name on the driver's license "Uhmmm...Miz Mary Elizabeth Oakes O'Brien?"

The young woman nodded and snuffled assent.

"My name's Malcolm Jones. I'm sheriff of this here county. Folks who like me call me Mack...and..." —using the top rail as a desk, the sheriff began to copy down data from the driver's license without looking up— "...this here's Dr. Lyon, he's county coroner."

Doc Lyon smiled gallantly. "Folks call me Amos, Miz O'Brien." His fingers twisted at the ends of his neatly trimmed, almost silver handlebar mustache.

"You can just call me Maggie." The young woman shuffled her feet nervously and blew her nose as she gave the pair a careful once-over. When she got home, she decided to tell her teen-age son and daughter that the pair looked as if they had walked right off the set of an old-timey cowboy movie.

"Well then...ma'am, uh, Maggie..." The sheriff peered over his little gold-rimmed spectacles and handed back her driver's license. "So you were on your way back from Palm Beach...just happened by on the spur of the moment, so to speak." He consulted his notes. "Your permanent address still Twenty-five Cochina, Wrightsville Beach?"

"That's correct." The young woman replaced the driver's license in her wallet and rummaged through the expensive leather saddlebag purse for a lipstick and a mirror.

"You met the, uh, deceased...ah..." —he referred to his notes again— "...Zoni Corbett...in Palm Beach? You were living in Palm Beach?"

"Not exactly. I move around. I'm a professional interior designer. I do large condominiums and resort hotels. I'm under contract with Lewis Warrant Enterprises, travel all over. I just finished SeaGrapes at Palm Beach. Ever seen SeaWatch at Wrightsville?"

"Hmmm...interesting. How long you known the Corbett woman?"

"Well, since just before Christmas. She moved into my condominium complex in Palm Beach." The young woman inhaled sharply and tried to pull herself up straight. She looked in the compact mirror and gave her nearly perfect saucy Irish nose a swipe with a Kleenex to brush away a new rush of tears. "I still can't believe all this. Zoni was just a kid...shy...very sweet..."

"Yes'm. Sometimes it's just plain hard to figure." The sheriff nodded sympathetically. "What else you know 'bout her?"

"Not much. She was originally from around here, near Lockwood Folly, I think. Since I grew up on Wrightsville Beach, we sort of hit it off."

"She's wearing a wedding band. You know her husband?"

"Nuh uh. Jimmy Lee was a preacher. Some kind of holy-roller missionary, old enough to be her grandfather. He just came back to the States this week. Gone a year, some godawful place like the Amazon jungle, I think. That's another reason we hit it off. Both our men were older and gone a lot." Maggie tried to muster a smile and failed.

"Was she having trouble with this preacher husband, mebby?"

"Well, yeah. Jimmy Lee came back two weeks early…quite a surprise…"

"Oh, I get it. She was pregnant. He'd been out of the country. Baby wasn't his, that it?"

"Well…yeah…worse, really…"

"Worse? What's worse? She committed adultery…She was a preacher's wife?"

"Believe me, it was worse. Baby's father was black…"

"Oh?"

"Yeah…Oh, ho, ho!"

"Was this preacher man violent? He didn't threaten her, did he?"

"Whoa! All that mess in there? She did that to herself, didn't she? You don't think Jimmy Lee…ah…"

"Murdered? Neah. We don't suspect anything like that. Pretty sure it's suicide. We just want to try to understand 'the why' much as we can. Cases like this, it never hurts to make double sure. Get the picture?" The ruddy-complexioned sheriff shifted the hefty wad of tobacco in his cheek with his tongue, leaned across and let fly another jet of tobacco juice.

The old doc cleared his throat irritably and pretended to examine his fingernails.

The sheriff reached for his bandanna again.

Maggie took no notice. "I understand. Look, Sheriff Jones, Zoni took the breakup hard. I only intended to stop off here to say a quick hello, try to cheer her up. I've been driving all night. I was just going to stop off here, say hi, grab the next ferry at Southport and be on my way. I don't know much else I can help. I need to get on up the road…I mean, I'm exhausted and my kids are expecting me."

Holding it by a slender pair of mosquito forceps so as not to put prints on it, Doc Lyon had been examining a little folder that looked like an oversized matchbook cover. Originally it had held physician's samples of Empirin with Codeine. All four pills had been punched out.

The old doc cleared his throat and gave the sheriff a meaningful look.

The sheriff caught his sign and nodded imperceptibly.

"I wonder ma'am, did Miz Corbett use drugs...other than for pain?" the distinguished-looking physician asked, uncomfortably.

"If you mean dope, no way. I never even saw her take an aspirin."

"Hmmm...You say you knew she was pregnant?"

"Yeah. When the abortion fell through, she went crazy."

"She told you she was going to get an abortion?"

"Sure. Her husband was a preacher who hadn't shared her bed in over a year. She'd had this fling with this sleazy Haitian folk singer with Miami Mob connections...been giving her guitar lessons. Dominique was light-skinned, like Michael Jackson. Oh...oh...dear God!" Her face registered enlightenment. "Is that what the awful mess in the commode is about?"

"Yes'm, but understand now, I'm not saying she had an illegal operation...more often abortions are spontaneous...they just happen." The old doc shrugged, then added, "Still, it looks funny, and she was right far along."

"Poor Zoni. What a screwed-up world. If the stupid President had been one day later, she would have gotten rid of it. No wonder she took a gun to her head. I should have seen it coming. After Valentine's Day, seemed like she was going to church twice a day. I really don't know any more than I've told you...I just drove up here an hour ago...found her and made the call. Look, sheriff, Wrightsville Beach's not that far if you need me. I'm on my last legs. Can't I just give you my number and get home to my kids, please?"

The old doc looked at the sheriff and shrugged.

"Sure, why not? Give her your card, Amos. If you think of anything, Miz O'Brien, just give Doc Lyon a call."

"Thanks." The young woman nodded. She put the card in her purse and lost no time making her way down the steps to her car.

The sheriff walked to the rail and spit. Before he could pull the red bandanna out of his hip pocket to wipe his chin, Maggie had lowered the top of the new Cadillac convertible and was backing out of the drive.

Looking slightly green from having thrown up over the rail of the deck overlooking the ocean after he'd seen the gruesome corpse, the young deputy, Clark Simmons, had quietly joined them on the rear deck to take the air.

Now he stood at the rail admiring the well-formed young woman leaving in the convertible. "Wow...that's really some piece of work," he said, half-aloud.

"Seems like you made a speedy recovery, Clark. Best we keep our horny minds on business. Find anything interesting inside?" Mack Jones good-naturedly pulled him back to reality.

"Not much. Bankbook showed she'd withdrawn eleven-hundred bucks Friday. Half-empty bottle of Jim Beam, some sandwich stuff and beer in the fridge and less than sixty dollars in her purse. I'm glad the ambulance beat us here. Driver'll make a good witness to my search," Simmons replied.

"Simmons, you gotta quit being so damn paranoid," the sheriff grumbled. "Anybody looks at that rundown trailer you call home would know you're honest. What'cha got there?"

The deputy was holding a clear plastic evidence bag.

"Contents of the trashcan in the bathroom. Here...take a look." The deputy handed over the bag.

Through the clear plastic the sheriff could see a soap wrapper, an empty Crest toothpaste carton, a discarded mouthwash bottle and—among other odds and ends—what looked to be an elongated insertion tube for a menstrual tampon.

"Whazzis?..." He took the bag and held it in the light and twisted it so he could examine the cardboard tube. "Says...G/uL Technologies... T3...ever hear of that brand of Tampax?...I thought she was pregnant. Could all that blood and mess be just menstruation, Amos?" The sheriff looked quizzically at the old doc.

"No way. G/uL Technologies is the name of a medical equipment manufacturer in Richmond, but I don't think they market menstrual tampons. Besides, she aborted all right. Mind if I take a look?"

The sheriff handed him the bag.

"Hey, Mack, how much longer?" the ambulance driver called from inside the house.

"Well...how about it, you two?" The sheriff directed the question to both the doc and his deputy, before he turned and spit again.

"Self-inflicted gunshot. Pure'n'simple," Simmons spoke right up.

"Yeah...I can't argue..." the old doc muttered half to himself. He was looking closely at the bag with the contents of the trashcan. "But not exactly pure'n' simple. Before she blew her brains out, she'd just aborted a two- maybe three-month fetus."

"You sure 'bout that, then?" The sheriff was still wondering about the cardboard tube.

"I'm sure. Closer to three months. She was definitely pregnant."

"So? What's the problem?" Young Simmons shrugged. "She's pregnant…a holy-roller preacher's wife. The Oakes woman said the daddy was a Neegra…she starts drinking and gets up the nerve to ram a rusty coat hanger up herself…gets scared…has remorse…puts a gun to her head…pow!…" The young deputy pointed his finger at his head and pulled his trigger finger. "Classic case of good girl…too much bad luck."

"Think that abortion was self-inflicted, Amos?" The old sheriff asked, refolding the red bandanna.

"Nuh-huh…we didn't find a coat hanger or knitting needle…nothing like that," Amos Lyon said.

"Hmm. Heard of anybody 'round here doing back-alley surgery since the goddamn abortion zealots started killing innocent people and the stupid president called out the guard?"

"Neah, not around here, anyways. Wilmington… Fayetteville… Myrtle Beach….maybe? Anyone around here was doing 'em, I'd know." The old doc shook his head. He knew just about everything that went on in his county.

The ambulance driver stuck his head out the door, "Well? How 'bout it, Mack? It's a good three hours' drive to Chapel Hill."

The sheriff looked to the old doc. "Amos?"

"Oh…sure…take her on up the road, Charlie." The taciturn doc was still preoccupied with the contents of the evidence bag. "Mack, hold onto this for a couple of days?" He handed over the collection in the bag. "And wait one second, boys. I want Clark to bag her hands. We need to get a paraffin test; wouldn't hurt to take fingernail scrapings while they're at it."

"Good idea. You thinking the same thing I am? The O'Brien woman said the deceased's husband had threatened her. Even a saint will commit a crime of passion."

"Well…I don't know about that, but there's something about all this that bothers me. And while you're at it, have that cardboard insertion tube dusted…and the gun…just in case?"

"No big deal. Always have the gun dusted in self-inflicted gunshots, anyway."

"Here, dust this, too, Mack." The old doc handed back the discarded pharmaceutical sample folder, careful to let him take it using the mosquito forceps.

"One thing I wish you'd do for me, Charlie." The old doc turned to the ambulance driver. "I'm going to call ahead to Chapel Hill and order some x-rays of the body. I'm gonna ask 'em to roll both hands for prints. I'll make sure they know we want those prints stat. I'd appreciate your waiting…so you can bring 'em back to me. OK?"

"Sure…" Amos Lyon knew the young driver would wait if it took all night.

Like everybody else who knew them, Charlie thought Sheriff Mack and old Doc Lyon hung the moon.

Chapter Five

A MILE OR SO EAST of the Northmoor shopping center, Buchanan turned off Six Forks and took Old Wake Forest Road north to U.S. 1.

A few miles further, nestled in a sheltering grove of pines along the left side of the highway, the creamy white architecture of the venerable old Plantation Inn radiated the influence of Charleston or Savannah or New Orleans. In the cold mauve-gray, pre-dawn light, the large landmark motel faintly reflected a hue of delicate-lilac.

Beneath the bower of pines, a sentinel row of gaslights flickered pleasantly from antique lampposts lining the sweeping drive. Buchanan turned left into the main entrance and made his way straight back where the semi-circular driveway branched and ran down the abrupt slope between the northern terminus of the motel and the matching colonial architecture of the owner's elegant cottage.

At the rear, the Inn revealed a lower level overlooking a small lake surrounded by pines and dogwoods. With practiced familiarity Buchanan drove slowly past the long row of cars parked in front of each door until he reached the far end and pulled in beside a highly-polished, brand new gray Buick sedan.

"Come in, Buck." The paunchy, balding man stood holding the door before Buchanan had a chance to knock.

Joe Acton always looked tired, much older than his thirty-seven years. Dressed in a fresh white dress shirt with no tie and the sharply-creased trousers to a remarkably unattractive fecal-brown suit, Joe's belly ballooned out over his belt, giving him a faintly Pickwickian air. The scraggly fringe of sandy hair above his tiny, flattened ears was still slightly damp from the shower.

The room reeked of AquaVelva. It was easy to remember the man was a redneck Baptist preacher's son. But, despite the cheap aftershave, Buchanan caught a pleasant whiff of fresh coffee before he stepped through the door.

"I had coffee sent over, some cheese Danish too.…" Joe was clearly ill-at-ease as he indicated a tray with a large thermos carafe and some cups on the desk against the wall opposite the foot of the king-size bed. "...Help yourself."

The invitation lacked the ring of sincerity. Joe obviously wanted to get this meeting over with.

"Don't mind if I do." Buchanan ignored the fat man's anxiety and poured himself a cup of the thick Cafè du Monde coffee blend.

"Well...uh...ah...have a seat, Buck...have a seat." The fidgety man eyed him uncomfortably.

Buchanan walked to the small round table in front of the window and took the chair furthest from the door. On the table was a lipstick-smeared glass and a half-empty fifth of J&B. The colorful molecular model of a new anti-cancer enzyme decorated the cover of the latest *Time* magazine. Buchanan watched as Joe went to the desk and refilled his cup. Joe picked up a plain manila folder before he returned and took the other chair.

"Well, uh...it's been awhile...let's see...the annual state neuropsychiatric meeting was middle of January, nearly two months now..." Acton made a halfhearted attempt to be companionable.

Buchanan had been prepared to make this easy on the other man but suddenly he was overcome by the utter hypocrisy of the entire situation. Now, all at once, he found it impossible to feel anything for the disgustingly misshapen, ineffectual man.

"Yeah, you really showed your ass that night, Joe. Had to leave your car at the motel in Durham. Angie Martinas was still here drunk and half-naked when we got back...Remember?" Buchanan's overriding rush of resentment spilled out.

Acton flushed and his hands shook as he sipped his coffee.

"By the way, Joe, how's Angie getting along?" Buchanan casually picked up the ashtray and examined the lipstick-stained cigarette stubs. He made no effort to hide his contempt.

A guilty look passed behind the fat man's slightly bloodshot eyes and the blush crept up his neck.

"Well...heh, heh...I...well...uh...you know how she can be..." Joe let the words trail off with a resigned shrug.

Pleased that he'd struck a nerve, Buchanan held back a smile.

"Don't say I didn't warn you. She may be a sex-machine but she's an alky, Joe...called me at home a few weeks back wanting to know when you'd be coming up here to work with me." He smiled a knowing smile. "Alma answered the phone. If I were you, I'd have a talk with her, Joe...before she starts calling you at home."

"Yeah...well...heh, heh...sorry about that." Joe put down his cup and picked up the file folder and started to finger nervously through the papers. "But, you're right. Maybe I should have a word with her…"

He avoided looking Buchanan in the eye.

Buchanan sipped his coffee and waited.

"Well…now…ah…" Acton cleared his throat and continued to shuffle the papers without lifting his gaze. There were beads of sweat on his forehead and upper lip now. "Buck…uh…I really don't know how to begin this. Hardest thing I've ever had to do…"

It's your show, Joe, just get on with it, Buchanan mused, silently. Finally, he said, "Yeah…why's that, Joe?"

"Well…I…uh…about two weeks ago, I got this call from Harvey in Englewood. The Food and Drug had raided a warehouse in Richmond and picked up a trainload of bootleg drug samples…and…well…they found some of ours. Not a lot of ours, really, but some. Enough…any at all is too much, really…" Acton stopped, made a wry face and took a sip of the coffee.

Buchanan just looked at him, unblinking.

"Well…to make a long story short…the investigation turned up a lot of names. Most of 'em were doctors or entrepreneurs who make it business to buy samples from doctors, but some of the stuff came from pharmaceutical reps." Acton's eyes flicked up at him just for an instant and then looked away again. He lifted a piece of paper from the folder and pretended, rather theatrically, to examine it.

Buchanan was reminded that Joe and Greta were big with some yuppie Charlotte thespian crowd. *Save it for the little theater, Joe*, he mused contemptuously but made no reply.

The silence lay between them like an anonymous overripe flatulence.

The fat man cleared his throat again and reached for a linen napkin and daubed the beads of sweat on his forehead and upper lip. When he took it away, he fumbled awkwardly to hide the lipstick on the stained napkin.

"Is it hot to you?"

Buchanan shrugged.

The fat man looked to the paper again. "Seems I recall Findlay Hanks, the Vitamerica rep in Roanoke, is a pretty good buddy of yours, Buck."

"I know him. We used to travel the same territory, have a few beers together on the road. Around town we never played golf or belonged to the same clubs, if that's what you mean…" Buchanan shrugged offhandedly, not changing expression.

"Well…uh…Findlay was one of the reps involved…seems like he made regular trips to Richmond…was doing a rather lively wholesale trade on the black market. They think maybe to other places, too...bought tons of samples from doctors' offices and maybe some fellow pharmaceutical representatives like...ah...yourself. A rather profitable enterprise, it seems." Acton glanced up at him but he still avoided strong eye contact.

Buchanan never blinked.

"Vitamerica fired him, of course. Well, uh...actually, the national sales manager came down from Philadelphia with two guys from the FDA in Washington. Hanks was lucky. The Food and Drug didn't want to prosecute...they just wanted his cooperation. They got his resignation last Friday. The Feds aren't out to put anyone in jail, or even get the press involved. They're just trying to put a stop to this wholesale misuse of samples..."

Tiring of the clumsy charade, Buchanan glanced out the window at the reflection of the trees on the lake in the silvery-lilac pre-dawn haze. Finally he looked back to Acton.

C'mon, Joe, get to the punchline.

"Findlay brought your name up, Buck." The fat man nervously met his stare. Then his eyes flicked away again.

Buchanan stared back at him, impassive.

"Well, don't you have anything to say?"

"What?" He showed a bemused look at Acton's irritation.

Acton's mouth started to open but nothing came out.

"Did I miss something?" Buchanan shrugged, waiting.

"Ah...uh...well...Findlay told the FDA that he'd handled some samples for you."

"Excuse me, Joe, but I don't believe you."

"Well, uh...Didn't you sell him some of your samples?"

"Cut the bullshit. If you're accusing me of something, Joe, why don't you just do it?"

"Well? Don't you have anything to say?"

"Not until you answer my question..."

"I thought I'd give you a chance to resign," Acton hedged.

"Why should I do that, for chrissake?"

"I told you." Acton was furious now. Cheeks puffed, his face was beet red. He still couldn't look Buchanan in the eye.

"You told me that somebody accused me of mishandling my drug samples. That's all. People can say anything they want to about me...about you...or...anybody...or anydamnthing they please. Doesn't make it so." Buchanan challenged. From Findlay's call, he knew Joe didn't have much of a case.

"You mean you deny it?"

"Deny it? I refuse to dignify any of this crap until I hear why you're asking me to resign."

"I told you…do you want an FDA investigation?"

"Now that you mention it, that might not be a bad idea. Sounds like I've been slandered. My reputation's at stake. I've got a family to think about. Maybe I should talk to the Feds…I could tell them some things. What do you do with the samples you're always boosting from me? I wonder what the other salesmen would say. I think you just might want to throw me to the wolves to take the heat off your own sorry ass…"

"Well, wait now, don't be irresponsible. Harvey talked to the FDA and they'd rather just let the whole matter drop as far as you and Lhamda-A are concerned. The Feds have a carton with your label and microfiche of Hank's certified check made out to you in the amount of thirty-five thousand." Acton averted his eyes. "We'll accept your resignation…just say it's for personal reasons. Harvey says we'll give you a good reference. They got that check. Hanks ratted you out, Buck."

"Bullshit, Joe. Findlay Hanks has no reason to lie like that. And, you'll give me a good recommendation, a clean bill of health? That's pure bullshit. You know this business. You can't keep something like this under a rock. Word's probably already on the street and you know it. On the street my name will be 'Feces' before sundown tonight—if it isn't already. And when people check my references, Harvey will just cover his ass. If you fire me, then at least I'll get a hearing from the unemployment board…maybe I'll get a lawyer to represent my rights. If someone's going to make a sworn statement about me, let 'em do it in court." Buchanan struggled unsuccessfully to keep a tremor of raw emotion out of his voice.

"C'mon, man. Why make a federal case out of it? The Food and Drug don't want any publicity any more than we do. Just resign and we'll give you a month's severance and a clean bill of health. I'll even help you get some interviews. Trust me…"

"Trust *you*?" Buchanan made a face.

"Aw, come on, Harvey ain't out for blood. We'll help…"

"Save your help, Joe. You may need it for yourself. How'd you like to answer some questions on the stand? I'll have the FDA and the IRS subpoena the whole frigging sales force…" Buchanan regretted the words before he closed his mouth. He didn't want to dignify this cretin by making idle threats.

"Look, Buck, we go back a ways; you wouldn't make a stink. Why pull a lot of your buddies down? What good would that do?" Acton tried to make a neat stack of the papers he held and fumbled some of the sheets onto the floor beside his chair. When he'd retrieved them he looked desperately back at Buchanan.

"And what about the FDA? How can you be so sure they'll just let this drop? They tell Harvey that?"

"Oh, don't worry about the Feds. They don't want to nail you. They just want the company to show good faith. I can assure you, you won't hear from them."

"Spare me the bullshit, Joe. Would you put that in writing, about the Feds, I mean?" Buchanan let the question die in his throat. It was an empty exercise now, anyway. He couldn't let Joe know that Findlay Hanks had told him about the crooked agent, Stanley Herbert.

"Writing? You know we can't. C'mon, Buck, trust me, please..." Joe looked at his watch. "We can probably still catch Harvey at home. Want to talk to Harvey, Buck?"

Buchanan shook his head. "No way. I hope I never talk to that anal sphincter again."

"Come on man, don't be like that." Joe daubed the napkin to his forehead again. This time he forgot to hide the lipstick stain.

Looking at the smeary napkin, Buchanan felt soiled just being in the same room.

The anger suddenly left him. Joe was scared shitless, but bringing these hypocrites down wouldn't help him now.

What was the use, anyway? Let them bear their own guilt.

"You going to be here tonight, Joe?"

"Well, yeah...I planned to stay over and work with Bill Rogers." Bill was the local rep. When Buchanan's promotion moved him to Raleigh, Buchanan was put in charge of setting up clinical research at the medical schools at Duke, UNC, and Bowman Gray in Winston-Salem. Research Coordinator was his official title. It elevated him above the salesman rank but Rogers and the other sales reps didn't answer to him.

"I'm sure Angie's glad about that."

"Come on now, Buck, let's leave Angie out of..."

Abruptly, Buchanan held up his hand.

"OK. I'll leave my resignation at the desk before the day's over. I'll pack up what samples I have and my records and the rest of the company stuff and leave it all with Bill Rogers this weekend. Tell Harvey Kearns I want three months' severance pay, and the use of the company car until I can find a job."

Joe's jaw dropped.

"Three months? Harvey said he might stretch it and give you six weeks, but the car? I don't know, Buck, there's just no way Harvey can…"

"I said three months, *and the car*…and tell Harvey I want my company insurance to remain in force. If you're all so interested in my future, I need to find a job. Tell Harvey I'll see an attorney if he wants to fuck with me. I'll need that car."

"Well, I don't know…I…" Joe stammered.

Abruptly, Buchanan stood and stepped in front of Acton. With the toe of his black Bass tassel loafers, he snaked the edge of a pair of peach-colored nylon panties from under the bed.

Joe turned an even deeper red.

"By the way, Joe, Alma always sends her fondest regards to Greta." Buchanan laughed a dry little laugh. "Now, when I leave here just get on that phone and tell Harvey what I said."

"C'mon Buck…I'll do my best…but I…uh…"

Buchanan bent and picked up the panties and examined the rather flamboyant embroidery.

"That's some fancy shoeshine rag." He looked back at Joe.

He spread the panties with his long slender fingers in front of the fat man's face and smoothed them out. The monogram read:

Angie

Little florets hovered at each side of the flowing script.

"Nice…You have Greta's done like that, too?"

"Aw, c'mon Buck…ease up…" Acton blushed.

"Oh…don't worry, Joe. Harvey'll listen to you, you ol' silver-tongued devil. I'll call in a couple of hours, after you've had a chance to clear this with Kearns. When he agrees, then I'll need something from you in writing. Make it read: Three months' severance, insurance in force for ninety days and the use of the car. I'll even pay the gas. You can leave it in an envelope at the desk upstairs and I'll check it out when I bring my resignation this afternoon."

"I'll meet you…give us a chance to talk some more…"

"No. I'll call you later this morning after you've talked to good ol' Harvey, just to make sure that it's all arranged. Then, you have a letter typed up and leave it for me."

He tossed the silken panties square in the fat man's face. The flimsy garment hung just for an instant on Acton's nose before it dropped into his lap.

Buchanan walked to the door, then turned to face Acton.

"Just leave the letter at the desk upstairs. I don't want to see you or talk to you…or Harvey, either…not ever again."

Chapter Six

ALMA WOKE UP EARLY. After she got the kids off to school, she was planning to meet Judy Edens and Marylee Castle at Cameron Village to do some shopping then have lunch at the Hofbrau. After lunch, they were going to see Leonardo DiCaprio's latest movie, a remake of *The Poseidon Adventure*, with Gwyneth Paltrow, Nick Nolte and Kathy Bates.

She looked resentfully out of the living room window at her four-year-old blue Tahoe sitting in the drive. That wagon was a disgrace. She couldn't remember the last time Buchanan had washed it. Saturday, when he got back from the park with the kids, she'd nagged and nagged that it would be nice if he'd wash the Tahoe for her. She'd pointed to Charlie Rodl across the street who had his kids out in the drive washing Betty's practically new Ford Explorer. They had been having a merry time.

She'd pointed out that she couldn't afford things like car washes since they'd moved to Raleigh because he'd quit using samples to pay for her charge account at the drug store and nowadays it was a struggle just to make ends meet.

Steadfastly, Buchanan had ignored her. He'd told her grumpily that it was her car and it was her responsibility to take care of it. "If you want it washed, take it somewhere and pay to have it done." The smart ass had handed her a twenty-dollar bill and told her keep the change.

That had started a fight.

He'd gotten mad and accused her of nagging him to trade samples again. He yelled at her and said he was sick and tired of explaining that it was the same as embezzling.

"Well," she'd reminded him, "your boss is an embezzler then. And, what about those high and mighty doctors? They all do it."

"It's not right," he'd said, "but, technically, it's not embezzlement for the doctors."

She'd heard that dumb news a hundred times before.

She'd pointed out that they had lived a lot better before he'd taken his precious promotion.

He'd launched his boring speech about how their four little boys were going to be college age before you could blink your eyes and if he didn't move up in the company, how were they going to educate them?

She'd told him time after time that her mother had bought her an insurance policy when she was a baby that had paid for her nurse's training. "If you weren't so hardheaded about buying insurance policies that would pay for the children's college, we wouldn't have to worry about all that," she'd said.

The whole dreary fight was so predictable.

Now, she fumed and lit a cigarette, remembering.

Buck Forbes had the nerve to say she'd asked him to steal.

How was trading a few samples of that hot new instant hard-on pill stealing?

And...how could someone who knew all that stupid stuff about philosophy and writers and history and art...and his precious folk music...and jazz...be so dumb?

Renaissance Man? Mensa, indeed...if they only knew!

And now her tacky old Tahoe was still a disgrace.

Maybe she'd have time to take it to the Jiffy Wash.

Up the street she watched enviously as Emily Biggers backed her fancy new Tahoe out of the drive. This year's model, Emily's SUV had power windows, a CD-changer and sunroof.

Tonight she was going to tell Buck Forbes she needed a new car.

Chapter Seven

FIRED!

The word echoed in Buchanan's brain like a primal scream.

When he left Joe, he drove around, simply trying to get used to the fear, the feeling of emptiness. Findlay Hanks' warning hadn't prepared him for this, not really.

Idly, he fingered the outline of the key in his pocket and thought about the booty he'd stashed in the mini-warehouse. At least he had the self-righteous satisfaction that Hanks had given him enough warning so he could engineer Lhamda-Alpine's unwitting donation to his young sons' college scholarship fund.

Poetic justice? Maybe? Still, at best it was a Pyrrhic victory.

He hated himself for having been so weak as to give in to Alma in the first place. Anyway, it was too late to worry about all that now. If he walked away from this, not Alma, not money or Chinese torture would ever make him cross that line again.

Well, maybe an occasional fudge on his frigging income tax. Goddamn IRS!

Driving aimlessly down St. Mary's toward town, the numbing

thought that the IRS might investigate his spending habits gave him a sudden chill.

"Stuck in Folsom Prison..." Johnny Cash wailed prophetically on the radio.

When the light changed at Hillsborough Street, he turned left and drove a few blocks east. Traces of spring buds were on the bare limbs of the huge trees overhanging the broad thoroughfare. Up ahead he could see the top of the old state capitol building caught in the low slanting rays of sunlight, brilliant against the cloudless morning sky.

"...and the Hunter of the East has caught the sultan's turret in his noose of light..." The image called to mind lines from the *Rubiyat. First Folsom Prison, now a noose.* He shook his head and snorted self-consciously.

It was not quite 8:15 when he pulled to the curb in front of a stately old red-brick mansion that had been lovingly restored and converted into law offices. Third from the bottom, on a vertical ladder of shiny brass nameplates all bearing the names of attorneys, the name H. Cameron Brawley, Attorney-at-Law was neatly engraved on one of the ten highly-polished plates mounted on a walnut plaque at the entrance. The name at the top was a former governor. The others below it displayed names long familiar to native North Carolinians—some representing family trees which were well-represented in the history books.

The former governor was Hildreth Reynolds Cameron. Cammie Brawley's father was founding partner of The Cameron Group, one of the most powerful law firms in the South.

Now, finding himself parked in front of her office, Buchanan realized that he'd never really thought about it before, but Cammie Brawley represented his best and most trusted friend. It was predictable that he had run straight to her in this time of personal disaster.

"H. Cameron Brawley, Esquire, an impressive name for an attorney. A name lowly judges have to reckon with." Buchanan had often teased the rather striking woman who laid claim to the title. They'd met early one morning nearly four years ago when she'd been the guest speaker at a breakfast session of the Northmoor Toastmaster Club.

Back then, moving to Raleigh had been, for Buchanan, culture shock and his brief association with the Toastmasters had been a transient, knee-jerk reaction.

The state capital, Raleigh, was home to North Carolina State University, the shirt-sleeve old state school devoted mostly to engineering and agriculture. There were also three time-honored women's colleges—St. Mary's, Meredith and Peace—which catered to the well-bred daughters of the state's favored families. And, there was Shaw, a fine old university with a proud history.

Leaving the decade of the nineties, business and industry related to manufacturing and shipping was still very low key in the staid old city. Buchanan had found Raleigh still to be more of an overgrown country town, composed of old families whose tradition was invested mostly in bureaucratic government jobs, political office, higher education or management. The rest of the middle class was made up of attending professionals: doctors, dentists, and lawyers, and the shopkeepers and merchants who served them all.

With health advances, now, more than ever, Raleigh remained an old folks' town.

After they'd moved from Virginia, Buchanan had given up his weekend golf matches. The golf had been a token sacrifice, really. Raleigh had limited legitimate country clubs anyway. Membership was on a waiting-list-only basis—waiting lists that prompted Buchanan to grumble, "...probably pre-date the Civil War."

Raleigh was just that kind of tight-assed town.

And, while the slightly over-eager members of Toastmasters hadn't held his interest beyond that one meeting, shortly after that first encounter he had run into Cammie Brawley again one Saturday morning when he'd taken his young sons to the playground at the public park.

With his constant travel away from home, his Saturday morning ritual at the park with his sons had begun as a grandstand gesture to give Alma some much-deserved time to herself. Although appreciation from Alma was usually short-lived and soon-forgotten, the brilliant little stratagem did earn him temporary brownie points—kept him treading water in the shark-infested deeps of the husband tank.

And, in truth, those weekend mornings in the park quickly became a time he treasured.

He soon discovered that being with four young male animals: Garrett, four; Grayson, six; Gregory, seven; and Granger, eleven, was a deeply satisfying exercise of the spirit. It put him in touch with a dimension of himself that he hadn't known existed.

Fatherhood.

A heady thing!

After their first encounter at the park, Cammie Brawley began showing up more often and—with their collective gang of energetic kids—they became regulars at the playground. Over the months the two of them had become companionable. Soon, their casual association became a much-anticipated thing. Then—at some point—the quality of their trust had deepened and they'd become confidants of a sort.

Even though she was eight years older than Buchanan and seven years Alma's senior, at nearly forty-three, Cammie Brawley looked years younger. Her skin had an unblemished, youthful glow. Although she was slender, even in bulky sweatshirts it was impossible for Buchanan not to notice she had disconcerting curves. Seen in shorts or jeans and sneakers, despite the tiny traces of laugh lines crinkling at the corners of her clear, pale-seawater eyes, Cammie, with a pony-tailed mane of slightly auburn-tinted hair, still looked more like a college girl than an attorney of growing reputation and the mother of two daughters—Tyler, seven, and Amy, going on eleven.

On more than one of those weekend mornings at the playground, he had contemplated the glowing youthfulness of the self-assured woman and philosophically pondered whether it was because of a genetic—rather than a deep spiritual—difference between the two women that Alma was already developing an older, more matronly look.

Sometimes it was downright difficult for him to keep his mind on purely platonic thoughts.

Cammie's husband was—by her own wry assessment— "...a rather pompous...society cardiologist." On the visiting faculty at Duke and politically ambitious in the hierarchy of the state medical society, James Erwin Brawley, M.D. spent little time at home with Cammie and the children.

In a corresponding vein, since their move to Raleigh, Alma had rejected almost anything Buchanan suggested. She was more involved in bridge club and the doings of the ladies of the church and not at all interested in books or sports or theater or art.

As time went by, Buchanan found himself enlarging on his friendship with Cammie by meeting her occasionally for lunch during the week. They often shared the opportunity to good-naturedly bemoan the ups and downs of their marriages and discuss important things like politics and basketball and the latest bestsellers...or sometimes...their career frustrations.

Their comfortable camaraderie was an unexpected kind of relationship. It had grown, seemingly without visible gender consciousness and most importantly it was exclusively theirs. It was unspoken between them, but there had never been any mention—from either side—of including their respective mates in an attempt to widen the sphere of the relationship.

Like his friend Lane Zoeller back home in Roanoke, Cammie tried to make Buchanan out to be smarter than he really was. He blushed now, reminded how she kept bugging him to take the Mensa exam...and she was always picking at him—to no avail—to take the test for the ever-popular TV show *Jeopardy*.

If she only knew how dumb he really was.

Now, Buchanan watched up ahead in the next block as a nondescript gray Ford sedan pulled to the curb and parked on the opposite side of the street. The car was rather unremarkable but it set off a warning tightening in his gut.

Had he seen that same car behind him at the traffic light back at Five Points?

FDA?

IRS?

Fingering the key in his pocket, he recalled his pre-dawn treks to the mini-warehouse.

Sweetjesus! Was he being followed? Had Acton set him up?

"...*stuck in Folsom Prison...*" Johnny Cash continued to wail.

Heart pounding, he got out and closed and locked the car door and walked up the wide brick sidewalk. The soaring Palladian fan-light edged with delicate stained glass above the exquisitely carved double oak doors seemed suddenly forbidding—severely judgmental.

When he entered the front door, Buchanan found the reception foyer empty and the desk unmanned. At this early hour, none of the lamps was lit in the waiting area.

The magnificent crystal chandelier suspended on a heavy chain from the second story ceiling was also unlit. His gaze followed the spiraling sweep of the staircase up to the gallery encircling the second landing. Although he'd seen Cammie's shiny new red Sunfire convertible parked in back when he'd driven up, the building had an eerie sense of emptiness about it.

All at once it occurred to him that he really hadn't thought this out very well. He was really taking quite a lot for granted.

He had never been in real trouble before. To think Cammie would be happy to have him drop in and dump his sordid little problem on her at the beginning of a business day was an ill-thought-out act of selfish desperation.

Did he really want her to know he was an accused thief?

Would he ever be able to face any of his friends...or his father and mother...or his brother again? And what about his sons? Suddenly overcome with doubt, he turned to leave.

"Helloooo? Can I help you? Who's down there?"

Buchanan froze.

Somewhere, just out of view, Cammie's voice drifted down from above.

He held his breath and slunk silently further back, beneath the overhanging balcony. He couldn't let her see him like this.

"Buchanan! Where're you going? Come back here. What's the matter?"

Too late! Cammie had moved around the upper gallery and stood looking down at him.

"Buchanan! Talk to me" Her voice was sweet with concern.

He'd never noticed before, but Cammie never called him 'Buck.' In a curious way it spoke more of intimacy than distance.

Oddly, that gave him comfort now.

Chapter Eight

AGENT DURWOOD FISHER left the engine of the gray Ford running as he watched Forbes leave his company Chevy and walk up the sidewalk and enter the converted old mansion on Hillsborough.

Fisher had picked up Forbes when he'd left the Plantation Inn twenty minutes earlier and followed him over a meandering route back down Old Wake Forest Road onto the Beltline and finally down through Five Points to here. With all his wandering about, at first Durwood thought Forbes had spotted him and was playing cat and mouse. But now Fisher was more relaxed.

"He just went inside…" Fisher radioed Bill Johnston.

"Do you think he spotted you?" his partner radioed back.

"No way. He's just been driving around, probably trying to collect himself from that little scene with Acton," Fisher answered.

He and Johnston had electronically monitored Forbes' meeting with Joe Acton from the room next door at the Plantation Inn. They tossed a coin and Johnston had stayed behind to listen in on Acton's phone conversations and tail him if he left during the day.

Washington didn't expect to discover anything really sinister from either man. Tax-wise, the whole deal was small potatoes. Some altogether amateurish misappropriations of drug samples which was now ancient history and mostly based on hearsay from Findlay Hanks, one of the major players in the FDA's Richmond bust.

Now that the boys from the Food and Drug had closed the Richmond operation down, it was the Service's headache. To Washington, the rest was mostly show, anyway. A joke really—the Service rarely prosecuted these prescription drug deals as tax cases.

More than anything, this little surveillance was strictly CYA—*cover your ass*. The FDA had stuck 'em with this mess and it would be rather embarrassing for the Service to mark the Richmond File closed only to have something major surface later involving either Forbes or Acton, or Lhamda-A itself. If there was anything else going on, Washington had to know.

CYA. Around Washington, the first commandment!

With constant Congressional hearings on the high cost of prescription medication making headlines, there was enough heat as it was. Now there were undercurrents and rumors on the Hill about the buying practices of the General Services Administration and the Veterans Administration. The usual headlines—rumors about kickbacks and lavish entertainment.

Everybody wanted to burn the hapless IRS employees.

Besides, all that had precious little to do with taxes. It was pure bullshit to the Service.

Politically—like the auto and liquor industry—doctors, pharmacists and drug companies were untouchable. Policy was: *Check 'em out and lay low*. Rousting physicians and drug companies would raise a stink that no one in Washington wanted to deal with.

Fucking politics.

Let Congress sort it out.

Although the Richmond bust had been a real blockbuster with the totals running into the tens of millions, typically, there'd been no press. The FDA closed down smaller but similar operations several times every year and passed on the information to the FBI and the Service. The only tax angles worth following up were those involving the principal operators. Tax-wise, secondary players like Findlay Hanks were small-fry and guys like Joe Acton and Buchanan Forbes were penny-ante compared with those solid, upstanding pillars of the medical community, the untouchable physicians and druggists.

Next to God, doctors and pharmacists claimed sinlessness. Finding one willing to cast the first stone at a dirty colleague was about as likely as finding a Democratic congressman anxious to burn a fellow representative or senator for handing out a few political plums to the brother-in-law of a heavy campaign contributor.

The average dumbass clod at the weekly Rotary would be aghast to learn how greedy some of their upstanding doctors and friendly corner druggists really were. If the Service wanted to start in on the physicians who traded out or sold samples, then the numbers would be staggering. That would open a Pandora's box no one would ever be able to get the lid back on.

And—Fisher shivered—a frigging nightmare for the Service.

As unbelievable as it was, the Richmond bust was just the tip of the iceberg. In the end, cutting off the source was the only hope of finding a workable solution. Congress and the FDA were always making noises about putting some pressure on the Pharmaceutical Manufacturer's Association to remedy the drug sample problem. But it was a joke to ask the PhMA, the APhA, and the AMA to police themselves and take control of the tidal wave of freebies that kept flowing out in an endless stream.

So far the Service had refused to walk into that minefield. Not even that new dumb, born-again president fucked around with the public's health.

On the seat beside Durwood was Les Standiford's latest bestseller. It was about the bumbling of hardworking IRS agents. In novels and the movies, men like him took a bad rap.

"This is a waste. Sometimes I wish I was back auditing tax returns," Durwood complained into the mike. "At least I used to get to put a little heat on a good-looking broad once in awhile."

"Yeah…but sitting behind a desk all day is a drag." The car speaker crackled a little from interference.

"Well, hell, sitting in a goddamn government-issue Ford ain't exactly my idea of fun." Durwood's eye caught a pair of magnificently-formed secretaries walking toward him, heading for work. "Whoa, bite my tongue, Billy boy. I wish you could get a load of the tits on this…"

"Spare me the details…bzzz.." The static came in again.

Durwood made a mental note to have the frigging radio checked out. If technicians could transmit full-color television pictures from astronauts orbiting Mars, why couldn't he carry on a conversation across a dinky little city the size of Raleigh? It was hard to figure.

"Ooh-la-la, Billy! I think I just died and went to heaven." A steady stream of attractive women in spring dresses were beginning to emerge from the parking lots along the street.

"Will you cut it out, Durr? We got a job to do…"

"Some job," Durwood whined.

What a bummer! It turned out that the Richmond operation had been owned by physicians—that ass-kissing PC bitch at Justice would never bring those "lily-whites" to court.

Washington had already run a routine check on Acton's and Forbes' finances and bank records. Both men lived a little out of their income bracket, but then, nowadays, who didn't—if you didn't include poor bastards like himself who were on the public payroll.

The audit hadn't uncovered any yachts or expensive beach property lurking in the background of either man, so now he and Johnston were stuck with playing "junior G-Man" for a few weeks just to make certain there hadn't been anything they'd missed. And to make sure these guys didn't try to pull a fast one.

"Mark my words, Durr-baby. This is just another friggin' wild goose chase."

"Well…don't be too sure. Sometimes a guy like Forbes will fool ya. He may try to make a final hit with whatever samples he still has in his possession. And, remember, that guy Hanks told the FDA he'd heard scuttlebutt that Joe Acton had dealt with Richmond."

"OK, it won't hurt to keep an eye on both of 'em for a few days. I admit Hanks' testimony is highly apocryphal information but, if he's right, there's always the chance that this Acton might take the opportunity to make a 'short' inventory of the samples Forbes turns in and bootleg those himself."

"Either way, we might get lucky and stumble onto something like another bootlegger the size of Richmond. At the very least, we might put the tax hooks into another 'fat cat' pharmacist." The radio was clearer now. Durwood would just be goddamned if he'd ask that smartass Johnston what *"a-pock-cra…whatever"* meant.

"So what? Guys like Forbes ain't even a pimple on the fat ass of white collar crime. Besides, I'll bet you five that Forbes or Acton neither one try anything funny. We're just gonna waste the next few weeks on a wild goose chase. We'll mark this 'Case Closed' before the end of the month."

"No bet…" Bzzz…hummm…pop. A car went by and the radio broke up again.

The last of the pretty state secretaries passed down the street.

Durwood waited a few minutes and then eased the Ford out into traffic and moved up past where Forbes' car was parked and turned down the side street running alongside the restored mansion. As he passed, his interest perked up when he saw that the mansion housed old Governor Cameron's law group.

Why would Forbes see an attorney? Was he afraid?

Or just maybe he was going to raise a stink with Lhamda-A?

The thought warmed him. Listening on the hidden mike back at the Plantation Inn, Durwood had loved the way Forbes made Acton sweat about the floosie, Angie.

"Hey Bill, Forbes went in a lawyers' building. You gotta give it to him, the guy's got balls. It must've been rough to get caught with his hand in the cookie jar and get canned that way."

About two blocks down, Durwood turned around in a private drive and drove slowly back and parked in a spot where he had a clear view of the rear of the old building. Looking across the shiny red Sunfire convertible parked in the lot at the rear, he could just catch a glimpse of Forbes' road-worn standard-issue blue Chevy parked at the curb in front.

"Fat-cat" Acton drove a shiny Buick. Durwood hated "fat cats"—fancy cars, fancy houses, fancy neigborhoods, fancy schools.

He liked the power of poking around in "fat cats" lives.

If Acton was dirty and was planning something foolish, he was going to enjoy cutting off his balls.

There were always rumors about agents who'd retired early by lucking up on some "fat cat" operator who wanted to cut a deal to get out of tax trouble. He'd often fantasized the idea of cutting himself a piece of the pie. Sometimes he'd lay in bed at night imagining little scenarios about having some really big-time "fat cat" by the balls and retiring to a nice little apartment around Lauderdale.

And, what would be the harm…really?

Those "fat cats" just wound up costing the taxpayers room and board at one of them fancy "white collar resort prisons." Hell, most of 'em got a light fine and two-years-suspended anyway. In less than a year they walked…moved to Switzerland or the Caymans to be near their loot.

Johnston came back on with static and a squeal. "Durr, guess what? Little ol' Angie-baby just drove up to Acton's room."

"No shit?"

He wondered if the guy Acton could be squeezed over the floozy. He and Bill had listened in last night. Angie was quite a performer in the bedroom. A "screamer" to the end.

Even if you had 'em by the balls, trying to shake down Rotarians like Acton was hardly worth the risk. Just his luck. He never lucked on to a "fat cat" that was worth any real money.

On the other hand, sometimes a dude like Forbes had everybody fooled. Idly he thumbed through the file folder lying on the seat. The hackles went up on Durwood's neck. The copy of a recent Lhamda-Alpine printout showed Forbes could possibly be holding an inventory of fancy pharmaceutical samples worth almost a half-million, maybe even more.

Chapter Nine

"BUCHANAN?"

Dressed in his best dark-gray, nearly black Perry Ellis business suit, ordinarily Buchanan would have looked right at home striding confidently into his daily appointments with the various department chairmen of the state's three prestigious medical universities. At the moment, however, he appeared indecisive, defenseless as an antelope poised at the moment of flight.

Standing almost straight above him, legs slightly apart, the slender, patrician woman was wearing a trimly-fitted brocade skirt of a lime and orange floral print which featured a fashionable slit at the center of the front hem. The slit ran up to well above the knee and was powerfully distracting. From this angle, he could see up the length of the inner surface of her long legs, beyond where the delicately patterned hose were fastened to her old-fashioned beribboned garter belt. The sight of her naked thighs above the tops of her nylons and just a tiny flash of the vee formed by the crotch of her peach-beige panties gave him a disconcerting jolt.

Momentarily, he found himself speechless.

Besides being scary bright, Cameron Brawley was an extremely sexy woman. Sometimes it seemed to Buchanan that she deliberately made it difficult for him to remember she was his best friend. To be confronted by her undeniable sexuality often confused him and made him feel slightly dishonest when he was around her. Now, despite the acute distress of the events of the morning, he was tongue-tied by the unexpected, inappropriate rush of his senses.

"Buchanan? What's wrong? Were you just going to turn around and walk out? Don't just stand there. Say something, damnit!" Cammie Brawley demanded.

"Uh?…I really shouldn't have popped in like this. It was thoughtless. I'm sorry, I was just driving by and saw your car. I wonder if maybe we could talk later, real lawyer-client stuff. I'll call Mae for an appointment." He waved half-heartedly and turned to leave.

"You'll do no such thing. Hold on, goddamnit. Forget about later, the timing's perfect. Come on up here right this minute. Let's have a cup of coffee. Don't just stand there, come on up. Nobody to bother us 'til after nine. After the last few weeks in court, I'm happy to see your friendly face. I've missed you. I can really use the therapy. Now, come on."

Reluctantly, Buchanan moved slowly across the foyer and started to climb the circular stair. At the top, Cammie took his hand and led the way along the antique Chinese Chippendale banister to where her office door stood open at the remotest back corner of the long gallery.

Inside she closed the door and indicated a group of chairs bracketed around a low cocktail table in the corner of the high-ceilinged room. A copy of *The New York Times Book Review* lay open on the table revealing a full-page ad for Anne River Siddons' new bestseller.

"Black…right?" She held up the coffeepot.

"Uhmm…" Buchanan stood by one of the chairs until she brought him the coffee and came around to join him.

"Now, what the hell's going on? You don't look anything at all like my dashing hero, Buchanan Forbes, the young jouster of windmills." She looked into his eyes anxiously and took a seat.

"Well…I…ah…I just got the shaft," he blurted. He hadn't meant to blurt it out like that, but the whole sordid tale spilled out of him—Hank's cryptic note…the damning phone call…this morning's meeting with Joe Acton…and a rather disjointed account of the history that led up to it. When he paused for breath, he gave a sigh and took a sip of the steaming black coffee. "I really feel like checking into a hotel and tying one on. I can't stand the thought of facing Alma. She'll never let me forget this."

"Oh, don't be silly. Alma will stand by you…"

"You don't know Alma. She's always expected the worst from me. In her mind I'm the reason for her failing to attain her high destiny in life," he said, resentfully.

"Well, she certainly has to share the responsibility…"

In his confession, he'd told Cammie all about Alma's deal to buy the house.

"No, no, not Alma. Alma could rationalize her way out of cold-blooded murder. She'd never admit any responsibility, and she'll never let me forget this now. Two months after I'd taken that money from Findlay and she'd gone merrily singing and chattering through all that 'wallpaper and carpets' stuff with the builder, she tried to act like she'd been a little drunk and had only been joking. She denied having any part in the way I'd gotten the money. But…don't misunderstand me…I've only myself to blame. She didn't put a gun to my head."

"Well, there are a lot of Almas—a lot of perfect people in this world. I was at a cocktail party last night at the Club. I thought I'd scream at that bunch of hypocrites with their Bible Belt-mentality. My darling jackass husband and my own parents, and a thousand just like 'em, who still proclaim, 'I don't usually drink alcohol, but maybe I'll have just one.' If the dishonesty didn't make me so damn mad, I'd laugh out loud. Most of 'em keep parroting that same stupid lie and go back to the bar until they finally leave knee-walking drunk. Same damn actors, same tiresome speech I've been hearing for years. It doesn't matter what the reality is, as long as they pretend it's something else. God knows, the way some of those fancy brain and heart surgeons put it away, I wonder why there aren't more malpractice and wrongful death suits."

"Yeah, that's Alma to a 'T.' That woman's never been wrong in her life, except, of course, when she married me. But then I don't care about that anymore. I'm scared to death that the Food and Drug, or worse, the IRS, might give me a hard time. I, ah..." He started to say something about the gray Ford but stopped himself.

Suddenly, he felt foolish. He'd been watching too much television and reading too many spy novels—he didn't want to come across as being paranoid.

"Letting that man give you a check was a mistake. Can you explain that check to the IRS?" Imperceptibly, Cammie's manner had subtly become more professional.

"Oh, yeah, I can explain it. But you're right. I knew the check was a mistake from the minute I made the deposit. At the time we had our house in Virginia on the market 'By Owner.' To cover our tracks, Alma wrote out one of those stationery store real estate contracts showing that Findlay and Louise had made us an offer and had given us a deposit down in the amount of Findlay's check. A few days later I wrote him a check to return the deposit like the house deal had fallen through. Findlay cashed my check and gave me the money back in cash. Then Alma dealt directly with the builder and handled all the details of the new house in cash. The builder was very creative with the contract. He didn't want any paper showing the actual amount of the transaction any more than we did."

"Hmm...sounds like you're covered there. Are there any other loose ends? Are you telling me everything?"

"Only Alma's charge accounts at the drug stores in Virginia." Buchanan shrugged. "She played bridge with several young doctors' wives. They all ran similar accounts and their husbands traded out samples with a friendly pharmacist."

"How much did those amount to?"

"Oh, over the period of months—a couple years, really—I guess it all could have come to a few thousand. But those deals were strictly under the counter and the tab was torn up on the spot as soon as it was settled. There were never any real records kept of those."

"Well, if that's all, I wouldn't worry. Sit tight and wait for the next move.

If your suspicions about your boss are true, I imagine he'll be just as relieved to let the matter drop as you will be. I think your bosses are probably very nervous. I doubt your company will go out of their way to make trouble. Are you going to fight this or resign?"

"Resign. I can't stay on now. I feel relieved, actually. Alma would never understand but I've felt like a common whore, for a lot more reasons than the tacky misuse of samples. From time to time, I've acted as a pimp for hundreds of prominent and very respected…and some not so prominent or respected…physicians and pharmacists. I'm just a glorified 'gofer' really, forever scouting up their football and basketball tickets…and theater tickets in New York. I've kissed a thousand pompous asses in a zillion degrading ways. I hate it. I've felt dirty for a long time."

"Then good for you. So, what do you plan on doing now?"

"Jeezie, Cammie…I don't know. Since college I've tried damn near everything…even did a brief turn as a commercial artist. Acton says they'll give me a good recommendation. But I'd be glad for a chance to get out of pharmaceuticals. And…you know I was a journalist. When I got back from Desert Storm I was accepted in med school but turned it down to take the job at Lhamda-Alpine. I'm a pretty good writer, I think…you've seen my stuff. I still turn an extra buck off and on doing freelance medical articles for my old editor back at the Roanoke paper. He's a head honcho at SNS syndicate now. What the hell, I haven't used my G.I. bill. I might just go back to school, maybe medicine or law. Do you think I'd make a good lawyer?" Buchanan nodded at her law books and diplomas.

"I think you'd make a crackerjack anything you set your mind to. Stick to your demand for three months' severance pay. If they try to stall, don't just roll over and play dead. Let's see how anxious they are to forget this thing. It's almost nine. Why don't you call your boss right now, while you're here? Tell him you're in your attorney's office and she'd kinda like to know what his next move is."

"Well, why not?" Buchanan laughed a nervous laugh. He moved to her desk and dialed the motel. After a pause the motel operator put Joe on the line.

"Did you get hold of Harvey, Joe? I'm in my attorney's office. We want to know where we stand."

"Attorney? Aw, shit, Buck! Why the hell did you go to a lawyer? You know we want to do you right. Harvey said he'd try to get you a couple of months' severance, but he doesn't think management will go along with your using the car."

Hearing Acton's excuses made his blood run hot again. "I want my attorney to talk to Harvey, Joe. She thinks you're screwing me over."

"Oh, come on, Buck. Why bother Harvey? Maybe I could talk to him again."

"Hold on. My attorney wants to talk to you, Joe." Reaching for the phone, Cammie practically wrested it out of his hand.

"Mr. Acton, this is Cameron Brawley. I represent Mr. Forbes and I'm not at all certain that he should resign in this situation. We have to consider damages to his professional reputation. He hasn't been given a fair hearing. He's told me some interesting things about you. Sounds to me like you're sacrificing an innocent man just to avoid the unpleasantness of a government investigation of your own activity, and there's the issue of possible collusion with a Federal agency. At any rate, you owe him more consideration. I want to talk to your corporate attorneys. Can you give me their names and a number?" Cammie stopped speaking. Acton had obviously interrupted her.

She listened intently and winked.

"Well, I have a court date at 10:00. If I haven't heard from you by 9:30, I'll call your corporate attorneys myself. My client is under a lot of duress. Our requests are reasonable. Mr. Forbes deserves some assurances. I want a quick resolution. After all, he has a fine record with your company, and there's his family to think of…" Cammie stopped in mid-sentence and listened again.

"All right. My unlisted number here is…" Cammie gave him the number and listened while he repeated it back. "I'll wait thirty minutes, Mr. Acton. Not a minute longer."

She hung up.

"Unless I miss my guess, you'll get what you asked for."

"Gosh, Cammie, I'm so grateful." Buchanan stood and turned away to the window, suddenly overcome with emotion. Seeing her belief in him, it was all he could do to keep from breaking into tears.

Across the back parking area he saw an anonymous gray Ford sedan parked at the curb on the side street leading off Hillsborough. There was a man sitting at the wheel looking over what appeared to be an official folder. It gave him a start. Suddenly the world was full of gray two-door Ford sedans. This one looked the same, or was it different somehow? Dirtier maybe?

Cammie went to a sideboard and brought back a cut-glass decanter of brandy and poured a healthy slug into his coffee.

"Jeez…Alma'll have a fit if she smells booze on me."

"To hell with Alma! Drink it…it won't hurt you," she insisted.

While they waited, she asked him some questions about the deal with

Findlay Hanks. She also asked him to explain his remark about pimping for physicians.

He shrugged and explained it was simply a process of getting some friendly leverage to cajole them into agreeing to do research projects with his company's drugs. A simple matter of getting to be golfing or drinking buddies with them or setting them up with basketball or football tickets, or motel rooms for their rather steamy little afternoon episodes with the office help or staff nurses in their hospitals.

Then he told her about fixing Joe Acton up with the Rex Hospital lab tech Angie.

She giggled when she heard about the panties under his bed.

"Do you still trade samples for Alma's charge account at the drug store? I know some of James' fancy doctor friends do it, but I guess what I'm asking is: Is our tail hanging out in the breeze in any way that they can come back at us?"

A shadow of guilt for his secret cache flickered behind his eyes like a hummingbird against the sun.

He hated to have to lie to her. But, best friend and attorney or not, some things a man had to take to his grave. Besides, what the hell? It was true he hadn't traded any samples for Alma's drug store purchases since they'd moved to Raleigh four years ago. If he pulled off this final coup, he was home free. Nobody could come at him from now on…he'd make sure of that.

"No, I'm clean." He beamed his best wide-eyed choirboy stare.

Before she could respond, the phone rang.

Buchanan looked at his watch. Twenty-eight minutes had passed.

"Speaking." She nodded, then listened.

"We'll want that in a typed statement, signed by you…hold on." She covered the mouthpiece with her hand and turned to him and asked, "Acton says OK to everything, and he'll leave the signed agreement at the desk like you requested. Is there anything we forgot?"

Buchanan shook his head. "Tell him to get it notarized. I'll be there sometime after 3:00 with my resignation."

Cammie repeated what he said into the phone, then added, "Mr. Acton, I want your personal letter thanking Mr. Forbes for a job well done and giving him written assurances that Lhamda-Alpine Pharmaceuticals will always be happy to give him the 'highest recommendation.'" She listened for a moment and hung up.

"If they give you a written commendation now, it will make it damn near impossible for them to come back at you. Looks like they don't expect any repercussions from the Feds. Well, you got three months' severance, your health benefits will remain in effect during that time, you can use your car to look for a job, and the corporation will compute your retirement account and make a lump settlement within sixty days after the three months is over. Not bad, I'd say. As severance deals go, that's about the best I ever heard. I have to give you credit. I don't know if I'd have been cool enough to make that sort of demand if I'd been in your shoes, but then I'm not surprised. You're a smart man, Buchanan Forbes, too damn good for those bastards. This is probably the best day of your life. You'll see." She smiled a reassuring smile.

"Tell that to Alma."

"Tell Alma I said she ought to thank her lucky stars. She should be so lucky."

"Thanks, but I won't waste my breath." Buchanan smiled halfheartedly. "I guess I'd better figure out what the next step is."

"Call me and let me know how things go with Acton. Promise?"

"Well, I wouldn't want to bother you at home."

"Damnit! Humor me, Buchanan!"

"OK. But I want to pay you regular client fee."

"Don't insult me with that garbage. You'll never know how glad I am to help you. I'm always here for you...don't forget it." She hugged his arm tightly and they bumped slightly at the hips as she walked him to the head of the stairs.

There was a disconcerting sexual electricity between them now.

As Buchanan left, Cammie stood and watched him descend the stairs. On wicked impulse, she deliberately widened her stance, hoping he would look back at her again and see her exposed to him the way she'd been when he'd walked in.

When he didn't turn before he went out the door, the slender attorney slumped against the rail and let out a hollow little sigh—not knowing whether she was glad or disappointed.

She felt a bit like a schoolgirl. She knew her mother would think her a shameless slut. So what? Schoolgirl or slut, she couldn't remember when she'd felt so alive.

Now, standing at the balcony, Cammie watched him through the ornate antique Palladian fanlight as he walked away. She was stirred by his athletic stride and economy of movement as he slipped into his car.

What kind of woman would push a man into such a mess and then refuse to stand behind him?

Once, she'd surreptitiously driven by his house and caught a glimpse of Alma, out working in the yard. In shorts and the cutesy tank top with the watermelon pattern, Alma looked a bit dumpy to her. At thirty-six, Buchanan's wife was already going to seed.

Buchanan Forbes was a fine man and a wonderful father.

Too damn good for the likes of Alma Forbes, Cammie fumed as she turned back to her office.

As HE DROVE AWAY, Buchanan checked the line of parked cars in the next block on the opposite side of Hillsborough. The gray Ford was nowhere to be seen.

Cammie had stood by him. Amazing.

Still, he felt terribly dishonest. Would Cammie still speak to him if she really knew the truth about what he was about to do?

Chapter Ten

OFFSHORE SURFSIDE, A FEW MILES SOUTH of Myrtle Beach, the embryo sun poked slanted rays through the broken clouds and the air, fresh-washed from a sudden shower, smelled of pungent salt marsh and early spring flowers.

"Today while the blossoms still cling to the vine..." From her stereo in the back bedroom, the sound of an old New Christy Minstrels CD drifted faintly down the narrow hallway of freelance journalist Inger Strauss Carlyle's orderly-kept mobile home.

Civil Strife Shadows Abortion Shutdown

Inger glanced at the headline as she thumbed the pages of yesterday's Sunday *New York Times* looking for the Travel Section to read her own feature on another hunt for sunken treasure in nearby Georgetown's Winyah Bay.

At the sound of the approaching car, she heaved a great sigh of relief. Putting aside the paper, she moved to the door of the neat, white mobile home in Glover's Trailer Park next door to the 66 Marina. She watched happily as the leggy young blonde climbed out of the rather road-worn yellow 1999 Pontiac Gran Prix coupe, raised her arms high and stretched and waved. "Hi...I thought I'd never get here. Oh, Miz Carlyle, I just love it already."

"I was worried to death. I tried to call around midnight and no one answered at the sorority. Why on earth didn't you call?" With just the hint of gutteral Germanic lilt, the older woman tried to sound reproving, but her relief at seeing the girl betrayed her.

"I'm sorry. I know I should've, but I didn't think about it before I left. It took forever to get rid of Elroy, then I was too anxious to get on the road. I was the last one to leave the sorority…locked the place up. Everyone, including Mrs. Davis, took off for spring break. After I got on the road I thought about it, but I didn't want to wake you. I'm sorry you were worried, Mrs. Carlyle. I didn't leave the campus until after midnight. I drove all night," Penny Wagner babbled, sheepishly.

Dressed in cutoffs and a faded blue sweatshirt, the attractively over-ripe forty-something woman came down the little concrete steps and walked across and gave the girl a warm hug. "Never mind, now. You're safe. That's all that matters. And forget the Mrs. Carlyle stuff. Away from campus, I'm Inger, remember? Let's get your stuff inside and then we'll think about breakfast. Are you hungry? You haven't eaten, have you?"

"Well, not really." Penny opened the trunk of the Pontiac and started wrestling with a bulging, tattered robin's-egg-blue Land's End duffel bag. "Elroy gave me some new diet pills. They make me feel like super-woman. I didn't stop for anything except to pee." She laughed and sat the luggage on the gravel before she reached inside for the rest of her things.

"That reminds me. The good doctor Elroy Goins called about midnight, and then again around four, and about every hour since. I just now hung up the phone."

"Oh, Miz Carlyle, I mean, Inger, Elroy means well, but he's such a jerk."

"Oh, that's OK. At least he didn't try to stop you or…worse… follow you. Did he put up much of a fuss?"

"Oh, sure. He pouted and nagged but I just let him. He'll get over it. He did threaten to follow me, but I told him I'd never speak to him, that the engagement was off if he did. I'll go call him right now." Penny handed Inger a smaller traveling case and the folding garment bag and closed the trunk lid. She picked up the large duffel again and a canvas beach bag overflowing an orange beach towel and the straps of the bra-top to her pink and white polka-dot bikini and followed the handsome older woman inside.

"Where's the phone?"

"Forget the phone. Just wait…he'll be calling again any minute. Let him put it on his quarter. He can afford it. Come along and I'll show you your room." Inger led the way back through the tiny kitchen area and sitting room past the bathroom off the narrow hall. She stood aside at the door to the first room on the right. "Here. It's all yours. Not very big, but it'll get the job done."

"Oh…oh, it's wonderful." Penny put down her bags and plopped on the full-sized bed, which took up most of the tiny room. "I could close my eyes and sleep the clock around… hmmm…" She purred and closed her eyes for a moment before she bounded back upright and took the bags from her hostess and put them on the bed and started to open them. "But I don't want to sleep spring break away."

"The drawers in the chest here are empty," Inger said and pulled the top two drawers out. "Just unpack and put your things away. Make yourself at home, and slip your luggage out of the way, underneath the bed."

"OK." Penny had already begun to busy herself. "It won't take me long."

"Take your time. I'll put some bacon on. Come in and talk to me when you're done." She moved into the hall.

"Will I have time to take a quick shower before we eat? I feel so grungy from the road. I'm just finishing my period. I'd like to feel nice and fresh again." She blushed, averting her eyes.

"Of course, take your time. I've laid out towels and things in the hall bath…it's all yours. I have my own little bath in my room." Inger turned to go. "How do you like your eggs?"

"Scrambled, or any way is fine. I'll only take a minute. Should I put on shorts? I mean what are our plans?" Penny referred to the fact that the older woman was wearing cut-off jeans.

"Plans? No plans. You're at the beach, remember? We just do what we feel like, OK? Shorts are good for day. It's going to be near seventy here. It gets cool at night in March, so jeans feel good, and I hope you brought a sweater."

"Oh, yes, I remembered what you said," Penny called to Inger's back as she moved out of sight down the hall.

Out of the shower, turning this way and that, Penny examined her naked form in the mirrored back of the bedroom door. Her hips were just a smidgen too heavy, she thought—just where the long thigh bones merged into her body, opposite where the v-shaped shadow of her blondish, almost translucent pubic hair curled around the ruffled edges of her labia.

Last night's precautionary Tampax had shown no traces of stain when she'd removed it prior to stepping under the shower. At least she didn't have that nuisance to spoil her peace of mind.

She hummed LeAnn Rimes' new hit as she dusted with powder.

Her first trip to the ocean and everything was working out like a fairy tale. At school, Inger chaired the Writing Program and was her mentor.

Since Christmas, Inger had been here on sabbatical, writing syndicated travel pieces and working on a new book about the famous Brookgreen Gardens.

Penny found a clean pair of white cotton panties printed with tiny pink roses and put them on. She bent forward and adjusted her breasts into a halter top and knotted the straps at the back of her neck underneath her still-damp ponytail. Her breasts were rather large, but quite firm. At least, her breasts would last...her mother's had...she reflected happily.

On a scale of one-to-ten her boobs were a nine...but her butt? A seven? Well, maybe a seven-and-a-half. The men down here would just have to take her as she was.

Turning this way and that to consider the curve of her buttocks, she wondered if she looked too hippy to wear the bikini.

Well, her behind couldn't be all that bad. Back home, the usually quite proper Dr. Elroy Goins couldn't keep his hands off her fanny. That reminded her that since she was engaged, it was about time she went to see a doctor about going on "the pill." Speaking of pills, it was time to take another one of Elroy's little black diet pills. They made her feel all sparkly.

Penny stuck out her hip in an arrogantly disjointed burlesque pose and cupped her breasts sensually with her hands. Wiggling into her shorts, she found an oversized Southeastern Tennessee University Football T-shirt. She giggled and essayed a lewd wink at her coltish, waif-like reflection.

Before she left the bedroom, she dug all the way to the bottom of her beach bag and extracted a copy of the latest *Cosmopolitan* with the article *Masturbate to Endless Orgasm* featured on the cover. With a tiny vibrator, she slipped it in the drawer beneath her undies.

"Oh...there you are. That was fast. I hope toast's all right." Inger was taking a sip from a can of beer and turned when Penny came into the edge of the kitchen and stood by the little serving bar. Inger reflected for a moment on the can and then raised it in a little salute before she put it down on the counter. "Breakfast of champions. I become depraved when I'm down here. Bless his heart, the good colonel would mess his pants if he knew. Want one? Help yourself." She leaned across and lifted the top of a big red Igloo cooler sitting by the door. It was filled to the brim with beer and ice. The tops of two bottles of imported wine showed through. "Or maybe you'd rather have a glass of white wine?"

"Well...beer sounds good. Elroy would have a fit. He won't touch a drop of *anything*. What a drag. After that shower, I feel like a million dollars. I can't wait to see the ocean." Penny reached in the cooler and pulled out a Corona.

"We'll drive into Myrtle Beach after we eat," the older woman said as she broke four large brown eggs into a bowl. She stopped and turned at the sound of the phone. "That's the good Dr. Goins, you can bet on that. Do you want to talk to him?" Inger wiped her hands on a dishtowel.

"Might as well. He'll just keep pestering us if I don't." The younger woman giggled and grabbed the phone.

"Elroy? Oh, hi, honey. Yes, all safe and sound, and I miss you already." She made a face and crossed her fingers.

"Be a good girl? Of course I will." Penny reached for her beer and winked at Inger.

Inger was grinning ear to ear.

Chapter Eleven

ALMA GATHERED HER PURSE from the coffee table and was turning to leave when she saw Buck come driving up. Moving to the top of the landing, she stood looking down on the foyer when he opened the door.

"What's the matter? I thought you were meeting Joe Acton. Did you forget something?"

"Well, I, uh, I don't guess there's any way to make this any easier. Joe fired me this morning." Buck blurted out the bad news even before he finished closing the front door.

"What?" The full meaning of what he'd said didn't hit home right away. She looked at him blankly. "What do you mean? Is this one of your bad jokes?"

He just stood there and shook his head. "No joke, I'm afraid."

Alma suddenly felt weak in the knees. "Fired? Why?"

The dumb jerk just kept standing there in the foyer with that stupid look on his face. She should have known better than to marry him in the first place. Now it was hard to remember that he'd been a star athlete...all the girls were after him. Even the teachers loved him. His grades were nothing to write home about, but everyone said he was so smart. Apparently he'd scored out of sight on the IQ thing. Those stupid old maid teachers were always pushing him to improve his grades. But, even in high school, he'd been so damn irresponsible...such a dreamer. Her sister Jan had warned her. "Buck Forbes doesn't live in the real world."

"Well, are you just going to stand there with your stupid mouth open? They fired you for what?"

"Uh, well, the Feds caught Findlay Hanks for dealing in samples," Buck began. She listened while he explained.

"Buck, you're such a dodo. Don't you see that Joe Acton's taking advantage of you? He's just trying to save himself."

"Well, yeah, I know he's scared of me, but it's past Joe now. The FDA took this straight to corporate in Englewood, but I stood up for myself…" Buchanan started to explain about how he'd negotiated for his severance pay and the car.

Alma interrupted hysterically. "Stood up for yourself. What if the government puts you in jail? I told you not to trust Findlay Hanks. You're so flipping stupid. You never listen. I warned you not to let him have that stuff, that you'd get in trouble. Serves you right," she shrieked.

Buchanan stopped her. "I can't believe my ears. You're the one who nagged me in front of Findlay and Louise that night at the Valentine's dance."

"Don't you dare blame me for this, Buck Forbes. And you keep bringing up that one little time when I innocently told you about Joe trading a few samples for Greta's prescriptions and household stuff. I never, ever, suggested that you get into any deals for cash. I never trusted Findlay Hanks and I never could stand Louise. She was so tacky, the way she used to drink beer out of a can by the pool down at the Bath and Tennis Club. And that whiny little girl of theirs, Ginnie Mae, or Sue, Ginny-something. The Hanks have no class…"

"Alma, are you going to stand there looking me in the eye and deny that you pushed me to let Findlay make that deal to get you the down payment on this place? You don't remember? You deny…?"

"Deny? I certainly do. You and Findlay and Louise made that whole thing up. You…you…all were drinking that night. Don't blame me. I had no part in that. And letting Findlay give you that check. I told you that was dumb. If I hadn't told you to make it look like a failed deal on our house, then they'd have you dead to rights. You wouldn't have a leg to stand on. At least give me credit for that," she reminded him. How dare he accuse her, anyway?

"Yeah, well, I do. And it was your idea to deal with the builder down here in cash. I can't believe that you're saying that selling those samples was my idea…" Buchanan stopped.

It made her furious that he would cheapen himself by blaming her. The fault was his.

"Don't you dare blame me for your stupidity." She drew herself up to full height and let her voice take on a hard edge. "Anyway, don't worry. Joe Acton wouldn't dare make trouble. We've got enough on him to hang him. Greta told me all about how he used his connections to trade out merchandise. And Findlay Hanks told you Joe was diverting samples. He'll back you up."

"Forget Findlay. He won't say that Joe Acton was involved or anything else. He can't. He has no proof. And anyway, I've already talked to Findlay. If he's telling me the truth, he stuck to his story about that cashier's check. Joe says the Feds don't want to prosecute. As far as I'm concerned, the less the Feds talk to Findlay about me, the better."

"I can't believe Joe had the guts to ask for your resignation. That sleaze. He's just as guilty as you are. Did you tell him you'd turn him in?" Ranting hysterically, Alma's voice—like fingernails across a blackboard—rose to a nerve-racking screech. She glowered down from the upper landing with the unlit cigarette in her hand.

"Lower your voice. Where's Garrett?" Resignedly, Buchanan made his way up the steps.

"He's next door, playing with Ronnie Sykes. Dolly came and got him. I was going to meet Judy Edens and Marylee at Cameron Village. We're going to shop and have lunch. Besides, this is a fine time to be worrying about upsetting the baby. Oh, my God, what will I tell our friends? I should call them before they leave." She sniffled as the enormity of the situation began to descend upon her.

Buchanan just stood at the top step paralyzed. Finally, he brushed by her and walked into the large open living room and plopped into his favorite chair in front of the huge picture window.

Alma followed, sounding like a record playing at the wrong speed. "Well, I hope you told Joe Acton that Greta told me all about his sample deals."

Buchanan didn't look at Alma and he didn't respond. He picked up his guitar from beside the chair and idly began bringing the strings up to pitch.

"Put down that damn guitar, Buchanan. What's the matter with you? Did you tell him?"

"Tell him what?"

"That he couldn't fire you, that you'd take them all down with you?"

"No. What's the use? One way or the other, I'm still going to be sacrificed. Even if they could stop it, my career's over, at Lhamda-Alpine at least."

"You mean you're just going to resign without a whimper, just like that?"

"Well, yeah. But don't forget the three months' severance pay and they're going to continue my benefits for ninety days. And the car...they're going to let me use the car to look for another job." Buchanan made an effort to sound cheerful.

"Did they agree to that? I don't trust them. Did you get it in writing?"

He explained that he was going back to pick up the letter, but he omitted telling Alma that he'd gone to see Cammie. Alma was suspicious of his friendship with the older woman.

"Three months. Hmpf! What then? What'll we do? Will we still get the bonus that you have coming?"

"I think so. I'm pretty sure. I'll ask him. I'll call him in a little bit."

"You're such a jerk. It's a little late to be changing the deal. And, what'll we tell the neighbors? I can't face my family. Buck Forbes, how could you do such a thing? I warned you not to sell those samples. How could you?" She stood in front of him now and leaned forward, her face contorted in accusation.

Buchanan went icy calm.

"Alma, I can't believe you can stand there and act innocent. Remember the charge accounts you nagged me into because Greta Acton said Joe did it? You've been after me for three years now to start it up again down here. Why, just last Saturday you wanted me to call Harland back in Roanoke..."

"Well, that's not the same thing and you know it. That was just for a few household things. Taking cash is another thing entirely. I warned you..."

BUCHANAN'S KNUCKLES TURNED WHITE on the neck of the guitar. He just looked at her and lightly picked out the melody to *Wildwood Flower.*

"How can you just sit there and play that dumb guitar when you've ruined my life?" She was livid.

"Don't you think you'd better call your friends and cancel your shopping? Let's talk about this while the kids aren't here. We need to make some plans."

"Plans? You need to find a job, that's our plans." Buchanan watched Alma disappear into the kitchen.

After a moment he heard her calling Marylee. "I have the cramps," she lied.

Buchanan tried to tune her out as she embroidered her excuse with a lacework of unnecessary dishonesty.

He fiddled with the chord change on the melody to *El Paso.* John had taught him the fingering. It was tricky.

"All right. If you want to talk, put that damn thing away." When he looked up, Alma was standing in front of him glaring down again.

Nation's Abortionists Are in Shock
A Number of Suicides Reported

He glanced idly at the morning *News and Observer* lying unopened on the large lamp table.

"I think I could get a job on the *Observer*. I have lunch with Bob Taylor, the managing editor, once in a while. Bob was looking for a medical writer a few months back. I could always write full-time for SNS, I guess." He tried to reflect mild enthusiasm.

"I thought you were glad you left journalism. Besides, the newspaper wouldn't even pay enough to keep up the payments on the house," she snorted. "Next you'll be doing the commercial artist bit..."

Buchanan had to laugh. Right out of Virginia Commonwealth University before Desert Storm caught up to him, he'd done a brief turn as a commercial artist with a grocery chain.

"Well, if things get tight, maybe you could do private duty at the hospital. You're always threatening to do that. Wouldn't you like to go back to nursing?"

"Not full-time...the boys need me," she hedged. The idea obviously intimidated her, and she was right about the boys, too. Alma was very good at the mother business.

"Well, if you worked part-time, what would you think about my going back to school, maybe medicine, or law?"

"With four kids? Get real. How do you think we could manage that?" She sniffed.

"Well, my active duty during Desert Storm qualifies me for a college grant. I'm not sure how much, but I could continue to do some writing to help supplement our living expenses."

"Where? Where would you apply?"

"Well? Maybe Chapel Hill, or Duke, even VCU. Either would do."

"Are you kidding? Where would we live? We'd have to sell the house and we only have one car."

"Well...I, uh..."

"Oh, come on, be realistic. Besides, we might as well make plans to sell the house anyway. We only have three months' income. No telling how long it'll take you to find work, even if you just look for another pharmaceutical sales job. You should go have a FOR SALE BY OWNER sign made up today."

"Oh, no, I mean, let's not panic. Let me look around first and see what's available. What the hell? I might get a job tomorrow. Besides, three months is a lot of time."

"Yeah, sure, and you might not find work for a year. Then we'd lose everything to the bank. With high-paid execs coming in for that big IBM expansion in the Research Triangle we might realize a $100,000 equity in this place. Do you want to just let that go back to the damn bank?"

"No, don't worry. I'd never let that happen." Buchanan fingered the mini-warehouse key in his pocket.

No matter what, his sons wouldn't have to do without.

"Oh God, Buck, how could you get us into a mess like this?" Alma screamed and stomped her foot. Suddenly, she snatched her purse off the raised slate hearth and rushed sobbing to the bedroom.

Watching her go, he suddenly realized there was no bond between them. There hadn't been for a long time. He wondered, fleetingly, if there ever had been. Clearly, he was on his own.

All at once, his guilt was replaced by righteous indignation.

He went into the kitchen and got a beer out of the fridge. Then he went downstairs, crossed the huge playroom and went into his office. He booted up his computer and started typing.

```
March 4, 2002

Joe Acton, Division Manager
13 Scaleybark Circle
Charlotte, North Carolina

Dear Joe:
     It is with a great deal of regret that, for highly personal rea-
sons, I am submitting my resignation effective immediately.
     I will always consider my ten years with Lhamda-Alpine as being
among the most satisfying periods of my life...
```

Satisfying?

In a pig's anal sphincter! He deleted the word and thought it over. The cache in the mini-warehouse crossed his mind.

Rewarding?

Perfect! Smiling, he resumed typing with a vengeance.

```
     ...most rewarding periods in my life.
     I am taking this opportunity to thank the management of Lhamda-
Alpine for paying me full salary and continuing my benefits and
extending use of the company car through the three months following
this date.

Sincerely,
Buchanan G. Forbes
```

He pulled the letter from the printer.

Upstairs he heard Alma walk heavily down the hall and descend the steps of the split-entrance foyer.

The front door slammed.

Outside, he heard her start the car. The engine noise faded as she drove away.

Face it, boy, you're on your own. The realization hit him like a fist.

He picked up a framed snapshot of himself in the pool at Myrtle Beach with his sons. Clearly, those boys worshipped him.

He caught his reflection in the glass of the picture frame.

Some hero now…not even in Desert Storm had he ever felt so alone.

Chapter Twelve

WITH THE CONVERTIBLE TOP DOWN, an errant raindrop splashed on Maggie Oakes O'Brien's nose as she drove Lewis Warrant's tan Cadillac across the drawbridge spanning the Cape Fear River at Wilmington. She'd changed her mind about taking the ferry from Southport. The shock of Zoni Corbett's suicide had left her shaking.

For the thousandth time since she'd left Palm Beach last night, she swore a silent vow: *No more lying, cheating, sweet-talking men for her.* She'd turned thirty-three in January. From now on, things were going to be different. She and the kids could make it without Lewis Warrant Enterprises for awhile. She would just look up her old contacts and go back to decorating again.

Headed for the beach, she passed the shopping area on Oleander and pulled into the Krispy-Kreme and bought a cup of low-fat French vanilla cappuccino. She resisted the temptation to buy a box of donuts for "the kids."

She didn't need the calories.

Back on Oleander, she pushed the stereo buttons looking for music. When she finally found the oldie station, Gail Garnett was crooning the sixties hit *We'll Sing in the Sunshine.*

Beyond Bradley Creek Marina, after she broke out of the tunnel of ancient bearded oaks at Airlee Plantation and crossed the drawbridge at Babies Hospital, the morning shower had mostly passed offshore. To the east, the reflected sun cast a brilliant corona on the fleecy tops of the high thunderheads. Lower in the sky she could see a perfect rainbow where the sun was trying to peek through the wispy remnants of the low overcast clinging to the bejeweled surface of the placid sea.

At the height of the bridge, she slowed as Wrightsville Beach spread out before her like a postcard. Southward to her right she could see the distinctive Blockade Runner Hotel and, beyond, a half-mile south of the old-fashioned water tank behind the rickety little town hall and police station, she could see the gabled roof of her mother's weathered old wooden inn.

Maggie happily sniffed the air and pushed down on the accelerator as the first suggestion of the sexy primordial seashore smells beckoned her.

No place like home. Her shaky hands were steadier now.

At the bottom of the incline of the drawbridge, she took the right hand fork leading onto Harbor Island. Just beyond LBJ's infamous old crony Bobby Baker's once-notorious Desalinization Plant, she turned right again and drove slowly past the Marina Restaurant to the edge of the water and turned into the parking lot of SeaWatch, the new high rise condominium towers overlooking the marina and shrimp docks beyond.

FROM HER OFFICE WINDOW, Naomi Fountain, the resident manager, watched as Maggie pulled the Caddy into the parking lot. She nudged her friend, Julie Hughes. "Lookie, lookie! Madame Butterfly's back again. Didn't take her as long to leave Palm Beach as it did the Caymans."

"Maggie's life and times would make a great 'soap,'" Julie agreed. "Call it: *As The Girl Turns...*"

"Got to hand it to her, that gal's always danced to her own drum." Naomi's laugh had a wistful ring. She really envied Maggie. They'd grown up on this beach together. Not many of their schoolmates were still around.

"Why does she keep going back to the bastard? Everybody knows Lewis ain't ever going to marry her." Julie shook her head.

"Maggie ain't looking for a husband, anyway. She told me that when she started seeing him. Just before she left for Palm Beach in January, she said that he was talking about a divorce now, but she told him she wouldn't marry him. He wouldn't believe her, pissed him off. Went ahead and bought her the old Knight house down the beach from her mother's little hotel, said she could have it fixed up. In January she said he was taking her to catch the Spice Girls in Miami. After that he was taking her to Duke or somewhere to have one of those space-age birth control gadgets implanted in her uterus. Said she was sick and tired of sweating her period."

"An IUD? Sounds exactly like Maggie, but the Spice Girls! And he's giving her the *Knight* house? Jeezus! She's crazy to turn him down. Do you know what Lewis' share of his daddy's estate was worth? Maggie's got to be nearing thirty."

"Thirty-three in January. You don't know Maggie. That girl's got an independent streak. Anyway, most likely she's just back to visit her kids. I think the schools are on spring break this week. This could mean Warrant will be showing up. By the way, when was the last time we heard from Mr. Wonderful?"

"He called last week from Miami. He was heading for the new project in the Caymans, never said a word about coming here."

"Uhh-oh! She's putting her luggage into the VW. Just like the last time. Betcha anything there's been another fight. I wonder if that damn Bug will start? Been sitting there for nearly two months."

They watched as the attractive woman in the skin-tight jeans transferred her luggage from the Caddy into the bright-yellow Bug. When she finished, Maggie took a set of keys and tossed them onto the front seat of the Caddy and slammed the driver's door.

With that, she got into the little yellow car and drove away.

"Well, the car started all right."

"Huh! There's no damn car brave enough not to start when Mary Elizabeth Oakes O'Brien turns the key." Naomi giggled as she watched Maggie leave.

Chapter Thirteen

BUCHANAN READ THE LETTER over and signed it. Folding it neatly, with a regretful sigh he slipped it into a Lhamda-Alpine envelope.

He finished the last trickle of the warm beer, tossed the can into the wastebasket, and went upstairs.

In the master bedroom he looked on the dresser top, expecting to find a note.

Nothing.

Alma was predictable...*uniformly hysterical.*

"Goddamn estrogen poisoning," he muttered under his breath. He'd first recognized and defined her syndrome eighteen years ago when he'd dated her in high school. A long-running exacerbation of chronic-acute PMS, Alma was a landmark case. *Totally irrational!*

Of course this time, in all fairness, he really couldn't blame her for being upset. Losing his job was more than a minor disruption—but it certainly was not the end of the world.

He went into the garage and got some empty boxes and returned to his office and started cleaning out his files and packing up his company manuals. He hadn't really meant to do a lot of packing right then, but he quickly became lost in the obsession to purge himself of the past.

When he finally finished and returned the heavy file and book-laden boxes into the garage, it was after one.

He dialed the motel and waited while the operator connected him.

"Buck, glad you called. I was just sitting here wondering if you'd like to have lunch."

"No way, Joe. You finished writing my letter?"

"Yeah, but I..."

"Does the letter simply ooze of good will and appreciation, like my lawyer said?"

"I took notes. Everything, just like she said."

"OK. Read it." Buchanan waited until Joe came back on the line and read the letter. It sounded all right. If death warrants can bring good cheer, this was the best he'd heard lately.

"Well?"

"Sounds OK. Just leave it in an envelope at the desk. I'll leave my resignation with the clerk. Be there no later than three."

"No hard feelings, Buck?"

"Just leave the frigging letter, Joe. And have it notarized, remember?"

"I remembered. Sure you won't have lunch?"

"Forget lunch, Joe. I don't want to see you." Buchanan pressed the disconnect button.

He went to the fridge, opened another beer, took it into the living room and picked up his guitar. He ran up the strings a little here and there to bring them back on key.

"*Someday the man I used to be...will come along and call on me...*" he sang, here and there humming along where he'd forgotten the words.

After a while he picked up the beer and finished it. Then he went in and fell across the bed exhausted.

When Buchanan awoke it was after 2:00. Even before he walked back through the hallway and looked out the front window for Alma's wagon, he sensed she had not returned. The house had an unmistakable hollow feeling, like some mystical aura of portending. He wasn't sure he really believed in ESP and all that New Age karma jazz, but he knew now that his days in this place were numbered. Some things were scary sometimes when he thought about it.

He picked up his suit jacket where he'd tossed it over the back of the sofa when he'd come in this morning and realized for the first time that he was still wearing his best suit. He'd been so caught up in purging himself of the remnants of his ten-year tenure with Lhamda-A that he hadn't bothered to change.

In the bedroom he undressed and carefully brushed and hung up his suit.

Without a job, his good clothes might have to last a while.

Stepping into the fancy bathroom with its overlarge mosaic tile shower stall, he took his time and let the warm water slowly bring him back to life. After he'd toweled dry, he splashed on a tiny bit of cologne and dressed in bright red golf slacks and a navy blue knit shirt.

With a devil-may-care wink at his reflection, he took a white alpaca cardigan with a red monogram from his closet and looped it around his shoulders with the sleeves hanging loose. He'd be right at home at Pinehurst!

> *"Back around four. Stiff upper lip.*
> *—The Phantom."*

He left the note on the kitchen table. *The Phantom* had been a warm intimacy between the two of them, pre-dating their honeymoon.

By the time he pulled up in front of the Plantation Inn it was nearly 3:00.

Inside, Grover, the day manager, handed him the envelope. Duly signed and notarized, the letter was just as Joe had read to him over the phone.

Buchanan gave the envelope addressed to Joe Acton to Grover and left him a couple of bills.

"Buy yourself a beer, Grover ol' sock. I owe you three or four. You take good care now." He waved as he went out the door to his car.

At a curb market on Old Wake Forest Road, he stopped and dialed Cammie's number. When Mae said she was still in court Buchanan was relieved. "Tell her everything went as planned, and tell her thanks. I'll be in touch."

It was just as well. He was so ashamed, he hated the thought of talking to her, anyway.

The sun was low when he turned on Rowan Street. He could see the gang of kids in front of his house riding skateboards down the hill. John Castle and Charlie and Betty Rodl were supervising, keeping an eye out for traffic. It was the rule of the neighborhood: No skateboarding without at least one parent to supervise. Fighting back a sudden rush of emotion, Buchanan stopped at the top of the hill.

Struggling mightily, he fought back a tear. If he ever got his life back on track, he'd never compromise again.

Finally, he took a deep breath, composed himself and let the car roll forward. At the driveway he tooted and waved and carefully avoided a skateboard that had been left sticking carelessly out onto the pavement.

Gregory, his second-born, followed him from the street back up the drive to greet him when he opened the car door. "Daddy, Daddy, Mama says we're moving tomorrow, back to Virginia with Nan and Granddad."

"Moving tomorrow? Back to Virginia? I think you misunderstood your mother, Greg." The boy had a dirt-smeared, angry-looking strawberry abrasion on his elbow. Fresh blood was still oozing in tiny droplets out of the torn skin. Buchanan reached out and grabbed his hand. "Not so fast. Come here, let's see that elbow."

"Aw, the elbow's OK, Dad, but, we're going to Virginia, that's what Mama said." The boy gave him a passing glimpse of the elbow and twisted it quickly away before Buchanan could fully examine the injury. "Mom called us all in the living room after school and said you were going to be a doctor, that you'd have to go back to school. She said doctors make a lot of bread."

"Huh? Well, now, Greg, don't spread that story around. Nothing's been decided," he called to the slender Huckleberry Finn as Gregory scooted back to pick up his skateboard and rejoin the fun.

"Come on. Ride skateboards with us, Dad," Greg called back as he ran down the drive.

"Maybe, later." Buchanan turned, and shook his head in bewilderment.

"Now what?" he muttered under his breath as he strode quickly down the walk.

"Alma, what's this nonsense Gregory's spouting about moving back to Virginia?" he called as he entered the foyer and climbed the steps.

No answer.

"Mama's on the phome." At nearly four, Garrett, the youngest, peeped his cherubic head around the kitchen door at the top of the landing and ran to him. His mouth was smeared with what looked like grape Kool-Aid. "Are we going to Virginia and live on the farm with Nan and Granddad, Daddy?"

"First I'd heard of it. A visit maybe, but *live?* It's news to me." He picked up the boy and held him high above his head. In the kitchen, Alma was on the phone. There were none of the usual signs of dinner preparation.

He glared at Alma and mouthed silently, "What's going on?"

She looked right through him and turned coldly away.

Bitch, he thought. *We're going to have this out.* Resentment blew over him like a hot wind.

Buchanan lowered Garrett to the floor. He wanted to get him out of the way so he could find out what this craziness was all about. "Cartoon time. Let's go see what's on the tube."

"No, no. Let's go watch 'em ride the skateboards. Will you help me ride with 'em, Dad?" Little Garrett pulled him by the hand.

"Soon, but we'll have to practice first, on a little hill. Go on ahead, Tiger. I've got to talk to your mama. I'll be out in a minute. Stay out of the street, all right?"

"OK, don't take too long. Mama says you're going to take us to MacDommald's, OK?"

"Maybe. Don't slam the door," Buchanan called to the slamming door.

When he turned, Alma was standing at the sink looking out the window.

"Would you mind telling me what's going on?" Buchanan tried hard to control his anger.

"What do you mean?" she said. She didn't turn to face him.

"What's this about moving to Virginia? What did you tell the boys?" Buchanan struggled to maintain control.

"I told them that we're going to move back to Virginia, with Nan and Granddad. I called your father this afternoon. He said it would be fine."

"You WHAT?" Buchanan couldn't believe his ears. "What's gotten into you? Have you lost your mind?"

"Hardly. It's the only sensible thing to do. We're stranded down here. You without a job and the government about to send you to jail? Somebody has to think of the children." Alma's voice was showing the raspy edge of a rising hysteria.

"Alma...I tried to tell you. Joe, and Findlay, too, assured me that the Feds aren't interested in pursuing this. I have three months' severance pay, the car, bonus, everything. Joe's letter of recommendation, it's notarized. There's nothing to worry about."

"Nothing to worry about? And you believe that? Ha!" She turned to face him, her face screwed into a Harpy mask. "And I guess I'm supposed to trust you. We have the house payment, the bills, and now we're broke. I want to get these children into a stable environment."

"Alma, listen. You're not making sense. In the first place, I just told you. We have three months, full salary, my hospitalization and my life insurance will remain in force until the first week in June. I have about ten or twelve grand bonus coming and at least forty or fifty in a retirement account. And I'll have the car to look for a job. That gives us at least a year's cushion. Nothing's changed. Before the end of the month, I could very well find something even better than I had. If I go back to a commission deal with one of the better companies, I'll probably make several thousand more than I'm making now. We need to stay right here and not jerk the kids around. At least let's wait a couple of months, until school's out, at least that. There's no need to panic. Trust me. Come here; it's going to be OK." He spread his hands and reached out to take her into his arms.

She knocked down his hands and snorted with disgust.

"Trust you? Never again." Brushing by him, she fairly rushed down the hall and slammed the master bedroom door.

In a few seconds she opened the door again and shouted through the narrow opening, "I promised the children that you'd take them to MacDonald's. I'm packing their things. We'll be leaving tomorrow after school. And don't you dare tell the neighbors, not anyone, that you've been fired. I told everyone that you've decided to go back to medical school." She slammed the door again.

Buchanan reached the door just in time to have it slam in his face. Before he could reach the knob, she had clicked the inside lock.

"Alma, let me in," he said and rattled the knob in frustration.

"Go away. Leave me alone…"

"Alma, what did you tell my folks? Who did you talk to?"

"I talked to your father, your mother, too. I told 'em that you'd decided to go back to med school. After all, that's what you told me, wasn't it?"

"Alma, I only suggested that that might be a possibility…there are several possibilities. I guess the obvious thing is to try to find another job in the industry. There's no need for this hysteria. We can keep the kids in St. Timothy's and…"

"No."

"Alma, listen."

"NO, NO, NO! I'm taking the kids and you stay here and sell the house. Then maybe you can find something back home in Virginia."

"Alma…"

"Go away, Buck. LEAVE ME ALONE!"

"I need some clothes, my jeans and my Keds and…" He rattled the knob lightly.

Nothing.

He rattled again. "Alma…"

The door opened and a pile of clothes hit him in the face.

The door quickly slammed closed again.

Buchanan stood there, dumbstruck by the hysterical outburst. In his rising resentment and frustration his impulse was to kick the door open and shake some sense in her. He'd done it more than once. The last time, he recalled, she'd thrown a tantrum over buying new draperies.

Finally he shrugged. *To hell with it...to hell with her!*

He'd had enough confrontation for one day. With Alma, patience was the wisest course.

Give her anger time to defuse.

Buchanan picked up the scattered pile of clothes and went to the bedroom downstairs and changed.

Then he walked outside and got his skateboard from where he kept it locked up in the garage and went to join the kids. When they saw him coming, John Castle and Charlie Rodl waved their approval and a little cheer went up from everyone. Kids and parents alike, everyone knew Buchanan Forbes was still the biggest kid in the neighborhood.

AFTER THEY'D BEEN TO MCDONALD'S and stuffed on burgers and fries, Buchanan brought the boys home and hustled them all through their baths and into bed.

Resolutely, Alma remained locked in her room.

Pouring himself a healthy slug of bourbon, he got a legal pad off the kitchen counter and sat in the living room and tried his hand at writing a classified ad.

EXECUTIVE HOME
NORTHMOOR. BY OWNER.
BEAUTIFUL 4 BR, 3 BA, DOUBLE GARAGE...

He had no heart for it and finally put down the pad and stared blankly out the window. Sipping his drink, he picked up the guitar and noodled the strings, aimlessly.

After awhile, when everything got quiet, he went back to the bedroom again. The door was still locked. Buchanan tapped lightly. "Alma, let me in..."

"Go 'way."

He fought back his anger and went in the kitchen and dialed his father's number.

"Dad. I'm sorry I haven't called before but everything has been crazy here today..." He started in and told his father everything. "This thing of bringing the kids up there, it's not my idea…" he went on, but his father interrupted kindly.

"Oh, let 'em come for a few days. We'll see how things work out. As far as we're concerned we'll be glad to have you come back and stay until you get yourself settled, if that's what you decide. Do you want me to tell your mother all about this? I wonder if it might not be best to let things stay the way they are between the women?"

"It's OK, if you think it best. I just didn't want Alma's lie between us, Dad. One thing for sure: However this plays out, I'm going to take a fresh view of my life."

"Good. Uh, do you think…I mean…is there any danger the government will try to…?"

"No. Everyone is anxious to let it drop. There won't be any trouble." Buchanan hoped he sounded confident.

"Do you need money? Anything?"

"No, no. Trust me, money's not a pressing problem," he assured his father.

After he hung up, he poured himself another drink and walked back into the living room. He stood at the window and watched as an unfamiliar car passed under the street light at the top of the hill.

A gray Ford? Dusky blue maybe? *World was suddenly full of 'em.*

Fear did funny things. He tried to laugh.

Distractedly, he picked up the legal pad and stared down at his abortive attempt at the classified ad.

He was in no mood to finish it now.

Sipping his drink, he idly started to think about people he could contact about job openings. He put down one name, thought a minute, then scratched through it.

Who, then?

He was about to give up when another name suddenly popped into his head.

He wrote it down, then another. Within minutes the list was five.

A good start. He put down the pad.

He'd get back to it, first thing tomorrow.

Still sipping his drink, he picked up the guitar.

"Times a gittin' hard boys, money gittin' scaze…Time don' git no better boys, bound to leave this place…" he sang, wryly.

His gut tightened as he watched a gray car slowly cruise under the street lamp again.

Another Ford? His throat went dry.

He took another sip of the bourbon and absently fingered the outline of the key in his jeans pocket with the folded inventory list.

He needed to stash that key and list…had to be a *perfect* place…

All at once, he put down the guitar and closed the drapes.

Smiling inwardly, he went to the kitchen to get some adhesive tape.

If he kept his wits, Buchanan Forbes wasn't dead yet, not by a long shot.

Part 2

Durwood

Chapter Fourteen

SATURDAY, MARCH 9, 2002: Agent Durwood Fisher carefully entered the date in his notebook.

From his vantage point on the street behind the Forbes house, Fisher watched as Buchanan Forbes carried an armful of trash out to the roller rack of garbage cans on the back stoop then disappeared back inside the garage. Five days had passed since Forbes' wife had packed up the kids and left for Virginia. Except to go pick up a FOR SALE BY OWNER sign, which was now prominently displayed in his front yard, the man had scarcely left the premises.

On Wednesday evening at the end of the second day, after Forbes had taken two carloads of samples and supplies over to the local Lhamda-Alpine rep, Bill Rodgers', house, Fisher had recommended that the department end the surveillance at the end of the week. But his partner, Bill Johnston, had been monitoring Joe Acton's phone calls from the motel and, from Acton's conversations with Harvey Kearns at the home office, they'd learned that the quantity of drug samples Forbes had turned over to Bill Rogers had been ridiculously low.

"Buck, what are you trying to pull? We both know that you should have at least ten times that much. There's no Virecta or any Macroten and what about the anti-cancer enzymes? What did you do with all that stuff?" Acton pleaded on the phone.

"That's it. That's all I had left, Joe. I took almost everything I had to Duke Hospital and UNC a couple of weeks back and left 'em for the med students and residents to maintain the patients on follow-up from the clinical trials in the OPC."

When Johnston played back the tape, Fisher asked, "What's the OPC?"

"Outpatient Clinic," Johnston said in his usual smartass way and shushed him so that he could hear the rest of Forbes' conversation.

"Oh, come on Buck. If you're trying to pull a fast one, you won't get by with it. The Feds are probably tailing you right now," Acton warned in a whiny voice.

When Fisher heard Acton say that, he couldn't help but laugh out loud. He wondered what Acton would say if he knew his phone was tapped.

"So what? Can I help it if the bastards got nothing better to do?"

"Can I come inventory your storeroom, just so I can get Harvey off my back?"

"Joe, what I'm tempted to tell you to do with that request is physically impossible. If you think I'm holding out, get a search warrant."

"C'mon Buck, don't be difficult…" There was a sharp click on the tape as Forbes hung up in Acton's ear.

Then Acton called Harvey in Englewood.

"Do you think he actually gave all that stuff to Duke Hospital? My God, according to our shipping records, he should've had a truckload of Virecta, Macroten and the other high-priced stuff. We're talking easily over a half-million wholesale, minimum. It would have taken him four or five trips to haul that stuff in his car and put it in the OPC at Duke. I think he's pulling a fast one. Goddamn it, Joe, I hope the Feds don't get our tit in the ringer over this," Harvey Kearns roared at Acton on the phone when he found out about the short inventory of samples Forbes had turned back to the company.

"Well, do you want me to go to his house? I could make up an excuse. Maybe he'd let me check out his garage. He had this big room specially built to lock those samples out of reach from the kids in the neighborhood."

"Sure, why not?" Kearns agreed.

When Acton went to see Forbes, he didn't even get inside the front door. Forbes walked the fat man straight back to his car and sent him on his way.

At 3:00 that morning, Fisher and Johnston had picked the lock on Forbes' garage storeroom and found it empty. Swept clean.

"The bastard's up to something," the deputy director concluded. "My guess is he stashed the stuff. Someone, maybe this guy Hanks, warned him, or, what the hell, he may have had a regular thing going all along. Anyway, if he stashed it, he can't lay low forever. Those drugs are dated. If the expiration date goes by, then it's no good to anyone. We'll wait him out." The bureaucratic brass had no choice now. Fisher and Johnston had to keep an eye on Forbes for a while longer.

For the first three days, keeping Forbes under surveillance around that fancy residential neighborhood was a first class pain in the ass. Initially Fisher found a spot on the street in back of Forbes' house and pretended to be doing a traffic count. At first, dozens of curious kids on skateboards and bikes and residents out for a stroll had asked him what he was doing and he explained that the city traffic engineers were trying to upgrade the traffic lights around the feeder streets leading to the big Northmoor shopping center.

After the second day, no one paid much attention.

Still, it was hot, tiresome work. And, nothing was happening on Fisher's end. At least Johnston was fat and sassy in that air-conditioned motel room watching game shows on TV. And the lucky bastard was getting his kicks eavesdropping on the orgy going on between Acton and the screamer, Angie.

Then Fisher had gotten lucky.

The department found a house on the street behind Forbes that was under foreclosure by the FHA and after dark Thursday he and Johnston had moved in and set up shop with a living room full of cameras and electronic gadgets. The previous owners, an older, childless couple—the man had been an English professor at N.C. State—had been killed in a plane crash and the place was still furnished. The place even had a double garage, so they could keep their cars out of sight when they weren't following Forbes or Acton around. Which hadn't been a lot lately, since Thursday around noon Acton had kissed the floozy Angie goodbye and checked out of the motel and headed home to Charlotte.

So, for now at least, tailing Forbes had become a two-man job. And last night they'd followed Forbes to the supermarket. While Fisher kept lookout in the parking lot, under cover of darkness, Johnston had slipped underneath Forbes' Chevy and attached a magnetic electronic beeping device on the frame, near the gas tank. If Forbes so much as cranked the engine, the signal device started putting out a steady beep. Now, they could trail him safely at a distance. He'd never know the difference.

Just for good measure, they had put a tap on his phone.

The game was on, cat and mouse.

They had the guy wrapped tighter than an Olympic figure skater's ankle.

Chapter Fifteen

CAREFUL NOT TO DISTURB the rather shapeless form of the man sleeping beside her, Maggie Oakes O'Brien slipped quietly out of bed. Naked, she gathered up her clothes and tiptoed into the living room of the elegantly furnished penthouse. She dumped the small pile of clothes on the sofa and moved to the wide expanse of glass and surveyed the familiar coastal panorama, which spread out in front of her as far as the eye could see.

Fourteen stories below and directly to the south, haphazardly patterned with tiny little grassy islands at either side of the main channel, was the wide silver-green ribbon of the Intracoastal Waterway as it ran along the length of the Greenville Sound.

Muffled by the insulated window glass, in the distance several insistent blasts of a boat's horn echoed across the water, signaling the bridge tender to raise the span.

Bleary-eyed, Maggie rubbed her eyes and located a lone, rather large Hatteras yacht with a high antenna-laden superstructure. The pristine beauty plowed a foamy wake past the mouth of Bradley Creek, her huge Covington diesels purring their way north, headed for her summer berth, most likely at Annapolis or Long Island, or on further north, to the New England capes, perhaps.

Looking straight down, almost between her feet, Maggie could see the pre-dawn activity of sports fishermen—local doctors, lawyers, and assorted Indian chiefs—busily preparing their fancy boats on the dockside of the boat-filled marina. There was a very good run of early bluefish this season and the cloudless, pre-dawn lavender sky promised a great day for it.

Just beyond, on the commercial shrimp wharves at the tip of the small point of land, most of the shrimp boats had already left hours before to trawl for the daily catch.

Westward, across the stretch of the verdant pine- and live oak-forested countryside, the spires of church steeples and the distant twinkling of streetlights marked the beginning of the outlying residential sections of Wilmington.

Now she turned back to the east and stood there still naked, looking out across the jumble of houses on the beach to the horizon where a laser-sharp edge of bright pinkish-orange traced a clean line between the sky and the ocean, promising the coming of sunrise.

A perfect day for the beach.

At the southern tip of the strand, near the skeleton of an old wooden fishing pier that years ago had led to the cavernous, once-famous Lumina ballroom, she could see the light already on in her mother's kitchen but the windows in the kids' bedrooms were still dark.

Ryan was fourteen and Mary Ellen nearly sixteen.

Who would believe it?

The mother of teenagers at thirty-three?

Sometimes she felt like their older sister.

More often than not they seemed more grownup than she was.

Spring break, they would lie abed 'til midmorning if left undisturbed. Dreaming of who knows what.

At that age, she'd had glorious dreams. Where had they gone?

Suddenly overcome, her body shuddered with deep, gasping sobs. Huge rivulets of tears washed slowly down her cheeks.

Finally, she stiffened and wiped away the tears with angry swipes of both forearms. With the flattened palms of her hands she roughly brushed the salty moisture from the tops of her breasts. She cupped her breasts and squeezed them and hugged herself fiercely, trying to stir some feeling back into her body. Her mouth tasted like sandpaper and her head throbbed dully. The leaden heaviness of too much champagne and too little sleep left her feeling as if she were swimming in a sea of glue.

Quietly, she slid open the wide glass panel and felt the cool rush of morning air. Trying desperately to come alive, she spread her legs a bit and stretched her arms toward the ceiling. Raised up on her toes, Maggie inhaled deeply of the pungent salt marsh-laden breeze. With a deep sigh, she moved back across the room into the kitchen and found a double old-fashioned glass and, unsparing with the vodka, she made herself a Bloody Mary. Without even setting the bottle of mix on the counter, she thirstily gulped the drink without taking the glass from her lips, then quickly made another. *Easy does it*, she reminded herself—she had an important client at ten. This time, she used a lighter touch when she poured the booze. She carried the glass back into the living room and sat it down and started putting on her clothes.

"Where do you think you're going?" Lewis Warrant's voice startled her. When she turned, he was standing there wearing his Jockey shorts. He was tanned, but poorly muscled...one of those men who was born looking a bit like he was made of yeast dough. Now that he'd passed forty-five, he was looking more like an amoebae every day.

Until this precise moment, Maggie never realized just how much she hated Jockey shorts.

"Home...where I belong."

"Why? I told you I'm going to ask Val for a divorce this time, as soon as she gets back from Europe."

"Yeah. I know. Last September in the Caymans you promised you were going to see your lawyer when she finished decorating the house in the Hamptons but then her mother got the shingles, or something equally chic. Then, in January when I moved down to Palm Beach, just before you took off to Cancun with her, you promised you were going to get it settled while you were climbing pyramids. Remember? *Deja vu*. It's over, Lewis. This time, it's really freaking over."

"Aw, you can't mean that, Magpie..."

"Don't call me that! How many times do I have to tell you? I hate that silly name. That ol' Buzzy, Binky shit may sound great at the Yale Club, but I hate all your artsy *Town and Country* airs. Come to think of it, I hate every inch of your lying, phony ass!"

"Uhmmm..." He picked up her drink off the glass coffee table and took almost half in one swallow. "You didn't hate it so much about three hours ago."

"You've got sex and love all mixed up, Lewis. But then you're not all to blame. You didn't hold a knife to my throat." Maggie reached down and snapped her bra closed in front and roughly twisted it around her body, stuck her arms through the straps and adjusted the solid masses of her breasts comfortably in the cups. Then she picked up her faded UNC sweatshirt and started shrugging into it as she made her way back into the kitchen to fix herself another drink. Lewis followed, trying to get his cigarette lighter to work, still sipping on the drink he'd taken from her.

"Look, it's different now. Didn't I come running back here from Grand Cayman as soon as they told me you'd left Palm Beach? I love you, Magpie...ah...uh...Maggie, I mean it. As soon as the lawyers can settle with Val..." He reached for her, but she ducked away.

"Look, Lewis, I don't know how to make this any clearer. I already told you, forget it. Don't divorce Val for me. I won't marry you. It's over. I don't want to keep on with this under any terms."

"Oh, calm down. You're just disappointed about Cancun. Could I help it that Val got Monty's revenge down there? You wouldn't expect that I'd hit her with talk of a nasty divorce and property settlements when she was throwing up her toenails and trotting to the loo every five minutes. It would have been extremely poor form. But this time, I..." He tried to hug her again, but she stood her ground and pushed his hands roughly aside. "Come on, Magpie, lighten up, quit pouting. Just think how wonderful it will be..."

"Save yourself a lot of trouble. When I look in the mirror and ask myself what's been so wonderful about all this, the answer keeps coming up a big zero!" Maggie plopped a couple of fresh ice cubes into her new drink. She sorted through the liquor cabinet and found an unopened bottle of Absolut. Tucking the bottle under her arm, she lifted her hand and licked her fingers where the drink splashed on her as she carried the bottle and fresh drink back into the living room.

Plopping down on the sofa, she put on her Keds.

"*Zero?* Well, I don't know about that. What about the beach house? Didn't I promise to put thirty thousand in your account to do the remodeling? And, you can keep the condo at Daytona, and the cabana in Cayman. I told you that, and I told you last night you can go back to decorating Flash and Filigree, the new inn in the Caymans and the other projects. The drawings on Joshua Tree, the spa in Phoenix, will be ready this week, four hundred rooms. You can fly out there with me." Lewis remained in the kitchen.

"I know I'm a fool to turn you down, but I'd feel too much like the whore I really am if I took the condo or the cabana, but I *am* keeping the house. I deserve something. But I don't want to work for you anymore. I'd just wind up half-drunk one night, wake up and find myself right back in the sack with you and we'd have to play this tacky, tired-ass scene over again. I'm going back to decorating for private clients. I have a waiting list. And, I'm going to paint again. The gallery at Daytona said they'd take all the watercolors I could send. No more Lewis Warrant Enterprises for me. I want out. I gave you three years of good work and a lot of fun and games. But no hard feelings, my eyes were wide open. I'll keep the house here and the remodeling money. We'll call it even, OK? At least I've been a high class whore."

"Well, sure, but…but…uuhh…" Lewis' voice was muffled. "Quit using that word…."

"No 'buts' this time, Lewis," Maggie interrupted. She finished her drink and picked up the extra bottle.

"Magpie, don't we have some caviar left?"

She glanced back as she opened the door. Lewis had his head in the refrigerator.

"In the back, second shelf, and, Lewis, don't take it so hard, OK? Ciao." Maggie quietly closed the door behind her and moved to the private elevator in the vestibule.

So much for brave goodbye speeches. Her bank balance was under five thousand dollars, but she hadn't deposited the latest child support check from her ex. The impressive list of waiting clients currently totaled one old-maid schoolteacher. The gallery in Daytona had sent her three hundred and fifty dollars for the two watercolors they'd sold, but they weren't begging for more.

Damn right, she'd keep the frigging house. She'd earned it.

Chapter Sixteen

GORDON LIGHTFOOT
In Concert
Entertainment and Sports Arena, Raleigh, NC
Saturday, March 9, 2002—8 P.M.

CAMMIE BRAWLEY PUT THE PAIR of reserved VIP tickets back on the kitchen counter and looked anxiously at the clock on the kitchen range: 8:03 A.M.

For perhaps the fourth time in as many minutes, she took the wall phone off its cradle and nervously fingered the instrument before she put it back again.

Buchanan had called her twice since Monday and she'd been in court both times. She'd been in the damned courtroom practically the entire week since he'd come by her office on Monday. The messages he'd left her secretary were merely some cryptic words of reassurance for his own well-being and something about Alma taking the kids to Virginia. Now she dreaded going to the park. She had this sad feeling that Buchanan's Saturday mornings in the park were over.

Perhaps her secretary had misunderstood...

And? If his wife had the kids in Virginia, perhaps he would go hear Gordon Lightfoot with her? It was a seductive thought. All week, Cammie had wrestled with the idea of calling him at home, but was reluctant. She'd done that once before and Alma had answered and started firing questions. "Who's this?" and "Can I tell him what it's about?"

She'd had no reason to feel guilty. Still, the prissy bitch had put her through a regular third degree.

"Come on, Tyler, don't be so poky." Back in the bedroom wing she could hear Amy, the older of the two girls, impatiently urging her sister to hurry.

Cammie finished her coffee, rinsed the cup and put it in the drain. Then she picked up the cooler, hooked the coffee thermos with her little finger and took both to the foyer and sat them on the marble floor while she opened one of the heavy double front doors, lovingly hand-carved in Spain.

"Come on, girls, I've packed a picnic for brunch," she called. "Be sure and close the door tight. I'll be waiting." She put the cooler and thermos in the trunk of the shiny red Sunfire convertible parked in the drive outside the garage. She started the engine and was putting the top down by the time the girls came bouncing up the walk.

"Is Mr. Forbes coming, Mama?" Amy asked. Tyler had a crush on Gregory Forbes, Buchanan's seven-year-old.

"I'm not sure," she said and her heart skipped a beat. "I hope so," she added, suddenly a little breathless, as she backed out of the drive.

"Ty's sweet on Greg Forbes, Mama." Amy, a sophisticated lady of nearly eleven, loved nothing better than to tease Tyler, who would soon be eight.

"Well, she's got a picture of Granger stuck in her diary, Mama..." — Tyler was used to her sister— "...and Mama, you should see what she wrote..."

"You little sneak. You stay out of my diary." Amy gave Tyler a push.

Tyler giggled. Amy turned red and looked away at the golfers putting out on the fourth green.

"When school's out, could we invite Mr. Forbes and the boys to the beach for a weekend, Mama?" Tyler asked unexpectedly.

When the girls were little, Cammie had bought a big old beach house at Pawley's Island below Myrtle Beach and every summer since, she'd marked July and half of August off her calendar. She took the girls and they'd spent their summers there.

It had become a tradition.

Sometimes their father came down on weekends and he usually joined them for the week over July 4th. But, as time passed, his time there had grown shorter and shorter. Last year he'd been too busy to come at all.

The girls had taken little notice.

James was like so many physician fathers of their friends. His life was medicine. It was his religion—an obsession.

"Yes, could they, Mama?" Amy chimed in.

"Well, I, I don't know, their..." She started to remind them that the Forbes boys had a mother but she let the thought die unspoken in her throat.

She reached across and turned on the radio.

"We'll sing in the sunshine, make love every day..." The singer painted a seductive scene. Cammie fantasized Buchanan Forbes and his sons, a pack of healthy male animals, running in the surf. They could take the kids to Murrell's Inlet, and get some shrimp and go crabbing by the bridge over the waterway.

Her heart soared. It would be marvelous fun. She caught her breath, just thinking about it.

She'd been saving a perfectly scandalous black maillot jersey suit she'd bought at a regional American Bar Association meeting in Miami last year. It did wonders for her breasts and legs.

Cammie pushed harder on the accelerator pedal. She could kick herself for being so afraid to call Buchanan at home. She resolved to call him from her cell phone at the park if he didn't show up. Buchanan was going through a bad time. After all, what were best friends for?

My God, she'd just spent a week pleading a capital case in Federal Court. Why was she so flustered about a simple thing like a phone call about some stupid concert tickets?

Why indeed?

Chapter Seventeen

AT THE TOP OF THE WALK, Chuckie Rodl, Charlie's six-year-old, was crouched down, peering beneath Buchanan's car.

"What's the matter, Chuckie? Lose something?"

"Uh-huh. Chester's got a dead mouse under there and he won't come out. When's Greg 'n' Gray coming home, Mr. Forbes?"

"Uh, I'm not sure. Let me just see what Chester's up to. I gotta move this car, but we don't wanna run over Chester."

Buchanan stooped low and caught a glimpse of the orange-striped tomcat, warily regarding the both of them, jealously protecting a little gray ball of fur under one of his front paws. The cat was firmly ensconced smack dab in the middle of the car, just out of reach.

"Hold on, Chuckie. I'll go get a broom out of the garage. We'll chase him out from under there." He started toward the side entrance door to the garage.

"Uh, Mr. Forbes? What's this shiny little gadget for?" Chuckie called after him. There was a curious note in the boy's voice. A warning light clicked on inside Buchanan's head and he turned back to look. Chuckie had crawled halfway up under the rear of the car and was lying on his back looking up under the frame.

"Wait. Don't go crawling under cars, Chuckie. It could be dangerous if someone didn't know you were there. Come on out now."

"But look, Mr. Forbes. There's a funny looking little box sticking up under there, looks kinda like a little radio."

"Where?" Buchanan flattened himself on the concrete and peered into the shadows under the car.

Chuckie pointed to the shiny—obviously new—matchbox-sized device clinging to the frame beside the gas tank. Buchanan caught his breath.

"Oh, yeah, that. Has something to do with the, the speedometer, I think. Come on out now." He stood up, brushed off his jeans and waited for the boy to scoot from under the car.

While all this was going on, Chester saw his chance. Mouse firmly in his mouth, the big tomcat dashed out from under the car and scooted back across the street into the Rodl's yard as if he was shot out of a Roman candle.

"Well, there goes Chester, Chuckie. Be careful crossing the street. Tell your folks hi for me."

"Tell Greg 'n' Grayson I wish they were back here." Chuckie headed after Chester.

Buchanan lowered himself to his knees and took another peek under the car. No doubt about it; he was being tailed. And someone was goddamn serious about it.

He brushed himself off again and got in the car and backed out into the street. When he'd gotten down to the foot of the hill, he remembered the funny clicks he'd heard on the phone last night when he'd called the boys in Virginia.

The key?

His heart was beating faster now. How far would they go? Could they search his house?

Legally? Not without a warrant. Anybody with four young sons who watched as many spy shows on TV as his boys did, knew that much. But, what was stopping them from snooping about while he was away? It was not likely during broad daylight. Still...

FDA...IRS...FBI? Laws or no laws, the new Court under the Christian Coalition had suspended all the rules.

He turned left on Carrituck, circled the block and pulled back into his drive.

Back inside the house, Buchanan picked up the phone and put it quickly to his ear. There was an unmistakable clicking sound on the other end. He dialed the number for the correct time.

"The time is eleven minutes past eight," the recording droned.

He listened as it began again and hung up.

His hands were sweating now.

No mistake. There was another click when he picked up again.

This time he dialed Cammie's number.

No answer.

Trying to order his thoughts, he moved to the kitchen window and stood staring out across the tiny creek that separated his back yard from the houses on the street behind him. Between the houses he watched idly as a gray Ford sedan backed out of the drive of a house across the next street and sat there, waiting at the curb. The man behind the wheel kept looking Buchanan's way. The driver seemed undecided and finally pulled back into the drive but still he sat, waiting in the car.

All at once, it hit him. The yard of the house where the car waited had been a jungle yesterday, or the day before, unmowed for many weeks.

Now, Buchanan recalled that the house had belonged to the couple that had been killed in an air crash. The sign proclaimed the VA or FHA had foreclosed. It had been sitting empty for several months. Nearby homeowners had raised a fuss with the local Feds about the careless upkeep. The unslightly appearance was spoiling the neighborhood.

Now the lawn was neatly manicured.

A not-so-funny coincidence.

Buchanan's gut did a warning flip.

Rummaging in the kitchen junk drawer, he found a roll of invisible Scotch tape. He tore off a strip about two inches long and taped it across the edge of the back door at the very top, taking care to rub it down tight.

Still carrying the roll of tape, he went into the bedroom and from off his dresser top he raked a substantial collection of nickels, dimes and quarters into his hand and put the collection in the pocket of his jeans.

Had to find an untapped phone. Cash left no trace.

When he went back into the kitchen, he tore off another strip of tape and left one end sticking to his thumb while he replaced the roll in the drawer. In the living room, he put his guitar in the case, and case in hand, he went back down the steps, out the front door. Without glancing either way he leaned the guitar against the brick and quickly stooped and affixed the tape across the separation between the double entry doors at the bottom. When he stood, the strip was invisible.

Satisfied, he put the guitar in the car and started out again.

Located almost all the way across town off Western Boulevard, the park was situated between N.C. State University and Dorothea Dix, the sprawling state mental hospital.

No sign of the gray sedan. Buchanan took no comfort in that. With the electronic beeper doing its job, there was no need for the driver to stay close.

It was almost nine by the time he reached the park's sparsely-popu-lated parking lot. At the sight of Cammie's red convertible, Buchanan's heart leapt up.

With his guitar case, he started up the path toward the playground area. He caught the sound of Amy's voice and Tyler's shrill giggles long before he topped the first long rise and saw the three of them higher up, by the picnic shelter. Cammie was setting out a picnic on a table under the shelter near the swings and seesaws, beside the big kids' slide and the sand-boxes.

He stopped and turned and looked back down at the entrance to the parking lot below. The gray Ford sedan slowed on Western Boulevard and went on by, down around the curve toward the entrance to the State hospital.

He smiled. It would be damned impossible for them to get close to him here.

Screw the bastards. Let 'em sit in the car somewhere out of sight around that

curve and look at girlie magazines and listen to their boring little lullaby of
electronic beeps.

As he turned and climbed on up the hill, Tyler spotted him and shouted and waved.

Cammie looked up from her picnic cooler. She broke into a wide smile and stood up on the bench and waved frantically like a schoolgirl. The sight of her brought an aching to his throat.

His mood brightened for the first time in almost a week.

He quickened his step and finally broke into a trot as he made his way up the gentle slope.

Things were looking better all around.

Behind the shelter were public rest rooms. Just out of sight from the street, there was a small kiosk with a pair of glass-enclosed phone booths.

A comforting sight indeed.

Chapter Eighteen

AT MYRTLE BEACH, Penny Wagner stood at the boardwalk rail, took a tiny black diet capsule from her purse and swallowed it with a sip of the cold beer from the big milkshake cup. Now that she was developing a taste for it, the beer tasted sinfully delicious. And the pills made her feel very sexy.

For March it was an exceptionally summery day at Myrtle Beach.

Wafted on the shifting sea breeze, the salt-laden late-morning air was filled with the vagrant aromas of hot popcorn, cotton candy, mustardy hot dog smells and—now and again—the subtle, clean scent of ocean spray was mixed with a wayward whiff of suntan oil.

Across the way, where the wide avenue dead-ended at the boardwalk, the jukebox in the amusement pavilion was playing "...*going where those chilly winds don't blow...*"

The beach was still so exotic to Penny. She blinked hard and looked again, trying to permanently etch the idyllic scene in her memory. The view of the ocean was breathtaking. Beyond the breakers, just off shore, there was a ragtag armada of boats of various shapes and sizes trolling up and down the strand. Earlier, Inger had pointed out the fishermen busily working the rods and lines. "The spring run of blues, bluefish. They've been killing 'em all week."

Just down the beach a father and his little boy had just sent a plastic kite climbing in the breeze. Dancing and darting against the almost cloudless sky, the red and black kite looked something like a prehistoric pterodactyl.

Up and down the length of the strand, everywhere she looked, there were smoothly muscled young men and pleasantly rounded young women in bathing attire.

A trio of young college-aged men walked by and looked back with a collective stare. One tripped and almost fell.

The attention brought a pleasant flush of excitement, made her feel like a beauty queen. When the trio had turned the corner at the avenue, Penny—smiling inwardly—stole a self-conscious glance down between the pleasing swell of her breasts spilling out over the skimpy bikini top.

Across the boardwalk, sitting on a barstool in the Ocean Front Grill, an open-sided hamburger stand, Inger Carlyle had struck up a conversation with a rather rough-looking man wearing well-worn khaki work pants. The pants rode low on his hips. They were bleached almost white by countless washings. The jeans were held up by a wide belt with a big buckle bearing the badge of the NYPD. Across his barrel chest, his equally faded black T-shirt displayed the Pabst Blue Ribbon trademark and, across the back, the catch phrase WHAT'LL YOU HAVE? was screened in large letters. The man's arms were well-muscled, like a weight lifter's, and his back and chest were massive, but around his belt line, he was beginning to show the tell-tale first little roll of a future beer gut.

There was a deep Michael Douglas dimple in the man's square-set chin and weathered crowfoots were etched at the corners of his eyes. Above the craggy Gaelic face, his thick black hair, mowed short and flat in a spiky military-style crewcut, glinted a random peppering of gray and was streaked silver at the beginning of the sideburns.

Penny guessed he was about Inger's age, maybe a few years older...late mid-forties, perhaps.

Dressed in a flattering pair of white tennis shorts and a green paisley tank top which seductively modeled her imposing breasts, Inger was striking, a fact which was attested to by the way the male heads turned as the endless procession of boardwalk strollers marched by.

Penny's favorite fantasy was to have an affair with an older man, but the one Inger was with was a trifle too...Cro-Magnon... too...earthy?

Whatever.

And, perhaps just a trifle old, but it was mostly the dull, vacant look of intellectual bankruptcy that put Penny off. Cavemen and truck drivers were not featured players in her fantasy scenarios.

As Penny watched them, Inger glanced her way and, then, as she did, so did the man. Penny pretended not to notice, but she suspected she was part of their conversation. All Inger's friends had been politely curious about her since she'd arrived here on Monday. She could see that the man obviously was not displeased by what he saw, but he wasn't leering either.

Not at all the look of a dirty old man.

Perhaps she had misjudged him.

By her body language, Penny could tell that Inger felt comfortable with the stranger.

More…

She liked him.

But there was nothing flirty in Inger's manner. She betrayed nothing physical in her reaction to the man.

A comfortable relationship.

He was sexy, though.

Penny turned her attention to the legions of young men moving in random patterns at random speeds, beach and boardwalk, in the surf, all around.

Baggies or cut-offs. Tank tops or T-shirts. Most were long-haired.

There was a rather unimaginative sameness about them.

Cardboard cutouts. One-dimensional, every single one.

Not at all like Dr. Elroy Goins. And yet…the same.

She shivered involuntarily when she watched the fascinating bulges in the swim trunks of three approaching college-aged boys. Just yesterday, she had added a copy of a recent *Sports Illustrated* featuring the leading male swimming prospects in the upcoming Nationals to her collection of erotica under her mattress back at Inger's trailer. Idly, Penny wondered what the good Doctor Elroy Goins would say if he knew she masturbated.

She looked back at the older man talking to Inger.

Crude perhaps, but nothing boring there. Yes, she'd probably misjudged Inger's friend.

Inger glanced her way and smiled.

"WHO'S YOUR MYSTERIOUS young protege, Carlyle?" Sharkey Mallone guzzled thirstily from the can of Blue Ribbon and nodded appreciatively in the direction of Penny standing across the boardwalk at the rail. He reached down and pulled up the loose sleeve of his T-shirt and wiped his mouth and chin. "That young woman ought to be against the law."

"She is, for the likes of you, Mallone," Inger laughed. "Anyhow, you've got more'n you can handle at home."

"You got that part right." Sharkey Mallone looked heavenward. "Still, sometimes God exceeds himself. There's a certain angel-devil look about that one. She's going to be trouble…" His words trailed off as he drank from the can again.

"Trouble?" Inger frowned. "She's may be sexy but she's as pure as the driven snow, a very talented poet. Editor of our campus magazine. You've been writing that blood and sex stuff so long it's given you a perverted view of life. By the way, I saw a blurb in *Publishers Weekly* that you're coming out of retirement. Is it true? You've got a new book coming out?"

"Yeah, in June. My publisher sent out the releases last week," Mallone shrugged.

"Well, it's about time. How long since the last one? A few years? I lose track. And, of course this one's automatic Book-of-the-Month selection. Pity the poor struggling writers like me, sweating in cigar-fouled newsrooms for twenty years. I was just reading in *Publishers Weekly* that Helen Hunt is going to direct and star in a remake of *Peyton Place*. Poor Grace Metalious died at thirty-nine, after struggling all those years to get *Peyton Place* published. The article said that so many publishers rejected *Peyton Place*, poor Grace lost count. And, then, there's you, a 'true crime' pulp magazine hack who comes along and sells his first legitimate novel right out of the typewriter. The great Sharkey Mallone, creator of the Sex and Sadism school of literature. Poor man's Raymond Chandler. Mallet O'Hara, private eye, modern day Philip Marlowe."

"Metalious was a freakin' lush, and Chandler couldn't hold my jock strap. Marlowe was a pussy compared to Mallet O'Hara…"

"That's what I love about you, Mallone. You're so full of love for your fellow man…and modest to a fault."

"It's my inferiority complex…I'm trying to overcome it…"

"I keep noticing…"

"You really read my stuff, Carlyle?"

"Yeah. Do I get a copy of the new one?"

"I have an extra bound galley at home. Stop in this afternoon."

"Well, thanks, I will. Tell me, Mallone, after *Solitary Judgement*, you had six all-time bestsellers in six, seven years. Why'd you just up and quit and leave New York and move down here to the boonies? How long has it been since the last one? Seven, eight years?"

"Ten years this month. It ain't complicated. I quit because I didn't need the money. Besides…" Mallone put the empty can on the counter and signaled for another "…don't give me that poor struggling writer routine. I don't know many chairmen of university journalism departments who also are on the masthead of a major magazine and full-time contributing editors for papers the size of the *Journal-Constitution*. Poor Inger, poor thing…" Mallone accepted the fresh beer from the counterman. "You're on a full-year paid sabbatical from that Tennessee cow college to write your book. I was eating Beanie Weenies and fighting off cockroaches the size of rhinos on the ninth floor of a coldwater Brooklyn walk-up when I wrote *Solitary Judgement*. Nobody was paying me a professor's salary to bum around Myrtle Beach and Pawley's Island while I filed travel pieces for the Atlanta paper and worked on a book about a fancy mansion with a yard full of naked statues. Poor Carlyle…"

"Oh, cut it out, Mallone. Do you know how much college teachers make?"

"Sure, but I also know that *The Atlanta Constitution* runs your travel feature every Sunday. And *Elegance Magazine* and *Holiday*, too, run your byline with some regularity. Didn't you tell me that they'd already optioned first serial rights on the Brookgreen Gardens book? Save the poverty routine, Carlyle. Who's the bird, anyway? Virgin or saint or somewhere in between? She's centerfold material. Trouble for someone."

"Her name's Penny Wagner. She's my star student, going to be a crackerjack reporter if she wants to, but has a real talent for poetry. One of her poems was picked up by *Southern Review*. Besides, she's engaged to P. Elroy Goins, III. He's only twenty-nine and already chairman of Pershing's board."

"Oh? Twenty-nine? Still wet behind the ears and the Colonel's chairman at Carlyle Academy? No shit? How's that?"

"You've heard of BankSouth, Nashville?"

"Oh, yeah…'P' as in Pruitt…P. Elroy Goins, Senior. Cover of *Forbes* magazine. I get it now."

"Get what?"

"She's engaged to the heir to the Goins fortune? Well, well, well, that does make everything a bit clearer. She's your protègèe? Talented huh? A real poet? Save the Pollyanna routine. I wasn't born yesterday, Carlyle. You're just playing politics for Pershing, the dutiful Colonel's wife. How are things in the private military academy business these days, Mrs. Carlyle?"

"Don't jump to conclusions. Penny's really special to me."

"I'm no fool. No wonder you've taken an interest."

"You're such a goddamn cynic, Mallone." Inger threw back her head and laughed. "This has nothing to do with business or academic politics."

"Let me guess. So, do any of the Goins boys, father or son, or grandpa, maybe, sit on the board at your precious Southeastern Tennessee academic cottage cheese factory by any chance?"

"Well, sure, but I'm telling you, Penny Wagner worked for me as an intern while she was still in high school. Her mother was a friend of Pershing's. They grew up together. I want you to understand, it's not like that…" Inger's voice betrayed just a hint of its Germanic lilt as her emotion crept in.

"OK, OK, just kidding. Maybe." The man laughed again and drank from his beer. "You gotta admit though, that having her for bait doesn't hurt Pershing's clout with daddy Goins's kid heading his board. Which reminds me, is he coming down anytime soon? Tell him I bought a new boat, a thirty-eight-foot Bertram. Tell him to get his worthless conniving ass down here. We need to do some serious fishing."

"He'll be tickled pink but he can't come 'til after this school session. The break between the spring quarter and summer school, the first two weeks in June are usually best for him."

"Well, that may be too late. My publisher has me blocked off on TV talk shows and book signings almost all summer. I have a contract, and with fancy toys like the Bertram, I do need the money now…"

"OK, I'll tell him. Penny's coming back down here the first of June to spend the summer and help me on the Brookgreen Gardens book. Maybe he could drive down with her."

"Good. So that one's going to spend the summer? What will the snooty Dr. P. Elroy Goins think when he sees you living in a trailer park?"

"He's already been here. His daddy has a house at Pawley's Island. Besides, he'd camp out under a bridge if it meant being near Penny."

"I'll bet." Sharkey Mallone took a long look at Penny.

"I made him promise. He can come one week over July fourth and again in August, before school takes up again. We got work to do. He understands that he can't hang around all summer."

"Uh huh." Mallone smiled a crooked grin. "And the rest of the time she'll just help you with research and sit at home at night and write poems about the surf and sand?"

"Oh, quit being such a cynic. Look at her. She'd never even seen the ocean 'til five days ago. What's the harm if we occasionally have a night out? I'll make sure it stays platonic. It'll be a lot of fun. I'll look out for her."

"If I were you, I'd dress her in an old flannel robe and chain her to the kitchen pipes. She's got a restless eye."

"Oh, that's absurd."

"You ever hear of estrogen overload, Carlyle?"

"She's a good girl. Mallone, you've got a dirty mind…"

"I just hope you know what you're in for, Miss Pollyanna Carlyle."

Chapter Nineteen

AMY AND TYLER RAN down the hill to greet Buchanan with a hug.

"Where're the boys?" Both girls started asking questions as soon as they were within shouting distance.

It made him resentful to have to explain that Alma had taken the boys to Virginia. He felt like a fool telling them he didn't have the foggiest notion when they'd all be coming back.

Arm in arm, they all began climbing the hill to where Cammie stood waiting near the top, under the picnic shelter. As they neared the top, Tyler took the guitar and ran ahead.

"I was hoping you'd show," Cammie said as Buchanan, arms around the shoulders of the still-chattering Amy, walked up to where she stood.

"Mama, Mrs. Forbes took Garrett and Greg and the boys to Virginia. Mr. Forbes doesn't know how long they'll be away." Amy burst into tears. "Maybe I'll never see Garrett again."

"Now stop that. They may be back any day." Buchanan tried to comfort her as he bent to lift her chin and brush away the tears.

"Oh, do you really think so? When do you think?" Tyler asked and tugged at his hand for attention.

"Well, I, uh, we'll just have to wait and see." He avoided making empty promises.

"Run along and play while I fix the food. Mr. Forbes and I have a lot to talk about." Cammie shooed them away to rejoin the kids they'd been playing with when Buchanan arrived.

"Will you stay for lunch? Please, please? Will you sing about the *Candy Bar* and do *Beans in My Ears*?" Amy pleaded.

"Well, I'm not going to just run away. Go ahead and play with your friends."

"Run along, leave your jackets here with me. It's getting warm." Cammie laughed and struggled to pull her own lightweight parka over her head.

Buchanan watched as she raised her arms, breasts jutting against the light cotton jersey.

Cammie was so youthful, alive. Coming up the path, he'd marveled that she looked like a college girl. That she was eight years his senior was impossible to believe. She radiated that well-scrubbed aura of the best Eastern finishing schools. Except for a suggestion of lipstick, she was wearing no makeup. Her well-worn jeans were faded almost white at the seat and the knees. Hugging her legs, they looked as if they'd been spray-painted there. Her panty line showed seductively as she moved. Her heavy breasts thrust arrogantly against the light fabric of the white turtle-neck. Clearly, her nipples were erect. Helpless to take his eyes away as she struggled free of the jacket sleeves, she caught him staring.

"What's wrong? Have I got bird plop on my jersey or something?" She laughed, self-consciously. Obviously pleased at the attention, she tried to hide it with a little joke.

"Not at all. I'm just glad to see you." Buchanan blushed but didn't look away.

She held his gaze and they both stood not speaking, until the girls had moved away.

"I'm sorry I didn't get back to you. I was in court all week, then last night and this morning I was afraid to call. For some crazy reason I guess I was afraid I'd have to explain to Alma, ah, well, uh, I'm not at all sure why."

"Well, you had no way of knowing, but she left Tuesday, just packed up the boys and left." He brought her up to date on Alma's little melo-drama.

"Couldn't you have stopped her?" She looked down and gave a little kick at a pebble and missed. "I don't quite know why I'm so upset. It's none of my business, anyway."

"I guess I could have, but she was irrational almost from the moment I walked into the house after I left your office Monday. Crying. Accusing. I warned you, remember?"

"Oh, I can picture it all right. Did you confront her with the truth of her part in all this?" Cammie kicked at the pebble again. This time she sent it flying across the shelter until it rattled off a large steel trash drum. The sharp noise made an eloquent statement of her disgust.

"Oh, yes. But I already told you. Her denial is impervious to the truth. I can assure you, if Alma had been in that well-known Biblical set-ting, she would have stepped right up and cast the first stone with a vengeance."

"Why do you let her get by with it?"

"Well, I'm not into exercises in futility. It's easier to put up with her." He spread his hands in frustration. "You don't know her. She's built this solid fortress in her head, a logic-tight compartment constructed with blocks made of other's mistakes—mostly mine—and her father's."

"Her father? I don't understand…"

"He's dead, drank himself to death, actually. A very successful, but a very uncaring, selfish man. He made Alma's mother's life a living hell, and Alma's, too."

"Oh, spare me that. Anyway, you mustn't let her make you take all the guilt. The way it's going, you're going to have to confront this sooner or later...that is, if you're going to continue to live together. Lousy childhood be damned, you can't just let her treat you that way. You're too good for her..." Cammie stopped. She was stepping into deep water now.

"Well, I don't know..." Her intensity took him by surprise.

"I just hate seeing you take all the blame for this." She looked for another stone to kick.

"Cammie..." Gently, he took hold of her shoulders. "She can't help that she's insecure."

"But, don't you see, it's you and the children that have to live with her self-centeredness. She's taken your boys...she'll ruin your life. Are you just going to stand by and let that happen?"

"Look, *my* life isn't the issue here. If it weren't for the boys, I'd have walked a long time ago."

"The kids might've been better off, and anyway, maybe you could still have the kids. There are plenty of women who'd make you a good wife, and a mother for those boys of yours..."

"Whoa, I know you're my friend. But, marry a man with four wild Indians? I'm surprised that you're that naive. Besides, I doubt I'd ever get married again. I think I'd rather be free to play the field..." He laughed and winked lewdly.

"You? Play the field? If someone made a play for you, you'd turn and run. I'd bet on it."

"Yeah? Try me. Rule number one for Buchanan Forbes, world-class stud, is: If temptation comes along, give right in." Chin out, he challenged her.

"Anyone who believes that, stand on their head." She shot him a look and tossed her head.

"Well, well, no wild embrace? I guess I called your bluff..." he began, but let it drop. This was leading into uncomfortable territory.

There was a momentary silence as she gave him a disgusted look.

"Well, anyway, what are you going to do? I drove by your house Wednesday and saw the sign in the yard. Are you going to run back to Virginia with your tail between your legs? I would have thought you'd be more of a fighter." Her attempt at a hard look gave way to a sly smile.

"Quit trying to get me stirred up. It's not necessary."

"Well, what about that sign in your yard? That looks like a flag of surrender to me."

She was baiting him now and he knew it.

"Not so. I admit that Alma ordered the For Sale sign, but now I've had a few days to think it over, I've decided to go ahead and advertise the house, sort of test the water. If the market's good, I could make a nice profit. It might be good to scale down my expenses. I could be without any money coming in at the end of ninety days. At least I will have made a head start, just in case I have to leave Raleigh, or if I decide to go back to school."

"You mentioned school before. Have you thought any more about that?"

"Yeah, but, I really don't know what I'm going to do. Alma told the whole neighborhood that I was going back to med school. When the neighbors ask, I just laugh it off and stay uncommitted. I made a list and called two or three contacts I have with other companies. The first two guys acted embarrassed when I told them why I was looking for a job…"

"You told them why you got the ax? Why would you? I thought your company had agreed to give you a clean bill of health…"

"Ho, ho, ho! Bad news travels fast. One of the men I called had already heard a rumor. Of course I could deny it, I guess, but I wouldn't want this to come back to haunt me. No. No matter what I do, this time I'm going to start off with a clean slate. In OCS they taught us never to compromise, never quibble or equivocate. I hope I've finally learned."

"That's a noble ambition, but I'm not so sure it's a reasonable expectation for most of us."

The shadow of the sample cache in the storage shed crossed his mind.

"Well, nobody's perfect, far from it. But I see this as an opportunity to make a fresh start. I'm going to try my damnedest to get my life back on track. Anyway, I'm not going to lie about what happened just to get a job in the goddamned pharmaceutical industry again and have it surface later. I really don't want to go back to that if I can find something else. After pre-med I studied advertising art. A long time ago, before I was ordered to active duty for Desert Storm, I had a laughable fling at commercial art. I drew great bean cans and bacon packages. But I was a much better journalist. I called Herschel Roberts, my old editor at the paper. Hersh is bureau chief for the SNS news syndicate now…I still do an occasional piece on medical related stuff for him…and last year, an editor at *Esquire* invited me to try him again…"

"Oh, that *would* be exciting."

"Well, I don't have anything to show a major magazine. Besides, I'm not holding my breath. Takes most editors six weeks to zip their fly." Buchanan took his guitar out of the case and ran the strings up to key and sang, *"You can't hear the teacher with beans in your ears…."*

[110]

Cammie giggled.

"Well, call your old editor again the first of the week. What did the other friend in the pharmaceutical business say? Did you tell him what happened too?"

"Oh, yeah. He seemed to take it pretty well, but he said he didn't have anything for me right now. Well, he did mention a territory in West Virginia, but I'm not that desperate. The third guy, Morris Earle, was an old college buddy. We grew up in the same town. I helped him get into the field. He's moved pretty high up now, home office just outside New York City, but he was on vacation. Two weeks, his secretary said. I left my number but there's no telling when he'll be calling back. Anyway, I'm not very interested in Morris' company. Although I got him the job...and Stribol pays higher than anyone in the business...I really don't think I'd like to work for Morris' outfit. Stribol has a first rate product line...antibiotics...the best. But they have a reputation for being very M-I-C-K-E-Y M-O-U-S-E..." He played the chords and sang the letters, then he held his fists at his forehead like mouse ears. "If you get the picture?"

"I'm not sure I understand..."

"You know, gung-ho, uh, like, well, they have their managers follow behind their salesmen like private detectives to check on the honesty of their call reports. They call them in the middle of the night and test them on their product knowledge...stuff like that. Morris has told me some horror stories..."

"Oh...come on, you're teasing..." She stopped when she saw he was serious. "Really? I can't believe that grown men do things like that. I see what you mean, Mickey Mouse is hardly a name for it. I can't see you putting up with that stuff. Surely there are plenty of good companies."

"Oh, Stribol managers aren't the only ones that do it. There's a lot of that Gestapo mentality around the pharmaceutical industry. Last year, Tabbitt Labs, one of the biggies, had their reps logging in on their laptops every hour during the day to give a report..."

"In-flippin-credible..." She turned back to the table and continued unpacking the food.

"Yeah, it really is."

"How about school? You mentioned law. I could help you there, guaranteed. Chapel Hill or Duke. Take your choice." She tossed him a jar of mustard. "Make yourself useful, open that for me. Do you like mustard on your country ham biscuits?"

He twisted the top loose on the odd-shaped jar and sniffed and rolled his eyes heavenward. "Was Shakespeare an Englishman?"

"There are some paper plates in the basket."

"Law school does keep crossing my mind, but I haven't really gotten my head screwed on straight yet, and…" He started to tell her that he was being tailed, but he stopped himself and started to separate the stack of paper plates.

"I brought coffee, but there's beer in this cooler." Cammie lifted the lid to reveal a half-dozen bottles of Rolling Rock poking through the ice. "I guess it's obvious I was hoping you'd show up…you can have a bite with us, can't you? The girls will never forgive you if you don't."

"Sure. I'll have a beer and a biscuit, but I can't stay long. I put a classified ad in the Real Estate section. It was supposed to start today. I should get back to answer the phone."

"Let me get those napkins." She tried to reach across and brushed against him.

His arm tingled where her breasts touched him. He dizzied slightly as he caught her fresh-scrubbed smell.

"I think I'll just go up and wash my hands. Back in a minute." He handed her a beer and started up the hill toward the restroom.

Watching Buchanan's gluteus muscles rippling against the beige-white denim fabric of his jeans, Cammie caught her breath.

She kicked at a pebble and missed again.

ONCE OUT OF SIGHT, Buchanan moved quickly beyond the entrance to the men's restroom and entered one of the phone booths off to the side under the trees. He set his beer down and quickly inserted five quarters and dialed. Bird calls and the sounds of children playing faded as he listened to the rings before the party picked up.

"This is Forbes. The stuff is ready."

"How much?"

"Five-oh-eight, five, wholesale."

"Wow." There was a low whistle. "How much you asking?"

"Two-fifty-five. It's mostly in Virecta and Macroten, a little Prostogen, fast-moving stuff."

"Uh, that's fair enough. But, with the Richmond bust, we have to be careful."

"Yeah…I should warn you. I'm being tailed, but I've got it all worked out. Tomorrow afternoon, OK?"

"Tailed? Shit! Better wait, lay low."

"No. If you don't want it now, I'll take it somewhere else. I want it off my hands. Besides, it's not that complicated, I've got it all worked out. Listen…" He quickly outlined his plan. Practically foolproof, actually.

Unless? His sphincter tightened and his breath quickened. Had they been tailing him before Acton fired him?

"Sounds OK. Are you sure?"

" I'm sure. It's my ass, too. And, don't forget: Stick to fifties."

"Jeez, that's a lot of fifties. How about some hundreds? They're all used bills."

"No. *Fifties*. Exactly fifty-one hundred of 'em. Wrap 'em tight. Go to a bakery…they'll fit nicely in a large birthday cake box…I already checked it out…seal it extra good with tape, OK?"

"Well, all right…"

"Tomorrow then. If we have to abort I'll have the signal out. I'll call again as soon as it's safe. If everything goes down, you won't be hearing from me again. Good luck."

"To both of us…" The line clicked dead. Buchanan drained his beer bottle and walked back down the hill.

"Have you heard from Alma?" Cammie asked when he reached the picnic shelter.

"Well, yeah…she doesn't have a lot to say to me. Except for the boys, we don't have much between us now." He looked down and worried a discarded bottle cap with the toe of his Keds.

"I don't know how to say this, but before I call the girls, I just want you to know you don't have to worry about anything. I've got plenty of money. Don't be a fool and let your pride prevent your coming to me…money is nothing…no problem. So, don't get pressured into making bad choices. There's no need to take a job just because you feel the press of money. If you're going to make a fresh start…make it right. And don't write off law school as an option. I was serious. I can get you in, probably arrange a nice scholarship with a stipend. There are always ways. In my circle of academia money's never a problem. Remember that. Do you need any money? I brought five hundred with me…"

"Huh?" He was frankly flabbergasted…and touched. "I…I'm OK. Truly…" He searched for words. "But don't think I'm ungrateful. I've just never had anyone, except my father, stand by me like that. I don't know what to say…"

"Just promise that you won't hesitate. Are you sure? The five hundred is in my purse."

"I'm OK, but thanks." Charity was a weakness. No use to try to make her see. She'd never understand his principle. Personal indebtedness gave people a hold on you.

Always be the giver. Then no one could have a claim on you. His father taught him that.

He smiled and gave her a friendly hug. Looking down at her, her face shone with intensity.

Just for a moment he thought he might kiss her.

The moment passed.

He blinked and swallowed hard. What would she say if she knew the truth?

Cammie gave his arm a squeeze and called the girls to eat.

At the table Amy and Tyler were full of questions. After he'd eaten, Amy shoved the guitar in his hands and he played *Beans in My Ears* and *Talking Candy Bar Blues*. The girls laughed and sang along.

Sitting beside him on the bench, Cammie reached to retrieve her beer and brushed against him. When she straightened, they were touching at the hips.

Buchanan felt an unruly tightening in his crotch.

"I really have to go…" He squinted against the high morning sun. He missed his sons. Embarrassed and restless now, he stood and busied himself by putting his guitar in the case.

"Remember, we'll be back tomorrow morning, too," Cammie said and stood to face him.

"Oh, I don't know. My newspaper ad is running. Sunday is the big day for real estate." He looked at her and swallowed hard again.

"We'll be coming early…" She left the thought unfinished.

"Maybe, we'll see. Bye, ladies." He hugged the girls.

He turned and started back down the hill. He wanted to turn around and tell her that he'd come tomorrow, but tomorrow there were tricky things to do.

"Wait, Buchanan…w-w-w-a-a-ait…" Cammie yelled and came bouncing down the hill so fast she stumbled into his arms. "I just remembered," she gasped, out of breath. "I…I have two tickets to Gordon Lightfoot at the Arena tonight. James is in Chicago. Would you like to go?"

"Uh?" He felt a drop of sweat drip down his back. "Do you think we should?"

"Are you afraid of what people might say? James wouldn't give a damn. What about all that talk back there a few minutes ago about Buchanan Forbes, man of the world? I mean we're adults. It's public, no big deal. If you're worried, you could always act like you don't know me."

Her body felt good against him. She didn't move away.

"Well now, I assure you, if you aren't worried, I'm certainly not. What time should I pick you up?"

"No. Let me drive. I'll come by around seven thirty."

"Come by at seven and I'll give you a drink and some peanuts or some such thing. We can grab a bite after the show."

She was still pressed tight against him and he felt himself respond. There was no way she couldn't notice.

"It's a deal then." She squeezed both his arms. Reluctantly, she finally drew away.

"A deal. Seven," he said and turned and walked slowly down to the parking lot. The feel of her lingering against his groin stirred a pang of guilt and sent his senses spinning.

The park had been a mistake.

Cammie was too vulnerable and his thoughts were getting out of hand.

Maybe he'd call her later and make up some excuse.

Chapter Twenty

"THE SIGNAL STARTED UP AGAIN. Forbes must be leaving," Fisher called Johnston on the two-way from where he'd been parked out of sight around the bend.

"Stay back now, Durwood. Let the beeper track him. Don't let him on to us…it'll blow the whole operation."

The senior agent, Fisher, resented that Johnston always talked down to him like he was the rookie.

"Don't worry. I was doing this when you were still in high school," Fisher snapped back.

"OK, OK, let's don't go into that again. I hope he's on his way back here. His damn phone's been ringing off the hook for the past hour."

"No shi…uh…no kidding?" Fisher almost slipped into a FCC no-no. "Wonder what's going on?"

"Probably the wife and kids calling from Virginia…"

"Maybe. I'm moving west on Western Boulevard now and he just topped the hill at the light moving west back toward Beltline. Looks like he's heading home."

"I hope so. His flipping phone's ringing again…"

"OK. Don't forget, put your vehicle in the garage," Johnston patronized.

Fisher had to bite his tongue. Johnston was getting on his nerves.

When Fisher walked into the house from the garage, Johnston waved his hand to shush him and pointed to the loud speaker on the phone tap.

"What kind of heat do you have?" A woman's voice was asking.

"Heat pump...handles both the heat and air-conditioning. All-electric...ever heard of a Gold Medallion Home? The electric company approves the insulation, the glass is double-glazed...all that. Very efficient, ma'am."

"I don't know...my husband says natural gas..." The woman went on talking about the house.

Johnston said, "It's that For Sale sign in his yard. That's what the calls have been about."

"Uhmm...I wonder..." Fisher moved over to where Johnston had strewn the Saturday morning *Observer* in a pile on the floor, sorted through the mess and located the Real Estate Classified Section. He found the ad almost immediately:

EXECUTIVE HOME. Split foyer. 4 bdrm, 2 ba, formal l.r., large din & kit up. Huge playrm, plus 1 bdrm and 1 1/2 ba and office down. 2,900 sq.ft., plus double gar. Call 584-9521.

"Here, this explains it." Fisher stuffed a donut in his mouth, poured a cup of coffee and went back in the living room and handed Johnston the paper.

"Oh, oh, yeah." Johnston just glanced at the ad. "I meant to tell you."

Fisher gave him a look. He knew the SOB was lying. Johnston always had to act like he knew everything. The Real Estate section of the paper hadn't been touched.

"Well, I don't know...Two hundred, sixty-two five sounds high to me..." the woman on the phone rattled on.

"I'm sorry ma'am...this is in Northmoor...at that price it's a sacrifice. I wish you luck elsewhere..." Forbes replied, coolly.

"Well, maybe we could drive by this afternoon...will you be there?"

"You're welcome to drive by, ma'am, but I won't show the house without an appointment. If you'd care to give me your name and phone number and make an appointment..."

"Well...perhaps we'll just drive by first...and maybe call if we like the neighborhood."

"Good idea, ma'am. I hope you have a nice day." Forbes hung up and his phone started ringing again almost immediately.

Another woman calling about the house.

"Oh shit...is this going to go on all day?" Fisher moaned.

"Say Durr, did you see this thing in the paper about them new IUDs?"

"What's a frigging EYE-YOU-DEE?" Fisher asked.

"You know, an intrauterine device. It's a little plastic curly-cue they stick up a woman's uterus to keep her from getting pregnant. They been around since before I was born."

"Yeah, I know. What about 'em?"

"Well, Graham/unLimited Technologies has a new space-age version on the market, supposed to be safer, more effective, all that. Says here in the paper that they found an East Carolina coed in Greenville dead in the woods...think she bled to death from one of them things. Don't know where she got it. None of the local docs admitted seeing her; none had used these new ones either.."

"So....what's the punch line? I don't get it."

"Well, the punch line is that she was about four months pregnant, they think. So if the damn things are any good, how come she was pregnant? Since they made abortion illegal, my old lady has been bugging me about these things. Wait'll I show this to Miz Know-It-All."

The conversation with the next caller was brief. The woman abruptly hung up when Forbes told her the asking price.

There was a break in the phone activity and the room was filled with an uncomfortable silence now. Johnston suddenly stood up and walked across the room and reached in a bulky briefcase sitting amid an array of electronics equipment near the speaker box and took out a button-like miniature electronic device. He held it up and grinned and rummaged through the box again and came up with several others.

"Let's bug the SOB's house."

"Why?"

"Why not?"

"But how? You're crazy...we can't go in there...we already made an illegal entry when we picked the lock on that storeroom. That was taking a crazy chance."

"Easy as pie. We make an appointment to look at his house. We'll call Marge Tufts in the Durham office and have her come over and go in with me. We'll look just like a couple of happy house hunters. Since you're doing the outside surveillance, we don't want to give him a close-up look at you or he might accidentally make you if you should get too close. I'll call Marge, the sooner the better. When you think about it, he might make a contact with a buyer for the drug samples under the guise of showing someone the house. Ever think about that? I've got Marge's home number somewhere." Johnston was already busy thumbing through his address book.

"Bill, you been watching too much friggin' TV."

The sound of Forbes' phone ringing came over the speaker again.

"Hello?" Forbes answered.

"Is that you, Buck? This is Morris Earle."

"Morris? Morris, good to hear from you...thought you were on vacation..."

"I am, good buddy, but I got your message and I heard from my mom that she ran into Alma at the drug store back home...said you're no longer with Lhambda A. Going back to med school, something like that?"

"Yeah, well the truth is that I got canned..." Both agents listened, unbelieving, while Forbes confessed to his friend what happened. *"...But none of those samples came from me. Joe Acton threw me to the wolves to get his own ass off the hook..."* Forbes was quick to deny his involvement.

"Well, don't sweat it. As far as I'm concerned, Acton's loss is somebody else's gain. How far is Raleigh from Wilmington... Wrightsville Beach?" Morris asked.

"Oh, two hours, more or less. Why?" Forbes replied, puzzled.

"My southeastern regional manager, Randall Wickline's here with me and he may have an expansion territory opening up in Wilmington. Do you think you could drive down here Monday? We'll be fishing that morning. We could get together maybe mid-afternoon. God, man, we've been killing the bluefish all week, never saw anything like it. Are you interested? What do you think?"

"Well, uh, what's he going to say when he finds out I had my company buttons cut off and was drummed out of service in public disgrace for selling samples?" Forbes sounded skeptical.

"He already knows, news travels fast. You're something of a legend in the business, you know. He says the same thing I do: Their loss, our gain. His exact words were: 'If everyone in this business who'd traded out a few samples got caught, there wouldn't be anybody left.' We got this cottage for the week. There's room here for you, that way you won't have to drive back the same night. Monday about three? Worse thing that can happen is that we can have a few beers, eat some shrimp and tell a few lies about the women we had in college. What do you say?"

"Well, uh, OK, sure. I can do that." Forbes brightened. *"Where'll I meet you?"*

Johnston grabbed a legal pad and wrote down the directions as Morris Earle gave them over the phone.

"See ya Monday. Update your resume and bring it along." Morris Earle said goodbye and hung up.

"Can you believe it? The SOB just got fired for stealing and his competition thinks he's a hero. Talk about a fucked up code of ethics." Johnston shook his head. "Anyway, looks like you'll be going to Wrightsville Beach on Monday. Some guys have all the luck."

"Sheee-it! What kind of luck do you call that? It could be the frigging Fontainebleau and I'd still be stuck listening to that goddamn tracking beeper."

"Let's call the Wilmington office and see if they can set you up with a place to stay near this address. Those beach houses are all on stilts. You

can just walk underneath and put a bug in there. And speaking of bugs..."
Johnston held up the small button-shaped electronic devices he'd found.
"Let me call Marge...we gotta go bug an 'Executive Home For Sale.'"

Chapter Twenty-one

SHERIFF MACK JONES was on the putting green chomping at the bit.
He'd already had the old doc's clubs put on the cart when Amos Lyon
pulled his faded red GMC pickup into the parking lot.

The homegrown pair of Mack Jones and Amos Lyon made an
unlikely team. From their appearance, outsiders would never have
guessed their histories. Growing up, they'd been inseparable. Spent a
carefree boyhood in nearby Southport roaming the beaches and woods,
swimming, hunting, fishing—just running loose.

After high school, Jones had played a season of football for North
Carolina State before he enlisted and graduated OCS at Fort Riley
right after LBJ escalated the bombing in North Vietnam. He'd flown
into Saigon shortly before the Tet offensive in '68. By the end of the
war he'd made full colonel in the MP's. Like many military men, he
liked the lush life in the Far East and had volunteered for Korean
occupation duty.

Wounded in Seoul chasing a ROK deserter in 1981, he'd finally
taken a generous disability retirement in '91. Since his return home,
every four years he'd been elected sheriff—unopposed.

Sheriff Mack Jones ran a tight ship...sent all his deputies to the best
training available. Usually went to Washington twice a year himself.
Locals were grudgingly proud that Mack stayed up on the latest crimi-
nology techniques at the FBI academy.

As unpretentious as he looked—and was—Amos Lyon was once celebrated internationally as a forensic pathologist. Despite his retiring
demeanor, before he decided to get out of the rat race and come back
home, old Doc Lyon had taught at several famous medical schools and
authored a half-dozen books. When he retired, the handsome physician
had come back home, met and married Sheriff Malcolm Jones' baby
stepsister, Rhonda June, the savvy principal at the local consolidated high
school who, at forty-three, was sixteen years junior to both men.

Aside from making Amos happy, Rhonda June's main dedication in
life—much to Mack's everlasting chagrin—was trying to find her step-
brother a wife.

Brunswick was a quiet, dirt-poor farming and shrimping county with little crime. In this rural, extreme southeastern corner of the North Carolina coast, the vagrant warming Gulf Stream meandered to within thirty-eight miles of the sub-tropical Cape Fear beaches. Their daily lives not overburdened with crime waves, there was only a handful of days when the two friends couldn't play golf afternoons at Caswell Beach with old Clem Farrell the Club pro, the mayor, the Methodist preacher, and the odd assortment of bloodthirsty local hustlers of all ages.

Along with Rhonda June's holy crusade to save Mack from single bliss, the good-natured war off and on the golf course between the oddly-matched cronies was a local legend.

"Wher'n hell you been, Amos? I just got through trying to call. We're off in ten minutes. Ben and Latham are already on the tee, waiting," the sheriff started bitching before the doc had covered half the distance to the green.

"We were both outside, I guess. Rhonda June's car wouldn't crank...had a devil of a time. Cables were corroded at the terminal connections. Salt air's hell on cars." The distinguished white-haired physician shook his head. "Speaking of Rhonda June, your darling baby sister said to tell you, 'don't forget about tonight.'"

"How'n hell could I forget? She's reminded me twice every day this week. I told her she might as well forget the whole damn thing. I ain't getting involved with no Barbara Morgan, or no other man-hunting female for that matter." The sheriff sniffed and turned his head and let fly a stream of tobacco juice that made a little crater in the sand beside the paved drive at the edge of the putting green. He reached in his hip pocket and extracted a blue bandanna neckerchief and fastidiously wiped his bushy salt and pepper mustache. Army OCS training had ingrained a well-disciplined sense of neatness in him. But now, despite the fact that his spiffy pair of expensive green self-belted golf slacks and immaculate white golf shirt with the logo of the famous Dunes club at Myrtle Beach embroidered on the left breast had been taken right out of the cleaner's bag before he left home an hour ago, the humidity was already taking its toll.

"She's your sister. You tell her."

"Half-sister. Besides, I have already, about three times a day for the last six months. Half-sister or not, I don't know how you stand her, Amos. When she ain't trying to marry me off, she's always giving me hell about chewing tobacco. Leastways, I don't have to live with her."

"Uhmm..." The old doc considered adding a comment of his own about the nastiness of tobacco, then dismissed it. He wasn't in the mood for jousting windmills. He'd lost five bucks on a side bet to Mack on

Wednesday. The lucky so-n-so had chipped it in on the 18th for a birdie. Today was going to be bloody war.

Amos Lyon walked over and extracted his driver and two long irons from the bag on the cart, and, holding them awkwardly bunched together, he started to slowly swing them back and forth, widening the arc a little each time, encouraging his muscles to loosen up. After a few minutes he finally quit swinging the unwieldy bunch of clubs and returned them to his bag.

He found a sleeve of new golf balls and asked, "Ever hear back from that paraffin test on that Corbett suicide Monday?"

"Yeah, called 'em yesterday. Doesn't seem to be any doubt. She had gunpowder residue on her right hand and forearm. She fired the gun, all right."

"Well, no sense in checking on the whereabouts of that Baptist preacher husband, I guess." The old doc examined the sleeve of new Titleists. "I got number ones here. What number you playing?"

"I won some Maxflis...think I'll give 'em a try." The sheriff rounded up the six balls he'd been putting and headed for the cart. "Just to be sure, I also checked out the Haitian folksinger boyfriend, the one what knocked her up. He's been playing in some second-rate nightspot in West Palm Beach. Seems he was locked up in Fort Lauderdale all weekend for taking a swing at a guy in a titty bar. Didn't make bail 'til Monday afternoon."

"Uhmm, well, if I had mob connections and wanted to have a bothersome girlfriend taken care of, I just might arrange to have myself locked up in a nice respectable south Florida jail...perfect alibi. But the point is moot, I guess." Amos Lyon shrugged and climbed in the cart. "Did you dust that little tube and that pharmaceutical sample folder?"

"Oh, don't think I haven't thought about that one... and...yeah...the prints on the sample folder matched the prints on the drinking glass beside her bed. They're hers, no question. But that little cardboard insertion tube was clean as a whistle."

"You mean wiped?" The old doc opened a little envelope and took out a new soft leather golf glove.

"No, not as best we can tell. It's like it came right off the factory assembly line, untouched by human hands..."

"Hmmm, what do you make of that?" Amos Lyon carefully pulled the glove on and smoothed it between the fingers.

"Oh, there were some Playtex gloves in the bathroom. Women are funny...maybe she was just fastidious." He pronounced the word fas...tiddy...us. "You know. Particular."

"Could be." The old doc nodded.

"What about the autopsy? Anything we weren't expecting?" The sheriff shifted his wad of tobacco with his tongue and spit a few loose crumbs over his shoulder.

"Nothing. Still haven't seen the x-rays, though. Called again last night. Chapel Hill says they're on the way. But I'm not looking for any surprises. I think you can safely say that my office'll be putting this down as: *'Gunshot-self-inflicted.'* Still, a young woman like that, killing herself over getting in a family way…and that aborted fetus did look sort of messed up. It bothers me."

"The O'Brien woman said Corbett was a strict Baptist. They're as bad as Catholics when it comes to hang-ups about morality." Mack Jones climbed in the driver's seat. "Besides, forget all that. Weather's fantastic. Let's take these turkeys to the cleaners."

"Same bet between you and me?" the old doc asked, automatically.

"If you're such a glutton for punishment." The sheriff turned his head and let fly another jet of tobacco juice.

They hadn't changed their bet in years.

Chapter Twenty-two

AT PRECISELY THE MOMENT Buchanan Forbes hung up the phone, in Roanoke his old editor, Heschel Roberts, walked into his low-rent SNS office overlooking the rundown warehouses lining Salem Avenue beside the switching yards of the N&W and the railroad's large old freight station.

Hersh was not in a good mood.

Bureau chief for Southern News Syndicate, a struggling but growing syndicated news agency in the South, was not a very glamorous way to earn a living.

Bad enough that it was Saturday. To make matters worse, he'd come straight from his overnight, overlong, and nightmarishly depressing trip to the West Virginia coal fields where, because his regular stringer in Bluefield was laid up from a car wreck, he'd had to personally cover a story on a coal mine explosion. To further complicate his life, he had wound up staying an extra day waiting for the last body to be brought out of the mine, filing sporadic dispatches to wrap things up. The whole thing came off all right, but too much George Dickel bourbon and too much late-night carousing at the local beer joints left him with a killing three-day hangover.

Hersh had promised his subscribing editors the final wrap on the coal mine disaster would go out on the wire today. They were all holding space in their Sunday editions.

That alone would have been OK, because he had the weekend to screw his head back on straight, but yesterday at the last minute Dorrie Metts, his girl Friday, called to say that one of his prima donnas was almost two weeks past deadline on a promised article on a Southern entry in the upcoming Indy race.

The entire syndicated network was waiting on the piece.

So now, because the Indy piece had been sent "special delivery" and would be waiting on his desk when he arrived this morning, he was going to his office instead of his cozy little house in a nice old neighborhood near the downtown library to mix a big pitcher of Bloody Mary's and nurse his wounds. Dorrie was meeting him and Plan A was to get the long overdue race car piece in shape and on the wire.

Dorrie was waiting with the Indy piece in hand when he walked in the door and she followed close behind, talking a blue streak, as he went straight down the hall to his office.

"Listen, it's a good thing you came in. Tolley Vernon called. He ran into Sharkey Mallone's agent at a publisher's party Wednesday in New York. Mallone's coming out with a new Mallet O'Hara book in July, and he's introducing a new spy character, Stalker MacKnight, in another novel slated for the fall."

Hersh answered to Tolley Vernon at the Atlanta-based syndicate offices.

"Stalker MacKnight? People really buy that shit?" Hersh's head was killing him. He opened his desk drawer and pulled out a bottle of cheap vodka. "God, what I wouldn't give for some ice and tomato juice..."

"I'll run down the street in a minute. But first, let's talk about Tolley. He wants an interview feature with Sharkey Mallone."

"Sharkey Mallone! He's a Yankee...besides, our readers don't read that sex and sadism trash..."

"Yes they do, and he lives in South Carolina now, been there for years. Trust me, boss. There's a real story here..."

"South Carolina? Mallone? Oh, come on. Mallone was pop culture...a flash in the pan..."

"Wanna bet? Sharkey Mallone has six of the Top Ten titles on the all-time bestseller list. Know how many titles he's written... total?"

"Twelve...fifteen?"

"SIX!"

"You shittin' me?

"Would I shit you?" Dorrie handed him a page of research Atlanta had sent on the wire. "Count 'em. Six! The only title ahead of *Solitary Judgment* at the moment is *Gone With The Wind. Midnight in the Garden of Good and Evil* just made it. Now, just what do you call a flash in the pan?"

Roberts shot her a look.

He ignored the question and took the Indy manuscript from Dorrie's hands. "This Indy piece any good? How much work do we have to do?"

"It's OK. Better'n that. I already put a pencil on it. One thing about Bledsoe, he may be late but he can sure as hell write rings around most of these prima donnas. I get nauseous at the mere thought of car exhaust and he had me thinking this damn race was something akin to the running of the bulls in Pamplona…"

"Where's that tomato juice and ice?" Roberts took a seat and started reading.

Dorrie headed out the door.

In five minutes she came back with a can of V-8 and a milkshake cup overflowing shaved ice. She took two paper cups out of the filing cabinet and made them both a drink.

"Uhmmm. Thanks. I needed that." He took a giant swallow of the strong drink and smacked his lips.

"Get this out." He handed back the race car piece.

Dorrie nodded. "Now, what do you want to tell Tolley about a Sharkey Mallone interview?"

"Is that actually true? About Mallone, six out of six on the all-time bestseller list?"

"Yeah. After that he just up and quit writing. Hasn't published anything in ten years."

"Ten years…why?"

"Nobody knows. In 1991, he joined some holy-roller religion and announced he was through writing. Quit giving interviews, left New York and moved south, somewhere below Myrtle Beach."

"He got religion? That's a bad sign. What about Mallet O'Hara, private eye, nose and penis…he going to get converted in the new book?"

"The agent won't tell me. Who knows? But Tolly says Mallone got divorced last year. He just remarried, a blond showgirl-cum-model…you know, showgirl as in Vegas… model as in the catalog for Frederick's of Hollywood."

"Well, that must be some religion he got himself into. They don't believe in polygamy by any chance?"

"No. I looked him up on the net yesterday. They're a bunch of hell-fire'n'damnationists... quite a paradox for Mallone..."

"Ten years is a long time between books. Tolley's really serious about this?" Roberts was still unbelieving.

"Bigtime. Six out of ten titles, thirty million in print. Stephen King reads him, Spielberg is an addict, rumor has it George Bush...and wiggly Willie, old Zippergate himself, even Oprah...everybody reads Sharkey Mallone. I watch Stacy Keach's *Mallet O'Hara* reruns on cable TNT. Hersh Roberts, are you telling me that you've never read *Solitary Judgment?*"

Roberts looked up under his eyebrows with an enigmatic smile.

"All-time bestseller sex and sadism author suddenly joins church, quits writing and goes in hiding in Crab Corners, South Carolina, for ten years. Then, like the Phoenix, resurfaces with a brand new sex queen wife and starts writing again. Sounds like Sunday Supplement material to me. We could give it a snobbish flavor, sorta look down our noses at his borderline illiteracy, wha'cha think?"

"Well, wonder why I never thought of that?" Dorrie said with heavy sarcasm.

"Hmmm, how far is Raleigh from Myrtle Beach? Maybe Buchanan Forbes could run down and do a couple thousand words on Sharkey Mallone for us, what'cha think? "

"You're a genius..." Dorrie's sarcasm lost its edge. Dorrie liked Forbes' work.

"Wait up." Hersh handed her his cup. "Fix us another transfusion before you get Forbes on the phone."

Chapter Twenty-three

SUDDENLY, HIS YOUNG LIFE was a fucking mess.

The decaying interior of the old hospital matched perfectly the young Marine lieutenant's state of mind.

The cracked plaster and the shades of depressing bile-green and fecal-brown paint clinging desperately to the corridor walls in the aging New Hanover Memorial Hospital were just as outdated and in just as bad repair as the weather-faded, grayish-beige brick exterior of the antiquated, rundown, patched-together, and added-onto collection of buildings which fronted on 17th Street in Wilmington. At this anxious moment for Second Lieutenant Walter Callahan, USMC, these forbidding surroundings called up—much too sharply—images of the primitive World War I European hospital as depicted in the scene from the cable re-run of Hemingway's *A Farewell To Arms* where Rock Hudson as Lieutenant Frederick Henry is walking away from the sad little provincial Swiss hospital where Jennifer Jones, in the role of Catherine Barkley, has just died in his arms after suffering the tortuous agonies of an ill-omened childbirth.

Callahan tried hard to erase the image from his mind as he stared at the goose-shit-green paint flaking off the battered double doors leading into the surgical suite. An ancient black man in a dirty-gray uniform dipped a filthy mop into a pail of thick, greasy-looking water and splashed the contaminated gray liquid on the cracked, badly-chipped tile floors.

Abruptly, the doors swung open and the lieutenant jumped to his feet as a distinguished-looking man wearing surgical greens strode into the waiting area.

"Lieutenant Callahan? I'm Frank Martin…"

"How is she, doctor?…" the lieutenant asked anxiously, as he shook the doctor's hand.

"She's lucky as hell…touch and go. If you hadn't gotten her here when you did, then we might have had a tragedy on our hands."

"Thank God, and thank you, doctor." He released his hold on the doctor's hand. "When can I see her? How long will she be here?"

"Well, they'll be taking her back to her room in a few minutes, but she won't be feeling very good for a few hours. You might as well go get something to eat, or whatever."

"You mean she can't have visitors now?"

"Oh…well, no, I didn't mean that. You can go on back in a few minutes. I'll find out which room they're putting her in. She should be OK tomorrow morning. I do want to keep her overnight though, to be on the safe side. You understand."

"She can go home tomorrow. That's great, thank you, doctor."

"How well do you know Beverly Ann? Are you two engaged, Lieutenant?" The questions dangled awkwardly between them.

"Well, no. Not engaged. We've been dating about six months… going steady I guess you could say."

"I'm not sure of my ground here, but she listed you on her release of information form. Did you know she was pregnant?"

"Not until today. I…we…were careful…"

"Not so careful, I'd say. Now, what can you tell me about the IUD?"

"IUD?"

"Intrauterine device. Where'd she get it done? Do you know who did it? She won't tell me."

"Uhhh, no, I mean, I had no idea…" The lieutenant avoided the doctor's gaze.

"You didn't know she had had that newfangled *G/uL Technologies T3*? That device was purposely inserted into a very pregnant uterus to cause an abortion. I'd stake my reputation on it. No physician worth his medical degree could have missed seeing she was pregnant. From the looks of that mess, almost three months, I'd wager. I think you know more about this than you're telling me."

"No, no, I don't know anything. What…what did she tell you?"

"She won't tell me anything. Well, one thing for sure, now she doesn't have an implanted IUD any longer. Her uterus was trying to expel it when it ripped that bleeder and it damned near caused her to hemorrhage to death."

"She'll be OK? Now, I mean?" The lieutenant asked again.

The doctor gave a nod but persisted. "Where did she go to have it done? She must have told you she was pregnant? Come on…if a licensed physician did this, he was totally irresponsible. Someone should answer. Where did she go?"

"Why are you asking me? I don't have the slightest notion what you're talking about. She called me this morning at the base and said she was bleeding and I left and rushed her here as soon as I could. She lives in a trailer near Holly Ridge…out toward Surf City. She said you were her family doctor. She felt she'd be better off here than at Onslow Memorial."

"Well, I'm going to let her rest now, but I'll have some questions later, you can bet on that. I'll go find out which room they're putting her in." The doctor turned and started back into the surgical suite. He angrily rammed the double doors apart with his elbows, like a pro football lineman blocking a training sled, then he wheeled and looked back over his shoulder. "Your career could be on the line if I wanted to make trouble. She's underage. You know that? Nobody, certainly no knowledgeable…no responsible…physician would shove one of those plastic things into a pregnant uterus. Whoever did this is a maniac. If it keeps up, he…or she…is going to kill somebody. You could help me put a stop to it. Think it over."

The lieutenant just looked at him and spread his hands in an exaggerated shrug of denial.

"OK, have it your way. Dr. Lindamood, our OB-GYN resident will be along after a bit. I'll have the nurse come find you." Frank Martin turned abruptly and the tired old double doors swooshed closed behind him.

A young doctor in a green scrub suit came into the operating suite from the dressing room near the back stairs. The hospital ID pinned to his chest read: *Eugene H. Lindamood, M.D., Chief Resident, OB-GYN.*

"Hi, Wooten," he said to the OR supervisor. "Dr. Martin left word in ER that he had a patient up here for me."

"You missed the excitement. What took you so long?"

"I couldn't leave ER. A four-car pileup around four this morning down at Monkey Junction...smells like a distillery and looks like a war zone down there."

"Friday night special. Regular thing around here."

"Where's the patient?"

"They took her into recovery. She's still under. Almost bled to death. Somebody shoved an IUD into a second trimester uterus. What a mess!"

When he idly glanced at the chart, the young doctor went pale.

"I've got to run back to the ER. I'll send Taylor up here on the double." He wheeled and headed for the stairs.

Chapter Twenty-four

It was mid-afternoon when Bill Johnston and Marge Tufts showed up for their appointment as prospective buyers for Forbes' house.

"Bill Johnston...my wife Marge." Johnston extended his hand.

"Buchanan Forbes." Buchanan took Johnston's hand and nodded politely to Marge.

"Nice place you got here. Real nice neighborhood. I'm in farm machinery. What kinda bidness y'all in, Mr. Forrest?" Johnston had gotten into "character" and was really hamming it up.

It was all Marge could do to keep from laughing out loud.

The Johnstons were the third couple to whom Buchanan had shown the house, and this was only the first day. The first of the two couples before this one was seriously looking for a house, but they were bargain hunting and this neighborhood was probably just out of reach for their pocketbooks. The second couple was merely out to kill a Saturday afternoon and Buchanan guessed that they regularly went house hunting in preference to catching a matinee at the picture show.

Almost before Johnston opened his mouth, Buchanan sized the pair up as unlikely prospects. Their car was last year's Toyota Camry and their clothes were J.C. Penney. Resigning himself to being polite and answering their questions, he resolved to give them a perfunctory walk-through.

But Buchanan was ill-prepared. He never knew what hit him.

The two agents went to work the minute they walked in the front door. Buchanan had hardly begun to walk them through when showing the place suddenly became a major management problem. He had just finished showing them the extra bedroom and bath and was walking them through the den to show the office when Marge impatiently interrupted, "This is nice for you men, but I want to see the upstairs, you know, the woman's part of the house." Without waiting for a response, she turned on her heels and headed for the stairs.

Buchanan looked at Bill Johnston.

Johnston shrugged. "Go on ahead with her...I want to peek at this nice neat office. I'll be along in a few minutes."

Buchanan gave in and followed Marge up the steps. The next thirty minutes, the two of them ding-donged him back and forth. The agents literally had him bouncing off the walls.

While he was showing Marge the master bedroom and bath, Johnston called him out into the living room to ask him if the fireplace smoked. Then, right in the middle of that, Marge called him back into the hall bath to ask about the faucets. And so it went.

By the time they'd left, Johnston and Marge had carefully bugged the office, the living room, the master bedroom suite and the kitchen.

Then, just for good measure, Johnston planted a device in the garage and another in the huge faux-Japanese-lantern light fixture which hung from the ceiling of the split entrance foyer. From the street, showing through the large rectangular fanlight over the black enamelwork of the Oriental double front doors, this lantern-fixture was the architect's *piece d'resistance*, the showcase feature of the faintly Oriental-modern architecture of the house.

Pretending to want to examine the plastic imitation-rice-paper covering of the lantern to make sure it was *fireproof*, Johnston had brazenly asked Buchanan to get him something to stand on and waited while his exasperated host had gone out to the garage and fetched a stepladder. Without blinking an eye, Johnston climbed right on up there and, palming the tiny electronic device between his fingers, he'd reached his hand up inside and attached its magnetic backing to the structural metal ring at the base of the large white pumpkin-like light fixture.

From a surveillance standpoint, having a bug so strategically placed right at the front door was a stroke of genius, but a large part of Johnston's motivation in doing it was simply to show off in front of Marge.

"Well...you sho-nuff got yo'sef a nice place heah, mistah, Forman... Me'n Marge'll talk it over and call ya if'n we'd like to take another look. "

Finished at last, Buchanan walked them to their car carrying the stepladder.

By the time the agents had driven the two blocks up to Six Forks and then around the corner to the Winn-Dixie lot at the shopping center and left Marge's car, then driven back around to the surveillance house in the gray government-issue Ford, their sides were sore from laughing so hard.

"I heard all that BS you two were laying on that poor SOB," Durwood was laughing when he met them at the door. He'd monitored most of the bugging exercise on the speaker, blow-by-blow.

"That poor guy's house has got more bugs in it than the U.S. Embassy in Beijing," Johnston gloated. "Hey, podnah, did you catch my act when I planted the bug in the master bedroom? Hee-hee-hee, that one was for you." Johnston could hardly contain himself remembering.

"Yeah, you rotten degenerate bastard, hee-hee."

"OK, OK, stop it you two. What's the big secret? C'mon now, tell me." Marge was miffed that she hadn't been cut in on the fun.

"Well, oh, you tell her Johnston, it was you that done it…"

"Neah, you tell her…"

Fisher shook his head and blushed. "Not me, it was your idea…"

"C'mon, damnit, what happened? What'd ya do, Bill?"

"When I planted that mike I gave it the acid test…"

"Huh?"

"He…he broke wind, right into the mike."

"You…you…?"

"Yeah, I farted right in old Durwood's ear."

Marge feigned embarrassment before she finally broke down and howled with laughter.

Before she could find a Kleenex to wipe away her tears, the sound of Forbes' phone came over the speaker.

"Hello?"

"Hello? Buck?" The caller's voice sounded metallic over the speaker.

"Yeah?" There was a rasping squeal over the speaker as the listening device that Johnston had just planted gave electronic feedback over the telephone bug into the speakers. Johnston quickly turned down the volume on the amplifier.

"This is Hersh, SNS."

"Oh…oh sure, Hersh. I've been meaning to call. I been wondering if you might have a little work…I have some time…"

"As a matter of fact I've got a little job I need done right away. Ever hear of Sharkey Mallone?"

Johnston looked at Marge and Durwood and a sly smile came over his face. "What kind of shit is this rookie trying to hand us? Who's he take us for? This is his contact for the drug sample deal, right? What a bush league tactic. Call and get a tracer…"

Durwood raised his fingers to his lips to shush him so he could hear.

"*Sharkey Mallone? Writer of blood, bullets and bosoms? Sure, he quit writing years ago. Seems like I read that he moved to some little fishing town down below Myrtle Beach. I don't have any idea where he is now. He hasn't published in a coon's age. What'd you have in mind?*"

"*Well…he's still down there. Rummell's Cut, South Carolina. He's writing again…got a new Mallet O'Hara novel coming out in July…I was looking on the map…Rummell's Cut isn't too far from you…three hours at the most. Would you like to go down there Monday and interview him? Do me about two thousand words? Mallone ain't exactly John Grisham, but you can't overlook him. Six out of six on the all-time bestseller list. Anyway, I'm looking for a rather straightforward personality profile for our Sunday Book Page editors. You know, Horatio Alger, Jr. come-from-nowhere success. A touch of cynicism for his rather unlearned prose style. Recent divorce from childhood sweetheart to marry a showgirl. Sex and sadism novelist has burning bush conversion to that holy-roller cult…get the picture?*"

"*Oh yeah, I'd forgotten…the oddball religion slant's an interesting angle.*"

"*Well, what'cha think? Can you run down there Monday? I want to run this on our member papers' June 7 Sunday Book Pages. Two thousand words, rush, rush. Deadline Friday, two weeks. Can you do it? I got Mallone's number, you can call him. His agent's already told him we're interested.*"

"*Well, I…I'd sure like to, but I've got to go to Wilmington Monday. I have an appointment…*"

"*Wilmington? Delaware? Ah shit, Buck, how important is it? Jeez, make up your mind. You just said you wanted to write. This is SNS. You know how many writers would like this shot?*"

"*No, I mean yes, I do want to write, but 'no,' Wilmington is Wilmington, North Carolina. Down on the coast. As a matter of fact, it's not more'n a couple of hours down to Myrtle from there. Could I go down there Monday night? Maybe you could set me up to see Mallone Tuesday, or even Monday night? Would that do?*"

"*That would be dandy, if you can get me two thousand electrifying words out Express Mail by the twentieth. That's Friday after next. It isn't any use if you can't. I can always get Bill Thompson in Charleston…I just thought…*"

"*Forget Thompson. I can do it if you can set up the interview Tuesday.*"

"*Here's Sharkey's number. Call him yourself and get right back to me here as soon as you work it out. I'll be here all weekend.*" Roberts gave him a number for Mallone and his own home number in Roanoke.

"OK. I'll try right now. Call you back…" Forbes hung up.

"Holy shit…Sharkey Mallone…holy shit…" The three agents could hear Forbes talking to himself through one of the bugs that Johnston had just planted. There was silence and then a clink of glass and a rattling sound.

"Fixing himself a drink. Our boy is nervous as a cat." Marge giggled.

"You think this is on the up and up, I mean SNS? Come on…" Johnston was skeptical.

"Oh…shut up, Bill. I'm going to take your detective novels away from you. Of course it's for real. Didn't you read Forbes' jacket? The guy was a reporter for this guy Roberts at the Roanoke paper before he started peddling pharmaceuticals."

There were sounds of cabinet doors being opened and closed and the unmistakable clinks of ice cubes in a glass. Finally, after a minute, Forbes picked up the phone and started dialing.

"Shit." Forbes misdialed the number and started over again. This time there was a ring as the call went through. *"Come on Mallone, be at home, goddamnit…"*

"Our pigeon's nervous as a whore in church." Johnston laughed at Forbes' fretting.

"Mallone." A man answered gruffly in the middle of the second ring.

"Mr. Mallone, this is Buchanan Forbes. I write for SNS. We want to do a major feature about you to run in our syndicated papers next month. I wondered if I could come down and do an interview on Tuesday…"

"Yeah, my agent just called. Tuesday? Sure. What time?"

"Whatever suits."

"Anytime. I'm up around five, but I usually write until around lunch time. Could we make it around noon? I'm usually ready for my first beer around noon. How're you getting down here, anyway? From New York or Atlanta, Myrtle Beach Express flies direct, four flights a day…"

"Oh, no, I live in Raleigh, but I'll be driving down from Wilmington Monday afternoon, late probably, maybe more like evening. Could you suggest a place to stay?"

"Presidential. Eighth and Ocean Drive. Friend of mine owns it. Caters to traveling trade. Nice place…next to the Pavillion…right in the heart of things. No problem, off season, really. Canadians are here, but not a ratrace down here during the week this time of year…Nick Adams…an old NYPD buddy runs it. Uhhhh…let me see…number is…" Mallone read out the number. *"See ya' Tuesday around noon…"*

"Wait, don't hang up. How do I find you…I mean, I have an idea where Rummell's Cut is but, as I recall, there isn't much there. Can you give me directions…?"

"Sure, it's easy. Come down Seventeen Bypass south about five miles past the airport exit. You'll see a sign for the turnoff to Seagull Beach. There's a restaurant, Livermore's, on the oceanside of Old Seventeen...about a mile on down, there's a Speedway station..." When he finished, Mallone asked, "Think you can find it OK?"

"No sweat. I'll call Monday night. See you Tuesday..."

"OK." Mallone hung up without another word.

"Hot damn..." The three agents could hear Forbes muttering to himself as he dropped fresh ice cubes in his glass. Then he dialed another number.

"This is Roberts."

"Hersh, I got Mallone. I'm set up for Tuesday at lunch time..."

"Great. I'll have my assistant send a research package...clips, bio ...you know...whatever background we got in the files. You'll have it before you get back to Raleigh..."

"Oh, great. That'll be a big help. I wonder..."

"Yeah...?"

"What do you pay for a piece like this, I mean being Sunday Book Page full-length feature, all that...?"

"A buck a word. Two thousand bucks. OK?"

"Uhhh, well, yeah. How about expenses, I mean, will you...?"

"Send me your mileage, hotel and buy him some drinks...dinner...whatever it takes. I'll have accounting add that to your check. OK?"

"Sure. I wonder...could I sell a spinoff to, maybe Esquire, Vanity Fair, or a similar market?"

"Yeah, not before July, though. SNS runs first. Call me after you've talked to Mallone Tuesday, all right? I'm counting on you. Call me, OK?"

"Yeah. OK. I..." Roberts had already hung up.

"Well, hot damn!" There was the sound of more ice cubes dropping in Forbes' glass.

Chapter Twenty-five

ALL AFTERNOON CAMMIE played CDs of old Gordon Lightfoot records on the stereo. Well aware that Buchanan was like a kid over the sudden revival of the 1960s folk music craze, she was barely able to contain her excitement.

By five she was already out of the shower, standing in bikini panties, still bare-breasted in front of the mirror in her dressing room, fussing over her makeup, intent on getting it just right. One after the other, she tried and wiped off an endless array of "natural" shades of lipstick, looking for that perfect, freshly-scrubbed Junior League look.

When she finally achieved what she judged as a dewy look of schoolgirl-innocence, she tried her hair first in a single pigtail and then quickly abandoned that as being too obvious. Finally she decided to catch it all up with a ribbon, high on the back of her head, and let it fall into a ponytail. This done, she stood back and admired her handiwork. But when she stepped closer again, she frowned at the stray glints of silver among the dark auburn strands.

"Damn!" she swore out loud and vowed to have her hairdresser start using a color rinse.

Catching a full-length view of her nakedness, she stood up to her full height and, turning this way and that, she posed, running her hands down over the firm, flat lines of her abdomen.

Two pregnancies and not a trace of stretch marks. She was quite pleased about that.

And her breasts were still good. Praise Allah. At forty-three that was a miracle.

"*It's not the pale moon that excites me…it's just the nearness of you,*" she sang and hummed happily to the Hoagy Carmichael classic from the new Willie Nelson album. Cupping her breasts in her hands, she leaned forward, stuck out her behind and puckered her lips, posing for the mirror again.

Now, all at once she stopped. Why was she acting like a schoolgirl? Suddenly it hit her!

She had a crush on Buchanan Forbes!

Weak-kneed, she plopped down on the edge of the bed as the realization swept over her.

It was ridiculous, really. But try as she might she could no longer deny it. Over the last year, she had become increasingly preoccupied with thoughts of him. And her dreams betrayed her.

Such dreams. God, such dreams!

Her breath came a little faster as she stood up again on unsteady feet. Heart racing, she began to dress.

Trying desperately to collect herself, she slipped on a bra. She finished buttoning the back of the plain white blouse she'd laid out on the bed, the one with the Peter Pan collar, and moved to the closet and took down the Cameron tartan kiltie skirt she'd had made in Scotland.

And her saddle shoes.

Cammie caught her view in the mirror again.

Awfully collegiate.

Too-too…much too very-very.

In that outfit she looked just like what she was—a silly, ridiculously romantic matron in her forties pathetically trying to pretend she was still young and desirably ingenuous.

Undressing as fast as she could, she tossed the clothes aside.

Then she pulled on a pair of fashionable gray stirrup pants and selected an offhand-tres-casual designer sweater she'd paid a fortune for at one of the exclusive boutiques on her most recent trip to a bigtime American Bar Association meeting at the famous Greenbrier spa.

Nowadays the cost of looking fashionably-offhand-tres-casual cost a girl an arm and a leg. At the thought, Cammie couldn't help but laugh out loud.

She poked around her closet and selected a pair of ankle boots.

When she'd laced them, she stood and looked in the mirror again. She made a face. The blocky low heels made her thighs look heavy.

She leaned against the closet door, unloosed the laces, slipped the boots off and reached for a pair of navy high heel mid-calf boots with a slouchy medieval air.

Right out of Sherwood Forest.

Just the proper statement for a liberated young professional on her way to a campus hootenanny, a woman very much in tune with what was going on in the world.

She stepped again to the full-length mirror and her heart skipped a beat. She felt strangely vulnerable, like a schoolgirl on her first date.

A crush, all right. Well, what of it?

All at once, she felt delightfully sinful about it all.

IT WAS WELL-PAST DUSK, and Buchanan's place was lit up like a carnival midway when Cammie pulled into his drive just before seven. The outside floodlights on the corners of the eaves illuminated the front yard and there was a lighted oriental lamppost beside the driveway, out near the street. In the foyer, the oversized faux-Japanese lantern made a dramatic presence, shining through the large rectangular fanlight above the double doors.

The drapes on the huge picture window in the living room were open wide and she smiled as Buchanan jumped up from his chair and set aside his guitar when he saw her turn in.

He was already standing on the front stoop, grinning nervously as she made her way down the walk toward him.

"Well, well, hi. You look just like a coed. Everybody in the neighborhood will think I'm a dirty old man. I didn't have any decent jeans, so I hope this is all right?" He spread his hands and self-consciously looked down at his outfit of Savane khakis and a plain blue button-down oxford shirt without a tie. On his feet were a pair of high-mileage tan tassel loafers. "I thought I'd wear an old navy blazer, or just a sweater with a poplin safari jacket maybe," he said, a bit uncertainly.

"Either's perfect. You look like a law student at Carolina or maybe a graduate assistant in the English department at Davidson." She laughed. "C'mon, you promised me a drink, but go light. Remember, I'm driving."

"Man, have I had an exciting day. Since I left you this morning, things have really started popping. It's all too unbelievable, really..." As they closed the front door and made their way up the foyer steps into the kitchen, Buchanan, slightly breathless for no apparent reason, told her about the phone call from Morris Earle. Then he recounted Hersh Roberts' phone conversation and the rather unexpected series of events that had unfolded during the afternoon.

"Sharkey Mallone! In...credible! A Sunday feature for SNS. Imagine..." Cammie shook her head in disbelief. "But...the job interview in Wilmington, Stribol? Isn't that the company you said was so...so, M-I-C-K-E-Y M-O...?" she sang the letters, mimicking the way he'd sounded that morning at the park.

"Yeah, that's the one, but I feel obligated to talk to them anyway. After all, I have my family to think about. Stribol pays the best. Otherwise I wouldn't even consider going back into pharmaceuticals. I mean if I didn't have the boys to think about. Well, anyway, I do..."

"What's Alma think about all this?"

"Huh? Oh? I don't know, actually. ...."

"You haven't called her? Why?"

"Well, I don't know. I mean, I haven't been offered the job, and I sort of wanted to think about it before I discussed it. I mean, sort things out in my own mind. She still hasn't forgiven me for getting canned..." Buchanan flushed.

"Oh, yeah, I guess you do need to sort out your feelings first." She tried to sound encouraging.

"Yeah, right." He brightened.

"I love your house. Right off the pages of *Architectural Digest*. Alma must be a marvelous housekeeper."

"She does a good job. She has a cleaning lady come in every week when the kids are here. You can just imagine what four young male animals can do to white walls. Since they left Tuesday, I've been busy. I repainted the kids' rooms, scrubbed and polished. Up at five every morning…spent the entire three days since she left putting the place in show-case condition…you know, to show to prospective buyers."

"I'm impressed. But, up at five?"

"Well, it's nothing special, my routine. The only time of the day when I can have quiet time to myself. And the work has been therapeutic, good for me. I love mornings," he confessed, shyly.

"Oh, well, I do know what you mean. I'm a morning person myself. Usually I get to the office around eight so I'll have an hour to get myself together."

"Yeah, it's great to get up early and have no one to bother you," he said sheepishly and laughed. "I guess I should feel guilty, but I've enjoyed being alone. I love my kids, still, I'm really glad to have some time to myself. I've thought a lot about going back to school, but I don't know. Anyway, it's been a sobering experience. I haven't had any time to really think about myself in a long time. I confess, I kinda like not having any-one to answer to."

"Sounds very human to me. Sometimes I run away to my place down at Pawley's. I spent a week alone down there last September, after the girls were in school. I loved it. Walked the beach, listened to some music and read some trashy novels, even read a Sharkey Mallone, as I recall. Maybe you could get him to autograph a book for me."

"Maybe so. Which reminds me, I've gotten in some writing this week too. Considering this afternoon's phone call, it was time well-spent. I'm sort of rusty." He handed her the drink he'd mixed, led her out of the kitchen to the edge of the living room and hesitated awkwardly. He was clearly uncomfortable, at a loss just what to do next.

"Come on, show me the rest of your house; it's lovely. You should have no trouble selling. I'm sure you know that IBM announced they're expanding in the Research Triangle Park. Of course Northmoor is among the best residential locations. My aunt and uncle live on Salterpath."

"Oh, that's two, three blocks, makes us neighbors. Well, come along and bring your drink." Buchanan started to take her hand, but then he looked anxiously toward the draperies standing wide-open at the picture window. Sheepishly, he dropped his extended hand and turned and led the way along the upstairs hall toward the bedrooms. After they'd looked into the children's bedrooms and peeked at the big hall bath, he led her into the master bedroom and turned on the light. The drapes were closed on the floor-to-ceiling front windows which bracketed the headboard of the king-sized bed and looked out upon the street. He hesitated and tried to hide his embarrassment as he self-consciously walked around the far side of the bed and pulled the cord to open the drapes. When he returned, he moved around the near side of the bed and opened the drapes on the other window closest to the door.

Then he stepped into the master bathroom and flipped on the lights and opened the louvered cafe-shutters on the single window.

That window also opened to the street.

"Nothing like nosy neighbors," he said and laughed a self-conscious laugh.

"Uh, oh, I see. After dark, a strange woman in the house. You want the neighbors to see that everything's on the up and up?" Cammie teased, half-heartedly trying not to show her irritation at his giving in to middle-class convention. "Wouldn't want anyone to let it slip to Alma that you were plying a mysterious woman with liquor in the master bedroom, huh?" She winked lewdly, but her voice betrayed a bemused edge of impatience.

"Well, you know how people are." Catching her reproving tone, Buchanan blushed.

"Oh, sure, but I would have guessed you'd be the last to play that silly game..."

"But, I haven't, I don't. C'mon, I'll close the blinds if you'd like to take advantage of me," he said facetiously and moved resolutely across and reclosed the blinds, fastening them with the tiny brass hooks.

She sensed his awkwardness and took his hand, pulling him toward the door.

"C'mon before we get carried away with all this foolishness." She flashed a smile. His awareness of her as a woman was a compliment, she guessed. Anyway, it was all harmless enough. *Or was it*, she wondered. Her breath was coming slightly faster now.

"Fix me another bourbon and branch but watch it. I get wild when I have a little too much to drink...we might just skip the concert. Sometimes, if I really like a guy, I'll let him kiss me on the first date," Cammie teased. Trying to break the tension, she squeezed his arm and pulled him along the hall.

She heard him suck in a deep breath, trying mightily to relax.

"OK, but I warn you. I don't handle rejection all that well. I'll probably pout the rest of the evening." His hands were trembling slightly as he stiffened up their drinks.

I should have known, she smiled, inwardly. *He's really shy, just a boy at heart.*

When she took the glass she noticed the clock on the kitchen range. "It's late..."

"Here. Pour our drinks into these. I'll run get my jacket." Buchanan handed her two plastic airline glasses and practically bolted out of the kitchen.

INSIDE THE CAVERNOUS Entertainment and Sports Arena, their seats were third row. Strictly VIP. Straight from the college chancellor's office. Buchanan was impressed.

The crowd went wild the moment Lightfoot came on stage. He was wearing tight, wash-worn jeans that left little to the imagination. The overall effect was more seductive than being bare-ass naked.

"Can you believe it? He must be seventy if he's a day. Who gives a damn whether he sings or not?" Cammie dug Buchanan with her elbow and whistled right along with a dignified, snowy-haired professor-ial-looking woman in the next row.

"Sexist pigs, all of you." Buchanan smiled, broadly.

When the house lights dimmed, she reached across and found his hand. She felt him stiffen, then relax as the music started.

Lightfoot opened with *Someday Soon* and closed with *In the Early Morning Rain*. As he sang the first words of the finale, Buchanan squeezed her hand and whispered in her ear. "Lightfoot was telling my life story when he wrote that song. I've been half-drunk and stranded in more goddamn airports than I could ever count."

Buchanan was still standing and whistling for more when Lightfoot took his final bow after what was probably his third or fourth reprise.

CAMMIE HAD PARKED in a private faculty slot near Hillsborough Street and afterward they walked up from the coliseum and went across to Player's Retreat to have a sandwich and a beer. In the popular campus hangout, Cammie looked around at all the young faces and the happy noise and snuggled closer to Buchanan in the booth so that they were touching at the hips and thighs.

He tensed but didn't move away.

I'm flirting, she admitted to herself.

Buchanan was flushed and beaming, his senses obviously still on overload.

So what's the harm? She snuggled slightly closer.

Looking at him in the soft light-music drifting in from where the crowd was dancing in the back room, her heart skipped a beat.

With the sixties revival sweeping the country, the kids were playing Chubby Checker twist tunes on the jukebox.

[139]

"C'mon, let's dance. I haven't felt this good in a long time." She gave him a nudge with her elbow.

"I don't know, I'm not much of a dancer..."

"Oh come on. I'm the granny here." She nudged him with her shoulder but she regretted calling attention to her age the minute the words slipped out.

On the dance floor, it was no surprise...he'd lied. He was good, knew all the dances.

Progressively, as the evening wore on, the music gradually slowed to a more romantic tempo. With Don Cherry crooning softly the words of another sixties hit, they danced slowly, barely moving their feet.

Intoxicated by the music and the drinks, now she snuggled closer, touching lightly at the belly. Letting her leg slip between his in the anonymous dimness, she felt his maleness stir against her pudendum.

Idly, she wondered what he'd say if she made some sort of move.

Her groin tingled at the devilish thought.

But time ran out and the evening ended, hardly before it really started.

In the car on the drive home, she could sense his discomfort with the raw sexuality between them. She tried to sustain a conversation about the concert but eventually they lapsed into silence.

When she pulled into his drive, he was obviously quite ill at ease.

"Well, I can't tell you how much fun it was," he began, "I guess it's too late to ask you in for a nightcap..."

The clumsy remark broke her mood.

"Well, it isn't too late for me, but I guess you're still worried about your neighbors?" She tried to contain her anger, but her voice betrayed her sarcasm.

"Huh? Oh, yeah. Wouldn't want to put you on the spot." He was totally confused by her unexpected reaction. He really didn't know how to respond to her now.

"Buchanan Forbes, you're a sweet man, but you've got a helluva lot to learn about women."

"Wha-a?" She hushed him by putting her fingers to his lips.

"Shut up and just listen. Let me tell you a secret about boys and girls."

"Huh?"

"Shh-h-h." She touched her fingers to his mouth again.

"You men delude yourselves that you're the aggressor. All that brave talk you were doing this morning at the park about not being afraid to take 'yes' for an answer. And now you're worried about my reputation? I don't think so. Some stud you are..."

"Aw, c'mon now, I…" he protested lamely, taken completely by surprise.

"Listen, my friend, there are no nice girls when it comes to men. A woman will take any man she wants, anytime she wants, any way she can…her priest, her kid's choirmaster, her best friend's husband. We're a ruthless lot. A man gets a few too many under his belt and pats his neighbor's wife on the fanny or sticks his tongue in her mouth at the country club dance and the next morning he wants to go to confession. You guys are a bunch of boy scouts when it comes to romance."

"Ahh-h, c'mon now…" His eyes bugged out with amazement.

"Well, thanks for a wonderful evening, my dashing swordsman. And, I think if I were you, I'd call Alma and tell her all the news tomorrow. But I don't believe I'd tell her about the concert and certainly not about the funky slow dancing…"

"Well, yeah, heh, heh…" In the ghostly glow of the dash lights his face looked green.

"Will we see you at the park in the morning?" she asked, more kindly now.

"I have the ad in the paper, better stick close, I guess…"

"Sure. Well, goodnight, and thanks for a wonderful time…" She put the car in gear and waited while he got out. Then she backed out quickly, fighting off her sudden rush of tears.

Chapter Twenty-six

IN THE POST-ANESTHESIA CARE UNIT, Dr. Martin finished writing orders on the Rivenbark girl's chart and handed it to the PACU charge nurse. "Did you find Lindamood?"

"Oh, yes, Dr. Martin. I meant to tell you. He was here while you were talking to the lieutenant. He took a quick look at Rivenbark's chart, then he just turned and left."

"Left? What do you mean? Where'd he go? I want to talk to him about this girl. If she starts to bleed again, I want him to find me. Where'd he go?"

"Back to the ER, I guess. They had a bad wreck down toward Carolina Beach early this morning, but he said that he'd send Dr. Taylor right on up here to see Miss Rivenbark."

"Did someone take my name in vain?" They both looked up to see a clean-cut young man in hospital scrubs approaching.

"Oh, Taylor, what happened to Lindamood?"

"Well, he had his hands full. There was a pregnant woman in that smashup at Monkey Junction. He sent me up here. Whatever happened to a scheduled day off around this place?"

"You want to be a doctor? Welcome to the wonderful world of medicine."

"Thanks...a heap..."

"Did Lindamood say he would be up here to take over when he was through down there? I mean, after all, he's the OB-GYN resident..."

"Uh...well...I'm the intern on his rotation starting tomorrow and I got the duty next month. He didn't say whether he'd be on up or not. Hell's bells, I was sleeping like a log. I didn't ask him."

"Let me call ER. I don't know who he thinks he is, anyway. The ER has their own house staff.." The older doctor went to the house phone and dialed.

In the ER, the charge nurse picked up the phone. "ER. This is Walton."

"Walton, this is Frank Martin up in Recovery. I hear you got a real mess on your hands."

"Yeah. Two came in DOA and another on the way up to surgery...closed head injury. Robert Moore's scrubbing for that one right now. If you ask me, that one ain't gonna make it either. We got the rest in bed or all patched up and out of here."

"Good. Let me talk to Gene Lindamood. I need him back up here..."

"Just a minute..." She put him on hold but was back on the line in a few seconds. "I'm sorry, Doctor Martin, he just left, less than five minutes ago..."

"Good. He's probably on his way back up here."

"No, he signed out. Grumbled something about his wife. You want his number at home?"

Martin glanced over at Taylor and the nurse waiting beside his patient "No, thank you. I've got to go." He hung up and walked back to where Taylor stood.

"Mark, did Gene Lindamood say anything about a call from home?"

"No. He didn't say anything to me except to get my fat ass up here on the double. Why?"

"Very peculiar. Not like Lindamood at all. Walton down in ER says he said something about his wife and signed out for home..."

"Well, I'm sure Gene has a good reason. You know that wife of his is a bitch. They separated once when we were in school at UVA. Then he found out she was pregnant. He was furious, swore he was going to get her aborted but he never did. She told my wife that he just came back to her because her folks have a lot of money. But he told me it was because of the baby. Lindamood loves that boy."

"Oh well. Anyway, unless we missed some bleeders, this one can go home tomorrow after rounds. C'mon out here, I want you to meet her boyfriend, a young Marine lieutenant. Name's Callahan. He brought her in. Try to get him to tell you who put that IUD in her."

"Is there trouble?"

"She was about three months pregnant and someone shoved one of those space-age IUDs in her. She damned near died."

"OK. I'll see what I can do. What does the girl say?"

"I asked 'em both. She isn't talking and he's playing dumb. They're covering up."

"You think someone meant to, ah…"

"The whole thing stinks. Not even a second-year student would have missed seeing that she was pregnant. I'd bet my bottom dollar that this was done deliberately to cause an abortion."

"I can ask the girl again when she starts to come out of it. IV barbs are like truth serum. Sometimes they talk when they're woozy," the nurse reminded them.

"Not a bad idea, worth a try. In the meantime, Taylor, you try to make friends with the lieutenant. Buy him some breakfast; he's had a rough night. Put it on my tab in the dining room." The kindly physician pushed his way back through the battered doors leading to the waiting room.

The nurse watched him leave. She turned to Taylor. "Did you see the way Lindamood acted when he looked at that girl's chart, Mark?"

"Yeah, I saw him. Turned white as a sheet. I think we hit some kind of nerve, don't you?"

"It crossed my mind."

Chapter Twenty-seven

AT 4:15 SUNDAY MORNING, Buchanan woke up in the throes of a profoundly pleasurable orgasm. He lay in the dark tightly caressing himself, clinging to the dream until his last frisson of ecstasy passed.

He had been dreaming that Cammie came to him in the dark and kissed him deeply while he was lying in bed beside Alma. In the dream he was so powerfully taken by the eroticism of the dream-kiss that he ignored Alma lying beside him and reached under Cammie's shortie nightgown and ran his hands over her naked breasts. The delicious feel of the warm flesh as he ran his fingertips down over the firm ridges of her rib cage and the delightful little swell of her abdomen still danced on the ends of his fingers. He had barely untangled the thatch of Cammie's soft pubic hair and parted the wetted lips of her vagina, letting his fingers slip up inside her, when Alma leaned across and took his penis in her mouth and started running her tongue around the glans. At that point in the dream, the flood of his juices had begun to erupt violently out of him.

He recognized that the dream was born out of the frustration and confusion of going with Cammie to the concert, especially the funky slow dancing afterwards at The Player's Retreat. The fantasy, he understood, was darkly Freudian, with undertones of hostility toward Alma. But, if he felt any guilt, for the moment at least, guilt was the most deeply-enjoyable thing he'd felt since his teenage sexual initiation.

Guilt, he decided, lying there, fingers still tightly wrapped around his throbbing penis, was something he'd definitely worry about later...perhaps on his ninety-ninth birthday.

Finally...reluctantly...he turned on the bedside lamp and got out of bed and took off his semen-soaked undershorts. Then he stripped the bed linen and—still painfully erect with after-pleasure—he rather sheepishly took a long hot shower.

After he toweled himself dry, he put on fresh underwear, slipped into his jeans and pulled a clean sweatshirt over his head. He located fresh linen and remade the bed. Barefoot, he went into the bath and gathered up the towels and replaced them in readiness to show the house later in the day. Satisfied that everything was in order, he picked up the pile of soiled linen and—still warm with the pleasure of the dream—took it all downstairs to the laundry room and started the washer.

Upstairs again, he walked around in a pleasant afterglow while he started the coffeemaker and turned on the intercom and adjusted it so that it would pick up from the Aiwa multiplex. Then he went into the dining room and turned on the Aiwa and put on a Gordon Lightfoot CD. Singing softly along with the music, he went back downstairs and, armed with a feather duster made of peacock feathers, he began a complete tour of the place. By the time he'd finished the dusting, the coffee was ready. He poured himself a cup and went back into the dining room just as the changer moved to the next Gordon Lightfoot. He set the coffee cup beside his laptop and sat down and began to read the opening paragraph of the novel he'd begun the morning before.

A bit self-conscious maybe…but not bad at all. He blocked out the last phrase he'd written, rearranged the sentence and then he began typing again, taking up the action where he'd left off.

Shortly after eight, the phone began ringing and by eleven he had already shown the house to a young lawyer and his wife. The man liked it, but Buchanan had the distinct feeling that the young wife had her sights set more on the Druid Hills section off the Raleigh-Durham highway out beyond the Carolina Country Club.

When he watched them leave the driveway, he went back into the kitchen and checked out the list of hourly appointments he'd already booked, on the hour, every hour until three…the next appointment after two was for three fifteen.

From where he stood in the kitchen door he could see his car parked in the driveway and his gut tightened with a curious mixture of excitement and a sense of danger when he recalled the small electronic box attached to the undercarriage. Fighting off his paranoia, he walked back into the bedrooms and, front and back, he looked out the windows, in every direction, trying to spot a spy.

No strange cars.

No strange people.

Nothing out of the ordinary.

ALL DAY LONG, Buchanan walked strangers through the house. But, as the minutes crawled slowly by, he kept a watchful eye on each vehicle passing down the street.

Still nothing strange that he could see.

He knew they were out there.

The game was cat and mouse. He'd show 'em which was which.

When the two o'clock appointment left it was almost two forty-five. Buchanan walked them around the outside and up to their car, answering the man's questions about the lawn and the roof and the type of paint. A handyman type, the man wanted to know everything.

As soon as he waved a final wave and watched them drive down the hill, Buchanan walked back inside and picked up his guitar and took it back into the master bedroom away from any casual observer who might catch a view of him through the living room window. Sitting on the bed with the guitar on his lap, he probed a finger deep inside the sound hole. A few scrapes with his fingernail loosened the tape and he pulled out the key he'd fastened there. When he'd separated the key from the tape, he laid the guitar across the bed, wadded up the tape and threw it into the trash basket beside the chest of drawers. Then he slipped the key into the little change pocket of his jeans, retrieved the guitar and walked back into the living room and leaned it against his chair.

His watch showed 2:55.

Hurrying now, he went down the steps, out the front door and walked nonchalantly out across the yard to where the garden hose with the sprinkler attached was resting near the curb.

Trying to look altogether casual, Buchanan's heartbeat quickened when he heard the sound of the truck as it turned off Currituck, almost two blocks away.

Perfect.

He stopped and picked up a fallen pine cone. When he straightened up again, the truck was just topping the hill. He slowed his stride to time his move toward the street to retrieve the sprinkler, carefully watching the Ryder van move down the hill and then start up the grade again.

The driver slowed and pulled up as he approached Buchanan standing near the curb.

Leaning across, the driver rolled down the passenger-side window and looked out at Buchanan.

"I'm looking for…" The driver read off an address on Rowan six blocks farther on up past St. Timothy's School, across Six Forks Road.

Walking across the yard, Buchanan had slipped the key out of his change pocket. Now he leaned in the truck window and without a telltale motion he casually opened his fingers and let the key fall on the passenger seat while he gave the driver directions.

"Thanks…sounds like a piece of cake." The driver tipped his hat. He waited until Buchanan straightened and stepped back before he let the truck move up the hill and out of sight.

Almost before Buchanan had moved the sprinkler, the 3:15 appointment pulled in the drive.

IT WAS NEARING SIX O'CLOCK when Buchanan bid the last of the house-hunters farewell and got in his car and headed for the Winn-Dixie at the shopping center. The store was crowded with late shoppers looking for last-minute items for Sunday dinner. He found a shopping cart and made his way back toward the produce section and located some leaf lettuce and stuffed it in a plastic bag. Picking over the tomatoes, he finally selected one and returned to his cart and started off again toward the bakery/deli section. He found a loaf of pumpernickel and moved to the deli counter and had the attendant slice a half pound of rare roast beef and an equal weight of swiss cheese. When the clerk had finished and wrapped the packages, Buchanan moved across to the huge magazine rack and located a copy of *Esquire* before he retraced his steps to the checkout counter.

It was beginning to rain as he carried in his groceries, opened a beer and set his packages on the counter top.

Placing the lettuce and the meat in the refrigerator, he removed the magazine from the bag. The remaining item on the counter top, a large cake box tightly taped and tied with string was marked with heavy red crayon: BAKERY —REDUCED/$2.95.

He carried the cake box downstairs to his office, untied the string and lifted the lid.

A sigh of pleasure escaped his lips.

Two hundred fifty-five thousand in tightly-bundled used fifty-dollar bills made a very nice piece of cake, indeed.

Part 3
Penny

Chapter Twenty-eight

UP AT FIVE AND OUT OF THE HOUSE BY SEVEN.

Driving south in the widely dispersed Monday pre-dawn traffic, by the time Buchanan made it around the Beltline onto I-40, he was sure he'd seen his tail driving the same gray Ford sedan he'd seen lurking on the side street behind Cammie's office, exactly one week ago—the morning Joe Acton fired him.

With the efficient little electronic device stuck in place underneath his car, there was no need for the tail to get too close. So, it was really no surprise that, for the most part, the driver of the Ford chose to lag well back, out of sight, to ensure that Buchanan could never get a good look at him.

It wasn't until he'd passed the Clinton exit—which Buchanan arbitrarily considered the halfway point—that it occurred to him whoever was tailing him might send someone to search his house while he was away.

The thought sent a chill up his spine.

Weren't government agents skilled at searching things out?

He shrugged, resisting the icy stab of panic and drove resolutely on.

The moment of truth. He tried to laugh it off. Now was as good a time as any to find out how clever he really was.

Driving along, he invented and rejected scenarios which might explain $255,000 in fifty-dollar bills.

A big night at one of the outlaw casinos in West Virginia near the Greenbrier, perhaps?

That one he dismissed hardly before it crossed his mind.

Better to have the Feds on his back than the mob.

What the hell? He shook his head. *Too late to worry about all that now, anyway.*

Besides, if they found the money they couldn't confront him.

That would constitute an illegal search and seizure. He'd just seen a play on TV that had hinged on the same situation.

Still, if they found it, they could leave it in place and get a warrant and come back. Couldn't they?

Well, he'd rigged it so that he'd know if the hiding place had been disturbed and he could move it right away.

But then they'd be on to him, watch him like a hawk. They'd make sure he never used the money.

So? With the cute little device beneath his car, they were watching him like a hawk anyway.

Besides, he could always...

He caught himself in mid-thought. Thinking about all the disastrous possibilities was a waste of time. Angrily, he tossed his head to rid himself of such depressing preoccupations.

He fiddled with the radio. The hot new rock group Cosmos was on the first three stations. The fourth had Willie. He finally settled for Ray Charles from the sixties revival.

What about Cammie? What would she say? If he got caught, she probably wouldn't even return his phone calls. And who could blame her?

Yet, what about her little speech after the concert Saturday night?

Had she actually been making a pass?

Not likely.

She'd had a couple of drinks.

All the same, she'd left him tongue-tied...

Women!

Too late to wonder about that now...still...the way her body had moved against him when they'd danced at The Player's Retreat. Recalling last night's dream, his penis started to swell...

Buchanan crossed the Cape Fear River at Wilmington with a glass-etching hard-on. It was just past ten when he pulled into a Seven-Eleven on Third Street to use the pay phone.

"New Hanover Hospital. May I help you?" the operator answered.

"Ring the pharmacy, please," Buchanan said and waited.

"Pharmacy. This is Mary Goodman..."

"This is Buchanan Forbes. I'd like to speak to Ted Harper, please," he said and waited.

"Who shall I say you're with, Mr...uh?..." she hesitated.

"Just tell Ted it's Buchanan Forbes, and it's *whom*." The whole world loves a smartass, he mused wryly, knowing that his tone left no doubt Ted would want to speak to him.

The woman sounded young.

Remembering Ted, he conjured up the image of an attractive, well-formed young female.

Big jugs, bet on it.

With Ted Harper it went with the territory. Ted was a regular Jekyll/Hyde. In his days with old-line Elias Aster Company, Harper had always been a competent professional on the job. But, even though he was married and had a grown son in med school in Atlanta, Harper had a reputation for being a chaser, an inveterate, relentless womanizer. On the road, after hours, Harper was a party animal.

When Buchanan moved to Raleigh, Ted Harper had been assigned to cover the medical schools at Duke and UNC at Chapel Hill and Wake Forest in Winston-Salem for the prestigious Elias Aster. Typical of most Aster reps, Ted was a registered pharmacist and had worked at old Grady Hospital in Atlanta before joining Aster and moving to Raleigh. Reliable sources said that before he entered pharmacy school, Ted, the son and grandson of a long line of Georgia physicians, had suddenly abandoned his medical studies at Emory University for some obscure reason that no one ever talked about.

In his regular travels to cover Bowman Gray School of Medicine in Winston-Salem, Buchanan had dropped in on a few impromptu after-hours parties. A small free-floating hormonal nucleus of med students, residents and nurses, ward clerks and a scattering of technicians from x-ray or the lab—to be from a Baptist supported school, they were a hedonistic lot—was a veritable meat market for the perennial hard-core of traveling pharmaceutical reps and medical salesmen out for casual sex. Invariably, Harper was always there. With the women, Ted Harper was a relentless predator, a legend in his own time.

"Buck Forbes, is that really you?" Ted came on the line in a matter of seconds.

"Does Miss Mary Goodman look as good as I imagine, Ted?"

"Huh? Well, yeah, I guess you *could* say that." Ted chuckled low into the mouthpiece.

"Good to know that some things don't change." Buchanan laughed an easy laugh.

"Where are you? You rotten no-good SOB."

"I just came across the bridge. Thought you might buy me a cup of coffee. How do I find you?"

"Sure thing. Where are you right now?"

"On Third...the Seven-Eleven..."

With Ted's directions, Buchanan located the undistinguished rectangular beige-gray brick high rise in no time. By the time he parked and walked up the hill to the lobby and found the steps leading down to the coffee shop, Ted was already waiting at a small table.

"Long time, no see, Bucko. I heard rumors about your, ah, your parting of the ways with Lhamda-A," the handsome, vaguely fortyish man in the white clinic coat said as Buchanan slipped into a chair facing him. "What got into Joe Acton, anyway? Hell's bells, you're the best I ever saw at setting up new clinical studies, and what'n hell brings you down here, for chrissake?"

Buchanan was not completely surprised that Ted had gotten the word. Drug salesmen were a gossipy bunch.

The reminder that he might be going back to that world brought an unpleasant taste to his mouth.

"Well, believe it or not, I'm down here for a job interview with Stribol." Buchanan swallowed his resentment and told the pharmacist about his three o'clock appointment at the beach. Then he added, "How's Stribol do down here, anyway?"

"Well, I hope you take the job. I have a truckload of outdated Stribol antibiotics to return for credit."

Buchanan was caught off guard by Ted's response.

"Why? I thought Stribol was tops in antibiotics. What about Staphopen, and Xantrek? My God, Cal Murphy is getting rich around Duke and Chapel Hill."

"That's part of the problem. They don't have a regular rep down here. That, and the eastern part of the state is so sparsely settled and so poor. Since the paper and fertilizer companies, the railroad and bigtime shipping barons moved their corporate offices, houses are a buyer's market. I just bought myself a mansion in Forest Hills for a cool 100 K. I mean a real live Tara with live oaks and four massive white columns, five blocks from the Cape Fear Country Club. You won't believe it. Dennis Hopper's revival of the old DeLaurentis movie studios in the late nineties have made this place a film capital. Movie people coming in and out paying big prices to lease these old mansions. I'm buying everything in sight. If you do take the job you can truly live in style. Get this. On either side, my next door neighbors are the leading internist and the chief of surgery here at the hospital. I just leased Spielberg a big old house I own, 10 K a month, six months in advance, enough to make a down payment on two more mansions."

"But what's this about the Stribol product line? Are you telling me that they have exclusive on all those miracle drugs and the local docs don't use 'em? What kind of medicine do they practice in these parts, roots and herbs? What about Stribol's new Spectropen, the new anti-viral broad-spectrum penicillin? The journals are full of it. When's it coming out? *Time* magazine says it's the breakthrough of the twenty-first century."

"Well, Spectropen just came out last week, actually. I've got it stocked, but so far there have been no calls for it. Someone needs to tell the urologists about it. They use some Xantrek now and then on resistant gram negs, but everybody's afraid of Xantrek's toxicity, even though nothing can

[154]

touch it in life-threatening situations. Surgeons will occasionally use some, and Staphopen, too. But Supraceph, Stribol's fancy phosphate complex of cephalosporin, is just too expensive for most of our docs. They don't believe it's that much better than the old-timey tetracycline hydrochloride." Ted pulled out a piece of the latest anti-smoking gum and popped it in his mouth. He shrugged sheepishly, "I can't seem to quit."

"Amazing. Well, I guess I'm not really that surprised about the expensive cephalosporin. Anyway, how's life treating you? You were about to have a doctor in the family as I recall..."

A smile lit Ted's face and he fairly bubbled as he told Buchanan that his son, Chip—properly, Edward Leonard Harper, IV—had just been offered an internship at Hopkins.

"Congratulations, and I'm glad you like Wilmington."

"Like? I love it. My wife even likes it. She's Junior League. Into the local arts council...on the Azalea Festival committee... and let me tell you this..." Harper's voice lowered to almost a whisper. "This place is paradise. I have this sweet little Sugarshack out at the beach with two other guys. Gene Lindamood, the chief OB-GYN resident here and Hank Long...Henry... Henry Ellis Long...part owner of Physician's Supply out of Raleigh...and me...the three of us have this hideaway at Wrightsville Beach. We run a non-stop party out there. Remember the high old times we used to have in Winston-Salem? The beach is jam-packed with pussy...aspiring movie actresses...school teachers...and nurses. Wild? These gals were born to spread their legs. I'm in hog heaven. Wait'll you meet our OB nursing supervisor, Janie Lockfaw...you wouldn't believe those tits..." He rolled his eyes heavenward. "It's like the good old days. Most every night...some of the swinging docs show up and local lawyers and some of the traveling drug reps. This is one swinging town, a regular Melrose Place. You'd like this crowd. Tonight's Monday...a big night...after everybody has been cooped up all weekend...played the family scene to get their merit badges at home. It'll be rowdy tonight. You should drop by. Give me a call when your interview's over..." Ted pulled out a hospital prescription pad and wrote down his number at home and another number and an address. "This is the beach number, unpublished. I wrote down the address just in case. If I'm not there, tell whoever answers who you are. They'll tell you how to find us."

"Well, I can't tonight. I have to run on down to South Carolina." Buchanan thanked him politely and tucked the phone numbers in his pocket. He was no prude but he had no interest in casual sex.

"OK, well, later. I hope the interview goes well. It would be great having you in the territory. You'd like living down here. We could sure use a Stribol rep in the area. I moonlight at The Apothecary downtown. Biggest prescription pharmacy in town. Slip me some samples now and again and I'll make sure Stribol is on the formulary. Know what I mean?" Ted winked. "Give me a call before you leave town and let me know how things work out. I better get back..." He stood and extended his hand.

Buchanan shook his hand and followed him out.

"By the way, if you're looking for a place to live, drop into Harbor Realty out at Wrightsville Beach, Rochelle Guest. She used to be a nurse, in charge of OB-GYN. Tell her I sent you. She negotiated the deal on the Sugarshack for me. Buy Roxie a beer...she'll treat you right."

When he got in his car, Buchanan retraced his route to Market Street, turned left and headed aimlessly back toward town. He'd purposefully come early to get a closer look at Wilmington. If there was any chance that he was going to be offered the Stribol job, he wanted to have a feel for living in the historical old seaport.

Regrettably, in the four years since they'd moved to Raleigh, he and Alma had rarely found the opportunity to visit Wilmington. Two or three times each summer they'd driven the boys down for a day at the beach, but the drive took two hours each way and by the time they made it back home, the kids were exhausted and everyone was at each other's throats. The kids loved it, but the excursion always left their parents tottering on the brink of a nervous breakdown.

Buchanan believed there were magic places that resonated enigmatically with a person's soul. Like Charleston, or Savannah, these old seaport towns whispered of dark and beckoning old brain stuff, stirrings that were forever double-helixed deep into his protoplasm.

For him, Wilmington held that magic.

Now, driving around slowly, the vibrations came rumbling into his psyche as if he was of another time, another place. The idea of living on the coast called up soaring flights of fancy.

He passed the old apartment building that had been a setting for the movie *Blue Velvet* as he neared Third Street. It was the main thoroughfare that had brought him in from the west and eventually led on down to Carolina Beach, terminating at Fort Fisher where the ferry jumped off to Southport. Buchanan could see the waterfront of the Cape Fear River and the dominating Hilton Wilmington Riverside. At the bottom of the gentle slope where Market Street ended three blocks further on, there was a magnificent old three-masted schooner anchored at the seawall.

The boat was something right out of a picture book.

A schooner, he wondered idly. A clipper ship or brigantine, perhaps?

Whatever. All sailing vessels were "schooners" or "clipper ships" to mountain boys like him.

Beyond, across the narrow river harbor, the ghostly hulking superstructure of the battleship North Carolina—her giant guns pointed menacingly straight at him—loomed through the hazy, blue-gray morning mists. Permanently moored there, the battleship was widely celebrated as a major tourist attraction. At night, he knew, there was a big light and sound show. Back in Raleigh, it was advertised on TV. His sons were forever bugging him to take them. Buchanan resolved to bring them the first chance he got, before they got too old to enjoy the adventure.

Waiting at the light at Third, he watched a long-legged flaming redhead swish down the hill in front of a storybook white two-story colonial house on the opposite side of the street. The house flew a Colonial flag from its porch and had an historic marker standing in front. The young woman's breasts bounced sensually against the light fabric of her blouse.

My-oh-my, would you just look at that? He sat marveling through the windshield at the redhead's saucy derrière. The memory of his erotic dream came sharply back to him. It had been almost two weeks since Alma left. Even for a man grown used to wifely neglect, that was a long time to go without.

He hadn't actually missed Alma, but he *was* human after all.

During Desert Storm he had attended to his lustful yearnings by the all-too-infrequent expedient of masturbating. Then, over the past few years with Alma's waning interest, he'd been forced to fall back on the same lonely exercise to keep his lust at bay when he stayed in motels.

Secretly he blushed, thinking about it now.

The car behind him honked impatiently. The light had changed.

Red-faced, Buchanan let the car move on through the intersection. As he went slowly by, he noted the headline on the historic marker in front of the little white colonial building:

CORNWALLIS HOUSE

This old port had seen its share of history. He recalled seeing another marker somewhere, a few blocks further east, down toward Carolina Beach. That one had something to do with Whistler's Mother. There were markers everywhere you turned down here, a number of them related to the blockade runners during the Civil War. Last summer on one of their outings, he'd taken the boys down to the ruins of Fort Fisher. With all the history and the beaches, Wilmington would be an exciting place to raise the boys.

Buchanan drove slowly through the downtown area and spotted The Apothecary Ted Harper had mentioned. Turning, he came back along the waterfront and pulled to the curb alongside the old "schooner." *The Eagle* was emblazoned in gold on the prow of the majestic three-masted vessel.

A portable sign on the sidewalk explained it was actually a "bark"—a training ship for the Coast Guard Academy. The poster advertised *The Eagle* was open to the public every afternoon from two to five. Catching a vagrant whiff of wood and rope, Buchanan's imagination soared.

He leaned forward and took a farewell look at the tops of the rigging falling in an orderly array from the tips of the tall oak masts as he slowly pulled away from the curb.

God! How his boys would love to scramble over the decks of that magnificent vessel—he sighed and his throat filled with longing. He really missed his sons.

Oh, well, he shrugged and decided that he might as well head out toward the beach and locate the cottage where he was supposed to meet Morris Earle and his flunky, Randall Wickline. He still had plenty of time to pick up a local newspaper and look at the real estate ads over a leisurely bite of lunch.

Driving away, he failed to see the gray sedan in the narrow alley beside the old Customs House.

Chapter Twenty-nine

FROM THE KITCHEN WINDOW Inger watched as Penny walked back by the trailer which served as the office of the Glover's Trailer Park. Since her first morning here, Penny had taken a daily walk to the beach, a half-mile beyond the marina. And, every morning right on schedule, Clem Glover popped out like magic and handed Penny the morning's mail.

Day or night, anytime Penny came within sniffing range, Clem always seemed to pop right out of the door. No doubt about it. Clem was a dirty old man—in his charming, completely harmless way.

So? What was wrong with that?

Inger smiled. She had a soft spot for Clem.

Penny liked him, too. Clem meant no harm and, looking now at the coltish figure of the gloriously tan young woman walking toward her, Inger could hardly blame any man for lusting after her.

Anyway, Inger felt certain Penny Wagner was quite able to take care of herself.

Inger looked at her watch: 10:25. The sun was beginning to burn through the light overcast, heralding a glorious spring day. She'd promised Penny they'd go into Myrtle Beach for the evening. They'd leave early…go check out the upscale shops and restaurants at Broadway. Except for the Canadians, the tourist traffic was light this time of year. If they went early, they could avoid the hassle of standing in line. Afterwards, the new band at the Bowery was supposed to be something special…old favorites and beach music…not too much rock and roll. Who knows, maybe they'd get lucky and find some nice young men to dance with? Friday night they'd run across a promising pair—a boat captain and his young mate, from a small motor yacht owned by a wealthy Long Island garment manufacturer who wintered in Palm Beach and moved his boat back and forth to match his migrations with the seasons. They'd danced the night away with the two ruggedly handsome men but afterward, much to Inger's disappointment, she'd had to turn down an invitation to accompany the captain back to the marina for a nightcap on the yacht. The captain, a virile man in his late fifties, was charming and enormously sexy. But, while the younger mate bore a strong resemblance to Leonardo DiCaprio, Penny had been less than enchanted with his coarse innuendoes and the cavalier liberties he took with his hands.

With her little finger, Inger hooked an oversized ceramic mug from the drain rack. She opened a can of beer and poured it carefully down the side of the mug to keep it from foaming over. She discarded the can and turned just as Penny came through the door.

"Enjoy your stroll?" Inger leaned around the counter for a better look.

"Oh, yes…yes, yes, yes. I wish I could stay here forever…and just write poems about the sea and the wind…and lost love."

"Lost love? Why not found love? Now that's a subject to take the chill off an old hag's bones…"

"Old hag? Why do you talk like that?"

"Uhmm, maybe you have something there. Dag Hammerskjold said, *'Do not seek death. Death will find you.'*"

"How depressing. What's gotten into you? You're as young and vital as any woman I know. It's a beautiful day, you're beautiful…here's a letter from the Colonel. That'll cheer you up." Penny sorted through the mail, separated out two envelopes addressed to her and handed Inger the rest.

"Ah, yes, the good Colonel Pershing Stuart Carlyle, I seem to remember him." Inger opened the envelope, quickly scanned the single page and tossed it on the counter with a rather enigmatic smile. "He's getting horny now. He wrote twice last week. Men are so predictable. He'll be bringing his little soldiers back from Florida soon. Says he may come by here for a few days during the school break."

"Ah? What?" Penny looked up from her reading.

"Oh, nothing, just rambling. I see that the good doctor, Elroy Goins, has kept his record intact, hasn't missed a day."

"Uhmm..." Penny made a face and handed the card over to Inger. "I wish I..." She left the thought dangling.

She opened the other envelope and began reading again. "My mother! She keeps pushing me to go ahead and set a wedding date. Since I've been gone, Elroy's been working on her, tells her marriage won't change anything. I can go right ahead and finish my degree...he'll pay the tuition. Good old Elroy..."

"Well, you can't fault him for persistence. And while we're on the subject, he's rich, he's a doctor...best family, good looking, well-respected, former football star, and still not thirty. When you get right down to it, he's damn near perfect. Every girl in Newbold, Tennessee, would kill to have him. You could do a lot worse." Inger took a deep drink from the mug. She swiped the foam from her mouth with the sleeve of her sweatshirt emblazoned with the legend: STAND UP F♀R FREED♀M ♀F CH♀ICE: RETURN Y♀UR RIGHT T♀ A SAFE AB♀RTI♀N.

Back home on campus, the shirt was taboo.

"*A lot worse.*" Inger emphasized the thought with a mischievous wink.

"But I'm not sure I love him. I mean, I do care about him—everybody looks up to P. Elroy Goins. He's sweet, but, well, you know what I mean. Marriage is supposed to be forever. It's scary. Forever is a long time."

"I know." Inger reached forward and patted her arm. She pulled out a stool and sat down at the kitchen bar and began opening the rest of the mail. "Let's go into Myrtle early tonight. My Brookgreen Gardens piece for the *Tennessean* has to be in the mail to Nashville today." She leaned forward and absently inspected the screen of the laptop sitting on the counter.

Penny pulled up a stool. "Were you crazy in love when you married the Colonel?"

"To tell the truth, no."

Penny's jaw dropped. "You're kidding..."

"No. Really. I was just looking for a ticket out of Germany. My parents had both survived the war as children and wound up on the Russian side in East Berlin. I was born in 1957 and my parents mysteriously disappeared. I was taken in by the wife of a high-ranking German official in the Russian occupation government. But by the time I was thirteen her husband had his eyes and hands out for me. She found out about him and blamed me. They left me to fend for myself. Afterward, one of his senior staff members took me in, thinking to make me his protègèe…until his mistress found out. By then, I'd learned what survival was all about. With the help of friends, I made it over to the American side of the wall. When I went to register for work, I was only fifteen but lied about my age. There was no way to check—all the records were on the Russian side. I went to work as a waitress in the American Officer's Club. When the Colonel came along, he thought I was nineteen. I jumped at the chance. He was only a major then, but sent from heaven. I would've done anything to get out. I would have married him if he had been a private and mentally retarded. Anything to come to America…" Inger pushed aside the mail and looked Penny in the eye. "But Pershing's been good to me. We're good for each other. We had…we *have*…a good marriage," she hastily amended.

"You learned to love him, then?" Penny leaned forward, eager to understand.

"Well, *ja.*" Dreamily, Inger's voice betrayed a trace of Germanic lilt. "I guess you could say that. But, don't think…I mean…" She drained the mug as she weighed her words. "There's a difference between loving someone and being in love."

She avoided looking Penny in the eye.

"Oh? How can you tell the difference? I mean you've been married to the Colonel since you were fifteen. Haven't you ever been '*in*' love?"

"Oh, now you're asking me a very tricky question. I don't know if I want to get into that."

Inger went to the Igloo cooler and took out another can of beer, but then she looked back at the little computer and sighed and put it back. "Guess I better finish that article before I get half-crocked."

She plodded back to her laptop.

"Is that all…I mean, aren't you going to tell me? How will I know? Elroy is good to me. But he's no fun. He took me to Knoxville to the opera last month. His sister and her husband went along to chaperone. Ugh! I really wanted to go to Atlanta and catch the revival tour of the Serendipity Singers with Bob Dylan, but Elroy says that's lowbrow. He's so darn stuffy. He's taking me to Boston to show me Harvard on our honeymoon. I told him that I'd rather go to Jamaica or Cancun. He says that would be a bore. There's nothing to do but snorkel and lie around on the beach. I asked him what's wrong with that? He just patted my hand…treats me like a child. Makes fun of what I read and never wants to see the movies I pick out. He's had his mother trying to teach me to play bridge...what a drag. Truth is, he bores me to tears most of the time. I really can't imagine having to put up with him day in, day out, forever."

"Uhm..." Inger found her little reading glasses and put them on. She regarded Penny over the end of her nose. "Well, one thing about being married to a doctor...they're never home."

"So, you think my mother's right...I should go ahead and marry him. Is that what you're telling me?" Penny slid off the stool, stepping defiantly forward with her hips thrust aggressively out, almost like a pugilist's pose. She stuck out her underlip and blew a sharp breath up at a stray wisp of her hair.

"Well, no, not at all. I just think you should take a long look at the advantages. You should be in no hurry. You'll graduate next spring. *Mein Gott*, you're only nineteen. Don't let your mother or Elroy rush you." Inger turned back to the laptop. Clearly she wanted to end the conversation.

"Do you have regrets? Did you ever meet someone who...who just filled you up with music and poetry? Did you ever miss your chance?"

"Well, no. I don't really have any regrets. Besides, I've had my share of music and poetry along the way and, if I'm lucky, I may again." A far-away look passed behind Inger's eyes.

"But, Inger, I can't imagine...I mean...the thought of making love to Elroy...of letting him...you know...I can't imagine that. I hate it when he kisses me. He's always trying to French me in the mouth. Ugh! Just kissing him on the lips is bad enough. In high school I went steady for a while with Ralph, the Reverend Boxley's boy. I liked it when he kissed me...made my toes curl up. Makes me shiver now, just thinking about it. Shouldn't it be like that when you're married?"

"Well, that's what the fairy tales say," Inger laughed.

"Don't patronize me. I'm too old for fairy tales. But I still believe in romance. What's wrong with that?" Penny asked, petulantly.

"Nothing. Not a thing. And give it a chance. Elroy might grow on you. You're so much younger than he is; maybe he's actually a red-hot lover, just afraid to show you his romantic side."

Penny gave Inger a despairing look. "Don't count on it. He's always trying to get his hand up my dress. Says it's OK, now that we're engaged. P. Leroy Goins, Mr. Excitement! He's about as smooth as a used car salesman. He buys all his clothes from Burberry, or some such snobby place in Boston, but he still looks like he shops at Sears' basement. Inger, I want someone who'll make me feel alive. Did you ever read *Lady Chatterley*? Does it ever actually happen like that?"

"*Lady Chatterley...ach, mein Gott,* that old book? Do you want to twine wildflowers around your lover's...equipment?" Try as she might to keep a straight face, Inger had to laugh.

"Don't make fun of me. Do you think it ever happens like that?"

"Well, yes. Yes. I know it does." She turned to her laptop to hide a blush. "Now, take the money and the grocery list there on the counter and let me finish this article in peace."

Chapter Thirty

BUCHANAN SPENT THE REST of the morning driving around, trying to orient himself to the lay of the good residential sections.

He discovered the university by following the signs. From there he retraced his way back to Oleander Drive and on out to Wrightsville Beach.

At the beach he parked his car at the tiny collection of shops, restaurants and businesses just across the old bridge from Harbor Island. He went into a large two-story red brick building situated—along with the laundromat, the post office and bank—on a little triangle of land where Lumina Avenue made a sharp zigzag and continued south along the Banks Channel, past the old landmark high-rise Blockade Runner Hotel, running all the way to the south terminus of the island at Masonboro Inlet. The sign over the door read Wings and the display windows running all the way around were filled with beachwear, mostly ladies' bikinis, and fishing equipment and kites and beach toys for the kids.

Wrightsville was a family beach. The buildings had all seen better days, but there was a mystical sense of permanence in the air.

Every building had withstood the brunt of Fran, a killer hurricane, which several years back had made landfall here. A few years before that there had been Hugo and dimly-remembered Hazel which—in the fifties—had hit, virtually full force, at high tide on the night of the full moon.

Looking north across from Wings, the Harbor Island Realty office of Rochelle Guest occupied the downstairs of a wooden building—a rambling old structure that obviously had apartments above it. Opposite, on the ocean side of the street, was a liquor store and gift shop displaying seashell doodads of every description. Further down he saw a rusty old neon sign mounted vertically over the door of a stucco corner building at the next side street to the beach:

The WIT'S END
Hamburgers • Pool • Beer on Tap

From a phone booth on the tiny greensward between the laundro-mat and the post office, he called Cammie's office, hoping he might hear a friendly voice, but Mae said she'd been in court all day. He told her he'd call back later and hung up.

Inside Wings he found a copy of the *Wilmington Morning Star*, paid the cashier and headed for The Wit's End.

By the time he'd finished his hamburger and coffee and read all the real estate ads, he still had an hour and a half to kill.

On impulse, Buchanan walked across the street and entered the tiny real estate office. As he entered, a bell tinkled somewhere in back. The door opened onto a small room with a desk, a small love seat and a chair.

"Have a seat...be right with you," a woman's voice drifted out to him through the door—curtained with seashells strung like beads—leading to the back. On the desk was a picture of the famous old-time golfer Sam Snead in a tux, holding a trumpet in one hand—ubiquitous straw hat perched jauntily atop his head, his other arm was tightly wound around the waist of a pretty little girl. Idly, Buchanan examined the array of framed business licenses and an old photo of a group of nursing students. The walls were warmly paneled in darkly-rich heart pine and covered with other photos. Each featured the same attractive female—an attrac-tive athletic girl posing with a variety of famous golfers, movie and TV stars—as she progressed to womanhood. Buchanan read some of the neatly typed captions centered at the bottom of each frame. Directly in front of him, Arnold Palmer was grinning down at the woman as a teenager—the caption read: Azalea Open — 1959.

Moving slowly around the walls, Buchanan recognized photos of dimly-remembered movie stars...Susan Hayward, Joseph Cotton, Sidney Blackmer and Ava Gardner. He stopped to examine a photo showing a not-quite-handsome, mustached man who had signed, *"Warmest, Robert."*

The face seemed hauntingly familiar.

"Can I help you?" The voice startled him out of his reverie. The slender woman, Buchanan guessed to be in her fifties, looked remarkably the same as in the photo with Tom Weiskopf which was dated April 1966, nearly thirty-six years before. Her ash-blonde hair was styled in the same closely cropped helmet—as fashionable now as it had been in the heyday of F. Scott Fitzgerald's *Gatsby*.

"Uh, are you Ms. Guest?"

"I'm Rochelle Guest. What can I do for you?"

"I wanted to ask about rental property, but I can't help but ask, isn't this Robert Ruark in this photo?"

"Yes. I didn't think anyone remembered poor Robert. That was taken the last time he came home. Right after *Poor No More* hit the best-seller list. That book scandalized the whole town."

"Oh, you mean those characters were real? I never thought about it, but he did grow up near here, didn't he?"

"Wilmington and Southport. He dated my grandmother in high school. Wilmington treated Robert's family like dirt. Robert settled a lot of old scores in that book...then he rubbed salt in the wounds." She laughed. "He was living in Spain back then. Came back here driving a gold and black Rolls Royce. Grandma told me Robert got a real kick out of that."

"A nice sense of poetic justice there."

"Yeah, but his liver went sour. His half-brother used to live right here, the apartment upstairs."

"No kidding. Did he write too?"

"No. The only thing he had in common with Robert was a love for the broth. But enough of that. Are you looking for a place?"

"I'm considering relocating from Raleigh and need a small place to rent. Temporarily, while I arrange to dispose of my place there and find a place suitable for my wife and sons. Ted Harper at New Hanover Hospital recommended you," Buchanan said.

"Oh, you know Dr. Harper?" She gave him a hooded look. "I gather you'd need something furnished, something just big enough for you, alone?"

"Just a place to sleep, really, with maybe a desk and a bath, and a kitchen. I wouldn't need much, you know, maybe one of those compact kitchen units like they have in the beach motels."

"Pullman unit?"

"Yes." he said. "I actually need something affordable."

"Hmm...define affordable?"

"Just something clean and comfortable will do," he said. "I'm actual-ly not even sure that I'll be making the move, but if I do, I would like to have some idea of my options..."

"Well, I have one little efficiency, and I do mean little, as in tiny. But it has everything you describe. Would you like to see it? If it doesn't suit, then we can take it from there. I know every available rental on the beach. Would you like to take a look?"

"Sure, I'm free 'til three."

Buchanan rode in the front seat beside her. He took in the neat rows of ageless cottages lining both sides of the street as they rode north along Lumina Avenue, paralleling the beach.

"How old are your kids?" she asked politely.

"I have four sons. The youngest will be five in September. The oldest will be eleven in May."

"You'll love it here. Wrightsville's a family beach, but you'd be surprised at how many people live here year round. There's a middle school on Harbor Island, near our once-infamous desalinization plant. The grammar school is just across the Waterway at Bradley Creek. If you came out Oleander, you may have seen it. It's on the opposite side of the road near the Marina."

"Oh, yeah. I did see it. The boys would love living at the beach. But I guess property's a lot cheaper in town."

"Depends. Sometimes you can pick up something pretty nice in the off season. Some of 'em don't have a good year-round heating system, but winters are mild. Most can be added on through the air-conditioning ducts. I have some things I could show you."

"Well, that would be good, but first I guess I'd better wait and see if I'll actually be moving down here." Buchanan laughed.

"Ah, here we are." The woman pulled the car to the curb in front of a neatly painted, two-story white stucco house. Without a word she located the key and opened the car door and started down a narrow sidewalk that led around the back, beside the house. By the time he caught up to her, she was standing at the door underneath a little aluminum awning which served as an entry stoop. "There's another, bigger downstairs apartment around back facing the lagoon. And the entire upstairs is a big three bedroom place that's taken by a young couple. She teaches school and he works out at the paper mill at Reigelwood. C'mon in." She stepped aside.

Buchanan walked in, ducking unnecessarily to avoid the overhang of the awning which was slightly higher than it appeared. Inside was a fairly large room that was all open and had a big old-fashioned iron bed at the front by the large window looking out on the street. He walked over and pushed tentatively on the mattress, testing it. Then he turned and sat on it and finally lay back and folded his hands underneath his head. "Not bad. I was up pretty early. I could go right off to sleep." He chuckled and bounced back up again.

A folding screen separated the room into two areas. Back toward the rear, the sitting area had a comfortable looking wicker sleeping-sofa and chair and a cocktail table. Lamp tables stood at either end of the sofa. There was a tall floor lamp by the chair. Buchanan moved across the room. The compact kitchen jutted off toward the back along the outer wall and a door leading to a bath occupied the similar space off the inner wall. Between the kitchen and bath was a roomy walk-in closet. Across from the sitting area was a tiny dining table with two chairs. The cement floor was covered not quite wall-to-wall with a heavy fiber matting. He tested the bathroom faucets. The plumbing in the metal shower stall was new and worked quite nicely.

"Well, what do you think?"

"This might do fine. All I really need is a place to do my paperwork and a dry place to sleep. I'd have to store samples, but I guess I could make arrangements for outside storage if I needed it. I could shove a lot of it under the bed. How much?"

"Well, how's four hundred sound? A month, I mean."

"How about three hundred? Is water and electric included?"

"Just the H-2-O, which includes garbage pick-up. Electric is up to you, but it isn't air-conditioned, so the electric won't run you much. And I own this place myself. If you needed to stay on a month longer, it would be OK. But, four hundred is firm..."

"Well, this is kind of rustic. What else do you have?"

"This is the low end. Do you want to see something a little bigger, with air?"

"How much are we talking about?"

"Well, the next thing is much nicer, larger and upstairs. I have one you could get for twelve hundred a month, but you'd have to move out on June first. In season, it goes for twelve a week."

"OK, OK, I get the picture. No need to look. If things should work out, this will do quite nicely, thanks. By the way, Ted Harper said he had a place out here. Is it nearby?"

"Just around the corner, on Lagoon, at the end of the cul-de-sac. You can't see it from here, but I'll show you. We go right by there. If you wanted to be near Ted...Doctor Harper...uh...well, you couldn't be much closer."

He started to correct her, but Southerners often called pharmacists doctor.

"Uh, no, not important. I was just curious. Mr. Harper recommended you highly..." Buchanan watched closely for her reaction.

"*Dr.* Harper is a nice man." Her face told him nothing.

By the time she had driven them back, it was almost 2:30. Buchanan thanked her, took her card and told her he'd get in touch as soon as he knew something definite about his plans.

He tried Cammie again. No luck. Back in his car headed south on

[167]

Lumina looking for the landmarks that Morris Earle had given him, Buchanan busied himself making a mental checklist of questions to ask about the job: Base Salary...Commission...Fringes...Hospital...Insurance... Retirement...

Suddenly he realized that he was not only hoping they would offer him the position, but that it would provide him with enough income and all the other good and valid reasons to justify moving his family here to the coast. As much as he hated the idea of going back to work peddling pharmaceuticals again, he grudgingly admitted that for the moment at least, this job offered a miraculous opportunity to get his life back on track, just when all seemed lost.

And...truthfully...he was just plain falling in love with the idea of bringing the boys to live at the beach. The kids would be ecstatic at the idea of living near the ocean, and the thought that he might be calling Alma with the news that he was once again among the land of the wage earners cheered him immensely. She would wind up with egg on her face over her recent hysteria.

And, what the hell, the job might not be so bad. After the rarefied atmosphere of academia, working a provincial territory would be a refreshing breath of air—poetic justice.

That Hersh Roberts had asked him to do the big feature article on Mallone was a miraculous stroke of luck, but he wasn't fooling himself when—just for the hell of it—he'd sent queries out to *Playboy* and *Esquire*. Originally, the thought of maybe breaking into the big time made his heart beat faster. But now that the euphoria of his fantasy had worn off, he realized that underneath he was just plain scared. What the devil did he know about writing anyway?

The odds that he was going to blossom overnight as the "Kandy Apple Kool-Aid Two-Fingered Typing Baby" ...a sensational new writing discovery who would burst on the scene like Tom Wolfe or Gay Talese did way back in the sixties...or...that he would become the next Ernest Hemingway...or Scott Fitzgerald... or...or...even a second-rate Sharkey Mallone...were on the same order of his chances of being the first man on Mars.

He was a long way from earning his way as a writer...but it was a romantic idea. The prospect intrigued him. And? If he was able to restore his earning power and get the family back together, then what was there to prevent him from trying his hand at maybe even a novel?

Just beyond the old-fashioned aluminum-painted rocket-shaped water tower rising behind the low cinder block building which served as combination town hall and police station, Buchanan slowed and found the street sign he was looking for and turned left toward the ocean. Wrightsville Beach stretched a scant four or so miles from the north end where the Guest woman had just taken him, to the south end, a mile farther on down where Masonboro Inlet divided it from the next little island in this vestigial section of the famed Outer Banks. It was wider at the north end, but even at the widest point, the intersecting streets spanned only two blocks on the ocean side and hardly more on the westward side, along the Banks Channel of the famous Inland Waterway. Here, the narrow pothole-pocked sand-blown street spanned barely two rows of tightly-bunched houses before it petered out and became a one-way track running along the salt-weathered houses fronting the beach. He proceeded slowly south, counting the houses, all raised high on solid creosoted pilings.

Ranging from tiny single-story boxes to sprawling weathered three-story seaside-Gothic mansions spanning as many as three of the tiny sixty-foot lots, the houses were a jumble of architecture. They stood like a line of rag-tag volunteer skirmishers, jammed tightly together, barely twenty feet separating the bedroom windows from the neighbors' kitchens and decks.

Just as Morris Earle had predicted, he had no difficulty finding the cottage and he pulled in underneath between the cross-braced stilt pilings beside the two other cars already parked there.

It seemed that his interviewers had already returned from the fishing.

Buchanan hoped their luck had been good.

He found his briefcase and, using the car window as a mirror, he straightened his tie. Taking a deep breath, he followed the sidewalk along the side of the house. Like most of the beachfront houses, the entrance was by way of the deck overlooking the beach.

Buchanan tried to tell himself that he actually didn't have anything to lose, but now, for the first time, he admitted deep down that he was lucky to have a second chance. This represented much more than just a pay-check. To get the chance to go back to work in the industry so soon would mean that his credibility would be instantly restored. Becoming a star performer with a top-rated line like Stribol in this backwater territory would be duck soup. It was a long way from the sophisticated ambiance of Duke and Chapel Hill, but that was in his favor. People in the business world had a short memory. And, best of all, if he could get back to work, he wouldn't have to listen to Alma's accusations about his dereliction of family any more.

If it weren't for his sons, he'd just tell her to shove it, anyway.

"Anyone at home?" he called out and, taking a deep breath, headed up the steps.

Chapter Thirty-one

WALKING OUT OF THE COURTROOM, Cammie Brawley tersely answered the reporter's questions. Cammie knew her client deserved better from her—it was a miracle that she'd won his case. Ever since she'd left him in his driveway Saturday night, Cammie's head had been abuzz with thoughts of Buchanan Forbes. Without breaking stride, she headed for the law library to use the phone.

Yesterday morning, she'd hoped against hope Buchanan might show up at the park, but somehow she'd known that he wouldn't. She'd wanted to offer him the use of her cottage at Pawley's Island on his trip down to interview Sharkey Mallone. In her confusion Saturday night, the idea had not occurred to her until afterward when she had been driving home. Then finally, when she tried to call him late Sunday afternoon, she'd received no answer. Afterwards, she'd wondered if maybe he was too embarrassed by her rather shameless—practically wanton—behavior during the evening following the concert and was avoiding her.

Truth was, when she thought about it, she alternated between being ashamed at her lack of self-control and being titillated at the memory of him getting an erection—well, at least he'd had a great start on one while they were dancing.

No doubt about it, she was dangerously attracted to the man. She adored the poor dumb jerk. He was heart-stoppingly beautiful...in every way. And, most likely a budding genius who had no bloody idea of his talent.

After Saturday, he probably felt sorry for her. Who wouldn't? Her hysterical outburst was, classically, the pathetic behavior of a sexually frustrated middle-aged female.

Stop it, Cammie berated herself. She had to quit this "poor me" binge. She was one of the top criminal attorneys in the Southeast...lectured at Yale. Come to think of it, Harvard too. Her social comings and goings were occasionally noted in *Town and Country*. She was certain that their friendship went deep enough. In her more rational moments she knew Buchanan Forbes really respected her more than that.

Now, she had decided that she had to back off and make him understand she was no threat to his marriage. She wanted him to think of her as a friend he could count on.

Cammie closed the door of the law library in the reporter's face and dialed the number.

"Mae, we won. Our client walked, no thanks to me. I have to go pick up a cocktail dress at Cameron Village so I won't get by the office before you leave. Have I had any calls?"

She held her breath and made notes as Mae read off a list of names.

"Oh, yes, I almost forgot. Mr. Forbes called…this is the second time. I just hung up. He said tonight he'd be in Myrtle Beach. Said if he got a chance he might try you again here later, if not he'd call tomorrow morning. He didn't leave a number."

"Thanks, Mae. I'll see you bright and early tomorrow. Have a good evening." She hung up and slumped against the wall and whooshed a sigh. "Oh, thank you," she said half-aloud to a God she didn't know. "Buchanan Forbes, you son-of-a-bitch. You could have left me some clue, you son-of-a-bitch…you beautiful son-of-a-bitch…at least you didn't forget me."

He'd told Mae he might call again. Now her heart was beating faster and her breath was shallow. If Buchanan called, she wanted to make sure he knew he could use the beach cottage.

She wondered how he'd react.

The idea of him sleeping in her bed was exciting. She hadn't changed the sheets from the last overnight stopover on the way to a regional ABA meeting in Charleston. She hoped her scent would still be on the pillows. Would he see the sexy lace panties she kept neatly arranged on the little open shelves in her closet? All embroidered, ivory-on-ivory, with her initials. She'd stirred him as a man on the dance floor…let him deal with her lingerie lying about.

The offer must have just the right ring of sincere friendship, but underneath she hoped Buchanan would understand it proffered an understood contract of deeper intimacy.

Ripping her notes off the telephone pad, she carelessly folded the pages and shoved them hastily inside her purse. Dialing the dress shop, she told the clerk she was on her way. She found her keys and headed for the door feeling deliciously sinful. She was playing a dangerous game.

Chapter Thirty-two

"YOU'RE LOOKING GREAT, BUCK, my man. Long time no see. How's Alma and the kids? C'mon on up here. I want you to meet some guys." Carrying a beer in his left hand, Morris Earle appeared out of nowhere. He stepped across the wide porch and was pumping

Buchanan's hand and clasping him around the shoulder hardly before he reached the top step.

Movie-star-handsome and athletically built, Morris Earle was hard-muscled, perhaps an inch shorter and ten pounds heavier than Buchanan. Wearing a T-shirt and track shorts, Morris seemed to always manage to have a deepwater tan.

Morris was an all-right guy but his old man had been president of both of the town's banks and an inveterate Rotarian—not to mention Grand Potentate of the Shrine and a deacon in the Methodist church. Even back in high school, Morris' voice always echoed vestiges of his daddy's hail-fellow, well-met stagy ring.

"Well, OK, I guess. They're up in the country with my folks until I decide what I'm going to do," he said, rather defensively, trying hard to lighten up. He was suddenly overcome with the realization that coming here to Morris with his hat in hand made him feel like shit.

"Let's sit out here. I love to look at the ocean. God, we're having a great time of it. We killed the blues today. Bluefish are so thick out there just past the breakers, you can almost walk on 'em. Fantastic. I'm tempted to take this territory myself...How about a beer?"

"No thanks, I'm fine." In suit and tie with briefcase in hand, Buchanan felt ill-at-ease.

"Ah, c'mon, Buck, lighten up; you're among friends. We're here to convince you to go to work for us." Morris winked and yelled back into the house. "Hey, Wick, c'mon out here. I want you to meet the notorious Buchanan Forbes."

Hardly before he finished the summons, the screen door opened and an unsmiling man came walking stiffly out onto the deck. He looked to be in his late forties and was wearing sharply-pressed khaki wash pants and a clean sweatshirt. It was obvious he wanted to make an impression.

Another, younger, very collegiate-looking man, immaculately dressed in white tennis shorts and a white Hilfiger polo shirt followed him out the door. Sleeves dangling loosely across his chest, an off-white tennis sweater with a red and blue-banded arm stripe was draped around his shoulders.

Right out of a Noel Coward play, Buchanan mused wryly.

Morris made the introductions. It came as no surprise that the older, unsmiling man was Wickline.

The cool dude with the tennis sweater was Hank Long.

"Hank owns Physician's Supply in Raleigh. We're using his boat. Hank and some local buddies keep a place up at the other end of the beach. We're going up there for some drinks later…you're going to stay here with us, aren't you? You don't want to drive back tonight. Besides, we have a lot to talk about."

"Good to meet you, Buck." Long shook Buchanan's hand. "I've heard about you from Ted Harper. Let me clear up one slight misconception: I actually don't own PS. My wife is VP and the president is my mother-in-law. C'mon over with Morris and Wick. I'm having a bunch of shrimp brought in, and, God forbid, there might even be some women. Here's to the longest-running, non-stop orgy on the Carolinas beaches." He raised his beer and smiled.

Buchanan remembered Ted Harper mentioning Long. "Well, thanks, that's very generous, but I'm afraid I have to head on down the coast. I have an appointment in the morning."

"Hey, don't be so much in a hurry. Maybe you won't want to make that appointment after we've had our little chat," Morris interjected.

Buchanan only smiled.

"Well, I guess I'd better get back up the beach…promised my partners I'd make a liquor run, and, I need to get cleaned up before the party starts. It's Monday, local studs' night out. Ted Harper and Gene Lindamood will be showing up early with some nurses, all of 'em pawing the carpet—hot to trot. Hope to see you later, Buck. The boys here speak highly of you. If they don't treat you right, come see me. You called on the medical schools, setting up research, I'm told?"

"That's right."

"Did you run into any studies on these newfangled IUDs around Duke and Chapel Hill? I know G/uL Technologies in Richmond has some studies going at Duke…did you run across that?"

"Just some scuttlebutt. With the holy-roller president circumventing *Roe vs. Wade*, unwanted pregnancy is suddenly a hot topic. Nowadays, nice, safe, clean, odor-free and invisible contraception is a very marketable idea. You thinking about getting into the market?"

"Already are. In the market, I mean. Since way back, around ninety-eight or nine."

"Oh?"

"Yeah, but this new G/uL T/3's going to be a gold mine. We're setting up a team of specialists to call on the OB-GYN's across the state. Keep that under your hat. We want to get the jump on the competition. I spent a week, back before last Christmas, up at the Medical College in Richmond learning the whole concept. Worked right alongside the docs. Learned the techniques. Even did some insertions myself. Ever look through a speculum right up the barrel of a nice clean pussy? Easy as sticking a straw through the top of a beer bottle. Here, take a look." Long fumbled trying to open a small box and a cascade of little white cylinders spilled onto the deck.

Buchanan helped gather them up and looked them over carefully. They looked like oversized milkshake straws or tampon insertion tubes.

"The journals say these are practically foolproof. You may be right. This may be a very hot product," he said as he handed them back.

"Bet on it. Anyway, I'm dead serious. If things don't work out, I'd like to talk to you. Here keep this." He handed Buchanan a slide rule about six inches long with the Physician's Supply logo on it. "It's a weight and dosage calculator. Keeps our name in front of the docs."

"Great idea...thanks a lot." Buchanan looked at the gadget with genuine admiration.

"You're welcome, and don't forget, give me a ring, if you're still looking for a job." Long turned and disappeared down the steps with a casual wave of the hand.

"C'mon, sit down, loosen your tie, Buck. Let's talk about working for the best goddamn antibiotic house in the world." Morris indicated a group of aluminum deck chairs by the railing. "Tell him what we...what you have in mind, Wick, before he gets too interested in selling space-age IUDs to doctors. I'll go get some drinks." Morris headed inside.

"Not to worry. I think your friend may be jumping the gun with that new IUD thing," Buchanan said. "I just read in a news magazine that G/uL Technologies and some other houses were having problems with so-called improved configurations of IUDs. There have been reports of serious hemorrhage, even rumors of deaths. The reporter suggested that the anti-abortion lobby had formed an alliance with the Planned Parenthood fanatics and were trying to cover it up. 'Misery acquaints a man with strange bedfellows.' That was Shakespeare, wasn't it?"

"Huh?" Wickline scowled.

"No beer for me, Morris. It's a work day." Buchanan called to Morris' back.

"Aw, c'mon. Relax. You don't need to impress us." Morris turned to reassure him.

"I know..."

"How 'bout a Coke?"

"No, nothing. Thanks."

"OK. Holler if you change your mind." The screen door slammed behind him.

"Morris speaks highly of you. And so does Cal Murphy, but what I want to know is why you resigned a cushy job with Lhamda-A?"

"I was fired." He quickly gave Wickline a rundown on what happened. He was sure Wickline knew. It irked him the man was testing him this artless way.

Caught off guard by Buchanan's honesty, Wickline was momentarily at a loss for words. Finally, he got his voice back. "So, you didn't have anything to do with the Richmond thing? And you've never sold or traded samples?"

"That's correct...I had nothing to do with Richmond."

"And you've never traded or sold samples, not ever?"

"I didn't say that."

"Well, I'm asking you. Have you?"

"Have you?"

"You're the one who's looking for a job."

"That's right. If you're looking for the man least likely to black market your company's drug samples, then think about it. Given the recent circumstances of my untimely parting with Lhamda-Alpine, you ought to have enough sense to know that man is me. I told you, I wasn't involved in the incident in question. If you want to go into ancient history, when I was about ten, I shoplifted a tube of toothpaste from Woolworth's, just to see if I could. I threw it in the river afterwards. In college I cheated on a physics exam once, maybe even twice. I truly hated physics. And, if it has any relevance here, I felt guilty. For the moment, my conscience is clear."

"Do you mind if I call Joe Acton to get his version of this?" Wickline leaned forward belligerently.

"Does it matter if I mind?"

"Not a bit."

"So, why ask? Here, be my guest." Buchanan took out an old Lhamda-A business card and scribbled Joe's number on the back. "I'd call the Food and Drug too, if I were you. The Richmond office is listed in the book...call long distance information."

"Are you trying to get smart with me? I know you're Morris' buddy, but I want to warn you. This isn't going to be a piece of cake down here. I need to have someone working this area like yesterday. The territory has been neglected and the competition is eating our lunch. You and Morris go back a ways but when the sales sheets come out, he'll come to me. It's my ass on the line and I don't fuck around. My men either produce or they don't last three months."

"Three months..." Buchanan snorted a derisive laugh.

"Is that funny?" Wickline obviously was not happy. Undoubtedly, he felt he was having all this forced on him.

Overcome by a sudden rush of contempt, Buchanan retrieved his briefcase and stood up. "Funny? Not at all, but three months is goddamn pathetic. I wish you luck, Mr. Wickline."

"What? Wait, where're you going? Sit down…you can't leave yet."

"Just watch me. As far as I'm concerned, you and I don't have anything to talk about. I'll just pay my respects to Morris and be on my way…"

"C'mon, man, loosen up. They told me you were the best. Not just Cal and Morris; I checked around. What's the matter? Job sound too tough for ya?" Wickline wheedled now.

"Yeah. I stopped in at New Hanover Hospital and had a talk with the chief of pharmacy, Ted Harper, this morning. Not even God himself can clean up this territory in three months. If you know anything at all about selling pharmaceuticals, you know that. I really do wish you luck. No hard feelings, but I'm not going to promise something I can't deliver just to come down here and have you on my back and then wind up firing my ass. Sorry." Buchanan stood over him and looked him straight in the eye.

"Well, OK. I guess I did overstate my case, but I'm a bottom line guy. I'm a hardass. My men all get results and they make money." Wickline gave him his best John Wayne stare and drained his beer. "Sit down, let's talk."

"Look, I don't mind a hardass, but, boss or no boss, I can't stand a bullshitter. And I won't be pushed around just so you'll know who's boss. I really do think you've got the wrong guy."

Wickline looked anxiously at the door, afraid Morris would walk in on them. "C'mon. Morris is high on you. Sit down. We'll get along. How much were you making with Lhamda-A?"

"Well, my base was just over forty-five not counting commission." Buchanan remained standing. He didn't tell Wickline that Lhamda-A's Research Coordinators didn't make commission.

"Wow. I guess you know we try to hire experienced men, the best. To get them, we always pay top dollar, but my tops is forty base. That's seven grand over industry average, but with us, the real gravy is in the commission."

"Are returns of outdated goods charged against sales when you calculate commission?"

"Of course. The idea is to sell it, not ship it back."

"Will the returns I'm going to inherit be charged against me or Cal Murphy?"

"You. But it's a tradeoff. For the most part Cal had stocked the territory with the line. The returns will be charged against whoever takes the territory. I can't change that."

"Then you know there won't be any commission down here for at least a year. Whoever takes the job will have to depend on base salary alone until he cleans up these returns. It might seem like a good salary to someone with less experience, but I can't live on forty, no way…"

"Oh come on. Cal Murphy isn't making much more base than that, but ask him about his commission…almost 25 K last year. Even more this year, from the looks of things."

"C'mon now, Wick, don't jack him around." At the sound of the voice, Buchanan turned to see Morris standing just inside the screen door. From the look that passed across Wickline's face, Buchanan knew Wickline wondered just how much Morris had heard.

"Well, Morris, I was just about to tell Buck here that we'd discussed the situation and because of his experience we could offer him…er…just what did we finally agree upon?"

"How's forty-seven-five sound?" Morris pushed the screen and came out with two beers.

"Well, not too shabby." Buchanan sat back down, opened his briefcase and loosened his tie. "Why don't you tell me *all* about the territory? And what about a car? And expenses?…"

Chapter Thirty-three

FROM THE PORCH Maggie could see the Banks Channel over the roof of the house Lewis Warrant had bought for her. It was down the street just past the Sea Oats, her mother's rambling old beachfront hotel. There was a small stack of new lumber in front of the garage awaiting the contractor's crew. Beyond, across the adjoining housetops, she could see Ryan and Mary Ellen were just getting off the school bus on Lumina. Maggie felt a twinge in the pit of her stomach. The kids had asked her some hard questions at the breakfast table this morning and she'd put them off with the promise of a powwow when they got home.

One thing about it: she'd always shot straight with her kids, even when they were little. Sometimes that hadn't been easy. But she'd never regretted it. They'd always been more than just mom and kids to each other. It was a miracle, but despite her more than several vagaries and indiscretions, they were her best friends.

"Hi, Mom," Ryan called as he came through the waist-high tangle of dunes grasses, weeds, and wildflowers on the vacant lot between the street corner and the soon-to-be-remodeled house. Maggie waved back but Mary Ellen ignored her. At almost sixteen, Mary Ellen was just now starting to blossom. Her face was changing dramatically from a freckled, chubby little-girl's face into that of a very pretty—and provocative—young woman.

On her sixteenth birthday, Maggie was going to give her some real lipstick.

Over the years when American Movie Channel and Turner Classic Movies reran the old 1950s Rock Hudson movie, *Written on the Wind*, everyone had told Maggie that with her pale-blue faded-denim eyes and pouty mouth, she looked a lot like the sultry actress Dorothy Malone. Secretly she loved the comparison. Maggie had taped the movie and tried to enhance the similarity. Every now and then, people still remarked about it. Looking at Mary Ellen now, she was suddenly struck by the fact that her daughter was fast becoming her own spitting-image.

Worst of all, Maggie suspected Melly had discovered boys. Predictably, with the youthful flood of hormones, she was on an emotional roller coaster lately.

Maggie remembered all too sharply the late Walter Huston's line from another old movie classic, *Duel in the Sun*, that also had been reissued recently and was also making the rounds on cable—the *USA Today* critic called it "Lust in the Dust." In the scene where Huston prayed over the sultry, hot-blooded Jennifer Jones he'd intoned the plea: *"God, help all those poor cowpokes who lay eyes on this thy creature."*

Maggie frowned thinking about it.

Mary Ellen was not at all happy with her mama.

Maggie knew she could thank her unhappy mother, Tillie Oakes, for most of that. Good old Grandma had been up to her sorry tricks again, trying to poison her kids against her. But then, Maggie had to admit most of her problems she had brought on herself. Over the years, she hadn't exactly been Mother of the Year. But, now, she was finally going to do something about that.

She glanced over at the house. She'd had the contractors over for remodeling estimates last week and she'd finally awarded the bid on Friday and given the man a check to seal the deal.

As for getting her career back on track, she was making the rounds of the local builders, paint contractors, wallpaper stores and furniture boutiques looking for opportunities to get some decorating jobs. New Hanover county wasn't Atlanta or Charlotte. It was slow going but she'd thrown a lot of business to local contractors when she was doing the SeaWatch job for Lewis' company and it was already paying off with the promise of a small job here and there.

"Hi Mom," Ryan said as his head appeared at the top of the steps. Maggie took the drawing board off her knees and leaned it against the railing. She'd already rinsed her brushes and put them pointing upward in the ceramic vase beside the box of watercolors on the taboret.

"Give me a hug, Tiger." She stood and held out her arms.

Boyishly embarrassed by open affection, Ryan moved across and wrapped his arms around her and gave her a rib-cracking squeeze. Fourteen and already taller by a half-a-head, she guessed he must have gotten his height from her own father because Ryan's daddy, Billy O'Brien, was a runt. Mary Ellen was still a few inches over five feet. More than likely, she was going to remain petite, more like herself.

"There's Cokes in the fridge and Grandma brought some cookies over…Toll House. I got Diet Coke for us girls, Melly." She looked over Ryan's shoulder as Mary Ellen started into the house. "Bring your snacks out here and we'll have our talk, OK, Shoog?"

"I don't want to talk about it anymore, Mama. It's always the same. What's the use?" Mary Ellen whined.

"Well, it's not always going to stay the same. Anyway, what happened? This morning you had some pretty probing questions. Seems to me that you said you were embarrassed because people were calling me a…a *whore*. People? What people?"

"Well, just people. Everybody."

"Aw, c'mon Melly, you know that ain't true. It's what Grandma said yesterday, down in front of Wings. Sometimes, I can't stand to be around her." Ryan objected and hung his head.

Maggie pulled him to her and hugged him tight again.

"I know. I had a talk with your grandma this morning. I wish I could say that it won't ever happen again, but you know better. It will. I'm sorry. Look, you know everything about me. I'm not proud of some of it. It may be a little late, but I'm trying to get my life straightened out. Besides, now we're going to have our own place." She turned Ryan around and pointed to the house. "See the lumber? Contractors are supposed to start tomorrow. If all goes well, we'll be in in a month or so. You'll have plenty of room and privacy. A place to bring your friends…"

"I was so ashamed. Someday somebody's going to hear her," Mary Ellen sniffed. "Why can't we just move back to Palm Beach again? Nobody knows us there." Maggie had had them with her at the condo in Florida for the entire summer last year. "Mr. Warrant said he gave you the condo down there. He said he'd get us a house if you wanted one. Grandma said he was divorcing his wife so you could marry him. I like Mr. Warrant, Mama. Why don't you marry him and take us out of here? Can't we just start over?"

[179]

"Well...I was—you all were, too—born and have grown up right here on the beach. It's our home," she began, trying to choose her words. "Don't you like it here? When the house is finished, it will be a dream...I've got thirty thousand just to spend on it. You can have your rooms the way you want them. And your friends, what about them? Greta and Beth? And how about Timmy? Do you want to leave them? You're a cheerleader next year...and on the honor roll...both of you. Do you want to start over in a new place? You won't know a solitary soul."

"But we were talking about moving to the islands last summer. You said it would be like an adventure then," Mary Ellen interrupted.

Maggie blushed. You couldn't get anything past these two.

"Sure, it would be an adventure...and sometimes we might have to move whether we want to or not...but it's not something to take lightly. You need to think things like this over. Besides, it's different now. And...I don't know if I could find work away from here...a lot of people here will help me, give me work..."

"I don't really want to move anyway..." Ryan began.

"But Mama, last week Mr. Warrant told Grandma when he was divorced, he was going to marry you. He's rich; why can't you go on working for him? He'll take care of us," Melly persisted.

Now Ryan brightened. "He said he'd ask you if I could have a car for my sixteenth birthday. He told Melly the same thing."

"Oh...he did, did he? Well, I guess I'd better have a talk with him about that."

"If he's going to be our stepdaddy, what's wrong with that? Why couldn't we? What would be wrong with that?"

"Listen Melly, it's not that simple. I don't want to marry Lewis anymore, and I don't want to work for him. Other than the house, I don't want to take anything from him. I don't want him to have control over me, over us. If I let him give you things then I'd be obligated."

"But I thought you loved him, Mama? You said you did..."

"Well, I guess I did, at least, I thought I did. But, things change sometimes. I do like Lewis...and he's been generous...and...he's not a bad person. He means well, but he really doesn't care about anyone but himself. He's like a spoiled rich kid. As long as he gets his way, he's all right. But, when he gets tired of me, he'll move on. There'll be no reason for him to hang around. I don't think he'd just dump me...he can't stand to have people think he's a bad person. He'd see to it that I was uh, compensated, taken care of...I...ah..." Maggie knew she was getting in deep water. She wanted to change the subject. "Anyway, he has been nice. He's giving us this house, isn't he? He owes me, but that's it. I want it to just end now. And who knows? There still may be a man out there for me, someone who would love me."

"Mr. Right, Mama?" Ryan looked down at her and winked.

"Yeah, Mr. Right." She rumpled his hair. "You two are almost grown…look at you. Both of you already working in the summer, making your own money. You'll be gone away to college before you know it. And, I'm not all that old. Maybe it's not too late for me…"

"But Mama, why won't you take the condo in Palm Beach or the other place in the Caymans? Mr. Warrant said he told you he'd give 'em to you, to us," Mary Ellen persisted. "He said, 'no strings.' He didn't say you'd have to marry him…"

"Then I'd just be what your grandma said I was," Maggie snapped back. "Surely you don't think he wouldn't be around? That's what this is all about. I want to be free of him. He's married. He just wants to keep me on his string, under his control…"

"But Mama, he said 'no strings,'" Melly protested.

"You don't think Lewis Warrant is going to just generously take care of me for the rest of my natural life and let me go merrily on my way, seeing other men—making a life of my own and having no obligation to him? He has a wife…a woman he goes to bed with…anytime he damn well pleases. And, while we're at it, his wife and I aren't the only women he's seen in the past two years. We're just part of an ongoing harem. I know of at least two other one-night stands. When I caught him the second time I said thanks but no thanks. If I'm willing to put up with that, doesn't that sound a lot like I'd be just selling myself? You're old enough to ask yourself a question. What's the difference between a mistress, a harem girl and whore, Melly?"

"Well, if he said he was going to marry you, and he took care of you…" the pretty teenager protested weakly.

"But, I don't want to marry Lewis Warrant. It wouldn't be any different. Don't you remember how it was in Palm Beach last summer…we had a great time, but Lewis was hardly ever around. About every fourth week or so, he'd call up in the middle of the night and tell me to pick him up at the airport and usually he was gone by the next night. The most he ever stayed was two nights. I want to see other men. I want to get on with my life."

"But, couldn't you just think it over? Maybe he won't do it again, maybe you're just jealous, or mad…"

"Look honey, I know you like Lewis, and that's OK. But I have my own life to live. Now, would you two like to grab a Coke and walk over to the house? I want to show you what I plan to do with the kitchen and you can tell me how you want your rooms. You can each have your own bath with a hot tub. The contractor's coming tomorrow."

"Oh, Mama, my own private bathroom and a hot tub. Do you mean it?" Melly made a tiny jump and clapped her hands.

"I mean it. And I'm going to have the garage finished off and there'll be room for Ryan's workshop downstairs. Upstairs there'll be a studio for my painting. Run put your books away and let's have a look." She released her grip on Ryan and turned to retrieve her drawing board to take it inside. The children scrambled ahead.

Just as they'd each grabbed a handful of cookies and a Coke, the phone rang.

"Run ahead. It's not locked. I'll get that. It may be the contractor." She went back inside.

"This is Maggie O'Brien."

"Maggie, this is Natalie down at the bank. Mr. Parks is in here with your check, but I can't cash it until it's co-signed by Mr. Warrant. Is he still in town?"

"Oh, no, you're mistaken. Lewis Warrant set that account up in my name. Thirty thousand…I have the deposit slip. I returned the signature cards Friday morning."

"I know the money's here and I have the signature cards OK, but the account is a joint account and requires Mr. Warrant's signature. I thought you understood."

"Understood? No, this must be some mistake…"

"No, Maggie, it's the way he set it up when he made the deposit. He said you'd be administering the funds, but the account requires that he co-sign. I got the idea that he was going to leave you some checks that he'd already signed. He made sure there'd be no risk with just his signature. It works both ways…he can't draw on the account without your signature, either. I thought you understood. The contractor is waiting here. What should I tell him?"

"Let me talk to Maynard…"

When Parks came on the line, Maggie apologized. "I'll locate Lewis right away and see if we can get this all cleared up. I'm sorry for your trouble. I'll call your office as soon as I can."

"Well, OK, Maggie, but I need to make this deposit before I go order more materials to start the job. You understand?"

"Sure. I'll try to get this straightened out within the hour. So let me get right to work on it." She said goodbye and hung up. Without having to look, she dialed a number.

"Mr. Warrant's office." Ellie Purcell answered on the first ring.

"Ellie, this is Maggie O'Brien. Is Lewis there?"

"Yes, but he's in a meeting."

"Get him out." Maggie was seething.

"But..."

"Ellie, ring through, or stick a note under his nose. He's going to be goddamn sorry if he doesn't talk to me..."

Chapter Thirty-four

IT WAS ALMOST FIVE **P.M.** when Buchanan pulled into the seedy roadside curb market on the outskirts of Bolivia. He went in and bought a six-pack of Blue Ribbon and got change for the phone booth.

"Hello..." Cammie answered her unpublished number on the fourth ring. The phone had just started jingling when she was halfway up the circular staircase. She'd fairly flown up the steps to catch it before the party hung up.

Please, God—she was certain it must be Buchanan.

"Cammie, at last. I was afraid I'd missed you..." Buchanan tried to crook the phone between his ear and neck while he fumbled to pull the ring opener on the beer can.

The can spewed foam all over his face.

"Shit..."

"What's the matter?" Cammie asked, alarmed.

"These goddamn pop-tops. I just got sprayed with beer. I hope I don't get stopped by the law." He sucked the foam off the top of the can.

"A little foam won't hurt you." She giggled with relief that she'd caught his call.

He laughed.

"Well? Aren't you going to tell me what happened?"

"Oh, I got invited to a wild party. Twice. The place is loaded with actresses. And nurses and secretaries and school teachers. Nymphos every one," he teased.

"Whoa, wait. Before you become the southern distributor of untreatable sexually transmitted diseases, what about the interview?"

"That *was* the interview. And I found a swinging bachelor apartment at Wrightsville Beach. I think I'm going to become a beach bum...might just buy a surfboard while I'm at it."

"Buchanan, how many beers have you been drinking? Where are you anyway?"

"You just heard the sound of my first beer today. And I'm in Bolivia, North Carolina. Know where that is? Besides, what difference does that make? Do you want to hear my suspense-filled story or not?"

Reflected in the glass of the booth, Buchanan watched a gray Ford pull into a gas station up the road.

"Sure, but from what you just said, I think I'd better send someone to rescue you," Cammie grumbled. "Now, would you mind starting from the beginning and going a trifle slower. What's this about a bachelor pad...and tell me about this job...I thought you hated the pharmaceutical business...particularly this outfit Stribol? Does this mean you took the job?"

"Well, not actually...I mean not yet, but as soon as I hang up, I think I'm going to call 'em back and tell 'em I'll take it, before they decide to offer it to someone else."

The Ford was too far away to get a look at the driver.

"Sounds like they made you a good offer."

"Even better than I hoped. I couldn't believe it. I mean I knew they paid top dollar, but this territory is hurting. It's never actually had a full-time rep. And the timing is divine. They've just released the hottest new antibiotic since the original penicillin. I mean right up there with the cure for cancer...or a retroactive birth control pill. Spectrapen is big news. And, they know that a Swiss competitor is coming out with the same drug in six months, maybe less. Much less. In other words, they're hurting down here. They offered more base salary than I was getting, and the commission could really amount to a big score. Of course, I'd get the usual automobile and fringes, all that. And, when I asked if they'd pay my moving expense, they didn't bat an eye. *Carte blanche.* I couldn't believe it. They'll even pay my living expenses for six months until I can sell my house."

"Whoa, Buchanan. Slow down. Are you sure you know what you're doing? You seemed so set against the idea...and what about the Mallone article for SNS? You'd be a fool to pass up the opportunity..." Cammie interrupted, obviously not at all happy he was thinking of dashing off down there to live.

"I know, I know..." Buchanan stopped her. "And I do really hate the thought of getting right back into the same rotten mess, but right now, getting my family back together is my chief concern. And restoring my credibility is an important issue here. If I go right back to work in the field, then my resume will look like I never skipped a beat. Even though the rumors are wild in the street, it would actually turn the tables on Lhamda-A, sort of leave them with egg on their face. I talked to an old buddy of mine, chief of pharmacy at the local hospital. It all looks too good to be true. As a matter of fact just hearing myself seals it. I'm going to call them as soon as I hang up. What do you think?" The words bubbled out non-stop. He was breathless at the end.

"Well, I don't know. I mean, Saturday you were so adamant about not going back to work in pharmaceuticals. You were reluctant to even have the interview. I thought you were so excited about the idea of writing. What changed your mind?"

"I haven't changed my mind, but I have to put bread on the table while I'm learning to become the next John Grisham. Surely you can see that?"

"I just hope you won't lose sight of your ultimate goal. I think you have too much potential. Your editor at SNS thinks you're a wonderful writer. The Mallone piece could lead to something. You're still young; now's the time to chase the rainbows." She struggled to keep the disappointment out of her voice. "If it's the money, I told you I can..."

"I know. I know..." Buchanan interrupted. "I appreciate it, you don't know how much. Anyway, I'm halfway to Myrtle Beach now. I haven't given up on the writing. I see Mallone tomorrow, remember?"

"Oh, yes. I'm so glad you caught me. I wanted to tell you that you can use my beach house tonight...tomorrow night...as long as you like. The key's in a flower pot in the carport underneath the house."

"That sounds great. I really appreciate it. How do I find it?"

"Do you know how to get to Pawley's Island?"

"Uh, yeah, but isn't that a long way from Myrtle Beach?"

"Well, Sharkey Mallone lives near Surfside. Pawley's isn't that much further on down the road."

"I don't know. It'll be dark by the time I get there and I already made a reservation. Sharkey Mallone told me about The Presidential. It's a new place right off the Pavilion that caters to traveling men. Seventy bucks a night in the off-season, and if you stay with 'em year-round, you get the same rate during the season. If I take this job, Myrtle Beach is part of the territory. I'll be down there one week a month. It will be a good thing to start staying with them before the season starts. You know, become a regular so they'll look out for me during the season..."

"Well, you could still use our place during the season, providing we don't have family staying there. That might become a problem..."

"That's really nice of you, but that's too iffy. I couldn't take a chance. I need to establish a track record with a local motel so I'll be taken care of during the season. But thanks, anyway. You don't know how much I appreciate the offer..."

Her silence was eloquent with disappointment.

"Cammie, surely you understand. I'd love to stay at your place. I hate motels; you must know that. But it's a matter of practicality. Anyway, thanks. I don't deserve a friend like you."

"Oh, poo, but I do understand, of course. I guess. Still, if I knew in advance what your schedule was, maybe we could arrange for the place to be available..."

"Surely you're not considering depriving your family the use of your beach house? Get real. They'd have you locked up."

"Well, I know you're going through a tough time. Besides, I'd rather you'd use it than James' family. I can't stand any of my snobby in-laws. It's easy to find just in case you change your mind..." —she went on to give him directions— "...the key is under the flower pot by the door to the storage room in the carport. You're always welcome," she persisted, hopefully.

"Well, it's going to get dark on me, and I really do want to call Morris Earle and tell him I'll take the job. They want me to leave for Utica next Monday for two weeks' indoctrination. Besides, I want to call the real estate lady and take that little apartment I looked at. I'll have to have a place to live while Alma sells our place in Raleigh. I gotta go. Morris and Wickline were going out to a wild party. If I hope to catch 'em, I don't have much time."

"You've made up your mind then? I guess Alma was happy to hear the news about the interview? Is she excited about moving to the beach?" She held on, reluctant to let him go.

"Well, I haven't called her yet. I'm sure she'll be glad that I got a job. I guess she'll be excited about moving. I know the kids will."

"Buchanan, I can't believe you..."

"What?"

"You'd better call Alma before you take that job. What if she doesn't want to move?"

"Well, just too goddamn bad for her. She said I was a bum, unemployable. I guess she won't have that to hold against me now. Besides, now is as good a time as any to get things straight between us. If it ain't gonna work, might as well get it over with..."

"Just the same, you'd better call her before you take the job. Don't you care about your marriage? Your boys?"

"I love my sons. My marriage ain't so hot."

Silence again.

"Buchanan?"

"Yeah?"

"Take my advice. Call Alma, please?"

"I'll think about it."

When he looked back, the gray Ford was nowhere in sight.

"Will you call me tonight at home? After you call Alma. I'm having dinner with James at the club but we'll be home by ten. I want to know how things went. I worry about you."

"Well, I don't know. I'm tired. If I'm awake. If not, I'll call you tomorrow afternoon after I see Mallone, OK?"

"OK, but please, won't you try to call tonight? I'll try to leave the party early."

"Maybe. I gotta go. And, Cammie, thanks. Don't worry about me, OK?" Buchanan hung up before she could protest.

Cammie slowly returned the instrument to the cradle and turned and looked out across the trees at the water tower on the campus of the state college. The park just across the hill seemed a distant country now.

Chapter Thirty-five

THWOCK!

Alone on the practice tee at the Oak Island Golf Club, Sheriff Mack Jones was the picture of concentration as he hit practice shots.

Damn Amos Lyon for marrying Rhonda June, his baby half-sister. And damn Rhonda June for being so damn set on marrying him off…and…well…damn all women in general!

Thwock!

For the past three years, Monday had been his night to keep his weekly date with Brooke Hankins, his simpatico young divorced nurse in Myrtle Beach. But, escorting Barbara Morgan home after they'd had supper Saturday night at Amos and Rhonda June's, she'd slipped her little hummingbird tongue in his mouth when she'd kissed him goodnight. Like some adolescent fool, he'd promised he'd take her into Wilmington tonight to dinner.

Thwock!

Jezzus! Goddamn duck hook! Ease off that old Harley-Davidson grip!

All he needed, besides a brain tumor, was a sticky relationship with a young, starry-eyed female. *"A sadder but wiser girl for me…"* He liked the wry wisdom from the old musical *The Music Man*.

Damn Rhonda June. She'd out-foxed him…fixed it so's he'd have to give Barbara a ride home Saturday night. Before he knew it, that little she-devil had asked him in for a nightcap…and… and…well…that sweet innocent little Barbara Morgan had been plumb full of surprises.

Thwock!

Gawdamighty, that curvy little package sure knew how to kiss. Most likely just a goddamnn tease…

Thwock!

Shit! Two frigging inches behind the goddamn ball!

Slow down. Remember your rhythm. Don't do any good to get in a hurry.

And, damn Amos Lyon, sorry scoundrel had gotten his hand in his pocket both Saturday and Sunday. Beat him all four ways on the Nassau. Two days in a row. Cost him a frigging bundle. Thinking about all that smacky-mouth with Barbara Morgan… couldn't concentrate a lick.

At his age, he should know better.

Thwock!

Then, this afternoon Barbara had stuck her head in his office and said, innocent as you please, "Mack, I hate to spoil your plans, but tonight's a work night. I was wondering if you'd just as soon come over to my place for a little supper instead of driving all the way to Wilmington?"

So? How could he lose on a deal like that?

Just Saturday, he'd driven into Wilmington and gotten his Virecta prescription refilled.

On the way here, he stopped off at the liquor store and bought a bottle of fancy Merlot.

Thwock!

Acting just like some high school kid…worse'n that really!

He'd been chewing bubblegum all day instead of Beech Nut chewing tobacco.

And…at his age…talk about a fool…

But gawdamighty! He kept thinking about that hummingbird tongue…

Thwock!

He wondered when Morgan had her last period. Too damn old to be sweating out girlfriend's periods. Why the hell hadn't he just stuck to good old Mondays with good old comfortable Brooke? Brooke was a nurse, had one of them implanted plastic IUD things. Well, next Monday he'd get right back on schedule.

Wonder if Morgan was on the pill? Should he get some rubbers? Judaspriest, Kirby's Pharmacy in Southport would have word all over town…

Besides, he could always pick up some rubbers from one of them machines in the men's room at the gas station he guessed…

Thwock!

[188]

Shitfire and goddamn! The bulldog sheriff watched the ball shank into the tangle of scrub oak and vines on the dunes, dead right off the practice area.

Now just where'n'hell did that frigging thing come from?

Get your frigging mind back on golf, you silly ass, and slow the fuck down...

Thinking of menstrual periods, his mind wondered back to last week's suicide down the road at Youpon Beach. So far he hadn't been able to I.D. that tampon insertion tube they'd found in the trash. *G/uL*-something. Graham/unLimited...multi-national corporation. Top 10 on the *Fortune* list. This morning he'd called up to Quantico. Someone there reminded him that Graham/unLimited got its start as a tobacco company, said it might be a wrapper for one of those controversial new smokeless cigarettes...he'd run that by Amos again when he saw him...

Thwock!

Well! Now that's more like it...

The afternoon sun was getting low. He pulled on his sweater, picked up the scattering of loose golf clubs and the empty heavy-wire ball basket and walked toward the clubhouse.

He'd hit the ball OK...he'd get even with Amos Lyon with a vengeance.

Head down, he almost walked into the old doc coming out of the pro shop.

"I been watching you. Where'd'ja learn that funny little pitchout I just saw you hit?"

Mack just glared at him. He wasn't about to dignify the smug old fool with an answer.

"Not talking, huh?" the old doc observed, wryly.

"Look, Amos, the sun don't shine on the same dog's ass all the time, so enjoy it while you can. But, if I was you, I don't believe I'd spend that thirty bucks just yet. You just might need it."

"Oh? Gracious sakes. I guess I'll have trouble sleeping now..."

The sheriff pushed on by, into the men's locker room and one-by-one he wiped his clubs and put them back in his bag leaning against his locker.

"You come over here just to check up on me?" he asked Lyon over his shoulder, as he sat down to change his shoes. They both lived on Caswell Beach, just down the road.

"Are you kidding? You just keep practicing your mistakes, Mack. Been at it for years."

The sheriff bit his tongue.

"What I came looking for you for, was to tell you I got the x-rays from Chapel Hill on that Corbett suicide. Now, I'm really puzzled."

"Yeah, and just why is that?" The sheriff resisted reaching for some bubble gum.

Amos would have a lot of fun telling Rhonda June about that.

"One of them IUDs planted up inside her…"

"IUD?…"

"Yeah, intrauterine device, latest birth control. Little plastic thing the doctor puts up inside the uterus."

"I know. But…I…uh…I thought she was…"

"Three months pregnant…" The old doc finished Mack Jones' thought.

"Don't make sense. You sure she'd just aborted a three-month fetus…"

"Sure I'm sure…"

"Then what about the Tampax thing? By the way, I called the FBI lab at Quantico today. They said it might not be an insertion tube for a tampon; suggested we check the possibility it might be a fancy package for one of them new G/uL smokeless cigarettes…"

"Interesting…" The old doc scratched his head. "A Tampax makes more sense. If she was about to abort, she'd be spotting. But there was no sign of a Tampax box in the place…her car neither…and nary a sign of a tampon in all that tissue that was expelled from her uterus."

"How do you figure that?"

"Beats me."

"So much for modern forensic medicine. See ya in the morning…" The sheriff finished changing and headed for the door.

Gawdamighty, what he wouldn't give for a big pinch of tobacco in his jaw right now.

Women. They weren't worth it. Still, wouldn't hurt to go find a pack of rubbers. You just never could tell.

Chapter Thirty-six

ALMA WAS JUST GETTING her car keys when she heard the phone ring.

Buchanan's father answered.

"Buchanan…I tried to call you this morning. We haven't heard from you in days. Where are you, son? You all right?"

Alma edged down the hall and into the kitchen and stood by the door listening to Grandad's side of the conversation. He looked up and saw her.

"Hold on, you just caught her." He motioned it was for her and put his hand over the receiver. "It's Buchanan. Something about a job."

Alma snatched up the phone.

"Buck? I was on my way to the hospital...I'm doing private duty. I just got called on a case. Gotta hurry. What's this about a job?" Alma snapped rudely, then fell silent as she listened to Buchanan's account of the day's events.

"Wilmington? You mean we'd have to move? No way, Josè. I just had to uproot the children and I'm not about to put them through that again."

"Well, I could put the house in the hands of a Realtor. You wouldn't have to bring the boys back to Raleigh 'til after school is out. That's only a couple of months. If we sold the house, it would be just in time to move the kids for the beach season... they'd love it."

"When are you going to grow up? What about the schools down there? How about the cost of living? What's the salary? Can we afford this? It'll cost a fortune to move...I'd have to get new drapes...Those drapes cost a fortune...Do you ever think of things like that?" Her protests came out like machine gun fire.

"Well, the move is paid for. It's a great opportunity and I can't take a chance on losing it. This will provide me with an unbroken history on my resume..." He tried to explain about the restoration of his credibility. "Besides, it doesn't have to be forever. I got a call from SNS..." He told her about the interview assignment. "Can you imagine, me doing an interview with Sharkey Mallone?

"How much does SNS pay?"

"Buck a word; that's two thousand, minimum. And, I might sell the same material to *Playboy* or *Esquire*. *Playboy* probably pays at least three times that for a cover feature, Esquire something less. Anyway, it could lead to other assignments if I do a good job. I'm on my way to Myrtle Beach right now. I'll be at the Presidential tonight. Want the number?"

"No, give it to your dad. I don't have time now...listen, call me tomorrow...mid-afternoon. I'm doing a double tonight. I'll be sleeping all morning. Somebody has to bring in some income."

"Listen Alma...don't give me that crap. I'm glad you have work, if that makes you happy, but my income has never stopped. Even if I take this job, Lhamda-A still owes me over sixty days days. We'll come out a sizable bundle ahead. I have it in writing my payout won't be interrupted."

"Well...you think money is everything. All you think about is money..."

"Geez, Alma you brought up the subject of money…"

"Quit twisting what I said. Call me tomorrow afternoon and we'll talk it over after I've thought about it. Tonight I'll try to make a list of pros and cons. We can discuss it. Besides, you could come up here and find a nice job. If you're going to write, then maybe the paper would take you back again. I can make a good income doing private duty. It's nice being back around my family…and your mother and dad aren't getting any younger, you know. You never think about anyone but yourself. By the way, will they furnish you a car? Which reminds me, I could use a new car. I'm going to have to have this one worked on. I gotta go. Call me tomorrow…"

"Alma, I'll call you tomorrow. But you don't make sense. It was you who bugged me to quit the paper when I got back from the war, and I thank you for that at least. If you need a new car, go get one. But as far as you supporting us? Hell's bells, do you think you can afford to buy us both cars and make house payments? Don't you understand? I've been offered this great job. They want me on a plane Sunday morning. That's five days. In the meantime, SNS's member papers are waiting for ten pages of thrilling words from me on the famous Mr. Sharkey Mallone. I don't have time to chitchat. I'm gonna call right now and tell Morris Earle I'm taking this job. We'll work out the details later."

"Don't you dare. I have a say in this. Suppose I refuse to come back down there. Suppose I just keep the children up here?"

"Well, I guess we'll have to discuss that later. In the meantime, I'm going to take the job. Let me talk to my dad."

"Buck, don't you dare…"

"Let me talk to dad, Alma. I want to talk to my sons."

Alma handed the phone to the senior Forbes. "Your son doesn't seem to give a hoot about what I have to say. He wants to talk to you. Maybe you can talk some sense in him. I'm late. Tell him I'll be back in the morning around eight."

Buchanan heard the sound of a slamming door.

Chapter Thirty-seven

TED HARPER CAME WANDERING OUT on the wide porch carrying a can of Old Milwaukee to where Morris Earle, Randall Wickline and Hank Long sat at a table eating shrimp and ogling the women. "Hank tells me that you interviewed my old buddy Buchanan Forbes after the fishing this afternoon. Is he coming to work with you?"

"Don't know yet. He said he had another interview down in Myrtle Beach tomorrow morning. Sounded pretty fishy to me...I think he was just trying to make us think he had a better offer," Wickline grumbled.

Morris pushed back a paper plate piled high with shrimp shells and turned sideways on the trestle bench of the white enameled picnic table so he could catch a better view of the sunset over the water. After a moment he turned and faced Harper on the opposite side of the table. "Tell me, Ted, you worked with him. What do you think of Forbes?"

"You'd be goddamn lucky to get him. Look, guys, the competition is eating Stribol's lunch in Wilmington. You'd better get a heavyweight in here. Forbes and I go way back; he's King Kong. He's kind of a loner, but he's head and shoulders above the pack."

"Did you hear that, Wick?"

"Yeah. Look, I know all about his reputation. I'm sick of hearing you and Cal Murphy tell Buchanan Forbes stories. But, it still bothers me that Lhamda-Alpha gave him the ax. I think he knows more than he's telling about that Food and Drug raid in Richmond."

"Forbes volunteered the information, remember? He didn't have to admit it. And, you called Joe Acton. Joe said he was a good man. He resigned for personal reasons. You talked to the FDA field rep yourself. They won't comment. If the Food and Drug isn't interested, why should we care? Besides, Buck volunteered the information. He could've just kept quiet."

"Humph..." Wickline finished gnawing an ear of corn before he wiped his mouth and answered grudgingly. "That open display of honesty is what bothers me; it's the old innocent act. He's pretty clever. News travels fast. Forbes knows the word is on the street. I know he's your asshole buddy...got you your first job with Stribol...all that. I still think he's something of a smartass. He'll be hard to handle. I think he could do the job, but he's not a team man. I've handled my share of prima donnas. I know the type."

"Look, if you don't want him, give me his phone number. He's just what I need to oversee my new IUD venture. I need instant credibility. Cal Murphy said he was an Army lieutenant, operating room specialist in Desert Storm...got a medal for doing an amputation under fire...saved his CO's life. A man with his medical background talks to the docs in their own language," Hank Long spoke up.

"Now, just hold on, Hank. I've got first call on this guy," Wick snapped. "I've already offered him the job. He's supposed to call us no later than noon tomorrow."

They all laughed at Wickline's sudden about-face.

Morris Earle shrugged. "Hey, guys, Wick's a realist."

"Well, I didn't say I didn't want him. I'm a bottom line guy. I know a good thing when I see one." Wickline wiped his mouth and shook his beer can. "I need a beer." He turned to Ted. "Don't be too obvious, but tell me who's that sexy, big-titted broad behind you, the one who just walked in with the crewcut guy in the monogrammed shirt and coat and tie? I saw you talking to them when they arrived."

"Oh...that's Jaynie Lockfaw. The coat and tie is Gene Lindamood. He's the OB-GYN resident. Jaynie's the OB supervisor. She's a stuck-up bitch, goes out with docs and lawyers mostly. But the word is that she fucks like a fox. Her name is mud among the doctors' wives around town. Lately, out here, she's paired off with several out-of-towners. Want me to introduce you? Tonight might be your lucky night. Hank's been out with her. Ask him."

"A gentleman never tells. Besides, I'm married to my boss. I only took the woman to dinner. I've been trying to get her to go to work for me, selling this IUD thing. Godawmighty, can't you imagine her as a sales rep?"

"These slender-hipped, big-titted women drive me nuts. Is she with the young doc in the coat and tie?" Wickline's interest picked up.

"Gene Lindamood? Naw, they just work together. You want to meet her?"

All heads had turned now to look at the woman standing near the center of the huge living room, just inside the open sliding glass doors. As they watched, another good-looking girl pushed her way through the crowd and asked Lockfaw something. Lockfaw shook her head and pointed toward them. Ted Harper gave a little wave. Lockfaw waved back and the other woman started walking in their direction.

"This is Kay Walton coming our way. She's one of the ER nurses. Kay's a real party girl. I'll introduce you. You guys should circulate... plenty of pussy to go around and the evening's young. Wait'll the actresses and the schoolteachers start to arrive. Hi, Kay, I want you meet some people..." Ted greeted the slender, dark-haired woman as she came out through the opening in the wide expanse of glass panels.

"Hi, Ted. Anybody here know a Randall Wickline? There's a phone call..." She smiled and put off the introductions.

"I'm Wickline...where's the phone?" Wick pushed back the bench and stood up.

"C'mon, I'll show you...I'm Kay Walton..." —she stuck out her hand— "...I'll be right back," she told the group and turned to lead Wick into the house.

[194]

As they passed by Jaynie Lockfaw and Gene Lindamood, Kay said, "I'm coming back soon as I show Mr. Wickline the phone. By the way, that was a close call with the Rivenbark girl the other day. Did you ever see her? I heard she was discharged this morning."

"Yeah, I saw her; she's OK," Lindamood said and watched her go on through the crowd.

Lockfaw shot Lindamood a look. "Heard Martin was pissed at you for running out on him," she said, and took a sip from her drink.

"Yeah, well, I can't be everywhere. I had to go back to the ER."

"Martin was livid. Said the Rivenbark girl was past three months, closer to four from the looks of the fetus. He was threatening to file a complaint with the Medical Society. Wanted to call G/uL Technologies, the manufacturer of the IUD. Jeezus. But Rivenbark refused to tell him anything. She'd almost completely passed the device before her boyfriend got her to the ER. I can tell you, Frank Martin was looking for blood. He was plenty steamed at you. Did he ever find you…I mean you never *really* saw Rivenbark at all, did you?" Lockfaw looked at him curiously.

"No. It was my weekend off. Today I scrubbed with Nicholson early and hung out in the OR all morning. I looked in but she was gone before I made rounds this afternoon."

"Do you think Martin was right? I mean, do you think she could've been more'n three months gone? Couldn't a doctor tell…I mean by looking at the cervix?"

"Not always. And, who knows? Ordinarily it still wouldn't be that dangerous. Hell's bells, folks been poking dirty sticks and rusty coat hangers in pregnant uteri since before written history."

"Well, I'm back. Where you been the last several days, Dr. Lindamood?" Walton stepped through the crowd.

"I went to the ACC basketball tournament in Raleigh. It was my weekend off. Excuse me, ladies. I think I'll mosey over this way for a minute…see you both later…" He patted Walton on the arm and headed across the room.

When Wickline came back out on the deck he had a fresh beer in his hand and a scowl on his face. "That was our pigeon, the high and mighty Mr. Buck Forbes."

"Oh shit, don't tell me…he turned us down," Morris said, anxiously.

"*Au contraire.*" Wick's scowl became a grin. "He's meeting me Thursday in Durham to process. I told him I'd have plane tickets to Utica in tomorrow's mail."

Chapter Thirty-eight

AFTER HE LEFT THE PHONE BOOTH in Bolivia, Buchanan saw no more of the gray Ford. In Myrtle Beach he had no trouble locating the Presidential. A scant half-block from the boardwalk, alongside the small amusement park across from the Pavilion, the unpretentious motel was almost brand-new. The rooms were surprisingly large and had Pullman kitchenettes.

It was nearly six P.M. when he dropped his duffel on the bed and pulled aside the drapes to look out on the pool. During the summer, he could bring Alma and the kids down with him. The boys all had sleeping bags and loved to sleep on the floor. To them it would be camping out. With a pool at the door and the amusement park right across the street, they'd be in heaven. He smiled at the image.

In Bolivia he'd stopped at the state-owned ABC store. Removing the bottle of Absolut and a bottle of tonic from the brown bag, he went to the small refrigerator and set both bottles inside to chill. Then, he put the remaining cans of beer he'd purchased at the curb market in with the booze.

When he'd hung up his clothes, he placed his Toshiba laptop on the desk along the wall. He plugged into the wall outlet and waited for it to boot. When it booted, he clicked up Microsoft Word, leaned over and started pecking with two fingers.

THE MALLET WIELDING
KNIGHT-STALKING TYPEWRITING BABY
Sharkey Mallone: A Profile
by
Buchanan Garrett Forbes

"Take that, Tom Wolfe," he murmured half-aloud to the mirror behind the laptop and stepped back and smiled.

So much for the new journalism, he mused as he fumbled through his briefcase for the pad with Sharkey Mallone's phone number. When he located it, he moved to the phone on the night table between the two double beds and dialed outside.

"Yeah?" After the third ring, a voice growled into his ear.

"Sharkey? This is Buchanan Forbes, from SNS, remember?"

"Yeah. We ain't supposed to meet until tomorrow, around eleven."

"Sure I know. I just wanted to let you know that I just got into Myrtle Beach and I'm at the Presidential. It's near the Pavilion, on Ninth, right across…"

"Yeah, right across from the amusement area. *I* told *you*, remember? Question is do you still remember how to find me?"

"I've got it written right here. Down old Highway Seventeen, past Livermore's and turn toward the ocean at the Speedway station, right?"

"Right. We'll have the place to ourselves. I was just taking Taffy to the airport. Her mother's in the hospital; she's going to New York for a few days…"

He knew from news clips that Taffy was Mallone's new wife.

"Well, I'm sorry to hear that. Nothing serious, I hope?"

"She's OK. She's having a D and C…and her tubes tied…"

"I hope everything turns out…" Buchanan wasn't sure Mallone was talking about Taffy or her mother.

"Hey, you had dinner yet?"

"No, I just got here. It's still early for me."

"Good. How about I come let SNS buy me a beer and a hamburger? The Bowery's the best hamburger in town. It's near the boardwalk, right across from the Pavilion. You like music?"

"Sure…"

"Good, they got a new band, starts tonight. Taffy and I were just going out the door. Airport's on the way. Plane's at seven. I'll be there about quarter-past. OK? What room ya' in?"

"Room 125, at the back. Should I dress? Do I have to wear a jacket?"

"Shit…they wouldn't let ya' in. This is the beach, man. I'm wearing a clean T-shirt, cause I have to keep my image up. See ya' in about an hour. Right?"

"Right." Buchanan put down the phone. All of a sudden he felt nervous. He'd never interviewed a real celebrity before.

Nothing like starting at the top.

What a day! He headed out to find the ice machine. He needed a real drink.

Back inside, he unwrapped a little plastic airline glass, dumped in some cubes and took the vodka from the fridge. Pouring himself a stiff shooter, he floated some tonic water over the top and stirred it with a finger. He polished it off without taking the glass from his lips.

"Wow, hotdamn!" He shook his head and shivered violently from the potency of the drink. Wiping his eyes with his forearm before he poured another, he left it sitting on the counter by the sink while he undressed. Without touching the drink again, he went in and shaved, then got in the shower and stayed under the spray for a long time.

He'd barely finished pulling on a pair of white sailcloth pants and a red and white striped sailor jersey—and had just picked up the drink again—when there was a knock on the door.

Shoes in one hand, drink in the other, he called through the door, "Yeah?"

"Forbes? It's me."

His watch read: 7:07.

"Mallone?" He took the chain off and opened the door to see the rough-hewn figure standing there grinning.

"I'm a little early. I always forget that planes board early. Taffy damn near missed that sucker. Anyway, if I'm too early, I could just…"

"No, c'mon in. Let me just put on my shoes. Look in the refrigerator…there's some beer…Blue Ribbon. I believe that's Mallet O'Hara's brand. Right?"

"You got it." Mallone was shorter than Buchanan had imagined. Five eight…five nine at the most. But he had a massive torso and the arms of a weight lifter.

"You actually read my stuff?" Mallone popped the top on a beer.

"Sure. I've read everything you've published to date. What's this new character Stalker MacKnight all about? You're not going to quit writing Mallet O'Hara, are you?"

"Oh hell no. I just got bored, and the double-O-seven movies got a lot of people buying spy stories. I just thought I might give my readers a little international intrigue for a breather. When you come right down to it, the ol' Stalker is just Mallet in a Savile Row suit."

"Oh, OK. You had me worried there for a while. I'm a Mallet O'Hara fan myself. Hell with James Bond." Buchanan looked up from tying his Keds. "Ready, or do you want to sit here and talk while you finish that beer?"

"I hate interviews and interviewers. Didn't they tell you?" Mallone turned up the can and chug-a-lugged the rest of the beer. "Let's go get a burger and look at the babes. Ready?" He winked and started for the door.

The crowd had already started packing in when they arrived at the Bowery.

"Locals. They got a local university right up the road. They flunk out in Columbia just so they can get their daddies to send 'em here to study the mating habits of jellyfish to get their grades up." Mallone waved across the room. Buchanan watched as a rather menacing hulk made his way through the crowd toward them.

"Sharkey, why di'nt yuse tell me yuse was coming?"

[198]

"Charlie, I want you to meet Buchanan Forbes. Do they call ya' Buck?"

Buchanan nodded.

"You'd never guess, but Charlie Mannerri here's from the old neighborhood in Flatbush." Mallone chuckled. "Used to wrestle under the name of the Masked Mutherfrocker, right?"

"Always kidding...it was the Masked Mauler." The tough guy ducked his head and blushed like a small boy.

Buchanan nodded and grinned.

The man stuck out his hand. It resembled the paw of a giant grizzly. "Good to meet yuse, Buck. Any friend of Sharkey's is a friend of mine."

"Good to meet you too, Charlie..."

"C'mon, I got a good table for yuse guys. Yuse don't wanna get too close to the band. They're good but the kids like 'em loud." They followed Charlie across the back, along the opposite wall and down the terraced steps to a table about halfway to the stage.

Charlie pulled back two facing chairs. The table was set up for four.

"Never can tell when yuse might run into some chicks in distress." Charlie winked.

"Charlie here's my kinda guy. Rotten to the core."

"Right. What're yuse drinking? I gotta get back to the kitchen, but I'll get yuse some drinks headed this way with your waitress." He pointed to one of the six or seven young women in white short shorts and nicely filling out tank tops stenciled with THE BOWERY logo.

They ordered drinks and Buchanan looked around the room.

The crowd was mostly college-aged. Just the sound of their chatter was almost deafening.

He looked back when he felt a touch on his arm. Sharkey was leaning across the table and gesturing, trying to tell him something. To carry on a meaningful conversation was hopeless.

"They're friends." Sharkey turned and pointed toward the entrance, which was crowded with people looking anxiously about for an empty table. He fairly shouted, "Do you mind if I ask 'em to join us?"

Buchanan shrugged. It was hopeless to tell who—in the sea of faces—Mallone was talking about.

Besides, there wasn't much hope of getting any real work done tonight anyway. He was sure coming here had been a waste of time. Maybe it would be best if Mallone did have some friends join them. It might provide him with the opportunity to make an early exit.

Now Mallone was standing and waving vigorously. He put his hand to his mouth and let go an ear-piercing whistle.

Buchanan covered his ears, still searching anxiously for a clue to whose attention Mallone was trying to attract.

Finally, he saw a rather handsome fortyish woman brighten and smile and wave back. She turned to the young blond amazon at her side and pointed at Mallone. They waved and slowly began picking their way down the clotted aisle toward them.

Mallone was tugging at his sleeve again. He leaned forward to make himself heard. "The older woman is Inger Carlyle...teaches journalism at some college in Tennessee...writes a travel column for the Atlanta paper...syndicated to about a hundred papers, I think. Husband's an ex-West Pointer, Col. Pershing Carlyle...owns Carlyle Academy. A fancy—winter in Florida, fall and spring in Tennessee—military school for rich boys. The good-looking one is her protégé...Penny something...studying to be a journalist. You and Inger ought to get along."

Buchanan couldn't take his eyes off the younger woman—she was hardly more than a girl, really. She glowed as if there was a theatrical spotlight following her across the smoke-filled room. Heads turned and mouths flew open as she moved. Now and then she turned and laughed when some of the young men tried to attract her attention with whistles and comments. She was wearing white shorts and a tank top made out of a clingy, cream-colored jersey. Loosely fitted, the outfit looked more like Victoria's Secret than beachwear.

She ought to be against the law, Buchanan mused, euphorically.

Hands down, she was one of the most beautiful young women he had ever seen.

Chapter Thirty-nine

AT PRECISELY 7:33 P.M., Alma made a note on the chart that she was relieved by the floor nurse to take a dinner break.

In the hospital cafeteria she bought a cup of coffee and took the brown bag containing the sandwich and fruit she'd brought from home to a table in the staff dining area and sat down and began to eat. When she'd finished eating half of a tuna sandwich and had started on a banana, she unfolded the Sunday Want Ad section from yesterday's *Roanoke Times* and started looking at the job listings under the category of Medical Sales.

"Lil told me you were back here with your kids. If you're looking for a job, come see me in the morning. I'll get you back on at the VA." Alma looked up to find Michael Gentry.

Mike had played ball with Buck in high school and Alma had dated him once or twice the year before she started dating Buck. Michael was now a cardiologist. They'd worked together when he'd been a resident at the VA hospital in Melas. That was during the time when Buck had been overseas. Later, Mike had been Buck's best friend and golfing partner before Buck had been promoted. She knew from hospital scuttlebutt that he'd recently become the "ex" of Lillie, one of Alma's close friends in the bridge club before she and Buck had moved to Raleigh.

Mike was holding a tray bearing a half-grapefruit and a cup of coffee.

"Sit down, Michael," Alma said without warmth. "I appreciate the offer, but for the moment I'm more interested in finding something for Buck."

"Oh? I thought Lil said he was thinking of going back to med school or some such thing? Did he change his mind? Is he looking to come back home?"

"Well, I think he's decided med school's out, but no, he doesn't exactly want to come back here, either. Not really. But, I don't want to go back to North Carolina. My friends and family are all here. I like being home."

"Hmm, so what *is* he up to then?"

"Well, he resigned the job he had and he's just been offered a job down on the coast in Wilmington. He knows I don't want to move back down there. I thought if I found something interesting I might convince him. Anyway, I've about decided not to go back, whether he takes the job down there or not. After all, I have the right to a life, too. Don't I?"

"Of course…" The boyish-looking man chose his words carefully. "I'm serious about the VA…I'd be glad to see you back…it's been a long time." He reached across and squeezed her arm.

"Look, Michael, please don't start bringing up ancient history. I'm happily married…well… married anyway and the mother of four sons, remember."

"Well, yeah. You've put on a little weight, but all-in-all you're still looking good. I have a hard time remembering that you have all those kids. Four boys…" He shook his head in wonder. "What I remember is the times we had in my office when Buck was overseas. Don't you ever think about that? Be honest, now."

"Well, I do…I sometimes wonder how I could have been so foolish. I had to have been out of my mind…" Alma sniffed and tossed her head. Unconsciously she smoothed her sweater over her tummy. She lit a cigarette and let the smoke drift out of her mouth and inhaled it back into her nostrils. "Besides, things were different then, and, well, that's ancient history."

"Hmm, well, you do think about it, anyway. And that last time, when we met in Richmond after the VA seminar on…what was it on…some dumb cardiomonitor, wasn't it? All I remember was that room in the old Jefferson Hotel...God what a night. You were married then too, right? And who did it hurt anyway? As I recall, you'd just caught Buck in a lie about some floozy he'd had lunch with out at the club. *'Sauce for the goose...sauce for the gander.'* Isn't that what you said? Anyway, you and I had our moments. You gotta admit, they weren't all bad."

"I don't admit anything of the kind. I was under a lot of stress, unhappy. And I had had one or two too many. That was an accident. Before that, it was different. I was alone. Buck was overseas with all those...belly dancers. I read the magazines, I knew what was going on. Left me back here with a brand new baby. Anyway, like I said, that's ancient history, eleven years at least. Forget it, Michael...it never happened. Besides, I hear you're taking care of every frustrated female in a fifty-mile radius."

"Not guilty. You know how rumors go around when there's a divorce."

"You mean Lil didn't catch you *en flagrante* with your office nurse?" Alma gave him a penetrating stare.

"Those stories were exaggerated...it was a misunderstanding."

"Well, just so we won't have a *misunderstanding*...it's been nice seeing you, Michael. I'm going to be working here, so don't come sniffing around. You know how people talk."

"Come on, Alma, what's a cup of coffee between old friends? I haven't seen you in a hundred years. Your husband and I are... were...high school teammates...and old golfing buddies. Back then Lil and I...and you two...we were a foursome. Goddamn, we had some high ol' times."

"Just the same...stay away. I don't want a peep out of anybody. I've got enough trouble with Buck as it is."

"Oh...I'm truly sorry to hear that. Were you serious about not going back to North Carolina?"

"Well, I don't want to but I have four kids to think of. I don't know. I have a life to live too."

"Are you separated? I mean officially?"

"I know what you mean. No, not really. We're just having a little rough spot in the relationship. He's so damn selfish...never gives a damn about me. Doesn't know I exist."

"You're just feeling abandoned right now. Why don't you and Buck join me at the club for dinner some Saturday when he gets in town?"

"Well, thanks, but Buck won't be coming back here 'til God knows when. He just told me this afternoon that he might be flying to Utica for two weeks. God knows when I'll see him. We never have any fun anymore."

"Oh, sorry. Hard to believe. Buck Forbes was always a fun sort of guy. The four of us used to get around. Remember the Greenbrier? We were all together at that medical convention two years in a row...and I recall the dances at the club...we used to have some wild old times. You're a damn good-looking woman, Alma. A terrific...dancer." He winked. "Goddamn, if you don't mind my saying so, even with the extra padding, you've sure managed to keep your figure...lose fifteen and who'd know you had all those rug rats? You ought to say something to Lil. She's let herself slip a little. Buck's a lucky guy. When you talk to him, tell him, 'Hi.' You sure are looking great."

Alma's hand went to her hair and she sat up straighter.

"Just can't believe that you and Buck are on the rocks," Michael continued. "You were always the ideal couple. Everybody always thought Buck was going places. Always the smart one. Studied art. Worked as a writer. Son-of-a-bitch could kick a football out of sight...might've made it in the pros if he'd taken a mind to."

"Buck's changed. He had a lot of promise before we left here, but since we moved to Raleigh, he hasn't exactly set the woods on fire. We never did join a club down there. We have practically no social life. He did have the offer of a promotion to the home office last year, but I wouldn't even consider moving to New Jersey...my God!"

"Sometimes a man on the way up has to take some opportunities in order to keep progressing. But, I can understand anyone not wanting to move up north. Still, it probably wouldn't have been forever."

"For me, one day up there is like forever...believe me."

"Was it bad? What was it like in New Jersey?"

"Oh...I don't know...I mean, of course it's bad. I didn't have to go up there to know that. I think we have to set our limits...establish boundaries, don't you?"

"I guess. But I think contempt prior to investigation is sometimes a dangerous thing. New Jersey's right across the river from New York City. You might have liked it. It might have been an adventure."

"I don't have to stick my finger in a flame to know I won't like being burned. The difference between humans and animals is that we can benefit from the experience of others. We don't have to learn everything the hard way." Alma sniffed again. She pushed back her chair and folded up her paper, rewrapped the remaining half-sandwich, and put the banana peel on the tray along with the empty coffee cup. She picked up her purse and took one final sip of coffee. Picking up the tray, she stood to leave.

"Good seeing you, Michael. Please don't come hanging around."

"Well, after all, I work here, too. No one would ever know, really. Think about Richmond sometimes when you go to bed. After your last kid, didn't Ogden Branch tie your tubes?"

Alma shot him a warning look.

"I'm late now. I've got a private patient up on the surgical floor. Bye, and thanks for the company."

"Bye...the VA job's always there. I mean it. Don't worry, things will work out. They always do. By the way, give Lil a call. We're still friends. I see her at the club for dinner almost every Saturday. I'm sure she'd love to see you again. Besides, you can come alone anytime you want to anyway. You don't have to wait on Lil. You're on the inactive roster. You're still entitled to privileges. When it warms up, bring the boys to the pool." Mike smiled encouragement.

"Well, I don't know, but I might call Lil' anyway. Lunch might be fun...gotta run."

"Don't forget me. Work on those extra pounds...you'd look great in a bikini."

She ignored him now.

Alma dumped her tray and headed for the elevator. As the elevator door closed, she had a final glimpse of Michael sitting at the table, sucking a trendy smokeless cigarette and waving to a table of nurses across the room.

Michael couldn't hold Buck's jock strap in the bedroom department, but, for a doctor, he hadn't been a total zero, either. And, in the real jungle, young doctors were fought over. She'd be damned surprised if Mike Gentry slept alone many nights.

Alone in the elevator, she reached down and smoothed her uniform over her abdomen and hips. Alma was glad she'd only eaten half of the sandwich.

Mike said she'd kept her figure.

She'd always been considered attractive. At thirty-six, she could still find plenty of company if she really wanted to.

She wondered if she should call Lil and wangle an invitation to the club Saturday night.

Chapter Forty

CONVERSATION WAS DIFFICULT over the noise in the room. When the women finally fought their way to the table, Mallone introduced them and moved around beside Buchanan so that Buck was seated opposite Inger Carlyle, the older of the pair. When Mallone told her he was on assignment for SNS, she wanted to talk about writing.

She asked him all about how he'd gotten started with SNS.

It was embarrassing to Buchanan, since he actually had no secrets to reveal.

"You mean you quit being a reporter, and now this editor is giving you a major Sunday Book Page feature? Do you realize how fantastic that is to me? I struggled for years before I sold anything to a major syndicate. Even then, it was just fluff travel filler on Germany for a minor newspaper chain. But, SNS? That must be some kind of sparkling prose you write," she gushed.

In the presence of two pros, Buchanan determined to keep the focus away from himself. He was afraid to show his ignorance.

Mallone and Inger talked books and publishing and Buchanan struggled mightily to keep his eyes off Penny. He couldn't decide how old she was. One minute she looked fifteen, the next twenty-five. She made him feel tongue-tied. Thanks to his lucky stars, the noise and music made it impossible to try to make conversation.

She was a golden tan and, except for just a touch of pink on her mouth, she used no makeup that he could see. On her, a shiny nose and the tiny freckles were something right out of a cover for *Cosmopolitan*. Underneath the clingy jersey tank top, those centerfold breasts had a life of their own. Where the tops of her breasts swelled beneath the thin straps, a light dusting of bronze freckles showed.

She caught him looking and smiled just the tiniest flicker.

He attempted a kindly smile but was distracted by the disturbing heaviness in his groin. Desperately, he turned his attention back to the conversation.

When the band started, Inger asked him to dance. The music was one of the new songs and Buchanan found it hard to find a beat, but she didn't seem to mind. Inger really wasn't half-bad on the dance floor, but she was aggressively sexual and he felt himself reacting again. Thinking back to the other night with Cammie, lately his penis seemed to have a mind of its own. He tried mightily to think about the new job...his sons...anything.

Over his shoulder he watched Mallone swinging Penny through the heavy traffic on the tiny floor. Watching her hips and breasts moving underneath the silky fabric did him no good. His rotten subconscious betrayed him again.

Back at the table, the talk turned to Mallone's books. Mostly Buchanan just listened. Once or twice, he caught Penny looking his way. She smiled again. His unruly penis was making him crazy. Could he make an excuse and just leave without hurting Sharkey's feelings?

No way. He was stuck. Might as well tough it out.

When the band took a break, the women excused themselves to go to the powder room.

The band was playing again by the time they returned. Two rather clean-cut young men came hesitantly over to the table. The locals obviously recognized Mallone. They were very polite and asked the women to dance. After the first number, they all switched partners and danced again before they returned the women to the table and thanked them. That started something and for the next half-hour, there was a steady stream of young men who made their way to the table to ask the women to dance.

In between, Buchanan danced once, nervously, with Penny to a fast old-fashioned twist tune. She had trouble following him at first. It was mostly his fault—he felt clumsy dancing with someone so young. Afterwards he apologized and she assured him it had been her fault.

"I love the sixties revival music, don't you?"

Could anybody be so freaking sincere? Looking at her tore the heart right out of him.

When the band took another breather, the women headed for the loo.

When the band came back, Buchanan asked Inger to dance to a slow tune.

"Penny thinks you don't like her. I told her she was wrong," Inger breathed in his ear.

"That's ridiculous...why? I've hardly said two words. I really don't know what to say to her. She's so young. I feel like her grandfather."

"You're hardly that. She's more mature than you think." Inger leaned back and looked up at him, questioningly.

"Oh, come on...eighteen?" he guessed out loud.

"Closer to...twenty-three. And surprisingly adult." Inger stressed the last. "She's old to be a junior in college. But of course she'll finish up right after Christmas. She started late...but she's truly bright. From start-to-finish in less than three years." Inger smiled up at him. "I'm afraid she hasn't had much excitement while she's been here. It's her first trip to the ocean and I haven't been able to introduce her to any men. Sunday's her last day. She likes you; thinks you're the cat's pajamas. You've really made an impression. Ask her to dance again...pick a slow one. Her daddy was a preacher...she's afraid to jitterbug."

"Cat's pajamas, huh? I translate that: Great-grandfatherly..." Buchanan laughed, but he felt a twinge of resentment. He would have preferred the girl found him...ah...*dangerous.*

When the music stopped, Buchanan waited until the band started playing again. The song was the old standard from the forties, *The Nearness of You.*

"OK, I'll ask her now. I love this tune." He steered Inger toward the table. Out of the corner of his eye, he saw the young college-type who'd danced with Penny earlier making a bee line for her table. He tried to hurry but walking with Inger threw his timing off and he got there a half-step too late.

"Thanks...but..." Penny was saying.

"Excuse me, Penny promised this dance to me." Buchanan moved in front of the boy and offered her his hand.

"Sorry..." She smiled prettily at the boy and followed Buchanan to the dance floor.

"You saved my life. I was tired of refusing him," she murmured in Buchanan's ear.

"*...It's just the nearness of you...*" She sang along and pressed closer. Through the silky fabric he could feel her thigh rubbing against his crotch. Her scent made him dizzy.

She smelled of soap...and maybe just a hint of powder.

Buchanan tried to hold her in a relaxed casual way, but she snuggled closer. She actually wasn't as tall as she appeared, five-eight, maybe five-nine, tops. Her head nestled nicely on his shoulder between his ear and his chin. Her breath ticked his ear lobe, wafting just a trace of mint. He stole a look at her mouth. Ripe, slightly swollen. What would it be like to taste her?

Help! He pleaded silently.

He tried to pull back from the distraction of her abdomen brushing against him.

"*...it's not the pale moon that excites me, that thrills and delights me...*" Her fresh breath was an aphrodisiac.

His unruly penis was an embarrassment now.

Buchanan was certain he could feel the texture of her pubic patch through the flimsy fabric. He tried to pull back looking down at her, trying desperately to distract himself with conversation.

"Inger says you're truly talented. Going to be a fine writer. What sort of stuff do you like to do?" he asked. Despite his effort to pull back, she remained glued to him at the hips.

"Oh, I don't know. I'd really like to write fiction, I guess. Journalism is hard. I don't know how you do it."

"Well, you forget, I'm relatively new. For me it's still sort of fun."

"Well, sometimes it's fun. But I edit the school paper and mostly it's just extra work for me. Oh, I love this song…" She snuggled her head against him, humming against his chest. "Are you married?" Her voice was just a whisper in his ear.

The openly inescapable entendre of the question put his head a-whirl.

Those heartbeats…hers or his own?

Suddenly, he was having a difficult time breathing.

"Well, yes, but she left me." The way he said it, he clearly meant it for a lie. He felt a fleeting twinge of guilt but he made no attempt to change the meaning.

Trying to seduce a college girl. What a fool. He was acting like a pimply-faced boy still trying for a tenderfoot badge. Too bad there hadn't been a Penny fourteen years ago.

His palms were sweaty now. Awkwardly, he tried to keep the pressure of her breasts away from his chest. It didn't help…made things worse, if anything.

Those tits were burning a goddamn hole in him.

"Do you like the beach?" he said, feeling totally adolescent, wishing for the music to end.

"Oh, yes. Did Inger tell you? I'm twenty-three and I'd never seen the ocean before. "

"No. That's incredible," he lied.

Two dances and it was getting to be second nature.

"Do you like swimming in the ocean?"

What moronic dialogue!

"Well, I'm actually not much of a swimmer. And the beach has been full of jellyfish. It's awful. Except for wading, I haven't been out in the surf. But, truthfully, I really like looking at the ocean. But I enjoy walking along the beach more than I think I would ever like to bathe in it. The salt makes me feel icky. I wish Inger had a pool. Where are you staying?"

"Oh? I'm at the Presidential. Just across the amusement park. You can see the sign from out front here, actually."

"Does it have a pool?"

"Yes, a big pool. The water is ten feet at the deep end. But no diving board. Hotels have quit putting in diving boards at all. Kids are crazy. Too much liability…"

Now he was sounding like an insurance salesman.

"Well, I don't care about diving boards, but I do love the feel of the water. Someday I'd love to have a house with my own pool…you know, truly private…so I wouldn't even have to wear a suit. I only wear a bikini now, anyway…" She wriggled closer as if her fantasy included him. "Do you dive off a board? I'd be scared to death."

"I did some diving in college. Not very good, I'm afraid."

"I'll bet you were. I watch the way you walk. You look like a gymnast to me…"

"Hardly, but funny, watching you move, I thought you might be a dancer. Do you take dance…you know…modern dance? All the girls at college took it when I was in school, but that was in the dark ages. You were only a little girl back then." Suddenly he wanted to remind her of his age, or was the reminder for himself?

"I took acrobatic dancing when I was a little girl. My mother made me. But, I finally had to quit. We moved around so much. And, then we finally had to leave my daddy…"

He suddenly realized the music was over.

"I don't suppose you'd like to walk outside for a little while…It's hot in here," she asked suddenly. "We could walk along the boardwalk…"

"Well, all right, but we should ask them to join us, OK?"

"I don't think Inger is much for walking on the beach, but I guess we do have to ask. Just don't insist, all right?" She squeezed his hand and giggled conspiratorially. "I've had it with togetherness for one night…"

"OK." He laughed. She seemed surprisingly adult.

She was right. Sharkey and Inger had no desire to take a walk.

"Go ahead, but this place closes down at midnight. If you don't make it back before then, meet me at the car," Inger said. "Don't be late. I won't be left sitting alone in a car late at night."

"Don't worry," Penny smiled. "I'll be on time."

Buchanan stole a glance at the Miller HiLife clock over the stage. Still over three hours 'til midnight! The idea of that much time alone with her put him in a panic.

Outside, she steadied herself by leaning against him and removed her thongs. "I love to go barefoot, don't you?"

"Well, by God, yes, I do…" Suddenly, he felt relieved to be out in the air.

What the hell. He moved to the boardwalk rail, put his foot up on the bench and removed his Keds. Peeling off the cotton socklettes he shoved them in the toes and rolled up his pants cuffs a couple of inches. "How's that?" He laughed.

"Much better…" They moved down the boardwalk. "Are you truly separated from your wife?" Her question came without warning. "Not that it matters. I really don't care. I guess you think I'm awful to ask…but…I…I…can't imagine why a woman would ever let you out of her sight."

"Oh, don't fool yourself. I can be a contrary bastard. She's living with my folks in Virginia with my sons. Just told me about three hours ago she was not going to move back down here. Except for missing my sons, I'd be glad really…"

It sounded like the truth.

Suddenly, he wanted to be free…and young again…if only for a night…

"How many sons do you have?"

"Uh…four." *Why lie about it?*

"Oh!" She was silent for a while. Then she squeezed his hand. "I want to have children…lots…I'd love to meet your boys. How old?"

"Well, the oldest is almost eleven. About the age you were when I was married." *Well, there it was.*

He felt old and terribly ugly—the magic was lost forever now.

Like a bad novel, the magic was something he'd made up. It had never really existed anyway.

"Quit trying to talk down to me. I'm twenty-three. You're not that old. Age is all a state of mind." She squeezed his hand again. It conveyed a delicious intimacy.

His imagination again.

Just let it go. A terrible sadness wrenched his soul.

They walked on past the sparse off-season crowd in the Pavilion.

She'd fallen silent again. Where their hips rubbed together it scorched him like a flame.

Get real. The thought echoed hollowly inside his head. Why torture himself like this?

"There. The Presidential…see the sign?" She pointed.

"Yeah. That's it, all right," he mumbled.

"Could we see your pool?"

Don't do this to me, he wanted to scream at her.

"Huh? Well sure." His breath was faster now. He hated all this goddamn innocence.

His chest was an empty canyon.

She stopped and slipped back into her thongs.

She squeezed his hand, then disentangled her fingers and moved closer, slipping her arm around his waist.

No choice but to put his arm around her now.

Crossing the street, Buchanan braved the pebbles but kept a sharp eye out.

Bumping at the hips again, she laughed as he tried to get into step.

"Hup, tup, thrup, fo'…" Blood roaring in his head, heart in his mouth, step for step Buchanan guided her across the parking lot and fumbled for his key.

Inside, he stooped to pick up his discarded bikini undershorts and stuff them into a plastic laundry bag.

"Don't mind the mess." He looked around with a self-conscious laugh. "I'd hardly stepped out of the shower when Mallone showed up. He was early. Can I fix you something…I have some vodka and tonic…and some beer in that little refrigerator?"

"I've had my fill of beer…I was really just nursing the ones I had. A vodka and tonic…what's tonic?"

"Quinine water. I have a little can of grapefruit juice in my bag…that might be better?"

"Sounds quite healthy, I think." She moved to the window and pulled back the edge of the drapes. "The pool is beautiful with the lights. I wish I'd brought my suit. We could go for a swim. Ever see those old swimming movies with Esther Williams? I read her book. I think she must have been a real sexpot, don't you?"

"Huh? Oh, yeah." When he turned with her glass, she had slid open the door and was standing outside at the edge of the pool. Against the pool lights, the shadowy outline of her legs showed through the loose folds of the flowing shorts.

He looked away and fixed himself a stiff shot of vodka over some ice and drank half of it straight without taking the glass away. Then he quickly refilled his glass before he walked out to where she stood.

"Here, try this on for size." He handed her the glass and waited while she took a little sip.

"Oh, wow!" She made a face. "That's strong. You're not trying to get me drunk are you…take advantage, maybe?" she teased.

"Well, Ogden Nash wrote: *'Candy's dandy/But liquor's quicker.'*" He raised his glass and laughed.

She reached in a pocket and took out a little black capsule and put it on her tongue and washed it down with her drink.

"Was that a Black Beauty?" He blinked in surprise.

"A what? It's a diet pill…helps me hold my figure. Would that make you want to hold my figure?" She laughed and took another sip. Her flirting was the pure light of innocence, made him feel like dirt. He wished she wouldn't play with him.

"What would you say if I went in the pool in my clothes?"

"Well, don't you think that would be uncomfortable…for later, I mean?"

"It's very tempting. Maybe we could dry my clothes over the air-conditioner." She seemed serious. God, what had he gotten himself into? He couldn't take all this frigging innocence. He wanted to just hand her the key and say, 'look, do whatever you want, but you can't trust me to be here.' Strange? At the moment his agony was curiously sweeter than any joy he could remember.

He just looked at her. He wondered about the booze and the black capsule of biphetamine.

"Well?"

"Well, that might be all right, but what would you wear while you waited?" The minute he spoke he wished he'd kept his mouth shut.

"Don't you have a robe, or I could wear a towel. I do at home all the time."

"I have a travel robe, but I'm not sure..." Was she serious? Now he really didn't know.

"Can we put more grapefruit in this?" She handed him the glass and walked back into the room.

He followed and poured some more juice on top and stirred it with his fingers. When he brought it back she had closed the sliding glass door and was just closing the drapes again.

"Put the drink by the bed." She waved her hand to brush an imaginary bug away. "Bugs. That's the trouble with walking on the beach at night. Not a good place to make love at all. All those silly romance writers obviously have never tried it." She took a step toward him. "Have you read *Lady Chatterly*?"

"A very long time ago. I think it's a powerful love story..."

"What would I have to do to get you to kiss me?" She raised herself up and leaned hard against him. Her arms encircled his neck.

She moaned softly and moved his hand to her breast.

For an instant he stiffened in surprise, then his hands found her buttocks and pulled her tightly against him. Probing with her tongue and biting...Buchanan tasted blood.

No hope for him, now.

After a time she pulled back and without a word she pulled her blouse over her head and with an economy of movement unbuttoned the waistband of her shorts and let them fall around her ankles.

Timidly, Penny looked at him.

"Do you like me?"

"Oh...Yes...YES..."

Have you ever given oral sex?..."

"Well..." *Are you freaking crazy?*

"Did you like to do it?. . ."

"Sometimes…" *This is a terrible mistake…*

"Then undress me…take me…I've never really had a man… teach me everything… please…"

It was way past talking now.

Part 4
Maggie

Chapter Forty-one

AS HE WATCHED the panel truck pull out of the drive, Durwood Fisher looked at his watch and made a note on the legal pad:

12:59 hrs–Sunday–March 17, 2002
Buchanan Forbes scheduled to depart RDU for Utica, NY
to begin training at Stribol Labs...

He placed the ballpoint and pad on his briefcase, poured a cup of coffee and sat down.

"Is that the last of it?" Johnston asked.

"All except the tapes and recording equipment." Fisher nodded, thought a moment and glanced across the kitchen table at Johnston. "Did you get all your personal stuff?"

"In the car. I'm ready anytime. But I don't feel good about this. I think Forbes put one over on us."

"Well, the boys in Utica are gonna keep an eye on him 'til he gets back. We left the bugs in and the monitors are still here. We'll pick him up again when he gets back in two weeks. The Wilmington office plans to keep an eye on him when he moves to the beach. But I've said all along, this guy has received more attention than he deserved. I think the whole thing sort of got out of hand. Personally, I'd hate to have to justify all the expense of that wild goose chase I made last week just to catch his job interview and a trip to Myrtle Beach to drink beer with Sharkey Mallone. That SOB has a horseshoe up his ass. I wish you could have seen that college girl, Penny Warner. A real centerfold! What she saw in him I'll never know."

"Did Knoxville check her and the Carlyle woman out?"

"Nothing there. She's a student at that college where the Carlyle woman teaches. But she lied to him about her age. Said she was twenty-three. You heard the tape I made at the motel. She's actually only nineteen. Her father was that holy-roller TV preacher that got caught operating a vice ring out in Kansas five years ago. Drug addict...con artist...a real sleaze. The mother took Penny and left him. The girl is one of those prodigy types. Anyway, her only crime is a lack of taste in men. Turned me down when I asked her to dance with me at that Bowery joint. What an airhead; she'll never know what she missed."

"That was stupid. It could have seriously jeopardized this operation if he'd spotted you."

"Shit, Bill. How many times I gotta tell you? The guy is dumb as hell. This whole thing has been a waste. You went over his place while I was down at the beach recording all that smacky-mouth and heavy breathing. Whadja find? Zilch. Zero. Nada. I warned you, right?"

"Look, I've already heard this. Doesn't actually mean a thing. He'd be a fool to stash a large amount of cash in that house. If he did make a big score with those drug samples he'd be feeling real spooky. Lay low for a while. And, quit your bitching. All you did was drive around the beach, drink beer and wind up eavesdropping on a child molesting."

"Well, you got that right. A real orgy. God, I never would have believed that it was humanly possible to go non-stop for over three hours. And that's no lie."

"I got to admit, for an ordinary pill pusher, this guy leads a charmed life. Writing for that newspaper syndicate…I'm surprised the Sunday book editors would want a piece on Sharkey Mallone. I thought they had too much class."

"Listen, don't knock it. Bill Gates…and a lotta other real intellectuals read Mallone. I'm a Mallet O'Hara fan myself. Too bad I couldn't figure out a way to get him to autograph a book."

"Look, Durr, you gotta get a grip. You're getting sloppy. This job ain't no two-bit cloak'n'dagger TV play. We're accountants…professionals…remember?"

"Don't worry about me. Washington's the one who's lost their marbles. I think it's ridiculous to have Forbes tailed in Utica. For chrissake, he's going be in a two-week indoctrination…new company…new job. But, I guess there's no harm in having Nell Batson keep an eye on him after he moves to the beach, just in case. Nell's single and practically lives next door…she already put a bug in that tiny pad he rented. She's going to tap the phone, soon as it's installed next week. Nell will have him wrapped tighter'n Gwyneth Paltrow's Danskins before he moves his first suitcase through the door. Still, it's probably just a waste of time."

"I don't know, something don't add up. For a guy who's just lost a job and has his house up for sale, and whose checking balance runs less than ten grand, he's never once seemed too worried about how he was going to make his house payment. And what about all that talk about going to Med school? Where was all the money coming from?"

"Probably got the GI Bill. He's a Desert Storm vet."

"Shit! That wouldn't even make his house payment. He's got four kids, for chrissake. I'm telling ya' there's more to this dude than meets the eye."

"Listen, we need to get out to the airport and get that bug out from under his car. Lhamda-Alpine is going to pick that car up while he's gone. We wouldn't want them to find that bug on it."

"No sweat. I'll do it tonight. Can we find out how his new company car's going to be delivered? We can stick the same bug back under the new one before he picks it up."

"Sure. Stribol probably leases their company fleet from Four Wheels, PH and H...or Globe maybe. Mostly, leasing companies deliver through a local dealer, but even if they buy up north and have a driver deliver direct, it should be a piece of cake to find out who it's coming through."

"Good. Having a transmitter on that car'll make it a lot easier on poor Nell. She'll be on her own after he moves to the beach."

Chapter Forty-two

BUCHANAN WATCHED as the TV monitor behind the USAir counter changed the ETA for his flight. According to this latest correction, it was already thirty minutes late leaving Philadelphia. This moved the estimated departure from RDU up to almost 2:00 PM.

He sighed and picked up his briefcase. Casting an eye to the pod of pay phones along the far wall of the ticket concourse, he wondered if he still might try to catch Cammie at home.

"Buchanan..." Incredibly, almost as if his thoughts had willed it, he turned to see Cammie running down the line of ticket counters toward him. In a fitted satin brocade suit in a tasteful tint of ash rose, she looked as if she'd just walked off the cover of *Vogue*.

Grinning like a schoolboy, Buchanan wheeled around and hurried back to meet her.

"Speak of the devil," he said when the gap between them narrowed so he didn't have to shout. "I was about to call you...again. You're hard to catch. I've called and called, you know."

"And every time I tried to reach you, you were out. This week's been insane. I'm glad you left Mae the time of your flight. Traffic was tied up by a bad wreck on westbound Seventy just before I reached the Angus Barn. I thought for sure I'd missed you."

"And I was just cursing the fact that my plane was going to be delayed. It must be some kind of omen when a flight delay is the first thing that's turned out right all day..." He chuckled. "Anyway, every cloud has a silver lining, they say. I can't tell you how glad I am to see you."

"I brought you a little going-away present. I slipped a flask in my purse, thought we could go into the snack bar and sneak a teensy *bon voyage* shooter of good ol' Jack Black?"

There was no table service in the little snack bar and Buchanan went to fetch some cups with ice while Cammie moved across and staked claim on a window table in the far corner of the room. When he returned, Buchanan took the flask and, discreetly screening his hands under the table's edge, mixed two fairly stiff shooters. He handed her one of the cups. "If you don't run for Governor, counselor, here's to a great future in bootlegging."

They touched cups.

"I think I'd prefer bootlegging. Most bootleggers I've had the pleasure of defending have had more integrity than most governors I've known." She took a tiny sip of the liquor and gasped.

"I'll drink to that. So, where were we? It's been a hell of a week."

Cammie wrinkled her brow. "Well, let's see. It was Monday and you were calling from Bolivia. You said you were going to take the Stribol job...and I said, 'You'd better call Alma before you take the job.' So...you took the job, obviously..." She waved her hand at the passengers in the concourse, scurrying to catch their flights. "I guess that means that Alma was glad to hear the news, right?"

"Not exactly. As a matter of fact she's madder'n a hornet. Says she won't move to Wilmington, won't even commit to coming down here in June, when school's out up there, to help sell the house. Refused to speak to me this morning before I left for the plane."

"That's quite a situation you have there. She's likely just mad because you didn't consult her. You hurt her feelings. Don't say I didn't warn you. But, it'll blow over..."

"I don't know. Believe it or not, I did call her Monday, just as soon as I hung up from talking to you. She said 'no' without even hearing the details. Then she hit me with the idea that she wanted me to move back to Virginia. I just said to hell with it and took the job anyway."

"Well, I hope you know what you're doing." She lowered her chin to hide her blush. "Tell me how it went with Mallone. What kind of man is he?"

"In the first place he was born to write fiction—a pathological liar. His version of the life and times of Sharkey Mallone is a lot grander than the facts. Got an ego as big as all outdoors. And, he's a cop buff. Wears this official NYPD badge as a belt buckle. To hear him tell it, the NYPD calls him daily to ask for his help. According to him he's unofficially helped solve most of the major crimes that happened in the last twenty years. "

"Sounds like you got to know him pretty well for just one day..."

"Well, two and a half, actually. I was able to spend more time with him than I thought. I called him when I got there Monday night. He was taking his wife to catch a plane so we went out to eat and had some beers at the local hot spot. Quite an evening. We ran into this lady—a travel writer friend who teaches at some college in Tennessee. Ever hear of Inger Carlyle? Had this girl with her, a senior student, a protègèe of hers." Buchanan was trying to sound offhand.

"The name Carlyle doesn't ring a bell. But tell me more about picking up some college women in a honky-tonk. No wonder you stayed an extra night. Mallone didn't get you into any trouble, did he?"

Red-faced, Buchanan raised his cup to hide a sudden pang of guilt.

"Neah, nothing like that...just a dance or two. Inger Carlyle is married to the headmaster of Carlyle Military Academy and this Penny Wagner's just a kid," he said, rather defensively.

"Oh? Who said anything about Penny Whozits? How old is she?" She was alert now.

"Twenty-something, I guess..." He tried to shrug the question off.

"Some kid."

"Oh, stop. It was all quite innocent really. Sharkey knows the Carlyle woman from way back. She's on some sort of sabbatical...doing a book...owns a house trailer down near where he lives. The girl's a promising poet...Carlyle's protègèe. We talked about writing..."

"Talked! Poetry in a honky-tonk?"

She was helpless to hide the sudden flare of jealousy.

"The girl's a journalism student. She was starry-eyed over the fact that I was writing an article about Sharkey Mallone, that's all. My God, I'm practically old enough to be that girl's father. Is this some kind of third degree?"

"No need to get defensive. I just don't think Alma would jump for joy if she heard you were out dancing with women in a honky-tonk. I know I wouldn't."

"Alma's practically filed for divorce. Why shouldn't I examine my options? I was just having some fun..."

"Oh, now we're examining options..." She was helpless to hide her morbid suspicions.

"Look, I already told you, we just talked. What's wrong with that? The kid has had a rough life...ever hear of a sleazy TV preacher, Milo Wagner?"

"Yeah. A real lowlife..."

"That's her father. On drugs and booze. Played fast and loose with the church funds, made all the papers. Big polygamy advocate...had a way

[221]

with the good women of his church…operated a regular harem under the guise of religion. Anyway, Penny's mother had already left Wagner by the time the curtain came down…" Buchanan obviously wanted desperately to drop the subject now.

"Sounds like you got her entire story. And you fell for that sad tale? I'm touched."

"All we did was talk…"

"So forget it; it's none of my business. But listen, I know that things haven't been exactly easy for you, and you're vulnerable. If you're going to live the bachelor life down at the beach, you'd better be careful. If you offer a shoulder to every pretty young thing with a sad story, you're going to get into trouble."

"I can take care of myself." He squirmed. "Don't be so damn cynical. It's unbecoming. My God, this girl had never seen the ocean. She's still a virgin."

"A virgin? Did she tell you that? My, my, that must have been some talk you had."

"You sound just like Alma. Women! You all think you know every-damn-thing."

Cammie sat momentarily frozen. She'd had no idea she'd strike such a raw nerve. "Whoa. Calm down. No big deal. I didn't mean to sound like such a know-it-all. I'm sorry. Come on, Mr. Buchanan Forbes, inter-national playboy, man-of-the-world…you should know that we women are naturally suspicious of each other. We're cats…always have our claws out."

She leaned across and touched his arm.

He scowled, sipped the drink, pouting.

"So, how long will you be in Utica?" She tried to change the subject. Still, the thought of him drinking and dancing with a young girl—and discussing the merits of her virginity—ran hot in her blood.

"Two weeks." Buchanan was still red-faced, partly from embarrass-ment, partly from anger. He swirled the ice in his cup with a wristy motion, struggling to get control of his emotions. "I don't know what I'm getting so stirred up about. I guess I'm a bit on edge. Having to go to Utica and sit through another of these tedious little schools for wayward pharmaceutical salesmen. Sitting in a room all day, listening to all that rah-rah stuff ain't exactly my idea of fun."

"Where will you be? I'll give you a call at night, just for your own pro-tection."

"Protection? C'mon counselor, give it a rest. Anyway, I'll be at the Hotel Utica. I don't have the number. I'd be glad to hear from you, you know I would...but I know you're busy..."

"No trouble. I'll have Mae call information." She tried to smile. "But you'll probably be out hitting the spots with the troops every night. I know how those things can be."

"I'm more a loner type..."

"That's even worse. Watch out for them big city women...I'll call just in case..."

It was getting awkward now but they still hadn't called his plane and she was loath to leave. "I could go by your house once in a while to make sure it's still there..."

"That would be nice but it sounds like a lot of trouble. I told the Realtor to have someone come in and dust once a week."

"No problem. I'll be glad to check it out."

"Thanks." He told her where he'd hidden the key.

"Well, it's about time to head for the boarding gate." Buchanan polished off his drink.

"Take this. I'd hate to pour it out." She handed him her cup and fished the silver flask out of her purse. "The flask is a little present..."

He gave it a closer look. "Sterling. Gosh, thanks a lot."

"Use it well, and think of me." They were walking along the concourse now. She bit her lip. She couldn't let him to see her cry.

In the waiting area around the boarding gates, she became increasingly uncomfortable, afraid he'd see how upset she was. "Well, I should run. There's a reception at the club. I'm running close. Bye. Remember...try not to listen to any sad stories...and...stay out of trouble..."

Hearing about that girl had put up a wall between them. Now nothing came out right.

He took a step toward her, not knowing exactly what to do.

On impulse, she raised up on her tiptoes and kissed him on the cheek and hugged him fiercely. He hugged her back awkwardly, then stepped away and balanced the briefcase and cup on the arm of a chair. Turning back, he smiled sheepishly and wrapped his arms around her and squeezed her tight, lifting her. When he relaxed, her body slid down the length of him until her feet regained the floor. The sensation set her all a-tingle.

"Thanks for everything," he said.

She pulled back and kissed him hard on the mouth. It was a wanton kiss.

He stiffened in surprise, then his lips went soft and he kissed her back.

When he released her she stumbled back. She blinked, barely holding herself together now.

"Take care," he said.

"You too. I really have to run." Giving his arm a final squeeze, she turned and rapidly walked away. In the parking deck, long before she'd reached her car, the tears were washing down her cheeks. It was all she could do to find the electronic release.

Inside, she slumped over the steering wheel. It was a mistake to kiss him on the mouth.

That girl. Only twenty-three. She was certain from his reaction that there had been more to the story than he was telling.

And he would be moving to the beach as soon as he got back.

There were bound to be others now that Alma was pushing him away.

Alma was a stupid bitch.

And Buchanan was such an innocent. If he needed comfort, then he deserved…

What?

Someone like herself?

What a joke.

Suddenly, she felt ancient…used up. Twenty years too late…

Almost forty-three…hardly a prize for a man his age.

She was openly sobbing now.

He had stirred to life a long-forgotten hunger. She was afraid it would never go away.

Chapter Forty-three

THREE PINK ENVELOPES addressed in a frilly feminine script were waiting when Buchanan arrived at the Hotel Utica. In the elevator, he examined the postmarks. One had been mailed on Wednesday the day after he'd left Myrtle Beach, and the second was dated the following day. The third was mailed that Friday from Newbold, Tennessee.

There were also two blue phone message slips leaving Penny's number in Tennessee.

He sent the bellman for some ice before he tipped him and sent him on his way. He unpacked his bags, found the silver flask and poured himself a drink. Then, fairly trembling with excitement, he sat down and opened the first of the envelopes.

March 13, Wednesday morning 1:30AM

Darling Buchanan:
We have only been apart for an hour and I think of you, back in that room—our room—lying on the bed still warm, fragrant with our love. Oh, how can I tell you that you've changed my whole life? When I met you, I wondered if there was any hope...any beauty left for me. My whole body sings with the memory of your touch.

Keep yourself safe. And don't worry, we'll find a way. With your own problems so heavy on your mind, I didn't tell you about mine. But, I have to finish school and you have your divorce and the problem of getting your children. I'll wait for you until you are free and then we'll have the rest of our lives.

I may never sleep again! But, I guess I must try. Tomorrow I must have a clear head and think of a way to resolve my own situation.

I know it's crazy...love like this only happens in cheap novels, but I'll never make fun of those corny stories again. If the way I feel is corny...so be it.

        I LOVE you, desperately,
        P

There was lipstick print covering the signature initial.

God, he mused, not unpleasantly. *Just what have I gotten myself into?*

Finishing off the drink, he went back to the dresser and fixed another before he sat back down and opened the next envelope.

The stationery showed spots where liquid stains...*tears?*... blurred the ink.

March 13, 2002, Wednesday nite, 11:00 PM

Darling, Darling Buchanan,
Excuse the splotches. I've cried and cried all day, and I thought I'd gotten all my tears behind me, but I can't write this without it tearing my heart out. Despite Inger's warning, I told my mother about you, and she's furious. I didn't tell you before because I wanted to get it over with before you found out, but I've been dating this man back home—he's really nothing to me—it was sort of expected, arranged. My mother pushed me into it. And, I don't know how to explain, but she's been through so much in her own life with the horror of my poor tortured father's problems, I felt it was the least I could do. Anyway, she's ordered me back home and I've just finished packing. I'll be leaving in the morning.

Don't worry. I can't think of a life without you in it. Once mother meets you and sees how beautiful and what a darling you are, it will be all right.

I'm sure she wants me happy.

I've been lying here with my eyes closed touching myself—do you think it's naughty if I imagine it's you? God, I want you more than life itself.

Love me, please...please...please...

> *I'm yours forever,*
> P (The lipstick seal again.)

Buchanan picked up the fresh drink and swirled the ice around.

Let Alma go straight to hell.

Buchanan shook his head angrily and picked up the final letter.

Tear stains? Again...This time much worse.

March 15, 2002

Darling...

I never thought I'd actually think about taking my own life. I've always thought it a sin. But the thought of living without hope of having you, I can't bear the pain.

I had hoped to spare us both this misery, but now I'm left with no choice and I guess it's a just reward for my dishonesty.

I don't know how to tell you, I hate it, but I lied to you before.

I am a senior and I'll graduate just as I said, in January, but I'm only nineteen, not twenty-three like I said I was. Don't blame Inger for supporting my lie—I begged her, that first night after I'd danced with you at the Bowery and knew instantly that I must try to make you like me, take me seriously. But that's not the worst of it. The man I told you about, it's more than I said it was. I'm engaged to him. It is true that I did it because my mother pushed me into it. I certainly don't love him—he's a bore. I can't even stand the thought of him kissing me. I feel so rotten that I've deceived you and this all has become so complicated.

I don't have time to explain all the circumstances. This is a small town and the man is an important young doctor. His father practically owns the place. He's on Inger's husband's board. This engagement meant so much to my mother to get her respectability back.

Anyway, I know the only way is to not write you or call you ever again. I will never, ever forget you. The best, the secret part of me will always belong to you.

Oh, Darling, this is tearing my heart right out of me. I don't know how I can stand the thought of living another day without you.

> *I LOVE...I ADORE YOU,*
> *Desperately,*
> P (Lipstick all over the place.)

P.S. Please don't write me...or call

Saved by the bell!

So, why wasn't he cheering? And what was that hollow aching in his chest?

Of course, he understood that absolutely the best thing that could ever happen would be that she would just put him in her memory book and from time to time sneak a fond look at the amusement park photo they'd had taken together.

The terrible sense of loss he felt was a death wish, but knowing that didn't help!

He took a big swallow of the bourbon and his eye caught the telephone message slips.

PLEASE CALL. PW. And her number.

He paced for perhaps ten minutes, then freshened his drink… lightly. Tomorrow would be a hectic day. A king-sized hangover wouldn't help.

Picking up one of the tiny blue slips with the phone message, he fingered the phone.

No!

He resisted, replaced the instrument and walked to the window and opened the blinds.

Sooty rooftops and a blackened airshaft. Utica at its aesthetic best!

Above the flattened surface of the rooftop, two stories below, a pair of women's panties, looking quite new—perhaps flung by some over-enthusiastic bridegroom, or some recently besotted fraternity boy—had caught on a TV satellite dish and waved like a flag of surrender in the half-hearted breeze.

A portent for an interesting two weeks?

He'd recently despoiled a virgin. He looked at the tear-stained pages in his hand. Now she was crying her eyes out.

From now on he made a solemn vow to stick to older women.

Less than three hours since he'd tasted Cammie's lips. His hands went to his mouth.

Well, to hell with Alma, anyway.

All of a sudden he was the man of the hour. Why didn't he feel good about that?

Well? Why indeed?

The phone startled him.

"Hello?" He held his breath.

"Oh Buchanan, darling…"

"*Penny!* I just got in. My plane was late. I was about to return your call…" he lied.

"Oh, darling, I hope you haven't had time to read all those silly letters. I know you think I'm crazy. And I am, crazy over you. Anyway, I've made up my mind. We will find a way to get out of all this. You have your problems to work out, and I'll work out mine. I can't live without the hope of spending the rest of my life in your arms. Do you think I'm crazy? Oh, Buchanan, do you love me? Please tell me you love me...do you miss me?"

"Uhhhh, of course. I do. I mean, I love you. I do miss you, terribly." Buchanan took a sip of the drink and sat down, slightly breathless.

"Will you wait for me, I mean, after you get your divorce?"

"Of course, but that's still a while...she'll hardly talk to me..."

Well, it wasn't a lie.

"I showed your picture to my two roommates here at the sorority, and they are absolutely dying to meet you. I hope you don't mind. Don't get mad with me, but one of them came up with a daring idea. I mean, I know it's a long way to come and you have articles to write and a new job, but I was wondering if maybe you might come to the final dances, the first weekend in June. I'm getting a new dress. I promise, you'll be proud. There's a small motel just out of town. Very secluded. Oh, darling, just imagine..."

"But Penny? What about your fiancé? And your mother? I don't understand. You're not thinking straight. We'll both wind up being tarred and feathered and run out of town on a rail..."

"We've got this marvelous plan. I live here at the sorority house. I only see my mom occasionally during the week, sometimes weekends. You could come as the date of my roommate. Her steady is in school in Michigan to play football and she won't be asking a town boy. Elroy... Elroy Goins, my soon-to-be-forgotten fiancé is a busy doctor, very professional, very much a nerd. He's easy to get rid of..."

"But what about your roommates? Do you think this is wise? Once you tell a secret, experience teaches me that sooner or later it will be all over school, all over town."

"Oh, don't worry. Peg...and Judy, too...they're closer than my sisters. I'd trust them with my life. Well, what do you think? Do you miss me? "

"Yes." He closed his eyes and remembered.

"Desperately?"

"Yes, desperately..."

"Good, here's the number of the motel. Go ahead and call them and make a reservation. Tell them you want something on the back. Wait..." He could hear someone whispering in the background. "Ask for Room 29 or something along that row...Peg's parents stayed there Homecoming weekend. OK?"

Buchanan made a note of the numbers on the hotel notepad.

"Sure, but I'll have to get a map and try to figure this all out. From Wilmington, it's got to be an eight-hour drive, at least."

"Judging from Myrtle Beach, that's probably right. Anyway, this is a pay phone and I've attracted an audience." She giggled. "I've got to run. I'll try to call again tomorrow night between seven and eight. Will that be OK? Don't forget, call and make a reservation."

"I'll call as soon as I hang up."

"Do you love me?"

"Yes," he said. He heard a kissing sound before she put down the phone.

Buchanan mixed another drink and picked up the phone and called the motel to make the reservation. "Room 29 will be no problem, sir. Mail us a check for ninety dollars and fifty-three cents to secure the first night and we'll send you a confirmation." The man hung up.

Buchanan walked to the mirror and spoke to the image staring back, "You've got to be crazy as a fucking loon..."

The next night and the night after that and again every night until the following Friday, he'd waited vainly in his room hoping for her call.

Cammie called almost every night. Despite his guilt, he thanked his stars for that.

The final pink envelope was postmarked Tuesday morning.

Tear stains again.

March 17, 2002, Monday. 11:30 PM

Dearest Darling, darling, darling,
 Your sunburned cheeks,
 My windblown hair...
 Rainy days and Sundays,
 Was it all a lovely dream?
 Were our footprints in the sand?
 I looked but I can't find them there.
 Did you really hold my hand?
 Mine seem so empty now.
 Did you really kiss me?
 Did it really happen?
 Did you ever love me?
 Rainy days and Sundays,
 Give them back to me.
 There's too much to explain and I can't make sense out of any of it. I'm just not strong enough...
 I will never forget you. I will adore you always.
 Don't hate me too much.
       Love, all of it, always, P

He dropped the page to the desk top and fixed himself a stiff drink and drank it down. From his wallet he slipped out the picture she'd sent.

Buchanan hung his head and shook as the tears came down.

Afterwards, he wasn't sure what the tears were all about. But the letter left him with an aching emptiness he was sure he could never fill.

He hung around the room again for several evenings. Cammie called several times—by now he'd lost count.

Penny never called again.

Chapter Forty-four

ALMA WAS FURIOUS. If Buck thought that by trying to wear her down, she'd just give right in to him, he had another think coming. Now that, finally, she had managed to escape from North Carolina, she had no intention of moving away from her sisters again.

Men were all alike.

As the youngest of her mother's ten children, all her life Alma had worn hand-me-downs and watched her selfish, domineering alcoholic father live the lush country club life while her passive mother and Alma's five older brothers and four older sisters took meager crumbs left over from his self-centered extravagances as the charismatic chief executive of a local printing company.

While Buchanan's drinking had yet to become alcoholic, just like her father—with no thought to his wife and sons—in his high-flown position, the charming, snobbish Buck Forbes traveled all over, entertaining the pompous hierarchy of the elitist Southern medical academia.

To begin with, it had been in a moment of extreme weakness that Alma had allowed herself to be seduced by the prospect of owning that dazzling dream house and had given in to agreeing to move when Buck had been offered the promotion to Raleigh. Then, in the cruelest betrayal of all, Buck suddenly refused to continue her harmless little charge accounts at the local supermarket pharmacies, and she'd found herself having to live like white trash in that fancy neighborhood where all her friends drove brand new Lexus SUVs and shopped at The Gap.

Now that she had managed to restore herself and her sons to their Virginia roots, she'd rot in hell before Buchanan Forbes imposed his selfish ways on her again.

She'd just come off a rather lucrative private case last evening and, all things considered, with Buck's sympathetic parents to take care of the kids, she was doing quite nicely without him.

But, she had to admit, this most recent case had been a particularly distressing one.

It had made quite a devastating psychological impact upon her.

Norma Randall—Norma Jenkins now—had been in her graduating class in high school and, even though they had not been close friends, it had been morbidly sobering to have to watch her die of an insidious cancer which had metastasized throughout her entire body like a raging whirlwind.

It had left Alma with a terrible foreboding.

To see from Norma's chart that the disease had remained asymptomatic until a scant two months ago when it first signaled its presence with an abnormal PAP smear was even more disturbing. Norma Randall Jenkins had had PAP smears regular as clockwork, once a year, every year for the previous five years.

Dead two months before her thirty-sixth birthday.

When Alma first accepted the case three weeks ago, she had been procrastinating overlong on having her own annual PAP done because of having to move the kids from Raleigh. Her checkup had lingered undone, almost three months overdue. The next morning she had rushed headlong to her gynecologist, Ogden Branch, and scheduled a PAP.

Last night, Norma finally died near the end of Alma's regular evening shift and Alma had sadly watched her poor husband lead his three young children quietly out of the room.

As a consequence, Alma had come home depressed and had passed a rather restless night.

Originally, she had planned to spend this particular Saturday at the hospital staff picnic with the kids. But at the last minute, Nan and Grandad had asked if they could take the boys on an excursion up on the Blue Ridge Parkway.

Alma had left it up to the kids, and Granddad and the Parkway won by a unanimous vote.

Just after breakfast—after waving to the Chevy van full of still sleepy but excited boys—she'd gone up and showered. Now, dressed in casual clothes, she was free for the entire day.

Then Buchanan called and spoiled everything.

"Alma, the boys will love the beach. Why won't you just come and take a peek? The beach would be a great place to raise the kids," he started in with his same tiresome plea for her to come down and take a look at Wilmington.

"Forget the beach...the kids just voted to go to the mountains with their grandparents, thank you very much..." she'd fired back and slammed down the phone.

Just like her father, Buchanan thought only of himself. Still fuming, she headed into town to buy some picnic food at the deli.

By the time she started up the narrow, switch-back road to the public park near the tacky ostentatious neon star at the top of Mill Mountain, her anger had almost vanished.

The idea of having the day to herself was secretly exhilarating.

Alma loved her kids, but with her newfound independence had come an increasing self-awareness. Lately, she had started to take better care of herself.

When she stepped on the scales this morning after her shower, she had noted with satisfaction that she had lost another pound. Almost a pound a day since she had consciously begun trying to limit her diet after Mike Gentry had made those snide remarks about her weight.

Talk about the pot calling the kettle black?

Mike was getting just the trace of a roll himself.

Why was it that men could let themselves go to pot and still expect women to keep their shape? What woman wanted to have some old walrus huffing and puffing on top of her in bed?

Grudgingly, she admitted that his physique was one of the few things she couldn't fault Buchanan for. He had the build of an athlete. He still did twisting somersaults off the high board at the swim club. And, reluctantly, she admitted he had always been a star in bed. Sometimes, ever more frequently now—especially late at night—she'd lie in the dark and touch herself and wistfully recall that he'd always known how to please her there.

But sex wasn't everything. And besides, if, ultimately, Buchanan decided to abandon her in his steadfast refusal to move back home, the world was full of desirable men.

As she rounded the final curve of the twisting road up Mill Mountain and passed through the gates to the park, she looked for Gentry's jaunty little red British sports car in the overcrowded parking area. Alma wanted to make certain the arrogant SOB saw her in the form-fitting stretch jeans she'd carefully purchased for the occasion.

No sign of him...

Still anxiously trying to locate his car, she pulled in under a grove of giant oaks. She gathered her picnic basket and headed for the large crowd of nurses and doctors variously engaged in volleyball and horseshoes and shuffleboard and pushing kids in swings.

"Alma Forbes, I thought you'd bring your kids." Startled, Alma turned, completely unprepared to hear Mike Gentry's voice behind her.

"Michael, hello, I didn't see your car…" She moved under the shelter and deposited her basket with the ladies who were supervising the setting out of the food.

"It's over there." He pointed to a new yellow Chrysler Sebring convertible parked comfortably away from the others in the lot. "It's new. You like it?"

"Of course. It's very…it's very, very you. But why so far away?"

"See how the trees are trying to pop their leaves? I didn't want the tree sap to ruin the paint. But where are your kids? Lil said you planned on bringing them."

"They took a vote and decided they'd rather be with their grandparents—mamas and daddies are a bore compared to grandparents. Anyway, I'm certainly not complaining. It's nice to have a day all to myself."

"Well, you're looking quite fit. Those jeans are something else. Lost a little weight, I see."

He made as to give her behind a pat but she skipped back out of the way.

"Michael! Don't you dare," she snapped and blushed.

"Oh, come on…just a little one, for old times' sake. It looks so nice I think it's a waste not to give it a little pat."

"Damn you, Michael. I told you I didn't want to be included in the gossip around this place," she fumed. But secretly she felt a flush of pleasure that he'd noticed.

"Well, anyway, if you don't mind my saying so, your ass looks great."

"Hush now. Just get away from me if you're just out to try to embarrass me. Besides, you'll have to excuse me. I see Sylvia from Ogden Branch's office. I want to see about my PAP."

"Your PAP? Why don't you let me do your smear? After years of practice, I've perfected a new technique."

"What on earth are you talking about now? Since when do cardiologists know anything about PAP smears?" She turned, momentarily confused.

"Well, I wasn't always a cardiologist. Besides, gynecology has always been sort of a sub-specialty of mine. My method is quite innovative. Most of my patients love it."

"Oh, come on. What's so great about what you do?"

"I collect the specimen with my tongue." He threw back his head and roared with laughter.

"You're disgusting." Alma stepped back and stared at him.

"Don't knock it unless you've tried it." She heard him still laughing as she turned and walked away, color creeping up her neck.

"Sylvia, I'm glad to catch you here," Alma called as she approached the corpulent young woman dutifully pushing an equally chubby little girl in the baby swings.

"Oh, hi, Alma. How are you? Your PAP came back. I tried to call you yesterday, but got no answer. Did you see Ogden? He was over by the horseshoe pit." She looked over her shoulder in the direction of the horseshoe players.

Alma turned. "Oh, yeah, I see him." Alma nodded. "It was OK, wasn't it...the PAP, I mean."

"Well, it was a Class Two, but there's not actually all that much to be alarmed about. Some hyperplasia, a few slightly abnormal cells. He wants you to come back after your next period. Why don't you go grab him? I don't think it's anything to fret about."

"Sure. Thanks. See you later," Alma called absently. Feeling a sudden chill, she started numbly in the direction of the silver-haired doctor watching the horseshoe players.

"Alma, what a nice surprise. Did Sylvia get you yesterday?" Branch gave her a big hug.

"No, but I just talked to her. What's all this about my PAP?"

"Nothing particularly alarming, but I'm the cautious type. Call and schedule an appointment for a repeat after your next period. Just routine...better safe than sorry. OK?"

"Sure." Alma felt as if her knees would give way, remembering poor Norma Randall.

Car-ci-no-ma...the word rattled in her head like the echo in a tomb.

Branch caught her reaction and took her elbow. "There's really nothing to worry about. It's not that unusual to see a bit of hyperplasia. If we did a smear every month on every patient, probably seventy-five percent would show at Class Two on occasion."

"I'll check with Sylvia in a couple of weeks." She tried to smile but she'd gone suddenly icy cold. Turning blindly away, she headed in no particular direction.

Cancer...

Suddenly numb with fear, Alma stumbled away from the crowd, trying to gather herself.

Intellectually, she knew what Ogden said was true. But too much had been going on in her life lately. Until this moment she'd had no idea just how vulnerable she'd become.

Moving aimlessly, she followed a path around the crest of the mountaintop toward the high skeletal framework of the shabby fluorescent star, towering above the trees.

In the daylight, the star reminded her of the superstructure of an electric generating substation...or some of the construction around the oil refineries she'd seen when Buchanan was in OCS out in southern Oklahoma...or a movie set from a story about a deserted space station.

Carcinoma. The wasted face of her dead classmate Norma Randall haunted her.

A chilly trickle of perspiration slid down her spine.

Virtually catatonic with fear, she moved across the catwalk to the observation platform at the base of the star and stood at the rail overlooking the serene panorama of the city. Before her, the Roanoke River valley stretched westward to the lavender mountains, ghostly in the distant haze.

"Alma, I'm sorry, babe. I didn't mean to run you off." She jumped at Michael's voice. He had come up behind her without a sound. "Look, I want to apologize. What I said back there was totally inappropriate. There's this terribly adolescent streak in me. I guess I'll just never grow up. I'm sorry. I truly am."

Shading her eyes against the brilliant midday sun, Alma could see Michael silhouetted at the top of the catwalk, against the high, almost colorless sky. For an instant, she remembered how he'd looked, standing underneath the goal posts when she'd dated him in high school.

"Here. Brought you a little something against the chill." He held out a large Coca-Cola cup. "I hope I haven't spoiled your day. C'mon, drink this. It'll put some music back into your soul." He walked across the catwalk and the cup with a boyish grin.

"What's in that?" She eyed him suspiciously.

Michael really was good-looking. Actually, he looked rather dashing in the bright red self-belted golf slacks. Neat and trim... actually not fat at all.

"Relax. Just trust me." He leaned forward with the cup.

Tentatively she took the cup and sipped. "Vodka? Collins? Thanks, not bad."

"It's the very least I could do."

She sipped the drink and told him about the patient who'd died and the news of her own abnormal PAP.

"I remember Norma, a rather shy, awkward sort of girl. I had no idea."

"It's not all your fault. How could you possibly know?"

"It seems that I'm always putting my foot in it. I'm sorry, I really am. Why don't we walk on back? They'll be serving food by now."

"You go ahead. I've lost my appetite. I think I'll walk around the other way and just quietly slip on off. I was thinking I might treat myself to lunch at Hotel Roanoke..." She looked at her watch. "It's not yet one. Lunchtime on Saturday isn't usually such a mob scene. I have a phone in my car. I can call just to be on the safe side."

"I don't think you ought to be by yourself in such a depressing state of mind. Why don't you let lunch be my treat? After all, we're old friends. And that dining room is the most respectable public place in the whole of southwest Virginia..."

"No. Absolutely not. Being seen at the dining room of Hotel Roanoke would be all right, but if we left here together, even separately in our own cars..." Alma paused and shrugged. "Face it, Michael, you've got a rather cavalier reputation. Can't you just imagine what people would do with that? I'm a respectable married woman. I can't afford the talk."

"Well, yes, but..."

"No buts. I'm sorry. Surely you can understand..." She turned and started walking back the other way. "Thanks for the drink. I'm feeling better already."

Alma made her way back to the car and left without bothering to make the call. The odds were really in her favor on getting a table on Saturday after one.

Her intuition was on target. The maitre'd showed her to a quiet window table in the back of the huge circular room. She ordered a champagne cocktail and a copy of *The Roanoke Times*. Sipping the wine, she thumbed through the paper and found the obituaries.

Norma Randall Jenkins

She scanned the notice intently.

Born, Melas, Virginia, June 1966
Died, Roanoke, Virginia, March, 27, 2002.
Graduated Melas High School 1984. Valedictorian.

Valedictorian!
She'd forgotten that Norma had been bright but not very popular in high school. Norma had been an orphanage girl.
Alma neatly folded the paper and put it aside.
Norma Randall. So little time.
Alma took the corner of her napkin and wiped away a single tear.
Enough! Straightening, she took another sip of wine and began to

idly browse the menu, recalling the times she'd been here with Buck.

Better times…golden days.

"Alma Forbes. I thought I recognized you. What a nice surprise…" She looked up with a start. Michael stood smiling innocently, holding a frosted mug of draft beer. "Mind if I sit down?"

"I don't see why not." She raised her shoulders with an exasperated shrug.

"You seemed so depressed back there. Besides, I wanted to prove I can be a gentleman."

"Won't you ever learn that sometimes 'no' just means 'NO?'"

"I can't stand to hear the word, not if I really want something that badly. I'd still like to put a gentle pat on your cute behind…"

She smiled, a little pleased now that she was out of public view. "You can't always have everything you want, you know?"

"Maybe not, but nothing ventured, nothing gained. Life's too short and our opportunities are too few." He gave her hand a little pat. "Life ain't no dress rehearsal…"

Alma looked out the window at the distant hazy mountains behind the downtown skyline.

No dress rehearsal? She wondered what Norma Randall would have said to that three months ago, when she was making plans for her summer vacation, or her next birthday? Now Norma Randall Jenkins was just another obituary in the morning paper.

"Michael, for once in your carefree life, you just might have said something quite profound…."

Chapter Forty-five

WHEN HE FINALLY UNLOADED the last of his things from the new company car, Buchanan found the box containing all the Stribol forms and reports he'd become familiar with in Utica and rummaged through the box until he found his daily desk calendar and located the date: Saturday, March 30.

He checked his watch. Not yet noon.

Everywhere he looked, the tiny apartment was piled high with a disordered array of the personal belongings he'd brought with him from Raleigh.

Locating his little cooler, he opened a beer.

His entire life—thirty-five years—reduced to what he could pack inside a shiny, new-smelling, oyster white Buick sedan.

Out with the old, in with the new. Buchanan found the thought comforting, somehow.

There was an implied freedom represented here. A new simplicity of life he found exciting.

But, for the moment, there was work to be done. By the bed was a small mountain of brown corrugated Stribol sample cartons that had been delivered while he was in Utica. With the kindly cooperation of Mrs. Guest, the shipment had been neatly stacked by the delivery man.

Conservatively, the ten cartons contained at least a quarter-million dollars worth of antibiotic samples at wholesale value. Very expensive stuff.

When he'd arrived in Raleigh late yesterday afternoon, he had wasted no time in getting his things packed. His phone conversations with Alma while he'd been in Utica had been exasperating.

She was unrelenting in her determination to stay in Virginia.

Thursday, the night before he left Utica, he asked if she intended to divorce him.

She howled. Tearfully, she accused him of desertion…irresponsibility…the whole nine yards. She hadn't missed much. She completely overlooked the fact that it had been her who had asked him the same question only the night before.

Good old Alma, she always had him—and her father—to blame for all her unhappiness.

At least she had conceded his point that the house in Raleigh was half-hers.

And, with that point won, she grudgingly agreed that she would consider bringing the boys back down for the summer, to try to help sell the place. From bitter experience, both of them knew that houses that were occupied and cared for had a better chance of selling.

And, as much as it hurt him to admit it, from all he could tell on the phone, the boys had made a good adjustment. Kids were resilient. They adjusted much better than most adults.

Tiring of his unhappy reverie, he finished off the beer and rolled up his sleeves.

When he finally came in from unpacking and moving the contents of the last of the sample boxes to the trunk of his car, Buchanan looked at his watch: 3:30.

He glanced around. Everything neatly stored and arranged. Not that there was all that much of it. Such as it was, it was home sweet home.

Almost. He'd saved the final touch for last.

He walked into the kitchen and found the hammer he'd placed in the drawer with his sketchy assortment of tools and located a picture hook.

Removing the row of three cheap Wal-Mart seashell prints from the wall over the sofa, he eyeballed the space and drew a careful bead on the center and lightly tapped in the nail that secured the picture hook.

From the bed, he picked up a massive casein watercolor. The stark scene dramatically depicted a powerfully-muscled black man, naked from the waist, swinging a huge hammer at a rail spike under a high, unrelenting sun. The red-clay delta land in the foreground was baked and cracked and the rails ran across the bleak landscape and disappeared into infinity. A distant stand of pines stood against the yellow-white sky and merged indistinctly with a horizon blurred by the harsh sun. In the background, perhaps two hundred yards behind the powerful figure, was a crew of gandy dancers carrying rails and swinging hammers. In the middle-distance the shadowy figure of a guard stood menacingly cradling a shotgun in the crook of his elbow.

This was the only thing he had painted since he'd given up trying to make it as an artist, six months after he'd gotten home from the Persian Gulf.

Eleven years was a long time between paintings.

He'd done this painting three months ago in a wild, frantic outburst of creative energy one January night when Alma had been laid low with flu. He had spent the dreadful, cold, rainy, thoroughly inhospitable day trying desperately to entertain his four restless little boys.

Verging on insanity, he had been rummaging in the garage looking for the dart board when he had run across the long-forgotten scrap of pressed white fiber board the builder had left behind. Earlier he had been playing *John Henry* and *Frankie and Johnny* and *Water Boy* and some other old Leadbelly chain gang songs on the guitar and the inspiration had seized him.

Excited by a sudden flight of fancy, he had piled the boys into the car and gone to the art store in the shopping center and bought six tubes of casein watercolors to make his palette.

"Yellow. Cobalt Blue. Red. Burnt Sienna. Lamp Black...and a giant tube of White, gotta have lots and lots of white." At the paint store he held them up, and named them, one-by-one like an art teacher with a class of beginners from the Junior League.

Sables and bristles...points and chisel ends...carefully, he selected a fistful of brushes. He handed it all to the clerk to put in a bag.

At the neighboring hardware, he bought a white enamel butcher tray to use as a palette.

Before they returned home, he stopped at the Food Lion and purchased a big tub of fried chicken, thick, greasy home fries and enough yucky fruit drinks and ice cream for an army.

Paper plates, napkins and cups to go around.

Back home, he had propped the large white fiberboard atop a chest-high bookcase, arranged the kids with TV trays and spread their food before them like a picnic on the floor of the downstairs playroom. He filled several canning jars with clean water and placed them near at hand.

Stage set, the high adventure had begun.

"What's the tray for, Daddy?"

"To mix the paint."

"What'cha gonna draw, Daddy?"

"How 'bout John Henry working on the railroad?"

"Neat-o, just like the song," Granger enthused.

"Well, I thought we might change things around a bit, use our imagination." He busied himself making light charcoal strokes to set the perspective of the rails and block the giant figure in.

"He looks like Superman, Daddy..."

"Are you gonna do Superman, Daddy?"

"John Henry was a kind of Superman, Garrett."

"Shut up, Garrett, let Daddy work!"

"What's all that yellow for, Daddy?"

"The sky..."

"But sky's blue, I never saw a yellow sky..."

"Hush up, Garrett, just watch, will ya..."

"This is like on a hot day, Garrett. Haven't you ever thought the sky felt yellow?"

"Hmm... Can I have some more Coke, Daddy?"

"I'll get it. Just keep on working, Pop..."

"What's the hole in the sky for, Daddy?"

"It's the sun."

"A white sun?"

"Maybe, we'll see..."

"Why didn't ya get any green, Daddy? A yellow sky's OK, but what about them trees?" Little Garrett was spellbound.

"Those trees, Garrett," Granger corrected.

"We'll mix blue and yellow to make green, Garrett. I have all the colors right here that I need to make any color you can think of. What I don't have in the tubes, I make by just mixing the others together. I really don't need this." He squeezed out a bit of the burnt sienna. "But it's hard to mix and get just right..."

"You mean brown, Daddy?"

"No, Garrett, it says Burnt Sienna." Granger read the label.

"What a dumb name. Why not just say brown, Daddy?" Greg, the seven-year-old, chimed in.

"Beats the devil outta me, Greg."

"Mama won't let us say 'devil,' Daddy," Grayson giggled.

"Hhmm…" He had struggled to surpress a smile.

"How can you make brown, Daddy?" Greg was enthralled.

"Just mix red and green. Then, depending on what shade, add a trifle yellow. See?"

"Gosh…"

"That's a big hammer…"

"Why's that man got a gun?"

"They're prisoners. Remember the chain gang song?"

"Who're all those other men, Daddy?"

"Gandy dancers. They carry the rails and put them in place…"

"Are they prisoners, too?"

He'd never seen that raving cub pack so well-behaved as they watched him work that night.

And he had worked like a demon, a man possessed.

A miracle all around.

All the intervening years of not having a brush in his hands seemed to have somehow, in some latently mysterious kinetic way, refined and matured his talent. He understood now that it had been because he had been so stifled with the fear of failure when he was younger, fresh out of school and trying to make a living doing layouts and uninspiring wash drawings of bacon packages and bean cans for the local supermarket chain.

Now he picked up the unframed painting and lovingly hung it on the hook and stood back to admire his handiwork. The agony of tortured effort twisted on the mouth of the heroic black man. Buchanan could almost hear his grunt, and feel his breath…

And hear his hammer ring.

Really excellent. *No, great!*

Even better than he remembered.

That he might reach this level again, he had no doubt. It was an exhilarating thought.

That rainy night had been a defining experience, a catharsis. Yet, he'd felt no strong urge to rush right out and repeat the exercise.

It had been a special moment. But, for the time being it had been enough.

Buchanan knew this painting would surely be hung if he entered it in a juried show. But he didn't want to be an artist anymore. That part of his life was over. Still, looking at it now, he couldn't help but wish Milton Hull, his old professor, could see it. It would knock his former teacher's eyeballs out.

He suddenly realized fear of failure no longer haunted him.

Free at last.

"Do us another picture, Daddy…" his sons had often begged him since.

This wouldn't be the end, he knew. He'd brought his paints with him. They were carefully stored in the enamel butcher tray above the refrigerator in the tiny kitchen.

Someday soon, he resolved to try his hand again. A portrait maybe…a woman, someone with a face that showed a lot of character. Or, maybe he'd try his hand at something that would capture the textures of the beach…the vagrant reverie pleased him.

But, now—for the moment at least—writing was the new frontier.

He opened another beer and took his guitar from the case and ran up the strings.

"Softly, I will leave you softly…"

His thoughts suddenly wandered to Penny and his chest ached with loneliness.

THWONNNGGG! With an outburst of anguish, he struck a loud discordant chord.

Buchanan put the guitar down, finished off the contents of the beer can and went into the kitchen and tossed it into the garbage.

All at once he felt exhausted.

He walked back in and fell across the bed.

Lying there looking at the meager space of the tiny apartment, he wondered fleetingly if he should risk moving his stash of contraband cash…

His thoughts faded into sleep.

Chapter Forty-six

BAREFOOT, WEARING CUTOFFS and a faded madras shirt, Maggie leaned on the bar at the Wit's End and pushed her glass across to Isis.

The tastefully dressed woman behind the bar took the empty, dropped it in the dishwater, filled a fresh glass and passed it back to her. "On the house. How's your love life? I haven't seen Mr. Wonderful around for quite a while now."

"Lewis? Oh, he still comes and goes. Flew in Monday and back out at the crack of dawn."

"Men are like hummingbirds, flittin' about, dipping their magic wands. How's the house remodeling coming?"

"I had some trouble getting started. But that's all settled now." Maggie knew that word was all over the beach that Lewis had held up the contractor's check for his signature. But she'd gotten that matter cleared up Monday after they'd killed a bottle of Scotch and eventually wound up in bed.

The remodeling account was totally under her control now. It didn't bother her that Lewis insisted the deed to the house was still held jointly. She knew she was a long way from breaking completely free. Besides, she'd won. All the joint ownership did was prevent her from selling it without his consent. All she wanted was to get it fixed up so she could move in and get out from under her mother's control.

She certainly had no thought to ever sell it. It would be a showplace. She'd worry about control later.

Maggie picked up her sketchpad and a stick of charcoal and started sketching Isis. "What're you so dressed up for?" she asked as she rapidly put lines down on the paper.

"Nothing special, actually. It's Friday. Thought I might go by that party up at the north end of the beach a little later."

"Where's that?"

"You know, that 'Sugarshack' those hospital types keep. You know. Ted Harper. He comes in here sometimes after work. Married, but has a roving eye."

"All the cute ones are married and have roving eyes. I think every one of those hospital dudes are married. That place is just a meat market."

"So what's wrong with that? When did you get religion? Damn, Maggie, you used to be a lot of fun until Lewis Warrant came around. If you ain't tried it, don't knock it. If you're really through with him, why don't you come along?"

"Neah. With this kinda of weather there oughta be a good weekend beach crowd. I thought I might do some sketches when the action picks up. I could use the money."

"Well, you could come later. That place runs wide open 'til God knows when. Come on, why not check it out?"

"Maybe later. Who knows? Mr. Right might come walking in and take me away from all this."

Isis looked at the Pabst Blue Ribbon clock over the bar. "Seven-seventeen. I gotta stay here 'til Jimbo shows—he's in love again. And Tory's runnin' late. He's gonna be a daddy."

"No kidding? Well, congratulations." Maggie beamed.

Jimbo was the regular bartender. Tory was Isis' only son, by her second, or maybe it was her first, husband. Maggie never could keep 'em straight.

"Me, a grandmother, at thirty-six. Can you believe it?"

"You're a lucky woman, Isis." Maggie smiled. *She believed the grandmother part but the part about being thirty-six? Never.*

"Didja hear? I'm gonna book some 'names' in the other room during the summer. Sixties Revival. Try to attract the country club clientele."

"Sixties Revival? Names? Like who, for instance?"

"Josh White, Jr. He's the first, and let's see…" Isis fumbled around under the counter near the cash register and came up with a legal pad. She waved it in Maggie's direction. "Here's the list of bookings. Printer picked it up yesterday. Josh White Jr., Saturday night, June sixth."

"No kidding? Who else?"

"We're negotiating to get Arlo Guthrie or Gordon Lightfoot, July Fourth. Nanci Griffith for Labor Day…" Isis read the list.

"You're really gonna make The Wit into a first-class joint. Be like Key West without the gays."

"Yeah, I can't argue. Say, there's this new guy who was in here earlier and grabbed a hamburger. Just moved on the beach a few weeks back. Been dropping by evenings to play guitar. Tallish and lanky…crew cut. Kinda cute. Even in jeans, he's a trifle preppy. Drives a brand new Buick. Said he might be back later."

"What's he do?"

"Works for some drug company. Said he knew Ted Harper. I asked him if he was going to be at Ted's tonight. Said he hadn't planned on it. I couldn't figure him out. He seemed kinda preoccupied or something. Name's Buchanan Forbes. Sorta standoffish."

Maggie pushed the sketch over to Isis. "What'cha think?"

"You got a nice touch, Magpie." Maggie had graciously left out a wrinkle or two.

Isis turned to some customers on the opposite side of the oval bar. "Ain't that good? Look, you oughta let her do you. Twenty bucks…"

She took it down to the end of the bar and passed it around. When she came back Isis winked. "I oughta get a commission."

"Well, I draw a crowd and people usually drink…" Maggie waved at some of her framed sketches of celebrities, former Azalea Queens and pro golfers that Isis had hung on the walls on both sides of the island bar.

"I'm just teasing…"

"About this new guy, Buck. Is he married?"

"Well, he didn't have on a ring. And he's living by himself. Not much of a talker. Just wolfed down a hamburger and a beer and said he had to go to the post office to mail some letters."

One of the couples at the end of the bar came over. The girl waved the sketch at Maggie. "Can you do me?"

"Sure."

"Twenty bucks?"

"Sure. If your friends want theirs done too, I'll do you for fifteen dollars."

"OK. But don't tell 'em. They'd be mad if they found out I hustled 'em. OK?"

"Sure, our secret. C'mon over here." Maggie led the pair to a group of small tables near the well-lighted back room with the pool table.

She posed the girl's head just right and started to work.

Within minutes, Maggie had gathered a small crowd. By ten 'til eight she'd finished the second sketch and was waiting while two women decided who was next.

Isis brought Maggie another beer. "I'm cutting outta here soon as Jimbo shows. By the way, he's back…"

"Huh?"

"You know, the new one, the guy I told you about. Buck something. He's over there at the bar, been watching you. He came over here once and looked over your shoulder, looked at all your stuff hanging on the walls. Said you weren't bad…said you worked a trifle tight for his taste…that you needed a looser hand but you'd be fabulous when you learned to trust your eye."

Maggie sneaked a look.

"Everybody wants to be a frigging critic. Sounds sorta swishy to me."

"Oh, calm down. I think he likes you. Said you reminded him of that old-timey actress, Dorothy McGuire…"

"Malone…" Maggie corrected.

"Oh, yeah. How'ja'know? You hear him all the way over here?"

"I've heard it before." Maggie looked up and caught another peek at this Buck, sitting at the near end of the bar. He smiled a vague smile as his gaze moved on past her.

Not bad, if you liked the over-thirty All-American boy.

"Who's next?" Maggie shrugged and picked up a charcoal.

When Maggie looked up again, it was 10:45.

"Thanks." She took a fifty dollar bill from the guy she'd just sketched. She stood to make change.

"Keep it…" He waved it off.

"Well, thanks, again."

"This is great, really great…" The man went away looking at the sketch, admiringly.

Maggie stretched again. Enough was enough.

She stowed her stuff in the canvas tote and took it over to the bar and asked Jimbo to stick it away for safekeeping.

Jimbo gave her a fresh beer and she walked back to where they were shooting pool. In the big dark annex to the left where the jukebox and all the booths were, she could hear a guitar. Idly she watched the pool players and dismissed them as real amateurs.

After a while she poked her head into the darkness of the big room and waited while her eyes adjusted to the light and the smoke, trying to make out who was playing the guitar. A narrow shaft of light from the other door nearer the bar slashed a rectangular pattern across the floor. When her eyes finally adjusted, she saw Tory and the new guy together at a table deep in the shadows. There was a small crowd around them.

The new guy wasn't Chet Atkins or Pat Metheny, but, then, who was?

Tory saw her and waved her back to join them.

She shook her head.

He waved again but she still resisted, feeling a strong resentment for the arrogant way this jerk Buck had criticized her work. Who did he think he was, anyway?

She turned and went in by the pool table. Standing by the bar, Goose Mapes waved.

"Shoot ya for dollar, get us dibs on the table..." The Goose called in a loud voice. He was already half in a bag.

Maggie waved back and went over to pick out her cue while the two clowns took turns screwing up easy shots on the eight ball.

At this rate, they'd be all night.

"Hi, Shoog. Looking good. Jimbo said they wore you out tonight. How'd ya do?" The Goose's eyes were crossed. He reeked of pot.

"Did eight or nine, I think. A couple of 'em tipped me a buck or so extra. A trifle over two bills. Not bad for a night's work and I didn't even have to drop my drawers."

"C'mon, let me get some of my money back." He grabbed a cue.

"Maggie..." Tory grabbed her arm. "C'mon in here. I want ya' to meet Buck Forbes."

"The Goose 'n me are gonna shoot pool. Maybe later, OK?"

"Neah, c'mon now. C'mon, Goose, you too. This guy's just moved here from Raleigh. He's writing a piece about Sharkey Mallone for a big-time newspaper syndicate..."

"No shit?" Goose gave his cue to one of the college kids. "He knows Sharkey Mallone?"

"Yeah, no shit. C'mon Mag..." Tory took her cue and stuck it in the corner pocket of the table. "What's the matter with you, anyway?"

"Nothing, Tory, but your mama said this cat worked for a drug company. What's all this writing crap? You sure he ain't bullshittin' you?"

"Trust me. He's doing a big piece on Sharkey Mallone. Over a hundred newspapers…"

"So? What's the big deal?" Grumbling, Maggie followed him through the door.

Chapter Forty-seven

IT WAS ALREADY AFTER TEN when Cammie called Nina Trask in New York. Nina had been her roommate at Duke. "Nina, I know it's late, but I need a favor. Anybody using your Wrightsville Beach place nowadays, like the end of May?"

"No. Why? You need a place?"

"Uh huh…Saturday to Sunday—May eighteenth to twenty-sixth."

"Are we talking about you? You personally, I mean?"

"Yes. Me, personally…"

"Well, sure, you know it's OK. I've offered but you never took me up before. God knows I owe you. How many times have I used your place at Pawley's? But I'm curious, why now?"

"Why not now?"

"You taking James Erwin and the girls?"

"No, just me. I want some time to myself. I deserve it."

"Cam, is everything OK? I mean you're all right, aren't you?" Nina betrayed concern.

"Oh sure, nothing like that. I just decided to take some time to smell the roses. I'm not getting any younger. I'll be forty-three May eighteenth, you know?"

"Ah-hah! So, that's it? So? Why don't you drag that stuffed shirt husband with you, have a second honeymoon?"

"Are you kidding? I can't take James anywhere. Even if he wanted to come along, he'd be on the phone the minute he found out. Before we even got here, we'd have a full social calendar. He's president-elect of the American College. There'd be dinner with some damn cardiologist from the good old days at PGH or MCV every night. That's part of what I'm running away from. If I took the girls and left him, it'd be six months before he'd realize we were gone."

"That's men for you. They're all bloody boors if you ask me. All they know is golf or the stock market. During the courtship, it's candlelight and wine…after the honeymoon, wham, bam, thank you, ma'am."

"That's James Erwin to a tee. But not all of 'em are like that, I assure you. There are still men out there who read books and love music and love their kids—and would love their women too, if they had the right one. Trouble is, I was too busy trying to help my daddy get over the disappointment he didn't have a son. I was too intent on Duke and Harvard Law. Jeez, I should've been out learning all about life. Maybe then I'd have found me a real man."

"Cammie? Are you going through the change? Sounds like you've been reading too much Anne Rivers Siddons. Listen, come up here and spend that week with me, if you're looking to have your fill of fancy-talking men. For women our age, the time is past for finding a real man. If they ain't already married with a zillion kids, then they're still being wet-nursed by their mamas. Last time I found a real winner, he was being held hostage by a dominating bitch who treated him and the kids like shit, took the Rolls and moved into the house on County Line Road in Palm Beach."

"How well I know, and, still, there's always hope. Some of 'em do get divorces…"

"If they do, the bitch strips 'em of everything they have and takes a second mortgage on the rest of their lives with child support."

"Well, that would be OK with me. I mean, he knows money would never be a problem."

Silence.

"He? Cammie? Who *he?*"

"Wait now! Don't jump to any conclusions…"

"What the hell's going on? You looking to shack up? Is that what this is all about?"

"No, nothing like that. You know me better. Besides…"

"C'mon, don't try to shit me. This is your ol' roomy, baby." Nina's voice took on that familiar tone of whispered intimacy. Cammie remembered the long secret-sharing nights in the sorority house. Nina had four brothers. She was the only girl in the Trask clan. Since college, they had remained like sisters. "C'mon 'fess up. You're having an affair? Who is he?"

"Well, I do know someone, just like you said. Wife's a selfish bitch, took the kids to Virginia. He moved to the beach. But it's not like you think. We're just friends…pals…confidantes…He doesn't have the slightest clue that I'm a woman."

"God, Cam! This guy's got you really hung up. It's in your voice. You got it bad, hon."

"No. But I am thinking too much about him lately. I just wish that a lot of things were different, Nina." There was an ache in her throat. She hadn't meant for this to turn out this way.

"Does he live at Wrightsville? God, I know everyone. Who is he?"

"You wouldn't know him. He just moved there from Raleigh. Look, Nina, let's just let it be, OK? I wish I hadn't..."

"C'mon, hon, it's OK. You don't have to tell me anything you don't want to. Anyway, the cottage is yours. Take a year, take as long as you want. Enjoy. I'll have Roxy Guest get someone to go dust and make sure the refrigerator doesn't need defrosting. Call her at Harbor Realty. Wait a minute...." She left the line, then came back on and gave Cammie Roxy's number. "Just call. Roxy will arrange to get you the key, OK?"

"OK. And Nina, thanks."

"Nada, just one thing."

"What?"

"Go for it."

Chapter Forty-eight

BY THE TIME ISIS got to the Sugarshack, the party was swinging. Jaynie Lockfaw saw her come in and took her back to the kitchen to fix a drink.

"Jaynie, the phone in the back bedroom's for you." The local nympho Betty Sue Willis sniffed unhappily as she came out of the back bedroom trying to straighten her skirt and smooth her hair. Some young Army guy that Isis didn't know followed Betty Sue down the darkened hall, trying to zip his fly. "Doesn't anybody ever hear the frigging phone out here?"

"Well, it's kinda noisy out here sometimes..."

"Having a phone in the bedroom's a loser, a real pain," Betty Sue grumbled, trying to button her blouse.

"Was it the hospital? I'm not on call."

"Somebody named Margaret, I couldn't understand her last name. She's calling from Tabor City."

"S'cuse me, Isis, only take a minute." Jaynie was already heading down the hall.

There was the vague muskiness of recent sex in the semi-darkness as Jaynie groped her way to the bedside table and found the phone.

"Margaret?"

"Jaynie, glad I found you. I got another little job for your friend, right away. First of the week, if it can be arranged..."

"I'll have to check, but I think it'll be OK. Can I call you tomorrow at home?"

"Yeah, but the sooner the better. Time's important here. That trouble with the last one scared hell out of me. The doctor got real upset when she wouldn't tell him who'd put that IUD in her. Anyway it ain't your guy's fault. The bitch lied to me. She was past three months, I'm pretty sure. Still, it looks like your man could tell by just looking. I mean, aren't there signs?"

"Sometimes." Jaynie didn't want to tell her about the Rivenbark case.

"Did you read about the girl last week near Rockingham? Paper said she bled to death at home. Paper said her uterus was trying to expel an IUD. You don't know anything about that one, do you? I mean our man?...You know what I mean?"

"No, that one has nothing to do with us. Probably some country midwife. Some old Lumbee squaws up that way still do a lively midwife trade. We haven't had any problems," Jaynie lied. "Look, there's always going to be some risk. You can't always tell. And sometimes, God help 'em, these country girls aren't even sure themselves how far along they are. Anyway, our doc knows what he's doing. He's careful as he can be taking their histories, but they all lie, bet on it."

"I know. Now, don't forget, I need to get this done right away. Prominent family. Got burnt fooling around on her husband. He's career Army, overseas. We need to get this out of the way. Hubby's coming home first of the month."

"I understand. I'll call you. Tomorrow without fail."

"OK. Don't let me down..."

Jaynie hung up and pushed her way back through the crowd of drinkers and dancers in the front room. The noise was almost unbearable. Someone had closed the sliding glass doors to keep out the bugs and the air-conditioning was struggling to keep up with the rising body heat.

Jaynie spotted one of the new interns across the room looking down the blouse of Francie Something-or-other, the new ward clerk on Four-South. Jaynie skirted the edge of the dancers and made her way over. "Have you seen Lindamood?" she asked when she got within shouting range.

"Not lately. He was here, but I haven't seen him for a while." The intern shrugged.

"He left some time ago," Francie volunteered.

"Know where he was headed?" Jaynie asked.

"Didn't say. But he was with some snooty new schoolteacher."

"Gene's got a nose like a hound dog." The intern laughed.

"Well, he'd better watch himself," Francie said. "Dr. Martin was bitching about him the other day. Said Gene was a damn good doc but wasn't always around when you needed him."

"If he's gonna practice OB-GYN he better get used to the idea babies don't wait to get born." The intern laughed.

Or unborn, Jaynie smiled to herself.

Chapter Forty-nine

BUCHANAN WATCHED as Tory came back into the semi-darkened room leading Maggie by the hand. She didn't seem too happy about the idea. Buchanan had seen her earlier when she was hard at work doing the pastel sketches over near the bar. She had a nice little talent for catching likeness but she worked a tad too tight—and, he could teach her a few things about flesh tones and color.

Watching her approach, the thing that fascinated him was how much her face resembled the honey-blonde, dreamy-eyed old-timey actress Dorothy Malone, Rock Hudson's leading lady in that late show classic *Written on the Wind.* Except for the color of her hair— Maggie's hair was auburn. When the light struck it, it glinted embers of a sunset.

An inch or two over five-feet, but nicely put together. Those god-damn cutoffs fit like a second skin.

If Alma got a look at that little package, she'd eat her goddamn heart out.

"*Cute,*" Alma would say, dying with envy.

And the way the fullness of Maggie's breasts pushed against the fabric of the faded madras blouse—and the way they continued to swell into her armpits—set his imagination working overtime.

"Maggie, this is Buchanan Forbes," Tory said. "And, Buck, meet The Goose Mapes here. Maggie's our local Andrew Wyeth and The Goose is Captain Eddie's mate on The Marlin Two. They're the world-famous sport fishing charter. Captain Eddie leaves the bottom fishing to the skippers down at Carolina Beach. Bottom fishing's strictly for Grandma and the kids."

"Tory says you're writing a piece on Sharkey Mallone. What's he like?" The Goose grinned and reached across Maggie and pumped Buchanan's hand.

"Just like you'd expect." Buchanan's eyes never left Maggie's.

"I saw your sketches. You're good," Buchanan said. "Tory says you play guitar and sing?"

"Only to myself," Maggie pouted, remembering what Isis told her Buchanan had said about her drawings. "I heard you in here playing. I'm not in your league."

The four of them sat around and talked like that for awhile, mostly with Buchanan answering The Goose's questions about Sharkey Mallone. Jimbo came in and said his new flight attendant friend had popped in and he wanted to go up to Ted Harper's party at the Sugarshack. He asked Tory to relieve him behind the bar.

Tory shrugged. "Sure, what the hell. But I'm warning ya', Isis is up there. I'm not so sure she's gonna like it."

"Leave yo' mama to me." Jimbo grinned and clapped Tory on the shoulder. "By the way, watch your talk. The guy with the Hawaiian shirt is a Fed, caught a flash of his ID when he bought a round."

"No shit? Think he's looking for pot?" Tory made a face.

IRS? Buchanan caught his breath and pretended to be occupied with tuning the guitar.

The Goose followed Tory and Jimbo out. That left Maggie, sitting there glaring uncomfortably across the table at him.

"Buchanan Forbes? Good name for a writer. I assume you do use your own name?"

"Huh? Oh, yeah, all of it. Buchanan Garrett Forbes." He didn't add that in outside newspapers he'd never been published before.

"Should I know your work? Doesn't ring a bell..." She was still steaming about what he'd said about her sketches.

"No way it would. Writing's just a sideline. I work full time for a pharmaceutical company—medical detail. It's actually just a fancy name for a salesman."

"Yeah, everybody knows what a medical detail man is. I've met a few. The beach is popular with traveling men."

"I bet..."

"Yeah, they're all looking to pick up women..."

"Something wrong with that?"

"Most of 'em are married. Take off their rings and lie about it. Their suntans give 'em away. Pretty sad, really."

"Yeah, I guess. I'm married, and I never wear a ring because, well, mainly, I just don't like to wear a ring, but I've never lied about it. Besides, not that it matters, I'm separated. Wife's got my kids in Virginia." Buchanan congratulated himself on the way he'd managed to keep the door open without telling a downright lie.

"Isis told me what you said about my sketches." Maggie spit out the words and shot him a venomous look. "Writer, musician, artist, is there anything you don't have an opinion about?"

"All I said was that I thought you'd be better if you were a bit freer with your strokes."

"So, you're an artist, too? I mean, is there anything you don't do?"

"In another life, I worked as a commercial artist. Trained at VCU. It was considered one of the best back then…"

"Virginia Commonwealth? Jeez, I'd give anything… But God, if you worked as an artist, why'd you ever quit?"

"Just being good is not good enough. I wanted to do figure illustration. Working on a goddamn computer, that's commercial art in the modern world. I hated it. And, as an illustrator, let's face it, I just didn't have it. Besides, I found writing for the paper was easier. Then my wife started having babies and the war in the Gulf caught up to me. So, here I am—a pill peddler who continued to write for his old editor when he took a job at SNS. Now I'm just about to get a serious byline on the Sunday Book Pages of over a hundred newspapers, I hope…"

"You didn't answer my question. Do you still paint?"

"Not anymore. Been years…" The thought of the John Henry painting crossed his mind.

"What do you mean about freeing up my hand? Come show me."

"Show you? Oh, no. Believe me, there's nothing wrong with your work. It's just a matter of style. You don't need me…"

"C'mon, I'll get my sketching stuff. Come do a quick study of me. Show me what you mean." She stood and grabbed his hand.

"No, my God, do you know it's been ten…eleven years. Lady, when I quit, I mean I really quit. I wouldn't know where to start."

"Bullshit. It's like riding a bicycle. You're either born with it or you ain't. C'mon, you're afraid…" She gave his hand another yank.

Her voice and look said, *"You got some nerve."* She was out to call his hand.

"Look, all this is going to do is show you that I was perfectly right in giving up art for good." Buchanan allowed himself to be pulled along, resigning himself to the fact that he was about to wind up looking like a fool and he only had himself to blame.

Back in the main room, she led him to the table she'd used to do her sketches. "Sit. I'll fetch my stuff." When she came back she handed him the box of pastels and started digging in the canvas tote for the sketch pad.

"What's that piece of dusty blue?" Buchanan pointed at a sheet sticking out of the bag.

"Oh, that's not for drawing. It's like a heavy matting paper with a rough texture.."

"Give it here. The rough texture's fine and I like the blue. Sit down." He opened the box of chalks and found a hard sienna stick.

"Wait, I have some charcoal…"

"Never mind. I'll just use this…" He took a squint at her and started slashing light strokes to block out the planes of her face.

Her face was easy, really. Great bones. He set the relationships of the eyes and nose and mouth. Recalling the night in January with the kids, the magic came flowing back.

Goddamnedest eyes he'd ever seen. "You really got some kind of crazy eyes…"

"How's that?"

"Like sea water, except they're lighter and bluer, like that translucence just under the curl of a wave with the sunlight filtering through when it breaks across a shoal."

"You write poetry too?"

He took colored pencils, put some sharp detail around the eyes… made them dominate.

He sketched in the mouth, lips slightly parted.

"Your lips look bee-stung…anybody ever tell you that?" He caught the slightly swollen characteristic of her lips, touching in just the flare of the nostril above her mouth, and the saucy uptilt of the Gaelic nose…

"Bee-stung?" She touched her mouth with her fingertips, self-consciously. "I guess you probably are a good writer; you're certainly full of shit."

He couldn't help but laugh out loud at that.

"There, what'cha think?" He put away the chalk and handed her the sketch.

The entire process had taken him less than five minutes.

Several patrons had gathered behind him as Buchanan worked.

"Fantastic," someone gasped.

Maggie stared, momentarily speechless.

"That's really something. I see what you mean now, about working free. This is reckless abandon." She looked at the sketch, then back at him. "You make my stuff look like honorable mention in a kindergarten show. Is it a trick? I mean how to get this freedom."

"Not really, you just let the chalk make love to the paper."

She looked across at him questioning and looked back at the drawing. "I think I see…"

"Natural. Like riding that bike you were talking about."

She caught his look and blushed and smiled.

"Would you look at my other work? The watercolors…"

[254]

"Sure, anytime."

"How about right now? I've got some beer, maybe some Scotch and gin, I think. It's not far, just up the beach…"

"Well, I don't know. Now is kinda late."

"Come on, it's Friday, not even eleven yet. My kids are at the Crest watching the third showing of some damn surfing movie. Come on. Just one drink. You can tell me what you think, OK? You can leave when the kids show up. Besides you've embarrassed me in front of my adoring public. You owe me."

Aware he'd hurt her feelings, he relented. *One drink, tell her her pictures are great, and make an early getaway—a sensible plan.*

"OK, you win. Where's your ride? I'll follow you."

On the way out, he scanned the bar for the Fed. *Nothing.* Thoughts of his secret cache brought a momentary twinge. Remembering the electronic device on his Lhamda-A car, he resolved to check out the Stribol car first thing in the morning.

The weathered two-story house sat alone near the south end of the island, across the street from a public beach.

Upstairs, the tiny living room of the apartment was stacked with sketches. Mostly landscapes, seascapes and old houses and buildings, watercolors. A definite preoccupation with quaint, mostly seaside architecture. She moved a pile of drawings from a chair but he ignored her invitation to sit and followed her to the kitchen door while she fixed herself a Scotch and handed him a gin and tonic.

When she squeezed by him at the door, the top of her head barely brushed his chin.

Drink in hand, he roamed the room, looking at the paintings.

"I think you've got real talent, really…" He tried to make amends.

Here and there he picked up a sketch and suggested how she might improve.

As she reached for a sketch he caught a scent of soap and dusting powder mingled deliciously with her woman-scent. Quite innocently, she brushed her breasts across his shoulder.

The sexy little fox.

He sipped his drink, talking art and other stuff. Leaving early seemed unimportant now.

He picked up a pad and began to doodle aimlessly a full-length sketch of her as she stood in the door frame.

Her thrusting breasts reminded him of a Eurasian girl who'd modeled nude for his life class in college in Richmond. That girl had been like a bronze sculpture. Unbelievable.

Pencil moving faster now, he shifted position to ease a nagging pressure at his groin.

He really should be leaving.

"Are you sketching me again?" She leaned closer to get a look.

"Hold still, just relax."

The slightest northeasterly breeze stirred the curtains in the kitchen behind her.

He caught a whiff of her scent again.

"There," he said and put the pencil down.

"Let me see." She moved around behind.

"What do you think?"

"Well, I *never!*" She refused to look him in the eye.

He'd sketched her in the nude.

"Don't you like it? I think it's pretty good. Here, tear it up if it bothers you." He held the drawing out to her.

"Do you want me to? Tear it up, I mean?" she stammered. "I didn't mean it isn't good."

"No, but I will if it bothers you..."

Silence.

Then, finally, "How'd you know to get the, uh, personal details just right?"

She looked away and blushed.

"Call it inspiration. I must confess those bee-stung lips aren't all I see..."

She glanced his way and smiled. Was there an erotic expectancy lingering there?

Too late now to think of turning back.

Now, all at once, Buchanan was aware that at some imprecise moment during the evening, a contract of intimacy had taken place between them. With great deliberation, he took a step closer and brushed his lips to hers. Her sweet hunger spilled into his mouth.

After a time she slowly led him back down the hall into her bedroom. The bed was a storm-tossed sea of disarray—redolent with female spoor. Discarded clothes were scattered everywhere.

Feet wide apart, she looked him squarely in the eye as she unbuttoned her blouse and let it slip carelessly to the floor. The swelling of her breasts overflowed the skimpy bra and curved impertinently into her armpit. The bra was semi-transparent. He could see clearly the dark circles and tiny bumps around the aureola.

Reaching behind, she undid the clasp. Feather-like, the flimsy garment floated to the floor.

Like the rest of her, her breasts were pure sculpture. Large and erect, nipples hard as nails.

With one hand, she cupped herself and with the other she pulled hard against his head and gave a little sigh.

He bent forward and licked each nipple, tasting her saltiness with his tongue.

Finally he sat on the edge of the bed, undid her jeans and unzipped the front. Slipping them slowly down her thighs, he waited while she steadied herself with a hand on his shoulder and stepped free.

"We forgot about the kids," he murmured.

"Forget the kids…" She reached back and locked the door.

He breathed into her navel, licking the little line of reddish hair, probing with his tongue.

"The light," she said.

"Forget the light." He pulled her panties down. She dipped her knees and the little garment slipped with a whisper to the floor. Moving first one foot, then the other, she scooted her legs apart, opening herself to the exploration of his fingers.

Laying back on the bed, he urged her forward on her knees, lowering her astraddle his face.

She gasped as he moved his hands behind her buttocks. His tongue found her crevice open, wet and yielding.

"Oh, God!" Her moaning began a low guttural chant, as her fingernails dug deep into the pillow behind his head.

"Yes…oh yes!" She arched upward and back, stretching her arms toward the ceiling.

Sometime later in the darkness, she murmured, "I won't fall in love with you."

IN RALEIGH, shortly before 2:00 A.M., Cammie was more than a little drunk when she finally gave up and put down the phone.

Chapter Fifty

ALMA STARED AT THE CEILING and gave an involuntary shiver as she felt Ogden Branch carefully insert the speculum. She had always wondered why nobody ever bothered to warm the damn things up.

"Let's have that spatula…" He spoke to the nurse. "…ah, there…just let me take some more from up here. Looks like the erosion may be healing. I could use a drop of silver nitrate, but let's wait. Actually, the os looks clean.

I know it's a lot of trouble but better safe than sorry. There…" She felt him ease on out. "Really, except for that one small place, you look quite fit."

When she had dressed and was sitting at his desk, he said, "I want to see you again in a couple of weeks. Give that little area a chance to clear up, OK?" He smiled and gave her hand a pat. "How's the family? Didn't you say you might be going back to Raleigh soon?"

"I'm thinking about it. Just a temporary thing, to sell the house. About a month, a bit longer maybe. Not until after the middle of June. School's not out until the fifth. The grandparents have promised the boys a trip to Williamsburg and I'll need time to pack. Moving four boys is like moving an army." She consulted the calendar on his desk. "So…this is Thursday, April twenty-fifth. I'll check about the PAP, when?"

"Don't bother. Sylvia will call if we need to be in touch. Nothing there to spoil your weekend, OK?"

When she left the office she found a pay phone in the foyer of the office building.

"Hello?" The voice was guarded.

"Hi, Michael, I'm through. Are we still on for four, your place in Catawba?"

"Of course. What did Ogden say? Are you going to live?" He laughed.

"Don't make jokes. You know I've been worried, but he didn't seem too concerned. The suspicious area looked better. Just the same, I'll sure feel better when I get a clean bill of health." She fumbled in her purse and lit a cigarette.

She wanted a drink bad.

"Quit worrying. Think beautiful thoughts. I'll meet you at four. Don't be late, OK?"

"All right, Michael, don't you be late. It's always me who winds up waiting…" She realized he'd already hung up. Searching her purse for an Atavan, she headed for the water fountain. She knew she had to break it off with Michael, but for now she was glad to have a friend.

Chapter Fifty-one

INGER TYPED THE LAST THREE WORDS of the sentence before she picked up the phone. If the goddamn thing didn't quit ringing, she'd never finish this frigging book. She was a journalist. Never should have started writing a damn book in the first place.

"Hello?" She tried to keep the sharp edge of irritation out of her voice.

"Inger, I'm glad I caught you. Sorry I missed your call. But things are crazy here. The second of May and finals start in three weeks. I miss you so, I wish I was back there with you. I wish I was anywhere, just a million miles away from here." Penny sounded so depressed.

"Oh, babe, don't sound so down. Soon as your finals are over, maybe your mother will let you come back for a few weeks. I have plenty from the advance on this Brookgreen book to hire you to proof the pages for me. It would be fun…"

"You know she won't. She's still throwing a fit over the last time. She watches me like a hawk. The way she butters up to Elroy, and the two of them bossing me around, makes me want to puke. And when he's not around, she keeps throwing Buchanan up to me. She'll never trust me again. Says I inherited this wildness from my rotten daddy. Inger, if I didn't live here at the sorority, I'd kill myself, I swear it." Penny sounded on the verge of tears.

"Well, I'd call her but I don't know what good that would do. I'm sure she holds me responsible. Right after you got back to school, she called and gave me an earful. Still, she was right. Buchanan Forbes was a mistake, and I blame myself. But no use crying over spilt milk."

"Have you heard from Buchanan? Has he been back to see Mr. Mallone? I think about him all the time. Elroy makes my skin crawl. Oh, Inger, what am I going to do?"

"No, he hasn't been back, but don't fret. I know it's hard to believe, but be patient; everything will work out. Things always happen for a reason."

"That reminds me, Inger. Didn't I tell you I'd just finished my period when I got down there in March? I seem to remember that I'd put in a Tampax before I left to drive down, just to be on the safe side. Do you remember? I just can't think straight anymore."

"Well, yes, as a matter of fact, I do remember. You were glad you'd just finished and you wouldn't have that to spoil your vacation. Why? You having trouble?" Inger was suddenly alert.

March…April… She did the arithmetic on her fingers. The numbers weren't good.

"Well, I'm such an airhead. I never pay attention. My mother was on my case so bad over Buchanan. But I don't think I've had a period since I got back and that's been almost two months. It's no big deal. I may just be a bit anemic. I've missed before." Penny sounded hopeful.

"You've been under a lot of stress. I'm sure it's OK. Are you gaining weight?"

"Well, maybe…I always do just before my period. Judging from my

[259]

disposition it should be any day now. I'm a bitch...I always am. I feel it coming on."

"Well, that's a good sign." Inger tried to sound cheerful, but she felt uneasy in her gut.

"I know I told him not to, but all the same, I wish Buchanan would call me. I'll always love him. Oh, Inger..."

"Hush, now. Don't torture yourself that way. Go outside and take a long walk. Write me a long letter. Write Buchanan a long letter, just don't mail it. Burn it. It'll help to get your feelings out. I promise."

"All right, I'll try..." There was a sigh as Penny hung up the phone.

Inger pushed back from the laptop, walked around the counter and looked at the calendar.

Penny had arrived on Monday, the fourth of March. That would have put her last period starting early in the last week in February...

She tried to remember the date they'd gone to the Bowery, the night that Penny had met Buchanan Forbes. It would have been Monday, March eleven. Twelve, maybe fourteen days total, give or take one or two.

The numbers bothered her...March...April. Almost eight full weeks.

She picked up the phone.

"Bonnie? Inger Carlyle. Remember you were telling me about this nurse you knew who knows a doctor...know what I mean?"

Chapter Fifty-two

MAGGIE COMPLAINED because Buchanan wanted to hang around and watch Eat My Dust win the Kentucky Derby. It was after seven when he finally gave in and took her to the Sugarshack.

The Sugarshack had been the simplest way to escape her bitchiness. She was due her period almost any day, with that IUD in place, regular as a clock, thank God.

Since his memorable first night at the beach, he and Maggie had become immortalized in local song and legend. Always looking for heroes, the local gentry had made them the greatest thing since Bogie and Bacall. Isis sweet-talked him into letting her have the fabled sketch he'd done of Maggie matted and framed. Now it hung on the wall, opposite the cash register. Isis even had him sign and date it and, to his complete amazement, she'd put a small light over it, like the ones you saw in the commercial galleries. Hung like that, it had become a legend of a sort.

Overnight he had become a local celebrity.

And, to tell the truth, he ate it up.

He knew it was crazy. If Alma relented and agreed to move to Wilmington, this thing with Maggie would prove to be downright suicidal. He was helpless. Maggie filled his soul with music.

Most weekdays he traveled overnight. But his weekends were like no other time he could ever remember. Maggie was incredibly bright and well-read. They read poetry to each other and passages from their favorite books. Starlight walks on lonely beaches talking religion…and literature…and film. She was a serious and insightful critic. Playing guitars and painting with watercolors…cooking…riding bikes…browsing quaint shops in downtown Wilmington in the revitalized Cotton Exchange. Rainy nights she fascinated him with tales about Mexico and the Caribbean and he taught her about Hemingway and Fitzgerald and Kierkegaard and Mencken.

Sex with Maggie was incredible.

For them both.

He was intoxicated by the textures of her skin and hair, the taste of her, her smells. Her laughter echoed in his dreams like silver chimes.

Shortly after their first night together, she had confessed to him, that, for the first time in her life, under his touch, she had become multiorgasmic. As a consequence, she'd become virtually insatiable, a dream come true. Incredibly, he had finally found a relationship where he didn't have to play games.

Maggie never used sex as a means to get her way.

"This is perfect, just what I need. No promises asked, no promises given." She had aggressively proclaimed her independence at the start.

But Buchanan was not completely taken in.

Nothing this perfect could remain that simple. There was always a payoff for everything.

"Have you thought about a lawyer?" Maggie suddenly remarked one night after she'd prepared a romantic candlelight dinner. He let it pass. Later in the darkness as he drifted near the edge of twilight sleep, she said, "You ought to file for an official separation. Alma could nab us for adultery. I went through that routine when Lewis' wife found out about me. I've had enough of that to last me the rest of my life. Take it from me, it's not nice."

Inevitably her hints became more frequent and insistent.

Toward the end of April, one Saturday afternoon after a picnic with her kids down at Fort Fisher, they were sitting on her balcony watching the pelicans holding almost stationary in the breeze at the surf's edge, searching for fish. "My kids are crazy about you, you know that?"

The not-so-offhand remark triggered a sudden puckering of his gubernaculum.

He continued staring off into the middle distance and made no response.

"You're never gonna leave those kids of yours, are you?"

"Doesn't look like I'll have much to say about it. Alma's has no intention of coming back," he hedged.

True, he hadn't been totally honest about Alma, but, still, he'd made Maggie no promises.

At first, borne of loneliness and separation from the family, he had been powerless to stop seeing her. Lately, he spent many nights building scenarios of a life with Maggie and having all their kids. It scared him to death that his feelings for her moved him so deeply.

Lately, her remarks and his guilt—and these troubling feelings of fondness and tenderness—were making him very vulnerable. He didn't want to start lying to her now.

"Well, why prolong it? Why don't you just get it over with? See a lawyer. I'm not about to waste the rest of my life waiting for her to name me as a correspondent." She got up and stomped into the house.

He understood that she was waiting for him to come make up. They'd played the scene before. It usually made the sex somehow sweeter.

But, now, Buchanan considered the situation soberly. He was a fraud. In a game like this, sometimes the best thing was to know when to fold your hand. It scared him how important Maggie had become. Still, he wasn't ready to confront Alma as long as he held out hope to get his kids back.

He simply got up and left and drove on home.

Maggie hadn't called for almost two weeks.

At first he'd been relieved. It was the decent thing, the perfect out.

But, soon, his nights alone were filled with devilish images of her in bed. No matter how he turned and tossed, he vowed to let it be.

Then, the second Thursday night when he'd gotten home from the road, the phone rang almost before he'd gotten in the door.

"I miss you. If we can't be lovers, at least let's be friends," she said without preamble.

It made him horny as hell.

"DIDN'T YOU MISS ME?" SHE ASKED, later in the darkness.

"Not much."

"Well, there for a minute you could have fooled me. I truly do love you, you jerk. You love me, too. Admit it."

"Uhmm…" He dared not confess his days were filled with fantasies of life with her.

Their relationship took on a frustrating pattern.

Friday was for making love.

Saturday was carefree...a day of fun and games...sportfucking like teenagers.

Sundays were filled with a tenderness and an intimacy that consumed him. But, invariably, as Sunday faded into twilight, the uncertainty crept back in. The tension was always waiting.

It went on that way. Maggie nagging him about Alma and his steadfast refusal to make any real move to make the separation official. It was a road to nowhere, he knew it.

He still hadn't made any overt commitments to Maggie, but they both knew he was living a lie all the same. More and more he tried to keep their relationship at home. Usually at her place. Her place was nicer. And now that the contractors were nearing the completion of the remodeling of her new house, much to his discomfort, she would drag him over to see their progress. It was a poorly staged charade, fraught with innuendo about how cozy it would be in this roomy new home.

"You could quit paying Roxy that awful rent. Think of the money we'd save..."

The virtues of togetherness...

So, this first Saturday night in May, the concession to drop in at the Sugarshack had been hard won for Maggie. Buchanan had talked her into eating at home but now she was on to him.

She knew he wanted to avoid being seen with her in public. It only made her more determined.

Reluctantly, he'd agreed to go along. The long-running party at the Sugarshack was preferable to making an appearance in a more crowded tourist place. Now that the vacation season was drawing near, more and more he'd run into people he'd known back in Raleigh, down for a weekend at the beach. While the Sugarshack was less visible than dinner at the Neptune or drinks at The Wit's End, Buchanan realized he was still playing a dangerous game. Word was leaking out. The Sugarshack was beginning to attract a lot of tourists hoping to rub elbows with Hollywood expatriates and out-of-towners looking for the action.

"C'mon, we might run into Sandra Bullock or DiCaprio." Maggie urged him out the door.

Buchanan smiled at the irony: This really was akin to switching seats on the *Titanic*.

Damned if he did and damned if he didn't...six of one and half-dozen of the other.

To parade Maggie into a room peopled with actors, directors, doctors and nurses and other professionals, occasional members of the mainland carriage set, just dug him a bit deeper into future jeopardy if and when he might talk Alma into bringing the boys down on an exploratory expedition.

This little exercise of social Russian Roulette was making him a nervous wreck.

But careerwise, his life was going even better than he'd expected.

The really good news was that the job was shaping up. It was no surprise to Buchanan that he would have trouble getting the territory cleaned up the first two or three times around, but, happily, he'd already begun to see an encouraging trickle of Spectropen prescriptions in the drug stores around the territory. And he'd discovered much to his delight that the Navy hospital at Camp LeJeune was already using large quantities of virtually every Stribol antibiotic on the current GSA contract.

The bad news was that things had gone from worse to dismal in his relationship with Alma. But he still wasn't ready to give up.

He routinely tried to call the kids twice during the week and usually early on Saturday night. While the news from the real estate agency was not hopeful, Alma had agreed to come to Raleigh after school was out, to see if she could speed along the sale of the house.

Secretly, he hoped that having her closer might somehow effect a miraculous reconciliation.

So, heart in his mouth, he was having serious misgivings as he followed Maggie up the steps to the cottage on Lagoon. But, much to his relief, the party turned out better than expected.

Maggie knew almost everyone, which made him even more anxious in the beginning. But, thankfully, she immediately drifted away to renew old acquaintances.

Buchanan breathed a sigh.

This lessened the chance of running into unexpected drop-ins who might know him from Raleigh, thus saving him from making guilty explanations.

Moreover, the evening turned out to be useful in a business sense. Ted Harper had dropped by for a few minutes and introduced Buchanan to Gene Lindamood, the Chief OB-GYN resident. Gene proved to be a likable guy who'd married a girl from somewhere in Virginia. The young doctor immediately took Buchanan under his wing and introduced him to a number of the other interns and nurses. Rochelle Guest was there. He remembered she'd once been an OB-GYN nurse.

Hank Long had attracted a small crowd, showing the group the tiny slide rule that his company was passing out to the doctors and nurses. They finally passed one over to Buchanan who had seen it before.

The slide rule did an exhaustive array of medical calculations, mostly dealing with determining dosages of medications based on body weight. It had the logo of *Physician's Supply* prominently displayed and made a very attractive promotional gimmick. Hank said he'd leave a quantity with Ted in the hospital pharmacy to pass out free to the staff.

Buchanan was impressed. He played with it, fascinated. "One of the best advertising gimmicks I've seen," he enthused.

An hour passed and he was getting restless.

"Are we out of Scotch, Hank?" The busty nurse that Ted Harper had introduced as Jaynie Lockfaw interrupted the group who was now alternating between a heated argument about the White House's abortion stance and raves for Nanci Griffith's new *Townes Van Zandt* album.

"Ted made a liquor run last night. Did you look in the back bedroom?" Hank nodded toward the back.

"I already looked. We're out. I think some of these freeloaders have been ripping us off."

"Could be. Are we completely out? If we have enough for tonight, I have some in my car but it's at the hospital. I could bring it tomorrow," Lindamood volunteered.

"We just broke the seal on the last quart. It's still early; it'll never stretch that far."

"Maybe we can ask some of the locals to lend us some?" He turned to Buchanan. "You don't have an extra bottle or two of Scotch you could spare, do ya?"

"I got bourbon or vodka. I never buy Scotch. Sorry."

Gene shrugged and looked at Jaynie. "Ask some of the others that live close by. God knows most of 'em have freeloaded enough of our booze. Don't be bashful...ask around."

Jaynie nodded and moved away.

In a few minutes she was back. She shrugged. "No luck. Where'd Ted go? We need his car to make a liquor run."

"He left about a half hour ago; went on home, I think."

"Well who's got a car? It'll only take about a half hour," Gene Lindamood asked the group.

No one volunteered.

"No Scotch drinkers here, huh?"

Finally, Buchanan spoke up. "Look, I'm riding with Maggie. You can take my company car. I'm parked right around the corner. C'mon, I'll walk you up there to get the extra set of keys."

"Can I ride along? I need to get a Chapstick." Jaynie slipped her arm around Gene's waist.

Buchanan suppressed a smile. He doubted Chapstick was the stick she was interested in.

"Sure, babe, you can drive my car back from town for me. I'll need my wheels back here."

Buchanan led them down the steps and up the street. Inside his place he quickly found the extra keys. Gene Lindamood eyed the stack of sample cartons that had come while Buchanan had been out of town. "Got any Spectrapen I.M. and capsules you can spare?" he asked.

"Sure, but I don't have time to rummage through these. C'mon, I've got some in my car."

When Buchanan opened the trunk, except for empty cartons, the space was virtually empty after the long week on the road. He quickly located the samples.

"Can I have that little box of pediatric suspension? I've got a kid at home." Lindamood pointed to a box.

"Sure. Say, there's only that and this box of Supraceph. If you want to, when you get to your car in town, just take it all. I have to make room for the new shipment anyway. They keep sending this stuff faster than I can get rid of it."

"If you want to get rid of some of that stuff, I can cut you a deal. I got a friend in Charlottesville, a pharmacist in a small hospital, no questions. I'll split fifty-fifty."

"Well, thanks but no thanks. It isn't worth it to me, believe me."

"Well, you got any extra left over, you know, if it starts piling up, give it to me. An OB-GYN resident's stipend is jackshit. I could use a few bucks, and I guarantee, I'll move your stuff like the wind in the hospital. That's legit enough. Who could complain about that?"

"No one. That's fair enough. I'll drop by with a nice little 'care'package Monday."

"Great. We'll be back with the Scotch in forty minutes, an hour at the most..."

When Lindamood took the keys, Buchanan admired the fancy monograms on the cuffs of the young resident's shirt.

"White on white, very spiffy. What's all this bullshit about a poor resident's salary?"

"It helps to have a rich wife. My snooty in-laws give me these shirts by the box."

"Take your time. Just lock up and leave the keys under the floor mat on the driver's side." He stood aside and waved as they drove off in the Buick.

Starting back to the party, Buchanan watched a young woman across the street locking her car.

Even in the poor light he could see that she was attractive. Sooner or later all the adventuresome local females checked out the action at the shack.

The overflow from the party had clogged the street with cars on both sides. The local residents frequently complained to the local gendarmes but as long as they were legal there wasn't much they could do.

Buchanan was grateful he could park off the street.

When he got back to the party, out of curiosity he wandered back through the hall into the bedrooms. The closet with the cache of booze was in the larger of the three rooms.

There was almost a case of J&B Scotch stacked with the rest.

Jaynie had made the whole thing up, a flimsy excuse to slip away.

It seemed a silly game to play. Certainly there were simpler ways to be discreet. But Lindamood was married and gossip travels fast.

It was a lesson he should take to heart.

He found Maggie and she introduced him to a group of attractive women—two school teachers, one flight attendant with Midway and two starlets from a TV revival of *Melrose Place*.

The fourth was the same woman who'd parked across from his place a few minutes before.

"This is Nell Batson. She works for Uncle Sam," Maggie said.

"Oh, which branch?" Buchanan asked, casually.

"That abominable Service, the one that pokes around in everybody's financial affairs."

"Well, someone has to do it, I guess." Shrugging casually, Buchanan took a closer look.

Chapter Fifty-three

SHERIFF MACK JONES shook his head.

It was just blind luck that they'd ever found her body in that swamp off N.C. 87, less than four miles before it intersected U.S. 17 near Town Creek. That jungle was no good for anything.

Even them snake hunters from the University had quit going in there.

The call had come in to the Brunswick County Sheriff's Office in Southport about 1:00 A.M. Friday morning. Jones' night deputy had called him at home over on Oak Island golf course.

The car full of teens coming back along the stretch of N.C. 87 going home to Elizabethtown from a Vince Gill concert at Myrtle Beach had been telling ghost stories about old Joe Baldwin hunting for his head before they tore up the tracks at the old Maco station.

More'n' likely the kids had been soaking up the beer. One of the girls needed to go potty, so they stopped the car to let her pee in the thick woods along the road. Nobody bothered to ask if she'd ever peed because when she stumbled and fell right on top of that body, she'd come back out of there screaming her pretty head off.

Right now, she was in the Brunswick County Hospital under heavy sedation. Poor kid would never be the same. No more ghost stories for that one.

"Probably scared the feces right out of her. Might never have another normal bowel movement again," old Doc Lyon remarked, wryly.

"So what do you think, Amos?" The sheriff examined his fingernails and opened up his buck knife. "Didn't look like they was a scratch on that corpse, but she was sure'n hell dead when she got to that place. Somebody dumped her there, I'd bet my life on that."

"Right."

"So? What killed her? She wasn't strangled. I've seen enough of them to know..."

"Ex-sanquination was the cause of death." A half-smile played across the old doc's mouth. "See a lot of it in Vampire movies."

"*Ees-what-....?*"

"*Ex-sang-win-nation.*"

"OK, I give up. Whazzit mean?"

"She bled to death. Somebody aborted her. Her clothes must have been a mess, and my guess is that she bloodied up quite a few towels and God knows what all. That body hardly had enough blood in it for the tech to run a blood group. I'd bet it was the work of a trained physician, or a nurse or a mid-wife maybe. Anyway, whoever did it has done it before, just ran into some bad luck. That squiggly little plastic IUD ripped a big bleeder."

"Ever see one of these?" The sheriff held up a small slide rule and went back to inspecting his nails. All morning he'd been thinking about how good a chew of tobacco would taste. Last night after she'd screwed his eyeballs out, that damned foxy little vixen Barbara Morgan had started measuring his bedroom windows for new drapes. Tonight he was going to put a stop to that.

"Yeah, I have one on my desk at the office. Some medical supply out-fit in Raleigh gives 'em away."

"You think it was a doctor?" The sheriff looked up from his nails.

"A doctor, yeah, but not a local, not in a hundred years. Of course, you never can tell. If it was a local, I reckon he'd 'a dumped her somewheres farther away. I'd guess this one's been dead several days. Four, maybe more," the old doc said. He'd like to thank Barbara Morgan for getting Mack off the nasty chewing tobacco.

"Body was probably brought here from Myrtle Beach or maybe somewhere west, like Florence or Fayetteville. Fayetteville would be a good bet. Around Fort Bragg there's got to be a lot of illegal surgery going on."

"But this wasn't an amateur. A doctor or paramedic did it. She's just a poor dumbass, misguided fool of a woman who ran into a crazy man and some bad luck. She have any ID on her?"

"No. We've sent her prints to Wilmington. Archie drove 'em up there about an hour ago. May take a month—maybe longer, maybe never. Unless there's a missing person report circulating on her. I ran over my files...nothing promising yet."

"Oh, well. It'll make *The Wilmington Morning Star*. Someone may read it in the paper."

"You thinking the same thing I am?" the sheriff asked.

"That Zoni Corbett case last month at Caswell Beach? Yep. I think we've got a situation here."

"Could be, all right. By the way, the Palm Beach County sheriff called yesterday to tell me they found the Corbett woman's Haitian boyfriend floating in a canal in Boca Raton. I still have doubts about that nice Baptist girl soliciting an abortion, then taking a gun to her head..."

"Me, too. Guess now we'll always have to wonder. It's sad, Mack. I can't help thinking, if those women could have had this done by a competent physician in a good hospital, this would have never happened. Wonder if we'll ever learn?"

Chapter Fifty-four

NELL BATSON WAS TRYING her best to be patient. Her first Monday morning appointment had already been waiting ten minutes. Durwood Fisher could be a regular pain in the ass when he wanted to.

In the first place, the Wilmington office wasn't staffed for intensive surveillance and this niggling request from Washington to *"keep an eye"* on Buchanan Forbes was a joke. Since way back when Bobby Kennedy had started playing cloak and dagger, every agency in Washington had started poking under rocks.

There was no way that Durwood Fisher could expect that she could spend her nights and weekends following Forbes around. She'd complained to her supervisor, but he was caught between the rock and the hard place. He already had almost twenty years in and wanted to keep his nose clean and that meant keeping the Washington powers-that-be happy.

And Nell did like her job.

Nell was only thirty and had her CPA license. Still, she'd already invested nine years of her life with the service. She was paying off the mortgage on a little storybook beach cottage she'd bought for a song after Hurricane Hugo had scared the life out of the Charlotte dentist who owned it. There were enough men in her life to make it interesting and she'd just joined Pine Valley Country Club and taken up golf.

For the daughter of a Brunswick County shrimper, she hadn't done badly for herself. As a matter of fact, if it weren't for having to keep tabs on this Buchanan Forbes, her life would be damned near perfect.

Nell resented having to put up with Durwood Fisher's garbage, but after all he was based in DC, and it never hurt to stay on his good side. The notion of taking an early retirement and doing some travel while she was still young enough to enjoy it conjured up visions of carefree cruises to exotic places peopled with darkly handsome men.

She listened patiently, then struggled to keep her voice calm.

"But, I'm telling you, Durr, he didn't drive the car. He loaned it to one of the local docs to make a liquor run. As a matter of fact, about the only time he's used that car on the weekends or at nights when he wasn't on his regular job was a couple of weeks back when he took this Maggie O'Brien and her kids on a picnic down to Fort Fisher. And once when we know from his phone conversations that he was going to Raleigh to meet the real estate agent. We monitor his phone, and I live right up the beach. I see him around the local watering holes. But, I keep telling you, I think we're wasting our time. There's no way we're staffed here to keep a tail on this guy."

"Well, from what you say, he's suddenly become quite a playboy."

"I'd hardly call it that. He's cheating on his wife, but from his phone conversations with her, she deserves it. He's begged her to bring the kids down. Besides, not even the local vice squad is interested in domestic hanky-panky in this enlightened age."

"What about cash? Is he a spender? He's maintaining the mortgage in Raleigh and paying for the rent at the beach. And he sends money regularly to his wife in Virginia. He's making a decent salary, but he's keeping a lot of balls in the air."

"Look, I told you, he's not throwing money around. You get my reports. Keeping tabs on his banking transactions is about as exciting as watching paint dry."

"Well, what about the transmitter on the car? Has he made any suspicious trips? Late nights, early morning jaunts, you get the pattern?"

"Durwood, I work all day long doing routine audits. Washington has me backed up with scheduled appointments through July two thousand three. I monitor the transmitter when I'm home. It's bad enough to have that damn beeper wake me out of sound sleep every time he decides to go home from his girl friend's during the middle of the night, but I can't follow him. Besides, I usually record his odometer every evening he's home and so far we've always known in advance where he's headed from his phone conversations. I thought we had an understanding. I'd try to keep an eye on him and report anything suspicious and then you guys could come back in. This is ruining my life. What else do you expect from me?"

"I know. I tell the chief all the time what a great gal you are, trust me."

"Yes, I trust you..." Nell was anxious to get off the phone. This was leading nowhere.

"I see on your report about him loaning his car to this Dr. Lindamood Saturday. What's that all about? Is there any chance this doc is helping Buck Forbes deal a few samples?"

"No way. I was in my car right across the street. I saw him give the guy his car keys and clean the empty cartons out of the trunk. I heard the doc ask him for some penicillin for his kid. He didn't have enough antibiotics left in that car to treat the common cold."

"Well, then, what was that all about? Why did he let the doc take his car in the first place?"

"The party up the street ran out of Scotch. The doc needed a car to make a liquor run."

"Well, judaspriest, from your odometer notations, that car was driven over three hundred miles from the time this Gene Lindamood borrowed it and you noted the mileage at..." Durwood searched the report for the notation, "...at...six thirty-five P.M. at the beginning of Saturday evening—three hundred fifty-nine miles to be exact—and you say, except to go to the post office down the street on Sunday evening, Forbes didn't use the car the rest of the weekend? How far is it to the liquor store, anyway?"

"Well, they weren't going to the liquor store. The stores were closed at that time. From talk at the party, Lindamood said he had some Scotch in his car over in town at the hospital. That's about twenty, maybe thirty miles round trip."

"You've got 'em leaving about ten P.M., right?"

"Yeah, I think it was around nine-fifty. It's on the report."

"You were at the party. What time did they get back?"

"They didn't, not before midnight. I left about then."

"Well, what time did the monitor pick up the signal that night...when they came back in range of the beach?"

"I don't know."

"Didn't it go off at all? Is it working OK?"

"Yes, it's working. If you must know, I didn't go home that night."

"Oh! Well, I wonder when they got back? Is there anybody who was at the party you could ask?"

"Maybe. What difference does it make? This Dr. Lindamood had Jaynie Lockfaw with him. They may have stopped to smell the roses."

"Roses? Oh, *that*. But three hundred fifty-nine miles...the roses must've been at Myrtle Beach."

She laughed. "I can tell you that the car was parked out in front of Forbes apartment when I came back on the beach Sunday morning around seven-thirty to have breakfast at the Palm Room. Later on that afternoon, I saw Forbes loading up the trunk with samples, getting ready for the coming week's work. It's his routine, does it every Sunday afternoon. Then he went to the Post Office and stopped by The Wit's End to have a beer and a hamburger. I ate there, too. I didn't feel like cooking."

"But aren't you curious?"

"About what?"

"All those miles on that Buick's odometer. Somebody went somewhere..."

"Well, now that you mention it, that reminds me. Sunday night at The Wit, Forbes was kinda upset about the car. I heard him tell Jimbo, the guy who tends bar, that Lindamood must have driven that car in the woods. He said there was mud and underbrush stuck all underneath the car. And he was complaining that they'd messed up the back seat, something about a stain. Anyway, Forbes was not a happy Samaritan. Said he'd think twice about loaning out his car again. Said it was goddamn lucky he'd put seat covers on to protect the upholstery from his kids, or else the company would make him pay the damages. If you ask me, Lindamood and Jaynie Lockfaw went to the boonies and bayed at the moon."

"That would explain it. Still..."

"Look, Durwood, why don't you tell the *powers-that-be* to give it a rest? Forbes is no saint, but as far as committing any federal crimes, he's clean as a choirboy."

Part 5
Cammie

Chapter Fifty-five

MAGGIE WAS RAISING HELL.

A non-stop fuss over nothing.

It never failed. Her period was due and she'd had a few too many Coronas last evening.

It all started over Buchanan's announcement that Cammie Brawley was coming to the beach for a week.

Alone.

Maggie had hit the ceiling. And she had kept right on drinking.

They started out to make love six hours ago, just after midnight when they got back from The Wit, but every time they got down to the nitty-gritty she flared up again.

Women! Goddamn estrogen poisoning. Bitch, bitch, bitch, ad infinitum.

"If you take that tight-ass bitch to dinner, we're through. And, why won't you introduce me?"

"She knows Alma, and you yourself said that you didn't want to be involved as correspondent in an adultery suit." Not truly a lie, but a world-class equivocation. A genuine artwork of rationalization, he wryly congratulated himself.

He was getting to be quite the expert.

"Well now, just maybe I wouldn't mind. Anything to get you a divorce."

"Oh, yeah, that would really be smart. The way things are, if Alma can sell the house, the money will be half mine."

"I'm tired of this charade. You have no intention of asking her for a divorce."

"Better than that. She's on the verge of asking me. It would be much better that way and you know it. That way I'll have more leverage; I'll be the negotiator, instead of being negotiated."

He congratulated himself again. Even as he fabricated the argument, the idea made sense.

"Goddamn it, Maggie, Cammie is maybe eight years older than I am. I told you we met in that park in Raleigh where I took my kids on week-end mornings. Our kids are playmates. She's just my friend, but a damn good one. A friend. Honest-to-God friendship. Now that's something I haven't had a lot of lately."

"Just friends, huh? And your kids are playmates. How touching. That's what she wants to be, your fucking playmate. If you think I'm just going to stand by while you fuck other women, you got another think coming, buster." She slapped him hard across his naked butt, kicked the sheet off the end of the bed and stalked into the bathroom.

Buchanan rubbed his butt. It stung like hell. It was already fully light, and he watched her sitting on the commode peeing. She tore off some tissue and kept right on running her mouth.

"It's bad enough that you're going to Raleigh next Friday to see your pretty little wife and kiddies. I know what you're up to. You're just going up there to take Alma to bed. You've had your cake and now you want to eat it too. Sweet little deal—move the wife and kiddies back to Raleigh and have a woman in every town. Just like Alec Guiness— *Captain's Paradise*—it was on the friggin' cable. Turner Classic Movies, in case you didn't know. Well, you can count me out. You've got to make a choice. No more playing me against the wife."

"For chrissake, Maggie. I haven't seen my kids since the first week in March. With one more week in May, that's three months. And, anyway, it's not for three weeks, June fifteenth, I think. And, let's get it straight. I am gonna see my kids. If you can't live with that, then to hell with it." He was getting tired of the conversation. They'd been going on about it off and on since he'd gotten back from a two-day sales meeting in Raleigh last night.

"Sure. And now, you want to date this fucking woman lawyer. If she's Alma's friend, how come she would have enough guts to call you and ask you out to dinner? She's got some nerve. If I had a friend like that I'd cut her fucking heart out. Just what kind of fool do you take me for?"

"Want a Bloody Mary?" Buchanan kicked off the covers and walked naked down the hall. His penis was still waving proudly at semi-attention. All this talk made him thirsty and he felt the jagged edges of a beer hangover coming on.

"No, I've had too much. So have you..."

"Might as well be drunk as the way I am. Looks like making love's out of the question."

"OK, I'll take one, but make it light." At the mention of making love, her tone softened. "Look, Buck, I understand about the kids, but, this thing about this Candy person—no way José. You can talk all you want to about your kids playing together and all that bullshit, but you must think I'm really stupid. You told me she took you on a date in Raleigh..."

"She invited me to a Gordon Lightfoot concert in a building that holds nineteen thousand seven hundred and twenty-two sweaty bodies for basketball..."

"Don't bullshit me. That's a goddamn date in anybody's book. That woman's out to get you in bed, if she hasn't already. I think you know it and can't wait to let it happen..." Maggie was whiny now. The mention of not making love suddenly calmed her down. "What kind of lawyer would have a name like Candy?"

"It's not Candy, it's Cammie. Hildreth Cameron Brawley. And look, what kind of crap are you handing me, anyway? You want to make all these rules about what I can do and just last weekend you had dinner with Lewis Warrant. Not once, but twice, for chrissake. Friday *and* Saturday! Went sailing down to Southport all day Saturday. What do you call that? All I'm going to do is take Cammie out to eat tonight, say goodnight early and come home and go to bed—maybe with you if you'll quit bitching. It's her birthday for chrissakes, forty-three, I guess. Did I raise all this fuss when you said you had to see Lewis. Well? Did I?"

He hated to admit it, but it bothered him that he still felt jealous over Lewis Warrant's visit.

"Well, you know it's not the same. Lewis and I had business to talk over. I needed more money to finish the remodeling on the house."

"This house thing is kinda strange, if you ask me. I thought it was your house...he gave it to you. Why do you have to have dinner with him two nights and spend all day sailing with the bastard every time the phone rings and he's calling from Miami or Phoenix, or Bumfuck, Egypt, for all I care? If you really wanted it to be over, he wouldn't be coming around. You're just using him. You were so nervous about me getting my things out of here before he hit town. What's all that about? Sounds more like a long-running shack-up than a date. If you ask me, you like having him around. He's your social security."

"You bastard..."

He heard her start the shower.

An optimistic sign. Maybe they could finally get down to some real business. He grinned to himself as he stirred the V-8 with his fingers. He was diamond-tipped horny now.

He didn't usually put up a fuss about Lewis when he hit town. Sure, maybe he felt some jealousy, the weak and watery sort of thing that bruised egos are made of. But in the cold light of reality, Lewis Warrant represented his main ticket out.

More'n'more in the wee small hours, he'd fantasized that maybe Maggie would ditch him and go back to Lewis. It would give him instant resolve, self-discipline. God knows, for the moment at least, he had become emotionally addicted to her, helpless to cut the cord by himself. He was not of the old Bogart or Cagney mold—not at all cut out for pushing grapefruit into women's faces.

The shower was no longer running.

When he brought in the drinks, Maggie was lying on the bed in all her naked glory, a sight which instantly got his penis's attention.

He set the drinks on the nightstand and bent and kissed her.

She pushed him away and sat up and pulled his pulsing penis to her and let her tongue slowly lick the entire length of its underside and then sucked the swollen head into her mouth.

She murmured and did it again.

He stroked her hair.

Finally, he pushed her back and lowered his head between her legs. She was still wet and slightly goose-bumpity from the rinse in the shower.

Scooting around, she spread her legs wide to welcome his exploration. "Oh...oh, my god, Buck...OH!..."

He felt her tense slightly as his tongue found her center.

Her little breathless gasp was followed by a waterfall of shudders. Without warning she came quickly to orgasm from just the sucking and nibbling of her clitoris.

Swiftly, he urged her up on her knees and entered her from behind. He caught her watching in the mirror across the room. Eyes vacant with desire, she was hot, moaning, talking dirty now.

"Oh...Buchanan!" She squealed and bit the pillow as he pumped into her and her ecstasy splintered into shivering aftershocks.

Unrelenting, he continued driving rhythmically against her exquisite little buttocks, his penis engorged and throbbing, unreleased. She began to respond anew. The silky lining of her vagina devoured the length of his shaft, as it slowly slid in and out. Bending forward he showered her back with tender kisses. His fingers found her breasts, lightly pinching her nipples.

In the door mirror, his image observed itself still joined, slowly thrusting—a granite stag mounted atop a marble fawn, writhing in sweet death agony.

Adam and Eve—in erotic innocence?

"Oh, Buchanan...I...I could hate you...I love you so much. I'm your slave. You really do love me...too. You do...admit...it?" she pleaded shamelessly.

Love? The depth of surrender in Maggie's voice touched his soul and he felt his raw lust sweeten with affection. The feeling of intimacy, the profound tenderness filled him with awe.

And stark, erection-numbing fear.

She always gave herself to him with childlike exuberance—it made him strangely paternal.

But love? A wary sense of vulnerability jarred him back to reality. First

Alma, then Penny…he understood the pain of rejection.

Love? His adrenaline rocketed into overload. This child/woman had cast a spell on him.

What did he, or anyone, know of love?

Chapter Fifty-six

BY SIX, BUCHANAN WAS GETTING extremely antsy waiting for Cammie. On the phone, she had insisted that she come pick him up. "I'm anxious to see your place."

He hadn't really thought much about it, but when she finally showed about 6:05 he found he was embarrassed to have her see the shabby way he had to live.

At first it was bit awkward for them both. But, if she was at all put off, she didn't show it.

"I know you must miss your kids, but don't you just love having a place to be alone? Oh, my! Buchanan…" —she spotted his John Henry painting— "…did you do this?" She went closer and examined his signature.

The curve of her panty line stirred him as she bent to study the painting.

Her tissue-thin cotton shirtwaist dress was a devilish thing—a miraculous understatement of elegance fashioned in the palest pink. Magically, the simple frock revealed more than it concealed. Must have cost a mint.

The strange interlude with Maggie had left him horny as hell. Suddenly, he was reminded just how attractive Cammie was. When she turned and looked up into his face, her breath betrayed a trace of wine.

"January, two thousand two? Four months ago?" She read the date. "I'd forgotten you were an artist. I didn't know you still did that. You obviously had some very good training."

"VCU, in Richmond. For just about a year…in another lifetime, I did commercial art. Mediocrity put an end to that." He shrugged, pleased she liked the work.

"Mediocrity? No mediocrity in that…"

"An anomaly, really. This was the first—the only—thing I've done in almost eleven years. I was just showing off to my kids." Eyes downcast, he modestly examined his fingernails.

He wished he could show her his celebrated sketch of Maggie hanging at The Wit.

A perverse whim of ego? *A death wish? Truly suicidal.*

As she moved back, she bumped into the small table holding his laptop and DeskJet and bent and examined the stack of pages.

"A novel? Page fifty-five...is it going well?"

"I'm not sure. Sometimes I think 'maybe,' then again I wonder if I really know what the hell I'm doing."

"Oh, you do all right. Can I read it? This much, I mean?"

"No. I'd just have to ask you what you thought, then I'd want to talk about it. Novels are to be written down, not talked out. Nothing to do with you...try to understand." He took a step toward her and reached out his hand.

"I do, I guess. But you're so talented. Have you heard from *Esquire?*"

Despite his superstition about ruining his luck, he'd told her on the phone.

"Not for a month. It's on hold, I guess."

"Oh, they'll want it. I know they will."

"Don't get your hopes up. They have Mailer, Dominick Dunne, Jim Harrison, Tom Wolfe at their fingertips. Hersh Roberts at SNS told me the big magazines have a lot of competition between the editorial staff as to just who gets whose writers published. Anyway, what the hell? If I'm rejected I'll just submit another query, maybe even the *New Yorker.* Who knows?"

"What about *Publishers Weekly,* or *The New York Times Book Review?*"

"Sure, maybe *PW. The Times Review?* Forget it. They'd never stoop to legitimatize Mallone. They were so critical in the beginning."

"Snobs..." She crinkled up her nose.

"Uhmmm...mostly, I agree with them. I guess we both know what that makes me." He laughed.

"God, it's so good to see you again. You're so tan, so fit. Give an old woman a hug?" Impetuously, she molded herself against him and gave him a seductive squeeze.

Awkwardly, Buchanan returned the hug. Pressing against her caused a twitch in his crotch.

"Nothing like any old woman I've ever seen. You sure as hell don't smell or feel like one." Reflecting anxiously on his rebellious male reaction, he blushed a deeper red and laughed self-consciously.

"Do you recall the night we danced at The Player's Retreat? I can't believe it! That's only been three months. Now it seems like another century." She seemed oblivious of his discomfort.

He flushed. How could he ever forget her famous free love speech?

Behave! Buchanan admonished his undisciplined anatomy, half-heartedly. In open rebellion over being denied this morning, his damned old centurion had a will all its own.

"So, what do you think? Can we do it again? Is there someplace we could get dinner and stay to dance?" She stopped and frowned. "I hope you've saved this night for me..."

He should call Maggie. Except to call, he'd made no other promises for tonight.

"Of course, but I wasn't sure. The Blockade Runner hotel has a nice dance floor and a very good band. It's early yet. Season's just started and the crowds are pouring in. Keep your fingers crossed. I could call and see if we could get a table."

"Sounds lovely. Go ahead, don't wait."

He nodded and dialed, "Maurice, my good man, this is Buchanan Forbes..."

Shamelessly, he affected an air of importance.

On the other end, the forewarned Maurice laughed. "Don't worry, Buck, old sock, come right on up. I'll see to it the lady's impressed."

Maurice was still chuckling as he hung up.

"We've got a table if we can go right now," Buchanan said as he put down the phone.

"Well, you seem to know your way around, but, then, I'm not surprised." Cammie was dazzled.

"Wait, I want to give you this..." He took a letter-sized manila envelope out of the top dresser drawer. "Happy birthday. It's just a token. The only other copy's in my file."

Cammie opened the envelope and pulled out a copy of the Mallone piece he'd done for the magazine market.

"*The Mallet-Headed, Knight-Stalking Typewriting Baby.* Move over Tom Wolfe, I can't wait to read it!" She hugged him again and kissed him lightly on the mouth.

"Read it later." He smiled, nervously. "C'mon, let's hurry and order drinks while it's still light enough to see the ocean."

As he turned to leave, Buchanan froze.

Feet apart, one hand upon her hip, the other holding a coat-hangered plastic cleaning bag...barefoot...cutoff jeans and a tangerine tank top without a bra...

Maggie stood blocking the doorway.

"Aren't you going to invite me in?" Maggie's smile was nasty-nice as she stuck out her hand. "I'm Maggie Oakes O'Brien. Sorry, I'm late. I had to wait for his stupid cleaning."

She walked across and handed him the cleaning bag.

"You must be Cammie. Buck's so rude, but I've heard so much about you, I'm glad we've met at last." She wheeled and gave Cammie's hand an aggressive shake and nodded at the envelope. "Did he give you a copy of that *Esquire* thing? Forces one on everyone he sees."

Buchanan sputtered, "Maggie is a local comedienne, quite a kidder..."

"Buck's so shy. I'm really his...his *intimate*," Maggie said, and winked. She looked around the room and made a face. "Well, thank God, Buck, you made the bed at least." She shot Cammie a look that was clearly just-between-us-girls. "If someone didn't look after him..."

Sadly, she shook her head.

The bitch.

Buchanan cleared his throat tentatively. "Well, we don't mean to be rude, but we have a dinner reservation...uhmm...running late. Maurice has a waiting list."

"You decided on the Blockade Runner then?" Maggie turned to Cammie. "I told Buck the Runner would be the best choice, unless of course, you have a favorite place. The Neptune perhaps? The owner's such a dear, but the Nep's a bit touristy for special occasions, don't you think?"

Cammie's lips drew a tight little line and showed just a pencil trace of white. "I don't know Wrightsville Beach at all. I usually go to Pawley's..."

"Of course. Wrightsville is so *por le populo*, a provincial family beach. But, still we have a certain charm. I do want to apologize for not joining you. I hope you understand. Buck's such a dear, but I told him you two have so much to talk about, your kids and everything. Anyway, so nice. I'll let you run. Call me later, Honeybuck, after you've had your little visit. *Ciao.*" She smiled at Buchanan, gave his cheek a painful tweak and went out the way she came.

Por le populo!

Honeybuck!

Ciao!

I'll put Ciao on your frigging tombstone, Buck fumed silently as he rubbed the place Maggie pinched.

Rolling his eyes at Cammie, he gave an exasperated shrug.

Cammie looked away.

"Well, that was quite a performance," he said with a sigh of exasperation as he tossed the cleaning bag on the bed and pulled the door closed behind them.

"I had no idea." Cammie stiffly let him take her arm. "I never thought that I might impose."

"I won't hear a word of that. If you knew just how glad, how very glad I am to see you. Maggie's such a..."

At the moment, Buchanan found his vocabulary was totally inadequate to tell Cammie Brawley exactly what Maggie was.

Chapter Fifty-seven

INGER WAS DOG-TIRED. She'd been up since before dawn, but she'd finally put the Brookgreen Gardens book to bed. She held the phone listening to the sound of the sorority sister calling Penny to the phone. In the background, doors were slamming, followed by footsteps on the stairs.

Penny was breathless when she came on the line. "I was afraid you wouldn't call. Did you find out anything?"

"Yes, it's all worked out. Time's crucial now. We need to get this done. I still think you should let me call Buchanan Forbes. I promise you, he'd want to know..."

"No. Absolutely not. I'd die, simply die, if he found out," Penny whispered into the pay phone in the downstairs hall of the antiquated sorority house. "I'm ready anytime. Set a date. I'll have to make up a lie, anyway. Mother is watching me like a hawk."

"It's all set up for June fourteenth, that's a Friday. I made the reservation at the motel, just like you said."

"The Presidential?"

"Yeah...I don't understand why you want to go back there?"

"You said the doctor prefers a motel. What difference does it make if I'm a fool?"

"None, I guess, but if you feel that way, why won't you let me get in touch with Forbes?"

"No. Let's not go around on that. Is this a regular doctor, like you said? I wouldn't want some quack," Penny whispered, hoarse with fear.

"Oh, he's legit, rest assured of that. Uses some new IUD thingamajig. I'm told it's a simple procedure now. Doctors use 'em everyday, all over."

"Well...why won't he just take me in his office, then? I read about those things in *Cosmopolitan* not long ago. They only cost around fifty dollars, even in New York. Why do I have to pay a thousand to have this done?" Penny sounded less concerned with being overheard.

"Well, to insert the thing in a non-pregnant uterus is birth control. Since the president shut down abortion clinics, to insert it in a known pregnant uterus is against the law, a major crime. We're lucky to have found a legitimate physician who'll take the risk."

"But if these things are legal, why couldn't I just find out who the legitimate doctors are who use them in Knoxville or Atlanta and make an appointment and have one inserted? Who'd know the difference? I mean, I tried to check around and from what I can find out, a doctor has to do a pregnancy test to tell if a woman's pregnant until she's at least three months along. Couldn't I just give that a try?" She'd lowered her voice again.

"No way. Bonnie says most doctors are reluctant to insert an IUD in a woman who hasn't been pregnant before. The problem is that the cervix has to be dilated on these patients in order to do the insertion and more often than not the uterus will expel the device. So we're stuck. But our main problem here is time. According to my calculations, you're two-and-a-half months gone. No doctor, not even this one, will do an abortion on a woman past the first trimester. Any doctor in his right mind is going to take a look at you and give you a pregnancy test."

"I guess you're right. I still can't believe that this has happened to me. I mean what are the odds, my first time for everything?" Her voice had a defeated sound.

"Not your lucky day. But, I'll take care of the expense, don't worry about that. Are your sorority sisters going to cover for you? Have you thought up an excuse to get away?"

"Yes, but Peg doesn't know I'm pregnant. She thinks I'm just sneaking down there to meet Buchanan. Her parents are in Europe, and her older sister's minding the fort in Savannah. Mama wasn't happy. She resisted at first but she's going to a retreat near Asheville with her new preacher boyfriend, so she finally gave in." Penny gave a hollow laugh.

"How about Elroy? Have you taken back his ring?"

"He's tried, but I won't take it back. My mother's furious, but now I think she's scared of me. She's afraid if she pushes me too hard, I'll never take it back."

"Maybe she's finally going to let go..."

"Don't count on it, but it's over, I'll tell you that. Money isn't every-thing. I just want to get this behind me and start my life again. I wish Buchanan had called. I mean, I'd never let him know about this, but maybe some day things will change. I'm young; nothing has to be forever."

"Well, you told him not to, remember? If you'd only let me call, he'd see you through..."

"NO! Don't worry about the money. I'll pay you back as soon as I get out of school."

"I didn't mean that at all. It's just that Forbes..."

"No. He'd just think I was trying to trap him."

"I don't know what to say about that."

"There's nothing left to say. I know what I have to do. When all this is done, there'll be time to call."

"OK. Then plan to come down on Thursday the thirteenth. Too bad I have to fly to Atlanta on Friday to meet my publisher, but we can visit for one night and I can get you checked in the room before I have to catch my plane."

"Well, OK. I wish you didn't have to be gone."

"I'll be back Saturday night on the six o'clock flight. You'll hardly miss me…"

"Will you call me again tomorrow? I'm so scared…"

"Sure, hon, don't fret now. By the way, I've been at it since five this morning, non-stop, but I'm finally done with this damn book. You can call me author now."

"Oh, Inger, how wonderful. And don't worry, I'll pay you back the money. I'll find a way, I swear…"

"Hush. The money's nothing…just get some rest and don't worry about a thing."

Chapter Fifty-eight

DRIVING TO THE BLOCKADE RUNNER, Cammie's silence was palpable. At the hotel, the valet took the car.

"I hope you don't pay any attention to Maggie. She's been trying her best to corner me," Buchanan lied, trying to ease his embarrassment.

"Oh, please, you don't have to explain…"

"But I don't want you to think…"

"Please, Buchanan, just forget it. It's my birthday, remember?"

"Well, Mr. Forbes, we don't see enough of you. How're things at SNS these days?" Trying hard to impress Cammie as he escorted them to the best window table in the Ocean Terrace Room, Maurice greeted Buchanan as if he were a celebrity.

"Is this table satisfactory for the lady?" Maurice outdid himself.

"Yes, it's lovely," Cammie said, straining to smile.

Buchanan slipped Maurice a five when Cammie wasn't looking. The young conspirator gave him a knowing nudge with his elbow.

After he was seated, Cammie avoided looking Buchanan in the eye.

When they'd ordered drinks, he took her hand and raised his glass. "Happy Birthday. I don't have the words to tell you how happy I am to see you and how ashamed I am for all that nonsense back there."

With her other hand she touched her fingers to his lips. "Hush. It really doesn't matter."

"No, listen to me, goddamn it! Maggie O'Brien isn't good enough to stand in the same sunlight with you. I'm serious. I need to make amends. I confess, I've bought her some beers and took her kids flying kites. She got the wrong idea, and now I can't seem to make her understand. The blame is mine, it's my fault that it happened. I'm just sorry that you had to go through that. I'm not asking for your blessing. There's no justification for any of it. But, I hope you'll try to understand." His little fiction was a minor masterpiece of sincerity.

Cammie wouldn't look at him. He followed her gaze out at the ocean. Sandpipers were chasing in the foam at the edge of the surf. Children were playing in the sand.

Finally, she squeezed his hand with just a trace of feeling now.

"I understand, really. I just felt I might have imposed." She finally looked him in the eye.

Now it was his turn to touch a finger to her lips.

"Not a word." He smiled his gratitude. "Don't you know that finding out you were coming down is the nicest thing that's happened to me in a long time? You'll just never know how I've looked forward to tonight." It was the truest thing he'd said all day. Things with Maggie had gotten out of control. He'd been thinking too much about divorce lately. Cammie was a welcome reminder of reality.

Cammie leaned forward and searched his face. "I know that your jealous little friend just wanted to spoil our fun, and I really don't blame her. But I'll just be damned if I'll let her have her way. Don't let's waste anymore time on her. I've got you now. Let's eat and drink and dance the night away." She gave his arm a squeeze and laughed a crystal arpeggio.

The tension gradually faded as they sipped drinks and ordered dinner. By the time the waiter whisked the last dish away, the sun was down and the lights had dimmed—the band had already begun to play.

Enchanted by the music and mellowed from the wine, they danced. Cammie simply stood in place and slowly swayed in time. Buchanan breathed deeply in her hair and tried to ignore the insistent rhythm of her crotch brushing lightly against his thigh. Helpless to stop it now, he felt himself swelling against her leg.

Awkwardly, he tried to hold himself away.

She looked at him and shyly laughed.

"Easy for you." He blushed.

"Perhaps if we went out for a breath of air, or we could take a walk?"

"A cold blast from a fire hose might help but I doubt it. Sorry. I'm only human after all. I hope you don't...I mean..."

"Oh, hush. I know this is shameless, but I'm flattered, I really am." She took his hand and kissed his fingertips and gave them just a nip. "Want to leave? I'm ready anytime."

Suddenly, it hit him. All at once, he saw where this was heading.

Deja vu!

Poor dumb-ass that he was, it had taken him until now to figure out she had been serious when she made the clumsy pass that night after the concert.

Momentarily, he held his breath.

Well, so be it.

Cammie Brawley was a big girl, capable of making her own decisions.

"I never thought to ask. Where are you staying?" His thoughts came back to reality.

"The south end, all the way, overlooking the jetty. A marvelous old showplace sitting on the top of the highest dune. Come on. If you're ready to leave, I'll show you. Is it too cold to swim, you think?"

"Not too cold for anything, I think," he laughed self-consciously. "But I'd have to skinny-dip, or perhaps I could get away with just my under shorts..."

"Sounds daring. I will, if you will..."

"Which? Skivvies, or skinny-dip," he challenged.

"Whichever..."

"Let's go...before you lose your nerve."

NINA TRASK'S weathered cedar shake beach house sat apart, perched atop the highest dune overlooking the new lighthouse built after last year's hurricane deposited treacherous shoals out from the rock jetty on the ocean side of the inlet.

Without making a light, Cammie led him inside and pulled him through the darkness back to the bedroom and raised the split bamboo blind to let the street light in.

"Lose your nerve?"

He shook his head.

In the darkness she made a pale-pink cameo against the shimmering waterfall of loosened dust motes twinkling in the slatted shaft of saffron streetlight pouring through the window.

She looked at him, shyly. Then, without lowering her gaze, she began to unbutton the front of the shirtwaist dress and with just the slightest sigh of hesitation she pulled the simple frock over her head and carefully shook it out and hung it on the bedpost. Clad now in her slip, she turned and waited for him to make a move.

Buchanan shrugged out of his jacket and walked over and hung it on the doorknob. He heard her suck in a breath as he slipped off his shoes and, holding on the door, removed his socks.

"Well," she encouraged him.

"Well, what?"

"You first," she whispered hoarsely.

He hesitated, then unbuttoned his shirt and hung it over his jacket before he walked back across to where she stood.

She watched as he loosened his pants, let them fall and stood naked except for briefs.

"Well?" He essayed a laugh and failed.

With a deep breath, she closed her eyes, pulled the slip over her head and threw it carelessly on the nearest chair.

They faced each other a step apart.

Bravely, she looked him in the eye and then she faltered and timidly looked away.

Then, shyly, she moved to him and encircled her arms around his neck and buried her face in the hollow beneath his chin.

Her voice drifted up, barely a whisper now. "I can't believe I'm doing this. Do you know I was thirty and had my own practice before I met James Erwin? I was still a virgin. I undressed in the bathroom and insisted that James Erwin turn out all the lights on our wedding night. I've never let another man touch me—and now I'm just about to turn forty-three, and here I am stripping to my best Victoria's Secrets in front of you like some two-bit floozy."

"Shhh, don't say that..."

"Why not? I'd gladly be your lover or your mistress. Don't you want me to be your whore? I mean, now that you've seen me almost naked? Are you disappointed? Am I such a fool? I know you have that sexy young girl throwing herself at you. Am I so ugly to your eyes?"

He could feel her begin to tremble. It drove him nearly mad to feel her body against him.

He pressed her closer. The texture of her pubic hair through the thin fabric of her underwear was no longer an imagined thing. Through the whispery satin of the bra her nipples felt like blunted spear points etching little circles into his chest.

"Hush. I want you for my lover not my whore," he breathed softly in her ear. She nuzzled his chest with her cheek as he smoothed her hair. "I always thought you were beautiful but, now, to see you like this, I never dreamed..."

For a time the silence was broken only by their breathing.

"It's OK, you don't have to tell me that." She groaned and hungrily pulled his mouth down to hers, devouring.

"If...you...only...knew..." Tiny kisses punctuated his words.

"Oh, God, forgive me, I'm not the innocent you think. I confess I meant to seduce you. I've fantasized..." Her mouth was probing now, her tongue went to his ear. "And now..."—she breathed wetly—"...after knowing that other..."—her tongue flicked in his ear again—"...little slut's been ahead of me...I still can't help myself...please take me...I'm shameless...I'll gladly be your whore..."

"I can't explain how it started with her. I mean before I knew it...it simply...happened. My marriage is falling apart, and...I...I don't want you to think I'm the kind of man who...Oh god, I wish I could tell you that I'm pure...but please believe me, I've never played around. I guess you'll never believe that now but it's true..." Confession...the cleverest lie of all.

He wanted desperately to hurt Maggie for the hold she'd put on him.

"Hush. I never want to hear her name again." Her voice husked with need.

"But, I never..." He began the lie again.

"Please, hush..." She found his mouth and pushed her pelvis wantonly against him.

Fingers cupped, he fiercely caressed her buttocks. Her trembling was lessened now.

"Oh, my sweet...sweet..." he murmured, letting his fingers trace themselves slowly up to touch her breasts where they blossomed out from the pressure against his chest.

At last, he pulled back and looked down at both of them standing nearly nude.

"So, what's next?"

"Well, for openers you could tell me that part again about how lovely you think I am." She laughed and slapped his face, a gentle loving little swipe.

"Oh, you are...so lovely you make me want to cry...and laugh...and laugh and cry again...I can't remember ever wanting anything so much." It sounded almost like the truth.

She hushed him with a searching kiss.

Then, pulling back, she shot him a serious look. "Save the talk, some things can't lie." She rubbed her pudenda hard against his swollen penis. "I guess you do like me a little." She giggled.

"You'll never know how much." The morning's unfinished business with Maggie had left him aroused. Now he was swollen to the point of pain.

"I'm getting the message..." She wriggled back and forth. "This is crazy...I just march in here and strip off my clothes and now I'm standing here virtually naked thinking about dashing out on a public beach in my underwear to go swimming with a man whom I've just actually kissed for the first time. The Camerons have this inviolable principle. The famous Cameron Rule." She gave his nose a tiny peck.

"And just what rule is that?"

"No skinny-dipping on just the first kiss."

"Well, if that's all that's bothering you..." He let his lips softly touch hers and held them motionless as their eyes met for a moment.

"Are we really going to do this?" She breathed the question into his mouth.

"Make love? You might as well start screaming rape. You'll never stop me now."

It would serve Maggie right.

"Don't fret. I won't stop you—I insist upon it. But what I want to know right now is, are we first going to go out there like this and go skinny-dipping in that damned ocean?"

"I don't know. Do you still want to? I'm not sure my old centurion is at all impressed with the thought of all that cold salt water."

"Oh, I knew it. You're all talk. You had my imagination afire with scenes of Burt Lancaster and Deborah Kerr rolling in the surf at Waikiki."

"You're serious?" Unbelieving, he could see she was.

"Hell, yes. I can just see the headlines in *The New York Times*, **Prominent North Carolina Attorney Caught Fucking In Foam**— double my practice, guaranteed." Laughing, she pushed him away and bolted like a schoolgirl. Dashing headlong through the house and down the steps, she sprinted across the wide white beach.

Buchanan didn't catch up to her until she stopped at the water's edge. The ocean was a mirror, with just the suggestion of a breeze.

Muted by a thin bank of low clouds, the filtered moonlight reflected dully on the softly-stippled surface. At dead low tide, the waves broke far out with a gentle shushing, sighing sound.

Coltish, emboldened now, she kicked up a little spray.

Ducking out of his grasp, she giggled, pointed to his swollen crotch and teased, "Skimpy underwear like that was never made for a man. And by the way, that's a rather arrogant display of apparatus."

"Behold Laird Buchanan, the bank walker." He stepped back and whirled around.

"Behold what? A bank walker? You mean like a bank guard? What on earth? I have a hard time following you sometimes."

"It has nothing to do with banks. Don't you know anything?" he scolded playfully. "Surely you must know what a bank-walker is. When

I was a kid skinny-dipping in the river back in Virginia, there were always some showoffs with oversized equipment who liked to walk up and down the riverbank calling attention to themselves. We called them bank-walkers. I always knew I had the temperament, and right now, I believe that what I lack in machinery I could make up for with sheer enthusiasm." He balanced on one foot and made to take off his shorts.

The new moon began to break from behind the cloud, bathing them in a pale light.

"Oh, Buchanan Forbes, don't you dare. I promise I won't laugh again. You qualify in every way. You're some bank-walker, all right. But right now let's don't press our luck." Cammie looked up and down the beach and anxiously pulled him toward the surf. "Don't you dare take off your shorts out here."

Contrasted with the chill night breeze, the ocean suddenly seemed seductively warmer. With the tide near dead low, hand-in-hand they splashed through the surf for a hundred yards before the water finally covered them above the waist.

Buchanan reached out his hand, but Cammie coquettishly ducked beneath the waves.

He turned in a circle all around until she popped up in front of him at last. Crouching low in the water, she kept her breasts concealed.

"Peek-a-boo." She laughed a trill of silver notes.

It drove him crazy not to see. He reached out again and missed.

Suddenly she stood erect and raised her hands above the water, waving her sodden pants and bra. "Ta, Ta! Can I be a bank-walker now?" She giggled and threw herself against him and fastened her arms tight around his neck.

Unloosed, her breasts seemed swollen, heavy, more roundly feminine than Buchanan had first imagined. Nipples squeaking wetly across the ends of the hair on his chest, the devilish feel of her drove him to distraction.

Now he struggled to loosen his shorts again. In an attempt to balance both their weights, he slipped out of her grasp, lost his footing and went under with a splash. Finally, out of breath, he struggled free and came up for air.

"Free at last..." He raised his shorts like a banner and waved them wildly against the pewter moonlit sky. In his exuberance the tiny garment slipped out of his grasp and went flying through the air and splashed into the water several yards away.

He dove and frantically splashed his hands about in the water trying to find them again.

"Oh, boy, I've done it now."

"Are you kidding me? Who gives a damn? C'mon back here." She stood up and waded brazenly to him in water up to her waist.

Mesmerized by the swaying rhythm of her naked breasts, Buchanan abandoned his search.

Taking his hand, she cupped it to her breast and with her other hand pulled his face down and urged him to take her nipple in his mouth. With his tongue gently sucking her, she moaned and kissed him on the forehead and licked the pungent sea water from her lips. He felt her wet underwear tickle across his shoulders as she threw her arms fiercely around his neck. Her legs came up and encircled him about the waist as she moved from side to side trying to capture him inside her with no assistance from her hands.

When at last his manhood found her center she was too tight at first, resistant to his swollen size.

"It's been so long, I'm sorry..." Cammie wailed and pushed all the harder. The warm sea water splashed deliciously against their buttocks as he moved gently back and forth in the sweetest agony, slowly inching, gradually gaining with every thrust. The sensuality of the velvety texture of her warm clinging flesh tightly sucking against his swollen member and the lapping of warm waves on his testicles was almost too erotic to bear. Struggling mightily to insinuate his way deep into her was virtually too exquisite to endure without exploding from desire.

Relaxing the hold of her legs around his hips she spread herself and welcomed him little-by-little, finally taking him all the way. Then she locked her feet around him again.

He took her hand and pressed it to her clit, forcing her to caress herself as he slowly withdrew almost to the very tip and let himself slide back in...and...out and...in and out again.

"Oh! Me-oh-my, where did you ever learn that...Oh my..." she gasped and caught her breath as she massaged her clitoris more insistently.

She pinched her little button and bit hard upon his lip.

Chapter Fifty-nine

"NEWFANGLED IUD, HUH? Looks like a plastic scorpion." Mack Jones examined the distorted little plastic device and handed it back to the old doc. Two weeks had passed and the Brunswick County sheriff still had no lead to the identity of the corpse of the young female they had recovered from the swampy undergrowth off the highway near Bishop.

About all Mack knew for sure was that someone, probably a physician or nurse mid-wife—anyhow, someone with a lot of up-to-date medical know-how—had inserted that plastic IUD into the woman's very pregnant uterus. Subsequently, she had started to have violent contractions and that tiny plastic squiggly-twisty-looking thing had ripped open a large blood vessel in her uterus and she'd bled to death.

"Even if I'm right and a regular physician inserted that damn thing, that in itself ain't a crime. They been legal since around sixty-four, but they're still controversial, even among the Yankee docs. In North and South Carolina, not a lot of docs use 'em. A handful of the fancy society doctors around Duke, and Chapel College and Winston-Salem, mebby." Ol' Doc Lyon was a Carolina grad and pronounced Duke 'Dook' and called UNC 'Chapel College.'

"Mostly their use is limited to hotshot society specialists in the bigger cities. Rumor is that this particular device, the Tri-Torsion Twist, Tee-Tee-Tee, or the new version, T3, was voluntarily recalled once, during the clinical trials, three, four years back. Its originator, Graham/unLimited Technologies—G/uL—in Richmond, had complaints of dangerous bleeding episodes, but the FDA took a look and it was redesigned and they subsequently allowed G/uL Technologies to put it back in trials. IUDs ain't a new idea—started with a German, Guttmacher, who used steel rings, back before the first World War or some such time as that. They can call 'em birth control if they want but it don't take a genius to figure out, it's just a built-in abortion. Just a newfangled version of a foreign body in the uterus. Same as sliding a knitting needle or a piece of rusty coat hanger up inside."

"'Zat a fact?" The sheriff wiped tobacco stained spittle off his chin with the back of his hand. He'd started chewing tobacco again when he'd had a big blowup with Barbara Morgan a couple of weeks back when she'd started to measure his place for drapes and talking about wedding plans. "Well, at least now we know what that tube with G/uL on it was," he said, referring back to the Zoni Corbett death.

Given the Corbett woman's boyfriend's Miami mob connections, the sheriff still hadn't officially labeled her death a suicide.

"You got any idea what a nulliparous uterus looks like?"

"NULLY-WHA...whazzat?" Jones wiped his hand on a bandanna handkerchief. Fleetingly he thought of calling the Morgan woman. The tobacco chewing had lost some of its old appeal.

"NULLY-PAIR-US! Uterus of a woman what ain't never been pregnant before? T'aint no bigger'n one of them roundish, big nickel balloons, you know, the heavy ones, twice the size of a silver dollar. And just about as flat—and near 'bout as thin and fragile. Imagine what that would be like with one of these here T3s jammed up in it. Wonder it don't rip 'em apart when they put 'em in." Amos grunted, looking at the IUD. "When fertilization takes place, then what chance does an egg have to stay implanted on the lining with an ugly thing like that poking around in that little ol' flat balloon? Picture this: By the end of two weeks a pregnant uterus is as grown over and filled up with new blood vessels as a piece of bread gets with new mold growing on it. Think of the hell something like that squiggly plastic scorpion would raise. Innocent looking little suckers, but closest thing to one hundred percent effective as we know in medicine." The old doc paused and held the plastic device up to light.

Old Doc Lyon knew his medicine. In days gone by, when the slender, mustached professor emeritus and widely-published pathologist spoke to large audiences in amphitheaters at places like Harvard and Johns Hopkins, he was considered one of the most erudite forensic pathology experts in the world.

But now he was out of the bright city lights and a simple county coroner, back roaming around close to his birthplace. At times his speech became as folksy and picturesque as a local shrimper or tobacco farmer. It was a whimsical affectation.

He took a final look at the IUD and put it in his pocket.

"No shit? No bigger'n that, hmm…who'da ever thought it?" The sheriff pondered this awesome bit of knowledge and spit tobacco juice at a squirrel nibbling on a piece of popcorn near the base of a gigantic live oak tree. He and the doc were whittling pleasantly aromatic cedar sticks on a bench in the park in Southport across from the old doc's office. "Well, by God, it may not be a capital crime, but they've had that dead woman on ice up in Chapel Hill for two weeks, and who…or is it whom…whomever…dumped that body is guilty of a sight more'n malicious littering, to say the very least. If we ever find out who—or whom—that butcher was, then, by jayzus, I think we've got a whole list of juicy crimes to charge the person or persons unknown with. Conspiracy to perform an abortion. Failure to report a death. Unlawful disposal of a corpse to conceal a crime, and if I have my way, voluntary manslaughter. Anyhow, if we can prove that the IUD was rammed up inside her to cause an abortion—which, by God, you told me was your opinion, Amos—we're gonna put that bastard behind bars."

The sheriff was highly agitated, mainly because phones had been ringing all morning. The national wire services had picked up the story and all the big Sunday papers in both Carolinas had stories about the alleged crime and an apparently related series of similar events.

The accounts all insinuated that Sheriff Mack Jones was incompetent and the good citizens of Brunswick County were dumb as possum shit.

It was the kind of publicity the local Chamber of Commerce could do without.

"Well, the Associated Press is sure making a case for that. Joe Jordan, that Wilmington reporter fellow, has dug up two other recent deaths and two or three recent hospitalizations due to IUDs causing hemorrhaging. He makes a strong case for some very questionable goings-on around these parts." Amos removed his faded Greek fisherman cap and wiped the sweatband.

He picked up a tattered legal pad on a clipboard and read the list: "Two known deaths: one in Rockingham and Greenville, both North Carolina. Four hospitalizations: Charleston, Georgetown and Florence, South Carolina, and Whiteville, North Carolina."

The sheriff leaned across and launched another jet of tobacco at the squirrel.

"All were inserted with G/uL's T/3 and George Lembeck, the pathologist at New Hanover in Wilmington says he's heard rumors that there have been several reports of private physicians having given office treatment for similar hemorrhage cases. But that's highly anecdotal at this juncture."

The old doc finished reciting the list and handed the pad back to the sheriff.

He grumbled unhappily as he turned the page on the legal pad. "The three best pieces of evidence we have on this butcher are: That little slide rule gizmo with the advertising trademark—it had that one partial print of an index finger; the plaster casts of the tire prints we found near the scene; and them Saran fibers we found stuck to a spot of dried blood on the corpse's backside. The state crime boys say they were probably off'n the seat covers of the car what dumped her."

The old doc turned away as the sheriff paused to spit again.

Mack Jones looked back at the clipboard and found his place. "We know that Physician's Supply in Raleigh distributed approximately six thousand slide rulers, and the partial fingerprint on this one is not on file in either of the Carolinas, so we're waiting on the Feds. The tire print can be positively ID'd as standard factory equipment on approximately seventy-five thousand Chevies, Pontiacs, Buicks and Oldmobiles manufactured after July last year. I'm told it would be possible to find out how many of those cars were shipped into North and South Carolina, but it would take months and what would we have when we found out, just a smaller round figure completely untraceable to a specific GM car or an area. The seat cover fiber is the same story. The manufacturer has shipped over forty-five hundred sets to GM dealers in the Carolinas alone in the last six months. It all adds up to jackshit!"

The sheriff spit out his plug with distaste. He wondered if he moseyed down to the county offices he just might run into Barbara Morgan and give her a chance to make amends.

"Well now, hold on, Mack, ain't exactly jackshit, either. If'n any one of those three pieces of evidence can be tied to someone who had motive or opportunity, then we got us a bono fide wrongful death case, bet on it. Don't forget that partial fingerprint. Besides, you're overlooking two other pieces of the puzzle that would help in building a damn good case. That woman had A-negative blood. That's pretty unusual. If we find a bloodstained car or clothing, it could be damning. We're checking donor lists to see if we might match the blood type to a missing persons report. And we know that the device was the improved G/uL T3. There have only been ten gross of those shipped into the Carolinas in the first several months since FDA approval. Six of the ten gross in the Carolinas were shipped to Physician's Supply in Raleigh. That's the same company that gives away the slide rule. So we have a connection that would sure'n hell get the attention of a grand jury, I'd bet on that."

"Well, yeah, but..." Mack Jones heard a shrill whistle and looked up to see his deputy's car pulled up to the curb. Waving his arms wildly, young Clark Simmons was coming across the village green dodging under the giant, grotesquely twisted live oak limbs at a dead run.

"Mack, we just got a call..." Simmons came puffing to a stop. "I think we may have ID'd that corpse...We got a match on a missing persons filed in Morehead City for a Hester Salter, nineteen. Her folks live in Sea Level. She's been living outside Jacksonville for two years, near a wide place in the road, place called..." —he unfolded a piece of paper and studied it— "...oh, yeah, called Hubert. She was engaged to a dog-ass gyrene who wrote her a Dear Hester when he went overseas. Since then she worked off and on waiting tables in local beer joints. Local cops have rousted her several times for soliciting around Camp LeJeune and Cherry Point Air Station. They printed her once for DUI. They're checking the prints now." Young Simmons had two years of college and had the makings of a damned good law officer.

"Do they say anything about..." the ol' doc began, but Simmons got his second wind...

"Blood type? Yeah, take a guess." Simmons beamed and waved a piece of paper.

"A-negative."

"Give the man a big fat cee-gar!" Simmons beamed.

Chapter Sixty

IT HAD BEEN THE BEST OF NIGHTS, but it quickly became the worst of days.

When they finally went to sleep in each other's arms, Cammie had lost track of how many times Buchanan had made love to her—or she had made love to him. After she'd walked hand-in-hand with him buck naked, glowing with pleasure from the warm surf and, flaunting all their natural glory, they'd waited for the crescent moon to duck behind a cloud and made their mad dash, whooping with joy, back over the dunes to the cottage. The rest of the night, they'd taken turns ravishing one another.

Sunday morning started with great promise. Buchanan had roused her awake around ten with a glass of champagne and pulled her into the shower and destroyed her again.

Sheer ecstasy.

"That's what ya get for lovin' me...da da, de, da da..." She'd sung the Gordon Lightfoot song as she dressed, contemplating the prospect of the coming week. No phones, no clients, nothing to spoil their perfect bliss.

But then, when the love-besotted attorney and her favorite bank walker finally made it to the Blockade Runner for brunch, the sugar had quickly turned to that well-known odious other thing. In the hotel gift stand, Buchanan picked up the Sunday *Raleigh News And Observer* and, over coffee, was reading the AP article about an outbreak of IUD deaths when Cammie caught a flash of a headline on the front page:

Senator Charles Graham Victim of Heart Attack

"Oh, my God, Buchanan, please, let me see this." She moved his hand so she could read.

The Senator's death had occurred late yesterday and the news was sketchy in the early report. The event was deeply disturbing, not only because the man had been her father's lifelong friend, but, also because he was a permanent fixture, a party stalwart, and was coming up for re-election in the fall.

Cammie was a staunch party member and as state vice-chairman she had become a power in the party hierarchy.

"Please excuse me, I'll have to call the Governor. This leaves us in a pretty pickle. When we're gearing up to make a run against that nut in the Oval Office, what a time to have to fill a vacant seat."

"Cammie, why don't you give it a rest? This is your dream vacation, remember? We're making romantic history. Don't let's spoil it now," Buchanan protested to no avail.

"It won't matter. I can't just hide. Mae has my number here. I unplugged the phone. Most likely she has been trying to reach me all night. There's no escaping in the end." She squeezed his hand and pushed back her chair.

"ROG, I JUST SAW THE NEWS. Have you talked to the Governor yet? What's the word?" Cammie asked as soon as she reached the party chairman, Roger Bowles.

"Well, the word is simple. Ol' Charlie has left us in a mess, I'm afraid. And God, I'm glad you called. Your husband's out of town, your kids have gone off somewhere, I can't find Mae and your daddy has no idea where you are. Where'n hell are you, anyway?"

"I tried to slip off for a few days of R and R. I should've known it wouldn't work...we need to meet. Call the Governor. The sooner, the better I think." In her mind she was weighing the gravity of the situation with her need to be here with Buchanan for a few more days at least. She'd suggest a compromise, she had decided.

But Roger interrupted and she never got the chance.

"I know, thank God you called. I already called the Governor. We need you here this afternoon at three. John and Claude are all coming in. And Ben, of course, will already be right here. We can't delay."

"Today...oh, no...not today, it's Sunday, Rog! I just got here," she wailed. "I could come tomorrow. Perhaps you could just meet without me this afternoon. Hell, the funeral's not until Tuesday, the paper says."

It did no good, of course. In the end, all her pleading was in vain.

Head hung down, she walked back across the dining room and sadly broke the news.

In the car rushing back to pack her things, Buchanan had thrown a minor fit. "Jeez, Cammie, I can't believe you've let yourself become such a slave. Screw the goddamn party. The only party that counts is the one we started last night. Don't you ever want a life of your own?"

But in the end, it was no use. Still protesting mildly, he kissed her deeply and squeezed her tight before she left. "Call me," he'd said and waved.

"I will, and if things go well, I may be back tomorrow, or Tuesday. You know I've marked off the entire week," she said optimistically and drove away.

Empty promises.

NOW, STANDING BY THE WINDOW in her office on Hillsborough, looking at the setting sun over the bell tower of a distant church, she turned and picked up the phone.

"Cammie, oh, I'm glad it's you at last. I've been waiting all day…"

"Me too, you'll never know…" she began.

"Well, what's the news? I bet the whole thing was a wasted trip…a lot of fuss over nothing. Can you come back tonight, you think?"

"Not now, I'm afraid. Something came up this afternoon…things have taken an unexpected turn…" She paused and sighed. "I've really gotten myself in over my head this time…"

"What's happened, for chrissake…" His voice was edged with exasperation.

"Just calm down. I'm dying to have you again right now," she pleaded. "I couldn't help it. God knows I tried, Buchanan, darling. I really did…"

Buchanan had already been alerted by her tone.

"What's the devil's going on? Don't tell that me you've let them push you into managing the new campaign? God knows you need a keeper— someone to protect you from yourself. Are you going to try to take that on?"

"No, worse than that, much more serious, I'm afraid."

"Worse? What could be worse that that?"

"Well, they're pushing me into running for the spot myself. Can you imagine? Me? Just think, they want me for a United States Senator. We're meeting again in half an hour." The euphoria bubbled in her voice now.

Silence.

"Buchanan? Are you there?"

"I'm here."

"Well, say something. Don't you think I can do the job?"

"I know you can, but that's the end of us…" She heard his disappointment.

"It doesn't have to be that way; we'll work it out," she said soberly.

"Surely you can't believe that? You're signing your life away."

"We will. I know we will. You'll see."

She fingered a tiny seashell she'd brought in her purse. Last night and the beach washed back over her like an erotic dream. The idea of having a secret lover was exhilarating.

"Well, listen. I'll let you go. I know you have a lot to do." His tone was flat.

"I can take a minute more..."

"Call me when you can. I'll miss you." There was nothing left for him to say.

"Buck, I love you so, I really do." Her shoulders slumped and she sat down. All at once her optimism vanished. "I'll never forget last night..."

"Keep well," he said, shrinking from her hollow avowal of affection.

He had already replaced the instrument on the cradle when Cammie asked the empty line, "Did you hear a funny clicking sound?"

Chapter Sixty-one

CAMMIE'S CALL LEFT BUCHANAN feeling strangely empty? Dishonest? Both? Whatever? Recalling her famous free love speech, he understood Cammie was only using him.

But then, hadn't he used her too? When he thought about it, he should feel relieved.

He moped around in his place for half an hour before he suddenly realized he hadn't eaten since his interrupted brunch. From her tacky little scene yesterday, he knew Maggie would be lurking about the beach, plotting to bump into him, but what the hell? He had to face her sooner or later. It was take a chance on that or starve to death. He considered the odds and took the chance.

And lost.

Or won?

It all depended on how you looked at it.

Didn't matter, anyway.

It was predictable. As if she had ESP, Maggie walked into The Wit less than five minutes after he had swung his leg over a barstool and ordered a beer and a hamburger.

She plopped right down beside him and demanded, "What did you two do up there all night?"

Without looking at her, he said, "Who two? All night where?"

"C'mon, don't lie about it. I was by there off and on 'til after 4 A.M. Her car never left the drive."

"So?"

"So, don't play fucking innocent with me. She drove you to the Blockade Runner and you went down to Nina Trask's place with her afterwards. Then you had brunch at the hotel this morning around eleven. So what do you have to say for yourself? And, where is she, anyway? Her car's gone since around twelve-thirty. I thought she was staying for a week?"

"She went to Raleigh. Senator Graham died."

"Oh. So, anyway? You going to tell me?"

"Tell you what?"

"Goddamn you. What did you do all night up there with her? You fucked her goddamn eyeballs out, didn't you? Admit it."

Feeling absolutely rotten, he ignored her and took a bite of his hamburger.

"Are you going to answer me?" Maggie hit him on the bicep with her elbow and made him slop his beer.

He rubbed his arm and shook his head. "Can't you see I'm eating?"

"You SOB..." She sat there for a minute. Then she finished her beer. "Well, fuck you, Jack. I hope your goddamn wife and fancy lawyer mistress kill each other fighting over who gets your worthless ass." With that she stomped out into the street.

"What's wrong with her?" Jimbo asked.

Buchanan rolled his eyes ceilingward and rubbed his arm again.

"Classic attack of estrogen poisoning."

"If you say so." Jimbo looked at him and shrugged.

Heroes die only once. Cowards die a thousand deaths.

Nothing like getting an unpleasantness over with.

He suddenly lost his appetite.

When he got back to the apartment, Buchanan showered and was struggling to get into the bound galleys of the new book that Sharkey Mallone's publisher had sent him.

The novel was vintage Mallone, a clinic in plot and pacing. Mallone surely knew how to move a story along.

"It's simple," Mallone had told him that first night at the Bowery. "You gotta start with the first word and seduce the reader, word by word, line by line, right to the very end. The first line sells the book you're writing, the last line sells the next one."

Buchanan vowed to remember the advice.

Idly, he picked up a framed snap of Maggie in a bikini with her kids on the beach. He thought his heart would break.

He looked at the picture of his boys in the park.

Goddamn Alma anyway, did she think she could just walk away with his sons?

He looked at the snapshot of Maggie again. Goddamn little witch. He didn't even believe in love. He couldn't make up his mind whether to laugh or cry.

What a mess. He slumped forward and surrendered to an overwhelming rush of tears.

The phone jarred him out of his cathartic reverie.

"Well, you're finally home at last. Where the hell were you last night?" He wiped his tears on his sweatshirt as Alma started right in without so much as a how-de-doo.

"I spent the night in Raleigh at the house. I was up there for a sales meeting Friday and took the opportunity to get the yard in shape," he lied. He was becoming a master at it. "I was about to call. How are the boys? How are you?" He tried to correct his oversight, but knew he'd only managed to call attention to the slight.

"They're OK, about to drive everyone crazy now that school is almost out. And I'm fine. I had a little scare about my annual PAP, but Ogden thinks it was a false alarm. Look, enough of this chit-chat. I need to buy a car. This one's shot. I warned you it was on its last legs."

"Alma, that car's only been driven fifty thousand miles. We bought it new. It's hardly broken in. Have you been taking it in for maintenance like I told you?"

Alma had never taken care of a car in her life. He'd nagged and nagged about the importance of routine maintenance and finally given up. Periodically he'd discovered the oil stick almost dry, and she never had a scheduled lubrication done. If it hadn't been for him, that sport wagon wouldn't have lasted twenty thousand miles.

"That car's four years old. And don't blame this on me. I told you the car was a lemon from the start…"

A lemon for a prune, he seethed silently.

"What did they tell you is wrong?"

"Oh, I don't know. They said something about re-boring the engine. Anyway, I asked 'em how much to trade on a new wagon and they made me a deal. I want to trade tomorrow before he changes his mind."

"What kind of wagon? Another Tahoe?" Originally he'd bought the wagon from Carlos Corazon, an old high school classmate. He trusted Carlos. He'd inherited the Chevy, Olds, Cadillac dealership in Melas from his dad.

"Yes, a Tahoe, but with electric windows and door locks—and a sunroof. George Fuller in Roanoke made me a good offer on a trade. My wagon and a little under twenty thousand. Not bad, don't you think?"

"Sounds like a lot of money to me. Why Fuller? I bought that car from Carlos. I think he'll do a better deal."

"No, I don't want to deal with Carlos anymore. I think he took advantage of you. You're so gullible. Your stupid loyalties cost us money."

"Did you check with Carlos? At least give him a chance and see what he'll do."

"No, I told you, this is my car. I want to do it my way."

"But I don't understand why you're on the outs with Carlos all at once. If you don't want to talk to him, let me try. Maybe he can save us money. Who told you that the cylinders needed reworking? At least let me get Carlos' opinion on that," he reasoned gently. "I'll just call him first thing in the morning. He'll take a quick look, won't hold you up..."

"Don't you dare. Carlos goes to my church. If you tell him I went to Fuller, you'll embarrass me to death. I can make my own deals," she sniffed, indignantly.

"OK, what did you call me for?" he asked, just to make his point. The question was rhetorical...they both knew the answer.

"Well, of course, you'll have to arrange the financing. Can you go to a bank down there? Just send me a check. The total is..." —he heard her shuffling paper— "...nineteen, five-ninety-one, twenty-five. Just call Fuller to work out the details. He knows all about it. And for once don't try to haggle him down. Fuller's a friend of Michael Gentry's. Michael said he'd treat me right."

"Michael, huh? Listen, Mike's OK, but I don't know...he's always after something. He's probably just trying to shill for Fuller so he can make a better deal on a new Cadillac. With Michael you never get something for nothing. You can bet on that."

"Damn you, Buck, why are you fighting me on this? If you want me to drag these children all the way back down to Raleigh this summer...take them away from their friends...then you'd better help me get a decent car. I've been through hell over this abnormal PAP. Quit tormenting me." She sounded on the verge of tears.

What was the use?

"OK, OK, just calm down. I'll call Fuller first thing tomorrow. Just fax me the sticker and give me his number. I'll call you as soon as I've got it all set up. OK?"

She read him the number.

"OK, now let me talk to my kids. Then fax the sticker."

Garrett, the four-year-old came on. "Daddy, Mommy's going to get us a new car..."

By the time the eldest got his turn, Buchanan's heart was aching to see them.

"You guys having fun?" he asked Granger, trying to sound all right.

"Oh sure, Mother's friend, Dr. Gentry, took us to Atlanta to Six Flags to ride the roller coaster and the bumper cars. He said he played football with you in high school. Do you remember, Dad?"

"Uh-huh. Well, goodnight and take care of your mom. She needs all the help you can give her. Tell Nan and Grandad hello." He said goodnight and waited as the fax came across.

That no good cocksman, Mike Gentry, suddenly turned good Samaritan. Now that was one for Bob Ripley's Believe-it-or-Not. He dabbed a vagrant drop of dampness from his cheek.

Buchanan looked at the fax of the sticker. With tax and license, he'd need almost twenty thousand.

He thought about his cache of ready cash.

NELL BATSON REPLAYED the tape and looked at the numbers on the pad: $19,591.25.

Twenty grand! A small fortune for a guy who was maintaining two residences, actually three, when you counted the money he mailed to Virginia each month. Funny…Forbes didn't seem to make all that much of a fuss about the money.

Chapter Sixty-two

AFTER NELL BATSON called to report Alma's decision to buy a car, Durwood Fisher had a premonition that Forbes might be about to dip his hand into his secret cookie jar.

Before he went to bed Sunday night Fisher arranged with the Wilmington office for Nell's schedule to be covered for Monday morning. He instructed her to stand by to monitor Forbes' phone calls and to keep him under close surveillance for as long as she thought it necessary to find out what arrangements he would make in the purchase of the car.

Up by six, she rushed through her shower. Experience had already taught her that most mornings the beeper signal on Forbes' car activated before seven, signaling his departure to work.

This morning proved to be the exception.

No phone calls or sign of life until shortly after nine when the beeper signal from the tracking device stirred her into action.

Taken completely by surprise that he had not called the car dealer as he'd promised Alma, she grabbed her purse and her jacket and headed out the door. Taking great care to remain out of sight, Nell had driven cautiously along, expecting he'd take U.S. 76 over the new bridge across the channel, but she was surprised again. Forbes headed south along the beach on Lumina and slowed just past The Wit and pulled off to the left and parked in front of Wings.

By the time she'd caught up and circled the small triangular block and taken a parking space back out on Lumina, Forbes was coming out of the Post Office. She watched from a distance as he walked into the isolated booth between the laundromat and the bank to use the phone.

Damn.

Nell fumed and twiddled with the radio for the better part of an hour while she watched him make a series of calls. In between calls Forbes hovered just outside in the awning shade of the laundromat while he waited for the phone to ring. Once or twice he had moved quickly back into the booth to warn away approaching callers that he had the phone in use. In each case he'd pleasantly directed the disgruntled party to the other booth across Lumina where she was parked by the dock where Capt. Eddie's charter sportsfisher Marlin II maintained a year-round berth.

At 10:55 Nell had almost decided to risk a quick dash into Newell's to grab a cup of coffee when suddenly Forbes left the booth and headed for his car.

This time she followed him across the Waterway, down Oleander and all the way downtown where he had to circle the block twice looking for a parking space on Front Street.

Now, she wondered if he suspected something. Why hadn't he made the calls from home?

Finally, she watched as Forbes parked on Market and she drove on past as he slugged the parking meter. Luck was with her, and she pulled into a thirty-minute loading zone and caught sight of him as he disappeared inside the main branch of the Wachovia Bank across the street on Front.

The outside walls of the bank lobby were glass, and Nell held her breath expectantly as she watched Forbes wait his turn behind the line of merchants and secretaries going about the routine of making the week's deposits and getting the day's operating cash.

The Wachovia made no sense.

Why hadn't Forbes used his local bank at the beach?

When he finally stepped up to the teller, her heart rate increased as she saw him hand the girl an envelope and wait while she removed and counted a sizeable stack of bills.

Where had he come up with all that cash? Durwood would wet his pants over this.

The teller turned and moved to the rear before she returned again and handed Forbes some paperwork. Forbes signed and then she tore the carbon out and put the slip into an envelope and gave it back again.

A cashier's check...

Her breath came faster now.

How much? No way to find out right now, but she had contacts. Later she'd get the exact amount. Tax and tags...with a trade, she'd bet the car was over 30 K at least.

Now her heart was thumping like a hammer.

Forbes paused on the sidewalk outside the bank and opened the envelope and quickly checked the contents before he put it inside the breast pocket of his light khaki poplin business suit. Glancing up and down the street, he shaded his eyes against the bright morning glare. Nell watched his reflection in the window of a dress boutique as he turned and purposefully set out again.

She waited until he had moved ahead and followed, keeping in the shade across the way.

In the next block, he suddenly veered and dodged through the light mid-morning traffic crossing over to her side, before he skipped up the steps of the main Post Office. Now, she had him on familiar turf. Her own office was in the federal suite on the second floor. Nonchalantly, she picked up her pace and narrowed the gap between them. Confidently she followed through the revolving door.

This time Forbes lost no time in getting his mission done. All business, he transferred the cashier's check to an Express pouch he'd picked up from the rack. He had obviously pre-addressed a label and took his place in one of the lines queued up at the long counter of postal clerks.

Nell slipped into the line two customers back but, try as she might, she was unable to catch a closer look. When Forbes' turn came, he paid in cash and waited for a receipt.

For the next hour Forbes' movements were boring.

To pass the time Nell sat in the car outside the big hospital and opened her laptop and completely typed out a report detailing the entire morning's activity up to the current moment. She considered calling the surveillance accomplished and was thinking about giving Durwood a buzz, but the clock on the dash told her it was not yet noon.

And what the hell? She was covered at the office for the day so she decided to go the extra mile and was rewarded for her perseverance.

At five 'til noon, Forbes came walking out of the hospital and headed straight back to the beach.

Nell was just walking through her cottage door when she heard him dialing the phone through the speaker monitoring the tap.

"Hi, Pop, how are things?" Nell listened as Forbes passed the time of day when his father answered the phone. After perhaps a minute or two, he said, "I promised Alma I'd call her about the car. Is she handy now?"

Alma came on the line near hysterics. "What took you so damn long? Did you talk to Fuller? Is it all arranged, when can I pick up the car?"

"Look, calm down, the car's all taken care of. You can pick it up around five this afternoon."

"Today? Oh, Buck, how did you manage to get it done so soon? You're a genius—sometimes—when you want to be." Her initial exuberance tempered to a more grudging tone.

"OK. Now listen, and don't get mad. I saved us almost seventy-five hundred on the deal and got a much better car. The very best model in the line. It's exactly like the new one Emily Diggers has, remember? The one you always liked so much. Much more interior room…blue, your color too."

"Buck, how'd you manage? I hope you didn't try to dicker George Fuller down. I'll be so embarrassed. He's Michael's friend. You probably treated him like some crook."

"Alma, did you hear what I said? I saved us seventy-five hundred on the deal. That's a lot of cash. It actually amounts to much more when you consider the model you're getting now is over five thousand more on the base price. Don't worry about Fuller. He doesn't need our charity."

"I might have known I couldn't trust you. You're such a clod. Nice people don't go around suspecting their friends of cheating them. George Fuller's mother is a member of my church."

"Well, that's the other part of what I have to tell you. You'll pick the car up from Carlos. I did the deal with him."

Silence.

"Carlos?"

"Yes, Carlos. It pays to do business with people you know and trust. Counting the more expensive model and all the extras, I saved almost twelve thousand in this transaction."

"Buck, damn you, I'm so embarrassed. How will I ever face Michael or Mr. Fuller again—and after they were so nice to me. You don't know how nice they treated me. Your stupid Carlos never took me out to lunch."

"I'm sure they were nice Alma, but business is business. Since when is lunch worth twelve thousand of our hard-earned cash?"

"That's so tacky! I'll not take that car. I'll just make my own deal. I have a right to a life."

"Suit yourself. I'll tell Carlos to tear up my check."

Silence.

"Can't you call Fuller at least, maybe…"

"Oh, I did. We went round and round on the phone this morning. He didn't really want to sell that car, not nearly bad enough."

"I'm so embarrassed. How could you? I hate you. Our friends will think we're cheap and Michael will be…"

"Alma, screw Mike Gentry. At least I owed it to you to give Fuller a chance to meet the deal Carlos offered us. After all, I understand you were negotiating in good faith. But I hate to tell you this, he was taking shameful advantage of you. And Michael Gentry should show better judgment, if indeed, he is your friend. He certainly didn't do you any favors here. Carlos will call you later this afternoon to let you know what time you can take delivery. The title will be in your name. All you have to do is sign the paperwork and drive it off the lot. That should give next week's trip to Raleigh an extra touch. A new car always puts a little spice in life. I hope you and the kids enjoy…"

"Well, I won't. You take the fun out of everything…" She slammed down the phone.

NELL CALLED DURWOOD and told him everything in a rush. "Listen, Durr, subtracting the seventy-five hundred Forbes said he'd saved by dealing with this Carlos person, that still comes to around twenty-six thousand and some change. That's a lot of cash for almost any working stiff to have to explain. I saw him get that cashier's check with my own eyes. That money will never show up on any tax return, I'll bet on that."

"*Bingo!*" Durwood practically shouted in her ear.

Chapter Sixty-three

DOC LYON WAITED until the sheriff put down the phone. "Well?" he asked, and watched while Sheriff Mack Jones jotted down some final notes.

Before he spoke, the sheriff turned and sent a jet of dark brown tobacco juice streaking across the room with unerring accuracy into a big old-fashioned brass spittoon.

The fickle widow Barbara Morgan was dating a widowed Baptist preacher now.

"Well, indeed! Things are really getting interesting in that Salter woman's death. Looks like that reporter Jordan may be on to something after all. There seems to be a definite pattern here…"

"How so?"

The sheriff wiped his mustache on a red bandanna from his hip pocket before he picked up the notes and spoke again.

He'd just be damned if he'd let that prissy Barbara Morgan get his goat.

"First of all, the State Law Enforcement Division in Columbia and the North Carolina Bureau of Investigation have found that in both of the other related deaths and at least five..." The numbers of reported incidents were increasing now that the situation had received national media attention. "...of the reported twelve hospitalized episodes of serious hemorrhage due to IUD's associated with an aborted pregnancy, the victim—or patient, whichever—had withdrawn or borrowed a relatively significant sum of money within two weeks of the reported incident. In four of the cases the amount was exactly one thousand. In the death near Rockingham, the woman was a solid citizen, a young clerk of the court. She had just taken a ninety-day note with a local bank for seven hundred fifty, but she'd also written a check for three hundred cash two days before she was found dead in her home in a pool of blood. The other women had made bank withdrawals or sold stock ranging in the neighborhood of seven to nine hundred dollars."

The sheriff reached for his bandanna, preparing to spit again.

To make matters worse, now Brooke Hankins, his faithful nurse in Myrtle Beach, had had her feelings hurt and was playing hard to get.

"Will you quit spitting that excrement and get on with it," the old doc prodded. "What about the Hester Salter woman?"

"According to the Jacksonville police, a retired gyrene gunny sergeant who lives in the same trailer park in Hubert loaned her the nice round sum of one thousand American..."

"Well, what do you know?"

"If'n ya' ask me, some enterprising doctor had hisself a regular gold mine going until things started going bad. My guess is that he'll go underground and no one will ever find him now. And, so far, the survivors refuse to talk."

"Look, women are dying. Sooner or later somebody will say something."

"Yeah? Well, the morning after the abortion, the woman they later found dead near Greenville told a close friend—a local coed at East Carolina University who thought she might be needing the same procedure—that her 'doctor' was a nice young man who had his initials on his shirt cuff. She'd said one of the initials was an 'E' and also told this friend that the doctor insisted on doing the procedure at a motel near Kinston."

"You suppose all of these cases involve the same guy?"

"There was at least one other woman, the one who was treated at the Cumberland County Hospital in Fayetteville. She was a hooker who's since moved to parts unknown, but she also mentioned the same thing about the fancy embroidered shirts to the technician in the ER when she showed up hemorrhaging. She said her doc met her in a motel, too."

"Well, if it turns out to be the same guy in the all other cases...we know we're looking for some fancy dude."

"What I can't understand is if these IUD's are legal and this guy's a regular doc, why a motel? If he's legit, wouldn't he just have these women come to his office, keep everything on the up and up? Then he wouldn't really be guilty of anything, would he?"

"Well, no, but most of these women, maybe all of 'em, have never been pregnant. Remember what I told you about nulliparous females? No respectable doctor is anxious to offer these things to those patients. The success rate is poor. I mean, a regular doctor could get by with this once or twice as an office procedure but sooner or later he'd leave a trail of hemorrhaging, aborting females, all of 'em questionable as to their appropriateness for the procedure..."

"OK, I get it now. It would ruin his reputation if he was doing it out in the open for fun and profit as a regular thing...like killing the golden goose, huh?" The sheriff interrupted and sent another unerring salvo flying at the spittoon.

Maybe he could call Barbara Morgan and apologize.

"Exactly, and not only that, the high end of the going rate for implanting IUDs at a hospital is only about four hundred bucks...with the hospital getting most of the loot."

"Ah, so, esteemed doctor-san...there's a lot of difference between four hundred bucks and a thousand, huh? And listen to this..." The sheriff turned his head away and sneezed and blew his nose on the bandanna, then he spit again. "...Henry Long, the guy who owns Physician's Supply in Raleigh and gives away them little rulers, is co-owner of a cottage at Wrightsville Beach. The place is known locally to the swinging crowd as the Sugarshack. A lot of married men go out there to meet the local unmarried women for exhilarating intellectual enrichment and spiritual meditation, mebby?"

"Yeah. Tell that to the women's auxiliary down at the Baptist church." The old doc guffawed and slapped the sheriff's knee.

Damn women in general. They owned eighty percent of the property and they damn sure owned a hundred percent of the pussy.

"Uh huh. Guess who one of his partners is?..."

"Ben Casey, or young Dr. Kildare?"

"A young doctor at the local hospital—a real swinger from what this report says. Married with a kid, but hangs out with wannabe singles at the beach. Has a reputation. In med school at Charlottesville he was a regular Don Juan with the nurses. Guess what his specialty is?" The sheriff wiped his mustache again and turned over the bandanna and examined it fastidiously and tossed it aside. He opened the bottom drawer of his desk and took out a clean one. This time it was blue.

The doc just looked at him.

"OB-STREP-TICS and GUY-NAH-COL-OH-GEE!"

"No shit, OB-GYN. Have they questioned the guy?"

"No, and this is strictly on the Q.T., you unnerstan'? So far the guy seems to have a pretty good alibi. But they're going to keep an eye on him...and guess what else?"

"Listen, can't you ever just tell me something? I'm tired of these..."

"He's been making regular deposits and has built up quite a sizable bank account separate from his joint account with his wife, mostly over the last three or four months. Most of the deposits were for around—how much you think?"

"Quit it, I tol' ya'..."

"OK, around a thousand, more or less...and he makes a lot of overnight trips out of town."

"No shit..."

"Wanna guess what his first name is, Amos?"

"Goddamnmit, Mack, will you stop?"

"Gene."

"Well, shit how does that help?"

"You used to be quicker'n that, Amos, you must be getting senile."

"The old doc's face screwed up in thought. "Oh! I get it, *Eugene*." His face suddenly lighted with a smile.

"With a friggin' capital 'E!'" The sheriff spit again.

Chapter Sixty-four

DAMN, DAMN, DAMN! He should have known better.

Win the battle, lose the war.

Although Alma had often thrown it in his face about how much she envied their Raleigh neighbor, Emily Diggers, for having exactly the same model, practically every day for the past two and a half weeks, Alma had called to complain about the new Chevy Tahoe. Listening, not too patiently, Buchanan recalled that it hadn't been all that long ago that he'd heard countless thrilling recitations about how nice the roominess and power windows and power seats and door locks of Emily's new wagon were for a mother with an army of small children to chauffeur about.

Buchanan had come to know by chapter and verse all about the sunroof. Alma could become quite emotional talking about how she simply adored Emily's new electric sunroof.

To hear Alma barely three months ago, to have to drive anything less was the equivalent of flagrant wife abuse and child neglect.

But now, quite suddenly and inexplicably, nothing about the new car could please Alma.

At first, the day after she'd taken delivery, it had been the size that bothered her. "I just can't find a parking space anywhere," she'd whined.

"Alma, it's on the inside that you get the extra room." When he pointed out that the car was a mere six inches longer on the outside, she'd ignored him.

"Read the handbook, you'll see. The specs are all right there."

She'd dismissed him with a sniff. "You're always confusing me with facts."

As days went by, the situation worsened.

"This thing eats gas. I was late for church because I couldn't find a gas station open on Sunday morning. I had to drive nearly into town."

By now, he'd learned that he'd never win, so he bit his tongue. Why remind her that the trip for gas was five times as far as the trip to the church which was a mere mile from his father's house?

Monday, it had been an errant window rattle. When he'd asked Carlos to check it out, it turned out to be a rat's nest of flashlight, old tools, an aerosol can with a loose top, a discarded cigarette lighter, a tire gauge and some toy soldiers she'd transferred from the old wagon and dumped into the glove box. It all clanged together when the car hit a pothole or a bump.

Tuesday, the dissatisfaction had progressed to an ominous engine sound—unspecified, of course—which made her "insecure."

Carlos, who understood by now the problem was not with the car but was related to the hormonal whims and the seething passive-aggressions of the owner, promptly brought her a loaner and kept the car all day. When he returned it, he offered to certify in blood that it was combat-ready stem to stern—fully prepared to negotiate a cross-country race in flood or snow or wind.

Buchanan apologized to Carlos for getting him into a no-win situation.

"No sweat, man. It's been too quiet around here lately, anyway—and after all I was married too, once." Carlos laughed the grateful laugh of a man who has had a brush with the guillotine.

First thing Thursday morning, a black cat had crossed in front of Buchanan as he made his way to the Post Office down the beach. Buchanan laughed a nervous laugh. He was not a superstitious man.

Besides, one more day and he was going to see his kids again.

He squinted against the morning sun as the cat dashed under a house and he labored hard to shake a free-floating feeling of impending doom. Beginning with the end of his bittersweet World War III relationship with Maggie, nothing had been going well since the Sunday after Cammie left, a few weeks back.

Secretly he had been relieved that he hadn't had to keep up a pretense with Cammie that his feelings for her reciprocated her romantic crush on him. And he'd put aside the guilt that he'd used her to insulate himself against his growing emotional attachment for Maggie. After all Cammie had used him too, and now that they had been intimate, he grieved the loss of her as his best friend.

And in that regard, just to make things even worse, he'd been conspicuously unsuccessful in his attempts to track Cammie down again.

So, against his building anxiety, all week long Buchanan had looked forward to tomorrow and the happy reunion with his boys. Home early Thursday afternoon, he packed his bags and tried to call Cammie again.

Still no luck.

"She's been in Greensboro and Winston-Salem all week, and now Washington. Due back tomorrow afternoon, Mr. Forbes," Mae, her ever-faithful secretary reported.

Disappointed, Buchanan hung up and called the boys to confirm Alma's final travel plans. He'd make sure to arrive in Raleigh ahead of them, with plenty of time to lay in rudimentary supplies and have the house in spotless shape.

"Well, it's about time you called. That damned car you dumped on me is a disaster. You always think you're so smart…maybe you'll be satisfied now," Alma started in without bothering to say hello.

Buchanan's heart sank. From her tone, the engine must have exploded or the transmission was lying somewhere in the middle of the street.

"Just calm down. What seems to be the problem now?" He dreaded to hear the news.

"Well, it's just not running right. I don't like the sound."

He breathed a sigh. "Oh hell, Alma, you're just nervous about the trip. Carlos told me Tuesday it was running like a dream."

"What did you expect him to say? After all, he's the one who helped you drop that lemon in my lap. Michael Gentry told me he'd heard that Carlos had been trying to dump that car. It was too gaudy and overpriced with experimental stuff to be practical. Besides, the local weather report is looking bad. What if it rains tomorrow?"

"What the hell difference would that make, for chrissake?"

"Michael said he'd heard that those sunroofs were bad to leak…"

"Sunroof leaks—what kind of crap are you handing me now? I haven't heard a single report of anyone's station wagon filling up with water and drowning the occupants from a leaky sunroof. And experimental? That's bull! Alma…it's the very same goddamn sport wagon, the very same identical equipment as the one Emily Diggers bought in January. You loved that car…said you'd gladly kill to have one just like it." It was an exact quote.

"I never said any such a thing. Don't you remember how much trouble Emily had with that damned wagon? Nothing ever worked the way it should. I always knew she'd bought it because she was just a stuck up fool, and besides, her sunroof leaked. You certainly remember that."

The very same sunroof you lusted for, he wanted to scream but bit his tongue instead. This was a combat he would never win. He'd never hear the last of this, not until that car was happily rusting in some forgotten junkyard.

"Don't worry. You'll be OK, and besides, I'll have it checked out again myself when you get to Raleigh tomorrow."

"No, I've been trying to get you all evening. You never stay at home. I wouldn't think of starting out with that car still acting up."

"What do you mean? You're supposed to bring the boys tomorrow…"

"I can't possibly start out with a car load of kids and the car acting up like this."

"OK, tell me exactly what the problem is."

"Well, I told you, it's just not right."

He should have seen it coming.

"I'll call Carlos at home right now and have him pick it up. He'll give you another car to make the trip while he makes this one right."

"I'd never stand for that. I'd rather wait. We paid a fortune for that car. I don't want to be stuck in Raleigh with the kids all summer, tied to the phone, trying to sell a house, and worrying about some worthless car. Michael is going to have George Fuller take a look at it tomorrow. He's got a much better service staff. Besides I have to go back to the doctor to let him check me again."

The doctor tomorrow? First he'd heard of it.

"Alma what's this about the doctor? You've known all along that you were coming to Raleigh. Be reasonable. You're not talking sense. Let me talk to my father. Maybe he and Nan will follow you and the kids, in case there's trouble with the car."

"Don't be absurd…I can handle this myself. Besides, I can't help it if Ogden Branch needs to look at me again," she snorted angrily.

"Then let me just talk to the boys…"

"No, not tonight. They're too upset because you stuck us with a no-good car and spoiled their trip."

"Alma, how could you? You're just using the kids to get back at me."

"How dare you blame me for our trouble? After all the misery you've brought down on me. If you hadn't gotten fired…You're not a fit father for them anyway." And on and on…

Finally he hung up.

The situation was getting grim.

No use trying to change her mind. And, now that he thought about it, that Mike Gentry was getting on his nerves.

Michael Gentry?

Hmm!…

No way! He considered and shook his head, too tired to think about it now.

He wasn't sure he really cared, anyway.

Buchanan grabbed his keys and headed for The Wit to drown his disappointment in beer.

Chapter Sixty-five

MISERY DOGGED BUCHANAN like a plague of locusts.

Sitting at the bar in The Wit, he listened with mild interest to Jimbo and Troy discussing the Braves' losing streak, trying to get the resentment for Alma off his mind.

"Well, at last, it's actually you. I've missed you, you dirty rat…"

Please God, Buchanan prayed silently. Perhaps it's just the alcohol that's befuddled my senses. Without looking, the voice sounded something like the old-timey gangster actor James Cagney's imitation of Maggie O'Brien—or, God forbid, the other way around.

Maggie touched his shoulder and slipped onto the adjoining stool.

"Hi Maggie," he said without warmth. He didn't want to admit how really glad he was to see her.

"Well, stranger, where've you been so long?"

"Out of town, mostly." He really didn't feel like talking now, least of all to her. Not much left for them to talk about anyway—he'd screwed that up right enough.

"I've been hoping I'd run into you. The house is all but finished. I've moved most of the new furniture in. It's beautiful. Come see it, Buck."

"You know we can't start all that up again." Softening a bit, his voice hoarsened, took a kinder tone.

"Oh, I know, but you can't just say things never happened, either. Look behind you on the wall." She pointed to his sketch.

He didn't need to look. She was right. It hadn't exactly been all bad. In fact it had been too goddamn good. Lately he couldn't sleep at night remembering just how good it had been.

"We had our moments all right." He felt a wayward tug of sentimentality and a powerful physical reaction.

"Buck, I'm sorry I acted such a bitch. I was just jealous. Surely you can't hate a girl for that."

He looked down at the dusting of freckles across her nose and those goddamned bee-stung lips. She was so smart, and funny, and tender. It broke his heart to remember.

"Aw hell, Maggie, you know I don't hate you. But, nothing's forever, so they say…"

"Yeah." She tried to laugh and failed.

"Well, if we can't be lovers again, that's no reason we can't be friends." She tugged his sleeve and gave him a hopeful look. "There's always rainy days and Sundays…"

A vagrant aching welled up in his throat. He hoped she couldn't hear his heart thumping.

Rainy days and Sundays with Maggie had been wonderful. Sometimes they had spent a rainy afternoon just talking or listening to music. God, he missed her something awful.

"No, no reason. I hope I'll always be your friend." He really wasn't sure.

"Well, that's a relief. At least I'm glad of that. Don't be a stranger, come see the kids once in a while. Ryan and Melly ask about you all the time." She brightened. Her smile tore the heart right out of him.

"I will. Tell 'em I miss 'em, too."

"Say, why don't you just follow me right now and let me show you the house? I've been dying to show it to you and it'll only take a minute. I'm leaving town tomorrow…Daytona. School's out, thought it might be good to have a change of scene. Please. Just come along and take a peek.

[316]

It's all but finished now. I'll be moving in when we get back. It would only take a minute, pretty please? OK?"

He waved a bill at Tory. "No, I better pass. Maybe when you get back."

"You'll never come. Come now, pretty please. It'll only take a minute. I won't bite, you know." She gave his sleeve a tug.

Watching her, he tried hard not to laugh.

"Look, Maggie, I told you we can't start all that again."

"Well, that doesn't mean we still can't…"

"No, no we can't. Alma's moving the kids back to Raleigh tomorrow so we can try to sell the house." He lied. He didn't trust himself with Maggie. He was desperate to make his exit now.

"I thought she was divorcing you. You're not going back to her…you can't."

"Well, I…" he hedged. "I'm leaving first thing in the morning. I want to see my kids. Now, let me get out of here."

"No. Buck, you'll see. We can work it out. I don't have to go to Daytona. I just said that to make you jealous. Don't you see? Let's give it another chance." She pulled his arm. "Bring your boys down here to see the beach."

"You know I can't do that. Let go, Maggie. I mean it now. I'm going to get my boys back." He pried her fingers apart to break her grip.

Maggie held on. "She's going to make your life a hell."

Maggie was wearing the shortest, tightest, whitest shorts and a halter, seductively improvised from a large red bandanna.

Her breasts filled the bandanna to overflowing.

Barefoot, what else?…

And, God help him, she smelled good.

Buchanan wondered now if she'd done it all for him.

It wasn't so much the stirring in his groin, as it was the tugging at his heart that warned him it was past time to go.

Chapter Sixty-six

BUCHANAN WAS STILL SHAKING from the hormonal rush when he fumbled with his door key hurrying to catch the phone.

Almost midnight. Had Alma had a change of heart?

"Hello…" he picked up in mid-ring.

"Oh, Buchanan, I've been on the verge of tears. I've tried and tried to reach you all night." Cammie blurted out the words.

"I'm sorry. I've called and called. It's almost two weeks now…"

"I know. Mae's told me. I've tried to call once or twice but I've hardly had a moment to myself. My life's not my own. I'm in Washington, but I'm coming back to Raleigh tomorrow afternoon. Is Alma still coming with the kids? I was hoping I might see you at the park on Saturday morning."

"No, everything suddenly has turned to shit." He spilled out the story of Alma's fictional car problems and her petty get-even schemes.

"That's some bitch you married. If it weren't for the kids you should count yourself lucky not to have to see her ever again. And what's between her and this so-called doctor friend? Doesn't that strike you as a trifle strange?"

"I don't worry about that. She'd never run around. Alma's just not built that way."

"Don't be so sure. Anyway, I guess that ruins my hope of seeing you, at least for now. I could cry. I suppose I've been kidding myself that we could ever be lovers. I think I'll hang up and pull the covers over my head. Tomorrow's Friday. I've managed to arrange to play hooky from tomorrow afternoon until Monday morning. We plan to make my candidacy official at a press conference Monday night. The girls have gone away to camp. And that darling husband of mine has gone off to New York again, thank God. I'd hoped to see you at the park at least. But with Alma back, it seemed the best we might manage, and I'll gladly take what I can."

"It would be better than not seeing you at all. And, there's really nothing to keep me from coming to Raleigh…" Buchanan paused. The way Cammie had said 'lovers' struck an erotic nerve. "Listen, Alma's canceled and there's nobody either of us has to answer to. Isn't there some way we could get away, somewhere away from there—or here—somewhere alone."

"What an intriguing possibility." Cammie's voice showed a sudden spark of interest. "What's to stop us? Who would know?"

"Nothing. No one." *To hell with Alma. To hell with Maggie. To hell with serious commitment. Up with the free-loving twenty-first century, and to hell with everything else.*

"Do you really think we could? This young jerk from New York has been practically keeping me a slave. Where could we go? Somewhere away from here, that's for sure. My picture's in all the papers and on TV, everywhere you turn…"

"We could take a plane." He thought about the expense of Alma's new car and his pitiful bank account. Then he brightened as he remembered his secret little cash reserve.

Should he risk a reckless move? He felt uneasy enough. This phone was bugged, he was sure of that. Too late now to worry about the Feds knowing about his romantic indiscretions.

"We could fly and meet somewhere away from prying eyes. Atlanta's out. New York might be the best."

"Why not Pawley's? I have my house, it's isolated. No one in half-a-mile. We'd just buy some food, everything we need. I'll meet you somewhere, drive down tomorrow night. We wouldn't have to show our face to anyone at all. Do you think we dare?"

"I dare, do you? You're the one whose career's at stake. I don't have a thing to lose." Soberly, he added, "This is very likely bordering on total insanity for you, you know?"

"I really should think this through. I'll call you tomorrow after I've weighed the risk in the cold light of dawn. OK?"

"What time?"

"Eight tomorrow morning. I have an early meeting and the plane leaves Washington at eleven. I'll be back in Raleigh around noon if everything goes as planned. I'll call at eight, OK?"

"You bet, OK. And don't worry, no matter what works out, I only want the best for you...always be sure of that."

"I know. Goodnight."

When he hung up, Buchanan's blood was roaring in his ears.

He completely missed the little clicking sound.

Chapter Sixty-seven

JUNE 14, 2002. 8:04 A.M. Batson jotted a note in the log the minute the monitor started recording the call.

"I hardly slept a wink, but I've decided I want to take the chance. Are you still willing?" Cammie's voice crackled with excitement, as soon as Forbes picked up.

"You don't have to ask. Now, what's the plan?"

"I'm not exactly sure, but I can leave tonight. I thought you could drive, or maybe fly and meet me at the airport in Myrtle Beach or Charleston, whichever works the best. Does that sound like the beginning of a plan?"

"Oh, sure, but listen: After you hung up last night, I checked out the schedules. We can both fly to Myrtle Beach and rent a car. There's a flight leaves here at eight; we'll be at Myrtle airport by nine. I know the flight because Randall Wickline, my boss, has used it before. And guess where it originates."

"Don't tell me, Raleigh?"

"Where else?"

"That settles it. The planets are on our side. I can picture it now. I'll just be sitting there on the plane as innocent as a lamb when you walk nonchalantly aboard. How marvelous." Cammie giggled at the conspiracy.

"Call from your room and confirm a reservation now. I'll do the same. I'll get us a rental car in Myrtle, OK? Call me. No, wait! I'll call you at your office at three this afternoon, OK? We'll play the rest by ear. You won't need to pack a lot, just bring the same swimsuit you wore."

"Oh, you devil. I can hardly get my breath just fantasizing."

"Remember, three. If you can't be there leave word when I can call you back. And don't forget, make the reservation now, check the schedule out for Sunday. You can probably return on a direct flight."

"All right. I love you. Now let me go. I've got a busy morning. I'll be waiting for your call."

When he hung up, he listened for a click but he couldn't be sure. He wondered if this weekend he should warn Cammie of his suspicions about the phone. He dismissed the thought with a shake of his head. He was paranoid anyway. As far as he could tell, he had not been followed since he'd changed jobs and moved down here. He resolved to check underneath the new company car to see if there was another tracking device installed.

After her candidacy became official, for Cammie's sake, he'd be more careful about the phone. For the moment, however, he was more concerned by Cammie's ever-increasing declarations of love. That memorable night at the beach she had coquettishly begged him to take her as his whore. He had not misled her, he knew, but now, it made him very uneasy when she avowed undying love.

But, for the present at least, that was the lesser of his dilemmas.

More than once, in unguarded moments he'd found himself breathlessly murmuring to Maggie, "I love you, too." Trouble was, his whisperings to Maggie had been the most natural speeches he'd ever made, as easy as breathing. Maggie had shown him an intimacy he'd never dreamed existed. Worse, she still haunted his dreams. Now, that was something to really scare hell out of him.

NELL WASTED NO TIME in ringing Washington on the phone.

She got right down to business the moment Durwood picked up the phone. "He's going to fly to Myrtle Beach to shack up with our senatorial candidate-to-be tonight. They're going to rent a car. A brand new car for the wife, air travel for his mistress. Our boy thinks he's rich."

"I'm not surprised, but he's a foxy bastard. I'll give him that. That god-damn certified check from Wachovia was for only nine hundred. Tags, tax, license and loan costs. Odds and ends. He financed the rest of his wife's new Tahoe with GMAC and the dealer took the other car as trade. But his payments are gonna run over five hundred a month; the man is living on the edge. He's smart, but just you wait. We'll get the bastard yet."

Nell looked at her notes. "By the way, I forgot to tell you. The other night, when that Dr. Lindamood took Forbes' car, he tried to feel Forbes out on doing a sample deal. But Forbes turned him down. Do you think we ought to take a look at the doc's cash flow too?"

"No way. Can't you just imagine how widespread the practice is. White-collar crime. It's like air pollution. The monster that ate Hometown, USA. Besides, the Food and Drug is pushing to get the manufacturers to work out their own solutions. That's the larger issue here. Most of 'em are already making the docs sign for samples and some have tried marking the samples. But it's an empty exercise."

"Why? Sounds like a good idea…"

"The markings have to be water-soluble. Damn bootleggers are already taking Q-Tips and hiring minimum wage personnel to remove the identifying marks. I mean, we're talking major bucks it's costing the manufacturers just to set up the special dies, and then the samples are cleaned and put back in the trade anyway. And, of course, there's talk around about doing away with samples altogether, but I wouldn't bet on that either. The docs love 'em. It's a form of professional payola. They get the samples, write prescriptions that create demand, then sell off their samples to help supply the demand. Private enterprise. It's the good old American way. Whole thing's diabolically elliptical. Old-fashioned greed is the ultimate marketing motivation, and marketing's the name of the game."

"Well, Lindamood always seems to have some ready bucks. It still might be interesting to check him out."

"No way…why bother? Don't start something you can't finish."

"All right. Still, it makes me boil. Do you know how much my pre-scription for birth control pills sets me back?"

"Write your future Senator. That is, if you can get her out of Forbes' bed long enough."

"You're a big help."

"Well, look on the bright side…one thing for sure, with Forbes flying off to meet the new senate hopeful, you'll have the weekend off."

"Thank God for small favors. And Durwood, if this Brawley woman does run for that Senate seat, the department might find these tapes use-ful. This coming McCain-Aaron Claibourne Powers race is going to be a dogfight. Wouldn't do to have a major party scandal down the road, ever thought of that? Better still, we could wind up with a Senator in our pocket."

"Batson, you've got the heart of an assassin. But never fear, old Durwood's always looking for the edge."

Chapter Sixty-eight

FRESHLY-SHOWERED and dressed in khaki Savane slacks with a pink, open-collared shirt, Buchanan walked to the mirror and took another look. The shirt had been a Christmas present from his brother. It bore the Pinehurst Crest for the 1999 U.S. Open. With his tassel loafers and a bright blue nautical blazer with bone buttons, he was every inch the low-handicap preppy out for a weekend on the links at Myrtle Beach.

All day long, he'd prowled like a caged animal.

Mid-morning, he'd driven out to the airport and paid for his ticket and arranged for a rental car at the Myrtle Beach airport with his American Express.

At 5:50 he drove to the Post Office to mail his paperwork. He used the public phone to order a Coastal cab for seven sharp, giving the dispatcher the airport as his destination and the address of the Sugarshack as his pick-up address.

Prudently, he'd decided to leave his car parked at home in case he was being tailed.

Back from the Post Office, he parked off the street and locked his car and took a final look around.

The sky was clear...the sun was warm. Not a solitary soul in sight.

At 6:15 he grabbed his leather duffel, turned off the lights, locked the door and ambled casually down the street toward the Sugarshack. The curb was already lined with cars—a strong contingent of early birds from the regular Friday crowd. When he climbed the steps and set his duffel by the door, Buchanan waved at Ted and Gene Lindamood across the room. Heading directly to the bar, he mixed a drink, careful not to start too strong.

"What are you all decked out for? And why the bag? Heading out of town?" Hank Long stood at his elbow waiting his turn to freshen up his drink.

Buchanan shrugged and smiled. "A family thing," he said.

"Well, too bad you've got to leave. The party's just warming up. New talent arriving every day now that school's out. Summer people. Fun and games. I love 'em all. Look at that pair of schoolteachers over by the corner of the deck. Did you ever see anything like it?" By the sound of his speech, Hank had already had a few. "By the way, how's the new job? Wickline's such a simple shit. Does he treat you right?"

"He's OK. Comes around once a month like clockwork and rides with me two days and tells me I need to work harder. I let him have his way until he's out of town. You know how it goes."

"I know, but listen, I'm still looking for someone to head up the IUD promotion. With the National Guard locking down all the abortion clinics, the new G/uL Technologies T3 is really catching on. Knew it would. Supply and demand. People fuck and fucking makes babies and babies ain't always in the budget. Know what I mean? Greatest thing since the pill, mark my words. I already been talking to the Welfare lobby and the State Health Department in Raleigh. If Wickline doesn't treat you right, I'll make you a deal. Keep it in mind. Come back one night next week. We'll talk."

"I'll think about it."

Buchanan nursed the drink and circulated until he finally arrived on the fringe of the group where Ted and Gene were holding court. Gene was trying to organize a late-night poker game. He turned to Buchanan. "How 'bout you, Buck? A friendly little game. Why don't you come sit in?"

"Can't. I'm headed out of town." Buchanan shrugged and looked at his watch: 6:47. "As a matter of fact, I'd better go on outside, make sure I don't miss that cab."

"Cab? Where's your car?" Lindamood showed mild interest now.

"I'm leaving it up the street, gonna take a plane. I really should go down and wait. I can't afford to miss my ride."

"Wait up. I'm going back to the hospital. Why don't I give you a lift. Call and cancel the cab."

"It's probably a little late for that."

"Go on, they're radio dispatched. You can cancel anytime. Why take a chance? It's Friday night. Cabs may be running late and planes don't wait. My car's right outside."

Buchanan hesitated. It was true. Friday night was bad for cabs. Feeling antsy, he said, "OK."

He called the cab dispatcher, gulped his drink before he grabbed his bag and went to join Lindamood on the deck.

Jaynie Lockfaw was just coming up the steps. "Did you get my message, Gene? You're not leaving yet? It's early."

"Duty calls. Got to go."

"Excuse us for a minute, Buck. C'mon over here, Gene, I need to see you for just a sec."

Buchanan watched as she pulled Gene Lindamood toward an empty corner of the deck.

"Don't be long. I got a plane to catch."

"No sweat. Go ahead. I'll only be a minute. Put your bag in the trunk. The dark blue Mustang convertible. I'll be right along." Lindamood tossed him the keys and turned back to Jaynie.

Buchanan found the car, opened the trunk and began moving aside a jumble of boxes of pharmaceutical samples to make room for his duffel.

"Here let me." Lindamood came walking up, pulling on a pair of driving gloves. He took the keys and helped make room for Buchanan's bag.

"Ever see these?" Lindamood opened a box labeled G/uL Technologies, Richmond, VA.

"Never took a real close look. Hank Long keeps trying to talk me into going to work for him." Buchanan took several of the small tampon-sized applicator tubes out of the box and turned them over in his hand.

"You ever implant one of these things?" He looked at Lindamood.

"Once or twice, before I left UVA. The G/uL research team came up to Charlottesville. We had a big study going. They're really easy to use and virtually trouble free. Better give me those." He took the tubes from Buchanan and replaced them in the box. "C'mon. Let's get out of here."

Hank closed the trunk. In less than a minute, they were moving down the street.

"Listen, Buck, the other night, what I said about taking a few of those antibiotic samples off your hands, if you ever change your mind, I can make it worth your while."

"Well, thanks, but it isn't worth the risk to me. I'd stand to lose my job."

"Not likely. Who'd ever know? I'd do the dirty work, no real chance of trouble. Besides, legally the law's vague. Technically, resale's not a crime as long as you don't repackage the material yourself. The Food and Drug are basically interested in protecting the integrity of the manufacturer's batch and lot numbers. It's the only way to investigate the product should safety problems arise. Even the pharmacist is in the clear. There's no law says he can't dispense if he doesn't cut open sample packages and mix them in with other lot numbers," Lindamood persisted.

"Sounds like you've looked into it." Buchanan was impressed. What Gene said was no news to him. But not many professionals—doctors or pharmacists—really understood the inadequacy of the federal regs. Gene had done his homework.

"I graduated pharmacy school at MCV before I applied to Charlottesville."

Surprised, Buchanan shot him a closer look.

On Market near the light at Twenty-third, rush hour traffic was already stacking up, but now time was on Buchanan's side. He had it made.

"Where ya' headed?" Gene made conversation while they waited for the light to change.

"Atlanta. Going to see family."

Buchanan was suddenly reminded of the spot of blood that Lindamood and Jaynie had left on the back seat of his company car, not to mention the sorry mess of debris and mud on the wheels and sides, the night they'd made their phony liquor run a couple a weeks ago. But the man was doing him a favor now, so he decided to let the matter drop.

"When ya' coming back?"

Buchanan was getting a trifle bothered by his nosiness now.

They were passing the bustling movie studios as they neared the entrance to the airport.

"Did you see Sandra Bullock at the Shack the other night? She's something else. We had quite a talk..." Lindamood was still embellishing his tiresome tale when he pulled up in front of the terminal. He hopped out, opened the trunk and handed Buchanan his bag. "I hope you have a pleasant trip."

"Thanks for the lift." Buchanan shook his hand and watched him drive away.

Inside the terminal he had a moment of panic when he found the plane was already at the ramp. Worse luck, his landlady was at the head of the short line boarding the new high-wing commuter plane.

When he finally climbed aboard the crowded plane, Roxy was busy putting her bag in the overhead and didn't notice him.

Heart still in his throat, Cammie was nowhere to be seen.

Finally he spotted her halfway down the crowded aisle in the window seat.

"Are you saving this seat, madam?" He coolly hid his smile.

"Not at all; just let me move my things." His heart was fairly racing now as he watched the slender woman in the denim skirt and tailored Laura Ashley blouse move the briefcase out of the unoccupied aisle seat and slide it underneath her seat.

He opened the overhead and slipped his bag inside. When he settled in his seat and fastened the belt, he turned and asked, barely able to keep from laughing with relief, "Thanks. I'm Buchanan Forbes. Are you going to Myrtle Beach or on to Atlanta?"

"Myrtle Beach." She suppressed a smile.

"I didn't catch your name," he said with a straight face.

"Well…it's Cameron Brawley, but…" She leaned across and whispered, "if you don't stop annoying me, you'll have to move. I don't like being chatted up by fresh men on airplanes."

She looked at him lovingly and gave his knee a furtive squeeze.

An unexpected chill descended over him, as he realized just how serious Cammie had become.

Out of the frying pan and into the fire.

Chapter Sixty-nine

SILHOUETTED AGAINST the bathroom light, Penny watched the doctor's shadowy form as he removed the surgical gloves and tossed them in the green plastic bag. "You're already bleeding a bit. Better put that pad on right now before you make a mess. Then you can put your panties back on and get dressed."

Woozily, Penny steadied herself and moved slowly off the bed, trying hard to hold back her tears. Shyly, she turned away as she adjusted the pad and stepped into her panties. Finally, she reached up to where her slip was bunched beneath her breasts and pulled it down. When she'd smoothed the wrinkles as best she could, she sat quickly down and struggled to hold back the tears.

The doctor folded the cheap sheets he'd brought and placed them in the plastic bag.

"How long will it hurt like this?" She sniffed, took a drink of the Cognac that Inger had left and shuddered, trying hard to regain control.

"Here, take two of these." He handed her some sample packages labeled Empirin with Codeine.

Penny wiped her cheeks with her fists, reached for a tissue on the bedside table, and gave her nose a gusty blow. Punching two pills out of the foil, she took them with a sip of Cognac.

"If you plan to drive, I wouldn't hit that booze too hard. You already took a Valium, you know?"

"You think it's OK for me to drive back down to Surfside tonight? It's only ten miles or so." She sniffled and blew her nose again.

"That's entirely up to you. Why don't you just lie here and rest a while? I've put you through a lot. Your cervix didn't want to let us in. Had to dilate it quite a bit. Are you still hurting?" He moved closer with a concerned look and put his hand on her forehead. "Almost three months is pretty far along. You may be a trifle shaky for a while. Lie here and maybe catch a nap. That would probably help a lot."

Unsteady from the drink and pills, Penny watched him roll down his sleeves, fold his clinic coat and put it in the bag. There was a laundry-faded stencil—University *something*—on the pocket of the coat. Her attention was drawn to a monogram on the cuff of his shirt. Something with an 'E' and an 'L?'

"I'd actually feel better if I was out of here. Wish I could just forget the whole rotten thing." She struggled not to cry again.

"Relax. Take your time. Your friend won't be back until tomorrow late, you said. Just lie back and take a nap. Give it an hour or two at least. The pill will make you better. Take another codeine in an hour or so if you start to cramp, and another Valium too. It won't hurt you. But be careful with the alcohol. Good luck." He turned to leave.

"I guess I should say thanks. I don't mean to be a perfect bitch."

"No one's perfect," he said and smiled. "Just remember, you're going to pass quite a bit of blood. This bleeding now is just a minor thing from what I did tonight. You'll start for real sometime in the next day or two. Don't be alarmed. It always looks worse than it is. I'll just leave these extra pads to get you through the night. Again, good luck."

"I'll remember." Penny watched him close the door before she took another drink.

Her eyes caught sight of the discarded IUD insertion tube lying on the carpet beside the door. It wouldn't do to leave it there. She'd better take it when she left.

Penny took the remote and tuned the TV to the Weather Channel and pushed the mute button before she pulled the bedspread down. Then she bent and checked the pad for blood again.

It was showing signs of soaking through.

So soon? And him hardly out the door.

Alarmed she took a closer look.

Flooding quite a lot.

He'd hurt her bad. She'd barely been able to hold still while he did his dirty work.

Penny opened up the vial and shook another of the Valiums out.

Wouldn't hurt, he said.

Washed right down. Careful with the brandy, he'd warned. A tiny sip was all she took.

In the bathroom she cleaned herself and changed panties and pad.

Rinsing her panties in the sink, she let the water run. Drying them half-heartedly, she left them lying on the sink, too exhausted to wring them more. Probably ruined, she thought.

Was there a dulling of the pain? Well, maybe, for now at least.

She found a large bath towel and spread it on the bed. From her purse she took the photo they'd taken that night in the Pavilion coin booth, just across the street.

They'd laughed a lot. The memory came floating back.

"Oh, Buchanan…" She looked at the phone number on the photo's back. He'd given it to her on the phone, the last time they'd talked when he'd been in Utica.

Looking around the room, it was unbelievable that it could have started here. Everything had seemed so beautiful then.

She hated the sight of it now.

So much for Lady Chatterly, she smiled, wryly remembering.

"Oh, Buchanan…"

*Turn out the light…shut out the world…*Penny pulled the covers over her head, buried her face into the pillow and let go an anguished howl. The tears began again and she slowly sobbed herself to sleep.

IN THE NIGHT…an errant stab of pain…the awful shaking from the chill.

Half-awake in the darkness, fumbling, she found two pills, located the brandy and washed them down. Still shivering, she drifted off again.

Chapter Seventy

IT WAS ALMOST MIDNIGHT when Michael finally called. Alma was still downstairs, the only one in the big house left awake.

"Hi, kiddo, I'm in White Sulphur Springs. A whole bunch of us came over for the golf. What's going on?" There was the sound of voices in the background. Michael sounded like he'd had a drink or two.

"White Sulphur? When did you decide to leave? Where's White Sulphur Springs anyway?"

"West Virginia. The Greenbrier. Just across the mountains from the Homestead. Slammin' Sam Snead country. Came over on the spur of the moment, after lunch. What's going on, my service said it was important? Said you'd been calling all afternoon."

"I'm scared to death. I have to go into the hospital Sunday—tomorrow afternoon. Ogden has to do a cone, a frozen, Monday morning at seven. He's already reserved the room. If it's bad, he'll take the ovaries and the uterus and resect all the suspicious nodes, of course. Oh, my God, Michael, I've got cancer. When are you coming back? I need you here. I'm going out of my mind."

"Whoa, just calm down, babe. You don't know for sure they'll find CA. Probably a false alarm."

"No, there were some positive cells on the latest PAP. And that place on the cervix is still there. I'm scared to death, Michael. Couldn't you come back and hold my hand? I don't want to be a baby, but I really need you with me now—it's all so unreal. And I can't get Buchanan on the phone."

"Oh, hon, just get a grip. I can't just duck out of here and leave these people flat. They're counting on me now. You'll be OK, you'll see. I'll look in on you tomorrow night if I get back in time."

"Michael, didn't you hear a word I said? Branch says I have CA. He's got the room and the team is standing by. I had a case just like this a few weeks back. They'd done a cone on her just like this and in two months she was dead."

"Alma, listen to you now. You're a nurse. That was just an isolated case. Don't come apart. Even if they do find an early cell, they'll get it all. Irradiate. Just hang on and get some rest. I'll pop in as soon as I get back. I'll try to get back early Sunday night. Do the best I can, OK? Now, stiff upper lip. I've got to go. We've got an early start."

"Oh…Michael, I don't think you understand. I'm not getting through to you."

"Believe me, babe, I do. Trust me, get a grip."

"But how about tomorrow morning? Maybe I could drive over there, just have a drink and lunch and talk. You won't play golf all day…"

"It wouldn't work. Spoil it for everybody here. Just rest. Relax, old Mike's giving you good advice. Have a nice weekend with your kids. I'll see you Sunday night if I get back on time."

"Can I call you tomorrow morning, just to talk?"

"I don't think so. I'm sharing a room, but if I get a chance, I might call you. We'll see."

"Oh, please do. Please, it means a lot to me."

"I'll try. We'll see. Now get some rest."

"*Mikey honey, get off the phone, come dance with me…*" In the background a woman's voice?

"Who's that, Michael?"

"Gotta run now. They're calling me. *Ciao.*"

The line went dead.

Alma stared at the instrument and slowly placed it on the hook.

She picked up the Merck Manual from beside her chair and opened it to ovarian cancers.

A torrent of tears spilled down her cheeks.

Chapter Seventy-one

"KEEP THE CHANGE..." Buchanan hurriedly paid off the cab and made a dash for his front door.

In the quiet of the Sunday twilight, he could hear his phone ringing all the way from the street.

"Hello?" Breathless, he picked up the phone before he put his duffel down.

"Buchanan. We've been trying to reach you all weekend. Alma has been desperate, Son."

Please, God, not my kids. The urgency in his father's tone struck instant terror in his heart.

"I was out of town, went down to Myrtle Beach. You know I've been working on that newspaper piece? What's the matter, Dad?" He held his breath, afraid to hear the news.

"Alma's in the hospital, going to have surgery in the morning. It's serious, but I don't understand exactly what's going on."

"What kind of surgery? What do you mean?"

"Oh, the female thing, something about her PAP. Cancer, I guess." His father sounded completely lost.

"*Cancer*? Where is she? Give me the number." He copied the number and read it back.

"Thanks. I'll call right back as soon as I've talked to her," he reassured his father and dialed as soon as he hung up.

"Alma? I just talked to Dad. What's this all about?"

"Buchanan. Where have you been? I've been out of my mind. You're never there when I need you."

"I'm sorry, I can leave right now..."

"It's too late, my surgery's first thing in the morning." She sounded woozy but on the verge of tears. "Where on earth have you been, anyway?"

"I was out of town. Sharkey Mallone lives below Myrtle Beach..." It wasn't a lie, but, remembering the stolen weekend, he felt a tug of guilt. "Now, are you going to tell me what's going on? What's this sudden surgery all about?"

"My PAP. Friday, Ogden Branch found some malignant cells. I'm terrified. I have CA. He's going to do a cone and a frozen and God knows what else," she wailed. "I'm so alone. Why aren't you here where you belong? You've made such a mess of things."

"I'm sorry, babe. I'm on my way...get some sleep. I'll be there to hold your hand when they take you to OR."

Cancer....

Poor Alma. His heart went out to her.

"Buck, you'll never make it now..."

"No, I'm on the way, so get some rest. You'll be just fine, I know you will. Just let me say goodnight, now. I'll be there by morning."

"Be careful. Do you still love me, Buck? I'll forgive you, you know I will."

"Don't worry, babe. It's OK." It was hardly time to tell her it would never be the same again.

"Buck, be sure and bring the card for our hospital insurance. Don't forget?"

"I won't. I'm on my way." He hung up the phone.

Buchanan grabbed the edge of the table. Couldn't stop his knees from shaking.

Alma had just turned thirty-six last month.

Could she die?

Not the mother of his sons...

WHEN SHE HEARD Buchanan Forbes hang up, Nell Batson tried Fisher at home again. He picked up on the second ring.

"Durwood, you're home at last. I've been trying since late Friday night..."

"What's up?" He sensed the urgency in her tone.

"Wish I knew. It's all so weird, I can't figure any of it out."

"Where's Forbes? Is he up to something new?"

"That's just it...I'm confused...you know he was supposed to fly to Myrtle Beach with the Brawley woman on Friday. Well, he left his car here and went with the doctor Lindamood to catch the plane and that's the last I saw of him, until just now, when he came back. I waited for his plane tonight and followed him. He took a taxi straight from the airport. But there's something very funny going on. His car went out Friday night around nine-thirty and I was too slow to pick up the trail. I lost the signal when I got caught by the drawbridge heading south..."

"What do you mean? I thought you said he flew. Where's his car right now?"

"Oh, it's right here. The monitor picked up the signal when the car came back around two Saturday morning. By the time I got dressed and got my car, it was parked right back there, pretty as you please, just like it had never left his yard."

"Was he there? Did he miss the plane and come back? You've got me all confused."

"No, no sign of him."

"How about the odometer? Were you able to get a baseline reading Friday night?"

"Yeah, that's just it. I was at the Sugarshack when he left with Lindamood. As soon as he left, I strolled around the corner and wrote it down. When the car got back Saturday morning, the engine was still warm and, Durwood, get this, that car was driven almost two hundred fifty miles!"

"Jeez. How far's Myrtle, or Pawley's, that's where he was headed?"

"Well, North Myrtle's eighty, ninety miles. Pawley's twenty or thirty further down..."

"Hmm, very strange. Do you think he missed the flight?" Durwood obviously didn't know quite what to make of it.

"Midway says he was on the flight. I checked on that first thing."

"Well, what the hell's going on? Who the devil took that car?"

"Beats me, but one other thing, I heard just now on my car radio they found that girl. I don't see how it could be related but it's a damn strange coincidence if you ask me."

"What girl's that?" Fisher asked absently, still trying to figure it out about the car.

"The girl Forbes had at the motel in Myrtle Beach when you tailed him in March."

"Found her? I didn't know she was missing." Durwood perked back up again.

"*Not missing*, Durr. They found her *dead* in Myrtle Beach this afternoon. Someone tried to abort her with one of those IUDs. Apparently they botched the job. She bled to death in a motel room."

"Judas Priest! What do you make of that?"

"I don't know. You know there's been a rash of moonlight abortions down here lately, all with IUDs. It's made the national news."

"I know, but I don't see. You don't think that Forbes is in on that?"

"Durwood, I don't know what to think, but there's something here that doesn't smell right. Who used that car?"

"Beats hell out of me. I guess I better come down there and get involved again."

"I could sure use the help...it's gotten way out of hand, too deep for me."

"Well, we'll see. Where's Forbes right now?"

"He's home, but he's cutting out almost any minute now....he just got off the phone."

"For where? What's that all about?"

"He's heading to Virginia. His wife just called. She's having surgery tomorrow morning first thing."

"You sure this is on the up and up? Should we check him out? Maybe you should jump on his tail?"

"Not a chance. I mean, that's three hundred miles. I'm certain that this one's legit."

"OK...give me the name of the hospital and get some rest. I'll have him verified tomorrow."

"What about the abortion death? Should I follow up on that? I mean, I don't know what to do."

"I hate coincidences. This is all very fishy. That death in Myrtle Beach...for the life of me I can't see how it fits, but it puts us in a bind. We may have information about a crime, yet we just can't afford to have word get out on how much we've spent on this surveillance. In the middle of this congressional election, too...we'd wind up on the street."

"Look, Durwood, I'm just a bean counter. This thing is turning too weird for me. I hope you're coming down here right away." Nell clearly wanted out.

"I'll do the best I can. I'll be in touch." Durwood said goodnight.

ON THE ROAD within the hour, Buchanan's head was in a whirl. He'd already passed Clinton before he looked at the mileage and came alert. *Was something weird going on?*

He'd logged the odometer reading Friday morning before he went to work.

Tired. His mind was playing tricks. He'd have to consult his notes.

Past Durham, he stopped for a cup of coffee at an all-night truck stop near Hillsborough. He noticed that there was a cigarette butt in the ashtray. He tried to remember who could have left it there?

Not Maggie...nor Cammie...neither smoked.

Jimbo, perhaps, or Troy? Someone from The Wit?

Oh well, he'd clean it out when he got the time. He rolled down the window on the driver's side to let the night air wake him up.

The digital clock showed 1:29 A.M., time to spare.

Now he was wide awake again.

The thing with Alma? Was it as serious as she said?

Was it really possible she could die?

She was the mother of his sons.

Part 6
Buchanan

Chapter Seventy-two

AT THE SOUND OF TIRES on the oyster shell drive, Inger rubbed the sleep from her eyes and finished off the shot of vodka before she met Puckett Crump, the Myrtle Beach police chief, at the door.

"Good morning, Chief, come on in. Coffee's on. Care to join me in a cup?"

"Don't mind if'n I do, Miz Carlyle. Just black will do for me. I know seven in the morning's a bad time to have to talk…"

"Well, you have your job." Inger showed him to a chair in the tiny living room and went to get the coffee. A breath of stale perfume mingled with vodka trailed behind.

"I'm awful sorry about the girl. I know you two were close. A student of yours, you said, last night?" The chief leaned forward and talked through the opening of the pass-thru bar.

Inger murmured an assent and came back around with a coffee mug in each hand. She handed him one. Wearing just a wispy summer robe over her shorty gown, she had on no makeup. She found a tissue in the pocket of her wrap and daubed at her swollen eyes.

A handsome woman, and so demure, the police chief mused. He averted his eyes when she showed a flash of white panties against the smoothly suntanned thighs as she took a seat across from him.

"I know I must look a sight…"

Embarrassed to see her grief, Puckett examined an imaginary spot on his shoe and cleared his throat before he spoke again. "I'll try to be real brief, but, well, there's been a wrongful death, and there are some things I have to find out."

"I'll help all I can, of course," Inger said. Her hand went to her hair. "I've cried 'til I don't think I can cry any more. I haven't slept a wink all night."

"I know this is hard, but going back to what you told me last night on the phone. You said you made the reservation for that room because you thought she was meeting friends?"

"That's right. Penny told me two of her sorority sisters were to meet her yesterday. She was…" She choked back a sob and took a breath to catch herself. "…coming here to stay a week with me as soon as I got back. I didn't have room here for the other girls, as you can plainly see." She nodded at the trailer's interior. "I'm on sabbatical leave from the school. My husband and I live apart. I keep this little place to work. I write a regular column for the Atlanta paper. It's syndicated around the country. I just finished a book on Brookgreen Gardens. That's where I was Friday. I flew to meet my publisher in Atlanta. Your deputy was waiting here last night when I got back. That's about all I know."

"Well, you say you had no idea she was pregnant, no hint at all?"

"Not a clue. I'm still having trouble believing it."

"Tell me more about this Forbes, the one in the photo she had with her. You say he travels for the drug firm out of Wilmington and does some writing too?"

"Yes. Penny and I ran into him one night back in March when she was down for spring break from school. Forbes was at the Bowery with Sharkey Mallone. We had a couple beers. Penny had a Coke. We danced a little. Mallone's an old friend."

"Yeah, I already talked to Sharkey. He says Forbes and the girl left that night to take a walk and didn't return."

"She was engaged to Dr. Elroy Goins, a prominent young physician back at home. Penny was only nineteen, awfully young. A brilliant journalism student but she didn't know her own mind. Her mother ruled her with an unforgiving hand. Forbes was almost twice her age, almost old enough to be her father. Anyway, that night we were talking writing. He was on assignment from SNS, a newspaper syndicate. Penny was quite impressed."

"So you didn't think there was anything going on between them, you weren't suspicious afterwards that anything happened?"

Inger resettled herself and re-crossed her legs. Puckett caught another flash of her nylon-covered crotch.

"We'd just met him. It was the last thing on my mind. At the time, the whole incident seemed harmless enough. But then later when she got back to school, the trouble started. I got a call from her mother accusing me of being...well...among other things, irresponsible. Mrs. Wagner and Penny have had a hard life. Penny's father was Milo Wagner, that disgraceful TV evangelist, if you know who I mean?"

Inger saw him nod assent before she continued speaking.

"Anyway, it seemed that the week Penny got back home, her mother found a letter she'd written to this Buchanan Forbes. The girl had formed a terrible crush and when her mother confronted her, Penny threatened to break off her engagement and run to Forbes. Of course, when her mother found out Forbes is still married and has a bunch of kids, all hell broke loose. And, you might know, I got the blame for everything. But, once her mother talked some sense into her, I thought the whole incident was forgotten." Inger took a sip of coffee and regarded the Chief over the rim of her mug.

"Well, her mother says about the same thing, but says she forbade her to come back here. Is that correct?"

"If she says so. Penny never told me that."

"You made the reservation at the Presidential yourself?"

"Yes. Penny asked me to see what I could do. The season's started, you know how high the tourist rates can be..."

"And she was here with you Thursday night?"

"That's correct. She got in late and we talked a little while then went straight to bed. The next morning I had to fly to Atlanta. That's the last I saw of her. She'd just gotten up and was still wearing the school T-shirt she'd slept in." Inger's hand began to tremble and she sat down her coffee mug and bent her head. Her shoulders shook as she choked back a sob.

"There, now, Miz Carlyle. I hate to have to put you through this, but there have been a bunch of other cases just like this, one just across the North Carolina line near Southport. We've got to stop this butcher before someone else is dead."

"I know, I want to help..." Inger got up and went to the kitchen and blew her nose on a paper towel. "This is so hard for me."

She tore off another towel and dried her tears as best she could.

"I understand." The Chief shuffled through his notes. "And Miss Wagner'd said nothing about an abortion. You had no clue?"

"I told you all that last night. It still seems impossible..."

"Do you think Forbes was the man who, ah, impregnated her? From what the medical examiner says, the timing would seem just right." The Chief pulled an ashtray over to him and took out a cigarette and raised it in front of his face, questioning. "Mind if I light up?"

"It's OK. I smoke myself, when I'm working, mostly. And, yes, I guess if it happened while she was here, it had to be Forbes. He was the only man she spent more than a passing word with the whole time." Inger fumbled in her pocket for a cigarette. The Chief offered her one and held the light.

"Thanks." Inger inhaled the smoke. "Penny never went anywhere alone, except for her morning walk to the beach. Occasionally she stopped next door at the park office to have a cup of coffee and pass the time of day with Clem."

The phone began to ring. She ignored it and looked at him.

He stood and waited until it stopped.

"Well, you don't think it might have been her fiancè? We called her mother and she refused to entertain the thought. She thinks Forbes raped the girl. What do you think of that?"

"Sheer poppycock," she snorted. "Whatever happened, there was no rape involved. I'm damned sure of that."

"OK. Thanks. One last thing, have you seen or heard from Forbes since that night?"

"No, well, yes. I mean, it wasn't just that night. I thought you understood. He stayed a second night. She went back by herself the next afternoon to swim with Forbes and I had him down here for dinner and let him take her back to the beach that next night, just to dance, she said. I had no idea. He was so...so clean-cut all-American. And there was such a difference in their ages. How was I to know?" Inger daubed at her eyes again.

"Well, thanks again. We can't figure out how she was able to arrange for the abortion doctor, or whoever it was. Did she know anyone else down here?"

"No, of course her fiancè was a doctor, but that's too farfetched to even consider."

"I thought of that. I'm going to check him out. He may be the only one involved...ever think of that?"

"No. I've hardly thought at all about anything, except she's gone..."

"Well, thanks. Sorry to have troubled you. If you think of anything, give me a call." He handed her a card and went out the screen door.

"I will. Come back anytime. The coffee's always on. I don't have much company."

"I just might take you up on that." Puckett Crump gave her a closer look.

"Please do."

As Inger watched him go, the phone began to ring again.

"Pershing? I tried to catch you."

"They told me...what's this all about? The press hasn't gotten to you, have they?"

"No, I doubt they will. I was in Atlanta at the time, you know."

"No. I didn't know. But are you in the clear? I mean you didn't? I mean...well?"

"No. This was all news to me. I was in Atlanta meeting with my publisher. Don't worry, there's nothing bad the media people can make of this. If it looks like the media wants to drag me in, I'll call my agent in New York and break my side with them, let them handle the wire services."

"I like that...a flanking strategy? Smart move. But I hope it won't come to that."

"I don't think it will. I just talked to the police, and I think that's the end of it."

"Well, if something happens be sure and call. We have the Academy's reputation at stake, you know. Our clientele won't tolerate notoriety of any sort."

"Don't worry. I'll call."

"All right then. Take care."

The phone went dead. But before she'd put it down, the phone rang again. "Inger, I've been afraid to call. Can you talk? Just say something about the weather if you can't."

"I'm OK, Bonnie, given the shitty circumstances. Did you call, just now? The chief just left."

"No, but what did you tell him? I mean, you didn't tell him anything, did you? God, Inger, we'll both wind up in jail."

"Don't be an ass. Of course I didn't tell. But if I ever get my hands on the imbecile who butchered her...now I understand there have been other cases botched. Did you know? God, I hope not."

"Don't jump to conclusions. This IUD trick is just a new wrinkle of the same old thing. It was just bad luck. Oh God, I'm so scared..." The woman started to bawl.

"Spare me that. I'm not in the mood. And put your mind at rest. But, if I were you, I wouldn't try to call here again. I don't think they would listen in; still, you never can tell. Better safe than sorry, if you know what I mean? Just forget we ever talked and no one need ever know."

"I'm so sorry that it turned out this way. I really am."

"Me too. Now let's just let it go at that." Inger hung up and went to pour another drink.

Chapter Seventy-three

OGDEN BRANCH was still wearing his green surgical scrubs.

"Just don't tell me fairy tales, Ogden. I want to know." Ogden had delivered all their sons. Buchanan believed him to be a straightforward man.

"Nothing's certain, but I think we got it all. We won't know what pathology says about the nodes for a day or two. Of course, after that, only time will tell." The distinguished-looking doctor chose his words carefully.

"Can I see her now?" They were standing outside the PACU.

"Sure, take a peek in if you like, but then go home and get some rest.

She'll be out for a while, and I've ordered nurses around the clock. I'll see you again tomorrow when I make my rounds."

The chilly Post-Anesthesia Care Unit reminded Buchanan of a movie morgue. He rubbed his eyes and blinked hard to chase the impression he was looking at her corpse. Shuddering at the thought, he bent and gently brushed back a wayward curl of Alma's hair. Alone on the stretcher in the green-tiled cubicle, she looked so pale, so fragile. A tug of tenderness welled in his throat. Putting aside her recent bitterness, for the moment he felt only Alma's fear and pain. He breathed a silent prayer to a deity he little understood, then turned and walked back outside to find a phone.

"Cammie, thank goodness."

"Oh, Buchanan, I'm glad you caught me. I only have a sec. I dreamed of you all night. Do you miss me…"

"Yes, I do, but I'm in Virginia." He blurted out the news.

"How awful. How're your boys?"

"Haven't seen them. I'm going up there now. I'll tell 'em you said hello."

"How long will you be there, you think?"

"No more than a day or so. I can't afford the time from work. Which reminds me, I haven't called Wickline yet."

"Won't you be coming back through here on the way home?"

"Sure. I'll call and let you know."

"Perhaps I could slip away for lunch. Can't promise anything. I'll be living in a goldfish bowl for the next four months. They may announce my candidacy at noon today. After that, my life won't be my own. Frankly, I'm having second thoughts right now. This weekend with you has me dreaming of tropical sunsets. I'm tempted to tell them to get someone else. A woman running in a senate race probably doesn't have a chance."

"Don't talk like that. You'll win, you'll see. And for me, things are even more uncertain now. Your whole future's at stake, and my situation is such a mess." He had no desire to lead her on. The stolen weekend at Pawleys had been revealing. His bedroom performance had been dreadfully uninspired. Might as well admit it. Maggie had ruined his erotic chemistry for other women now.

Cammie babbled on. She had no clue what he meant. "Don't worry, we'll work it out. I have to go now…they're waiting. Don't forget to call, leave word."

"I'll be rooting for you, Senator."

He reinserted the phone card and quickly dialed again. Wickline's wife answered.

"Hi, Chloe, this is Buchanan Forbes. Is Wick there?"

"Buchanan, where on earth are you? Wick just called in from Wrightsville Beach. Did you forget? You were supposed to work with him," she blurted out the words.

"Work with him? Wrightsville! Wick knows I was scheduled to be in New Bern today. Did he leave a number where he can be reached?" He tried hard to conceal his anger.

Wickline had gone to spy on him. The bastard was notorious for playing private eye.

Buchanan took down the number and read it back. "Thanks, Chloe, I'll call right now. But just in case I miss him, my wife's just had surgery. Tell him I'll be at my father's." He gave her the number and briefly told her about Alma.

"I'm so sorry. Wick will understand." Chloe seemed a decent sort. He dialed the Blockade Runner, wondering how she could stand the man.

"Randall Wickline here…"

"Wick, this is Buchanan…I just talked to Chloe."

"Where are you, you asshole? I want to work with you."

"How was I supposed to know that?"

"I told you in Raleigh last week." Such a lie was not only insulting; it was stupid.

"No, Wick, you have my itinerary. It clearly shows New Bern. Call Morris. I always send him a copy. Besides, it wouldn't have made any difference. I had an emergency." He tried to keep the anger out of his voice as he explained Alma's circumstance.

"Well, you could have called last night." The mention of Morris had a discernible effect.

"Sorry, but there didn't seem to be any need to wake you. Besides, you just sent out a memo raising hell about weekend calls, remember?"

"I didn't mean you couldn't call me over something if it was important enough. How come you didn't know all this in advance, anyway?"

"I was out of town. I didn't find out 'til last night around midnight. Your itinerary shows the usual office day. I assumed I could call you at home this morning."

"Out of town? That mystery writer again? You're spending too much time on that writing stuff. I never can get you evenings. You need to take a serious look at your social life. The territory needs attention."

"I know my job. Twice around the territory is not a lot of time to make a miracle."

"Well, I'd say three months is time enough for most of my men. Remember, you're on probation. So how long will you have to be up there holding your wife's hand?"

"I just got here, but if all goes well, I'll come back Wednesday night. Do you want to meet me there?"

"No, too late. I've got to fly to Utica. Just don't let me catch you fucking off, you understand? If you don't produce, not even your precious Morris will protect your ass. If I were you, I'd be trying to get back to work. If your wife has cancer, you'll need your job."

"I'll do the best I can." Buchanan hung up before he completely lost control.

Exhausted now, he turned and headed out into the morning traffic. He could hardly wait to see his sons—three months seemed like three years.

DRIVING SLOWLY out of the city, boyhood memories came flooding back. On the outskirts, the pavement narrowed and followed a winding course along the torpid Roanoke River as he moved into the country and neared his father's place.

He slowed as he passed the swimming hole where he'd gone skinny-dipping as a kid.

Back then he'd had such youthful dreams.

Fleetingly, he wondered about the *Esquire* query as, momentarily, all his vainglory settled around him like a wintery gloom.

But, when he turned into his father's drive, his momentary depression vanished in a puff.

He couldn't help but laugh out loud at the sudden explosion of moving arms and legs as the exuberant army of boys all came running from the porch, waving and shouting as he made his way up the narrow drive. He had to stop the car to keep from running over them. Pulling open the doors front and back and crawling across the seats, they swarmed inside, assaulting him from all sides.

"Daddy...Daddy...this car is new...where you been so long?" A thousand questions and a hundred happy hugs.

"Whoa, take it easy, guys," Buchanan protested happily as four pairs of arms tried to encircle his neck all at once.

"Did you see Mama? Is she all right?" Granger, the eldest, asked as he leaned over to get a manly hug.

Before he could answer, Garrett, the baby, said, "Dad, can we have a dog?"

"Mama's doing fine, but I don't know about a dog."

"When are you coming back to live with us?" The question came as a chorus.

"I want you all back to live with me again. Remember when we went to the beach? That's the place where we'll be living now."

"Oh, Daddy, I love the beach. Can we have a dog at the beach?" Garrett clapped his hands.

"Well, we'll have to wait and see." His heart melted with regret for having been away so long.

"WELCOME HOME. How's Alma, Son?" When he'd finally moved the car up to the house, his father beamed and clasped him around the shoulder.

"Do you really think she'll be all right?" his mother asked.

"Ogden seems optimistic. Let's hope he's right."

The boys had run to play with the toy airplanes he'd been saving for when he saw them again.

"Alma wants you to move back here to live. Do you think there's a chance?" his mother asked, hopefully.

"Not likely, Mom. I've tried to make her understand. As soon as we can sell the place in Raleigh, I want her to bring the boys and live on the coast with me, but she keeps putting me off. I just don't know what's going through her head." Buchanan shrugged. "And, now with this, well, who can say? She has her sisters here. We'll just have to wait and see, I guess."

"Well, these boys miss their dad."

"Not half as much as I miss them." He waved his arm and pointed. They'd all but forgotten him as they were sailing their toy planes in the enormous yard.

He played with the boys until after lunch, then showered and took a nap.

"When I get back, we'll go out to eat. What's your favorite place?" He left them arguing over where they'd eat as he took Alma's new Tahoe wagon and headed back to town.

Alma's *problem* car drove like a dream. He wryly shook his head.

IT WAS JUST AFTER THREE when he finally got back to the hospital. The private nurse was standing by to steady her as she slumped forward, sitting precariously on the side of the bed.

"Oh, there you are. Where've you been? You're never around when I need you," Alma wailed and was suddenly seized with retching.

The nurse wiped her forehead with a damp cloth, then helped her lie back down. She really looked like hell. "When I do that it feels as if my insides are spilling out." Alma rolled her eyes and groaned and clasped her abdomen gingerly. "Ogden said he got it all, but he's gonna start cobalt right away, to be safe, he says. Oh, Buck, I'm so scared. Do you think I'll be OK? I don't want to die. Will you come back home and take care of me?"

He moved around and held her hand. "You'll be just fine. Try to get some rest..."

Suddenly she sat up and began to gag again and the nurse waved him aside.

The nausea came and went. Finally the nurse went out and came back and gave her an injection. In a few minutes Alma relaxed and closed her eyes.

"Compazine. She'll stay out a while. Come back in the morning, when the nausea from the anesthesia's worn off," the nurse advised.

Happy not to have to stay, Buchanan nodded passively. He was useless here, anyway.

When he got back to his father's place, the boys were getting dressed.

"The Magruders are coming by. Can we have some money, Dad? They're gonna take us to a movie," Granger said.

The Magruders were neighbors. They had five kids of their own.

"It's somebody's birthday," his father shrugged. "I tried to talk them out of it. It seems a shame since you haven't been around in such a long time."

"Oh, they're just kids." Buchanan tried to hide his disappointment, waving at the van disappearing down the drive.

"You're a very lucky man," his father said.

"Well, they're getting along without me OK. I should be glad of that, I guess." Buchanan tried to sound cheerful.

Later, after the boys had returned and he'd tucked them safely in their beds, he went outside and sat with his father in the cool darkness on the porch.

They joked about his impetuous youth.

He loved his dad.

Inside he thought he heard the phone.

"Buchanan, it's a Mrs. Brawley...she said she's a friend." His mother stood in the door silhouetted against the parchment light.

"I'll get it, Mom." He hurried inside, pleased by Cammie's thoughtfulness.

"Buchanan, have you seen the papers or heard the news?"

"What do you mean?" He squeezed the phone when he caught her tone.

"That young woman, Penny Wagner—the one you met down at Myrtle Beach—they found her dead."

"*Dead!* Are you sure?"

"I'm sorry. I thought you'd seen it on the news by now."

"But, how?"

"The reporters say it was a botched abortion, something to do with a newfangled IUD. That Wilmington reporter Joe Jordan's linking her death to a rash of other cases. Remember the body they found down south of Wilmington somewhere?"

He remembered vaguely, but his head was suddenly filled with images of Penny. "I'm sure there must some mistake. An abortion? Penny Wagner? No way. The woods are probably full of Penny Wagners." His words were weighted down with dread.

"Well, I hope you're right. It happened in some motel in Myrtle Beach. I just thought you'd want to know."

"Oh sure, but I'm certain there's some mistake. I'll check the papers here."

"Buchanan, do you think...I mean, it wasn't you..."

"C'mon, Cammie, give me a break." He hoped he sounded more convincing than he felt.

"I just couldn't help but ask. I hope you understand."

"You can just put that right out of your head." He wondered if his bravado betrayed his fear.

"Of course. I'm sorry. Wish I'd had better news. And, oh, yes, they decided to delay the announcement of my candidacy until later in the week. Something about a survey of my name recognition, whatever that means." Disappointment was heavy in her voice.

"Oh, that's just politics. Some men still haven't heard that women won the vote."

"I'm having second thoughts. Maybe it's for the best. Do you know yet when you're coming back this way? I could use a hug right now."

"Me too. I promised my boss I'd be back to work Wednesday, so if Alma has no complications, I'll start back tomorrow after lunch. I'll give your office a call when I know for sure, OK?"

"OK. I miss, you darling. I wish we were back at Pawley's right now." There was hesitation in her voice.

"I'll call before I start back, OK?"

"We could have coffee, like old times. I'll try and work something out. Sleep tight."

"EVERYTHING ALL RIGHT?" his father asked when he came back out on the darkened porch and put his feet up on the rail.

He told his father about the call. "She was really beautiful. I only met her once." He played the whole thing down.

"We're back to doing abortions in a motel. World's gone mad. Nineteen? Hardly more than a child herself," his father said with a despairing sigh.

"It's a waste of time to try to figure any of it out," Buchanan said. "I gave up a long time ago."

For a time, they sat, just quietly listening to the night—frogs, crickets, the mournful cooing of a dove, the far-off whistle of a train.

Echoes of a less-troubled time.

"We miss you, Son. I wish you could be with Alma and the kids."

"I know, Dad, but a man's home is where his job takes him...you taught me that." Remembering the morning's conversations with Wickline and Alma, he wondered if he believed it was actually true.

"Alma's going to need someone to look after her. She's going through a lot."

"I'll take care of Alma, but I need my job. She needs to come back with me so we can be a family again."

"A man has to do what he has to do."

Buchanan nodded.

The smell of honeysuckle was heavy in the air.

The train sounded closer now.

Leaning out, he looked up at the stars. The moon was rising through the branches of the massive sycamores by the river across the road.

Jeannie Bryant had placed his hands on her breasts, pressed close against one of those trees, one night when he was twelve.

He'd always love it here, but for him *You Can't Go Home Again* was more than just a catchy title to a book.

"You've done all right. I'm very proud of you, you know," his father said.

He knew his parents loved him. No matter what, he could count on that.

He thought about his sketch of Maggie hanging in The Wit...and Cammie...the musical sound of her voice still echoed in his ear.

The thought of Penny lying dead superimposed itself upon his fleeting image of Alma lying in a coffin.

He shook his head, his mind suddenly a black hole, filled with dust moats of free-floating anxiety.

"I love you too, Dad." He cleared his throat. "If Alma's all right, I'll be going back tomorrow afternoon. I'm too new on the job to take the time. Besides, I may need time later more than now."

"Sure, but I didn't think you'd have to leave so soon. The boys will be heartbroken."

"Don't worry about the boys. I came out second best to a picture show and ice cream tonight. They'll forget as soon as I'm out of sight." He shrugged and laughed.

"Don't be too sure. They need their dad."

"Well, I have to make a living. If this thing with Alma should turn bad, I'll need to keep my job, you know?"

"Sure. I didn't mean to question. I'll just hate to see you go so soon."

"Me too." It was a lie. He wanted to run away and hide. He leaned across and gave his father's arm a reassuring squeeze. "You don't know how grateful I am that you've taken my family in. I hope it won't be much longer now." He stood and stretched and yawned an honest yawn. "I think I'll find the paper and fall into bed. I've about run out of gas."

"I understand. In the morning then." His father gently touched his hand as he watched him go.

Inside, Buchanan went to find the paper. Penny was heavy on his mind.

Police Question Mystery Writer In Abortion Death

The headline filled him with dread. The wire report had the byline: Joe Jordan, *Wilmington Morning Star.*

*Abortion...Penny Wagner...Sharkey Mallone...Inger Carlyle...*the words jumped out at him.

Buchanan scanned the brief report again before he turned out the light.

Tennessee coed. No mix-up there.

If she was in trouble, why hadn't Penny called? Deep inside he wanted to scream, but he was too frozen with horror to release his pain.

Cammie knew the blame was his. He'd heard it in her voice.

Penny. So young. So sweet...so dead.

Chapter Seventy-four

THROUGH THE WINDOW behind the desk, the Capitol dome soared above the trees against the cloudless June morning sky as Durwood Fisher turned the last page of the yellow legal pad and raised his eyes to meet the gaze of the Director. He'd been talking almost without interruption for over half an hour.

A trickle of sweat ran down his spine.

The Director cleared his throat and tapped his pencil on the desk and glanced back through the stack of Fisher's unofficial reports.

Fisher waited.

"And no one else—besides you and Nell Batson—are aware of this?

How about Johnston, I thought he was in on the Forbes surveillance too?"

"Only up until when we debugged the Raleigh residence and transferred the tracking device to Forbes' new automobile after he came back from the Utica training with Stribol. After that I passed Forbes along to Batson for casual observation and routine intelligence from the Wilmington office."

"Looks like you got carried away. This is more than casual observation to me. Something on the order of the Spanish Inquisition." The Director stood and walked around his desk, across the richly-paneled, deeply-carpeted office to straighten the President's picture hanging on the wall. He returned and stood with his back to Fisher, looking out over the morning traffic in the streets below.

Finally, he turned and sat back down at his desk before he spoke again. "Well, what's done is done. We've got to cut our losses here. No way do we want it known we were ever involved in this kind of operation. Electronic surveillance and a wiretap. Godamighty, we're sitting on a bomb. This is going to be the most bloodthirsty election year in modern history. Talk about dirt, with Democrats and Republicans throwing Aaron Claibourne Powers and Jerry Falwell down each other's throat and *The Washington Post* and *Time* reporting every time a government employee farts in church or has a spat with his wife, I'm scared to go to confession. And you can bet the President will never forget we raked him over the coals with the probe into the Habitats for Christ tax probe. If he got wind of this, he'd tear us limb from limb. Every man, woman, and their dogs hate what we stand for. So far, since we weathered the congressional shit-storm in ninety-eight, we've managed to stay out of the public eye. This presents a potential departmental self-destruct. The bleeding-heart White House would just love to have our balls. We've got to be extremely delicate here."

"I know, but, originally, the case was referred to us by the Food and Drug. We were just doing our job. How could we have known? If you'll look at the file, I recommended we drop the case at the end of the second week. This turned out to be entirely something different. But now I think Forbes might have been putting one over on us, after all."

"Look, it doesn't make a shit. What could Forbes possibly have gotten away with, anyway? A hundred grand? A quarter mil? Forget it. Hell, we're talking a tax bite of less than fifty thousand. How much time and money have we put into this cloak and dagger operation already? Goddamn it, man, we've got to burn our bridges and fade into the sunset quick. If it ever comes out that we have information that might bear on this abortion death—not to mention the natural history of just how we just happened to come on to it—we'll be the laughingstock. How are we going to do the right thing for the local law and still keep our name out of it? That's the issue here."

"Well, that's why I came to you."

"OK. First off, close the Forbes file immediately. I want that folder buried so far back in the archives nobody can find it. But, before we quietly fold our tent, we've got to point the Myrtle Beach law in the right direction on this abortion death. The best way is the simplest. We'll simply play the anonymous informant's role. Tell that Myrtle Beach cop just enough and let them do the rest. There's no need for us to be involved any further in the investigation of that death, or deaths, as may be the case."

"So?"

"So you have to fly to Wilmington to handle things. You say Forbes is in Virginia because his wife had surgery? When's he coming home?"

"I don't know. He's new on his job. My guess is he won't stay long."

The Director pushed the intercom and asked his secretary to check the flights out of DCA to Wilmington.

"Do you think he's involved in this IUD abortion thing?"

"Him personally? No way, but, I'll bet he's the father of the kid she was aborting. You heard that tape I made of them in that room in Myrtle Beach. And, there's certainly a mystery about his car. That thing about the mud and interior stain, the night he loaned it for the liquor run, and who used it last Friday night? If, indeed it was him who got on that plane?"

"What about this doctor…" —the Director flipped through the stack of paper— "…the one who drove him to the airport Friday night? Batson says he's the same one who borrowed the car for the whiskey run."

"Eugene Lindamood. That's correct." Fisher looked at his notes.

"He seems to get around. And you said Lindamood has a nice little nest egg stashed in a Charlottesville bank."

"Yeah. There's something smelly going on with him. Batson heard him try to talk Forbes into letting him deal some of his drug samples."

"Goddamn, Durr, I told you, drop that, it's not your job anymore. Now let's get you to Wilmington and bury this one in the back files as soon as we can. OK?"

"Yes sir!"

"Now it's up to you. As soon as you get down there, make the call. And, Nell Batson must be debriefed on this. No leaks. 'Mum's' the fucking word. If this comes back on the agency, you'll be lucky to be auditing pig farmers in Buffalo Hump, South Dakota."

[351]

The director's secretary buzzed him back on the intercom. "The next flight's at noon, Midway two nine five. Change in RDU. Arrives Wilmington at two thirty-five. After that there's only one at five. That one connects in Raleigh, arrives Wilmington at nine p.m."

"Book Agent Fisher cabin class on the noon flight and send around a car. He'll be down in fifteen minutes."

Fisher checked his watch: 10:59.

The Director frowned and shrugged. "Gladys, have his ticket waiting at the boarding gate." The director turned off the intercom and watched while Fisher gathered up his things.

"And Durwood, about the other thing, that intriguing bit of intelligence about Forbes and H. Cameron Brawley, the ex-governor's daughter who's going to run for that vacated senate seat. Are these the only copies of those tapes? And what about the reports? Were copies made?"

"I'm sure Batson has copies of the paperwork and the logs. Those tapes are the only ones we have."

"Good, get all that paper work involving Brawley and put it under personal lock and key the minute you get down there. I'm going to drop this juicy tidbit in the party's ear, at the very highest level. For an off-year, it's going to be a bloody election this fall."

Chapter Seventy-five

"GUESS WHO JUST CALLED?"

At 3:15 P.M., Mack Jones walked into the Brunswick County Coroner's office, closed the door, removed his hat, wiped the sweat from inside his hat band with a bandanna, and sat down beside the old doc's desk.

"What's up?" Dr. Amos Lyon sat up straight. An open medical journal slipped off his lap. He'd been half-dozing off and on since lunch.

"I just got a phone call from Puckett Crump, the chief of police at Myrtle Beach? Said he just received an anonymous call. Had some very interesting information about the latest IUD death down there. What'cha think the caller had to say?"

"Cut the quiz, Mack. Get to the bloody punchline just for once, OK?" The old doc was ill-tempered from being rudely interrupted from his nap.

"Crump says we ought to check out a guy at Wrightsville Beach, name of Buchanan Forbes. Also mentioned that young OB doc at the hospital in Wilmington by the name of Eugene Lindamood." The

Sheriff pronounced the name YOU-gene.

"Our mysterious initial 'E.' The one who's tight with Physician's Supply, the Raleigh IUD distributor?"

"The very same. And guess what else this mysterious caller had to say?"

"Mack, just cut the crap."

"Said Buchanan Forbes flew Midway to MBA Friday night, the night the Wagner girl checked into that motel, and this Forbes rented himself a car."

"MBA...what the hell's that?"

"Myrtle Beach Airport. Don't you know anything, you old coot?"

"Well, why can't you just say so? I hate all them goddamn acronyms. Ever since FDR with his CCC and WPA and..."

"And the TVA and the FDA. Goddamn it, Doc, sometimes you sound just like a broken record. Why bring that up? That was a hundred years ago."

"Well, how about the FBI, OAS and AFL-CIO. And in Boston you ride the MTA. Now it's even airports. It's getting worse." Dr. Lyon shook his head. "So, anyway, this guy Forbes flew into Myrtle on Friday, so what? There must've been a bunch of folk flew into there, and who's Forbes anyway? And how's that tie in with this young Dr. Lindamood?"

"Lindamood drove him to the airport, but that ain't all that's funny here."

"Eh? What else?"

"The caller told Puckett that about an hour after that plane took off, somebody took Forbes' car across the drawbridge on U.S. Seventeen headed south. The car didn't make it back until after two A.M., and by then the odometer had turned up about two hundred fifty miles."

"Say, what the hell's going on here? How come this informant has all this information? Sounds like someone's trying to set this Forbes up... or..."

"Or what?"

"Somebody's been keeping a careful eye on him."

"I thought of that. What'cha think? FBI? Local law?"

"Could be. Forbes got a record? What's he do to make a living, any-way?"

"Sells drugs, pharmaceuticals. I got his military record. Oh, yeah, he writes stuff for newspapers. Seems clean, but I don't know."

"Well, what'cha waiting on? Why don't we just go ask this Forbes a question or two?" Doc stood up.

"Can't. This anonymous informant says Forbes is out of state. His wife's had cancer surgery. In the hospital up in Roanoke."

[353]

"Virginia?"

"Yep." The sheriff looked around for a place to spit and eyed Doc's spotless white enamel trash can.

"Don't even think about it, you filthy ol' fart. Use the john." He thumbed him toward the rear. He was tired of Mack's tobacco chewing.

Disgruntled, the sheriff shuffled off to the toilet. He spit and flushed. His returning steps made a hollow clicking on the immaculate, white-tiled floor.

"Don't mess around. Why don't you get a fugitive warrant and have the Virginia law arrest this Forbes and send him back to us?" Doc leaned forward and grabbed the sheriff by the arm as he walked back by.

"Amos, you know better'n that. For all we know, this caller's just some goddamn crank trying to set this Forbes guy up. What if he turns out to be as innocent as a mother's kiss? Besides, we really don't know anything. It's too early to tip our hand." The sheriff reached for his hat.

"Where you headin'?"

"I'm gonna see Lew Dowdy out at Wrightsville Beach and find out what he knows about this Forbes guy. Lew rides herd on that Beach crowd like the FBI or MI5…or the KGB. They don't call him Snoopy for nothing. The man's got a book on everyone. Besides, Lew's men will need to keep an eye out and call me when Forbes gets back. Want to tag along?"

"Does a possum defecate in the swamp?"

"I reckon so, all right."

Chapter Seventy-six

WHEN HE AWOKE, Buchanan sat woodenly on the side of the bed and reread the item about Penny's death.

Real enough, when seen in the cold morning light.

What had Sharkey told the law? What would Inger say?

Fear slithered inside his gut like a slimy worm.

It all seemed a nightmare. His depression deepened when the boys said they'd rather go to the Vacation Bible School picnic than let him take them to visit their mother and then go fly a kite in the park before he had to head back home.

Even the cosmic architect seemed against him now.

Trying not to let on his feelings were hurt, Buchanan reluctantly drove them to the church and put them on the bus.

"Bye, Dad, wish you didn't have to go. Be sure and tell Miz Brawley to tell Tyler, 'hi.'" Greg gave him a snappy salute and climbed aboard the bus.

"Come back soon, Dad. Don't forget, tell Mom it's OK to get a dog." Little Garrett gave him a hug, and Granger helped his little brother with the first high step to climb aboard.

"When can we visit you at the beach?" Granger asked before he turned to join the rest.

With that optimistic sign, the sun suddenly seemed brighter.

"The sooner the better. I'll talk to your mom," Buchanan promised and turned to wave.

"We miss you, Pop. I wish you'd move back here with us and Mom," Grayson called back out of the bus window.

"Next time you come, we'll fly the kite." Granger stuck his head out of the bus window with a final word.

How quickly the child becomes the father of the man, Buchanan reflected, not too happily.

He waved and smiled, trying hard not to betray a wayward pang of loneliness as he watched the bus pull out of the parking lot.

At the hospital he found Alma sitting in a chair beside the bed. Her hair was freshly combed. A blue ribbon caught it in a ponytail and hint of lipstick made her color return a bit.

"About time. Where are my kids?"

"They had other plans. The Bible School picnic won out."

"Well, they could have canceled. That picnic wasn't life or death. You come marching up here with me in the hospital and in just one day you've spoiled them all over again. At least you could have brought my kids."

Buchanan let it pass. Alma was making a remarkable recovery, indeed.

"I asked Ogden about the cobalt treatments and he said it takes less than a month. He thinks you'll be right as rain soon enough, long before school takes up again. I wish you'd let me come up and drive you and the kids down to see the beach. We could take a good look at Wilmington, look at houses and schools. When we sell the house, we're going to come out way ahead. You wouldn't believe the mansion Ted Harper bought down there for under 200 K. I'm sure I could get someone to help you until you're on your feet again." He hoped to draw her out about her plans.

It proved to be a futile exercise. Her mind was closed.

"A trip would be a total waste of time. No way am I moving all the way back down there. I wouldn't know a living soul. At least I have your parents and I have my sisters here. Why do I have to make all the compromises? Don't you understand, I could die. Why don't you ask Morris

Earle? Maybe he could find you something back here?"

"Coming back here would be a dead-end street for me. I'm making progress where I am. Things look good. The *Esquire* editor liked the Mallone piece, and, I'm trying to write a book."

"A book? Oh, not the Hemingway routine, again?" She laughed a scornful laugh. "How much would a magazine like *Esquire* pay, anyway?"

"Well, I'm not sure. But Roberts at SNS likes my work. He pays a buck a word—two thousand for Mallone—and already asked me if I had something else I'd like to do. He says I can have steady work, if I want to take other assignments like Mallone."

"Don't you see how naive you sound? They have all the professional writers they need. You're not a real writer. You should be out making doctor calls instead of chasing empty dreams. I'm not going back down there just to have you get fired again."

"Well, if you won't come back to me, where does that leave us?" He stood at the window and looked out between the tops of the buildings to the mountains disappearing like rows of lacy ruffles variegating blues into violets into the distant haze.

"Are you asking for a divorce?" she snapped. "If you are, I warn you. I'll get the house. You lost your job, disgraced us all. You owe me and the children everything."

Divorce?

The word hit him like a fist.

"Disgrace? I already have a better job. I've sent you money, paid all the bills on time and hardly missed a beat. And, I don't care what you say, I may make it as a writer yet. I hardly think you could claim that I've ruined your life. It seems you're hell-bent on making it the other way around and anyway it was you who just up and left. My attorney could probably make an iron-clad case for desertion. Don't think I'll just stand idly by and give up my sons."

He couldn't tell her that he'd gladly give her everything—except the boys—if she'd just let him go.

"Attorney? Desertion? How dare you to come in here when I'm facing a horrible death, wanting to simply walk away and leave me alone. Have you already found someone else? Michael said you probably had. I know you don't care a thing about me. You'd be better off if I were dead."

She was obviously looking for a fight.

"Look, no sense in getting upset. Let's talk another time. Can I get you anything before I go? I'd best be getting on the road."

She gave him a list of magazines and other little things she needed and, gratefully, he went out to shop.

"Take care. I'll call." It was after one when he awkwardly squeezed her hand farewell.

A shadow of hatred passed behind her eyes. She turned away when he tried to kiss her.

He left the room as quickly as he could.

On the elevator Michael Gentry was heading down. "Hi, Michael. Guess you know about Alma's scare."

"It's really sad. She's no spring chicken. Without her ovaries her skin will go and she'll lose what tone she has. She's feeling pretty sorry for herself."

"I guess she has a right to feel a little sorry for herself. How'd you feel if someone found nodules in your balls? I bet you'd look real sweet when your titties started to grow." Buchanan couldn't hold back his sudden rush of anger.

"Guess you're right. I wouldn't like that much." Michael looked at him warily, now.

"If what I hear is true, I guess about half the women in Roanoke County would go in mourning if they heard you'd lost your nuts."

Mike self-consciously smoothed his hair. "Oh, not quite that many, I'm afraid."

"Alma tells me you've been a real friend to her. You make quite a pair." Hostility scorched the margins of his words.

"Now wait a minute, don't believe any of that."

All at once, Buchanan saw he'd inadvertently struck a nerve. "Didn't you volunteer to help her buy a car?"

"Oh, yeah, that. But that wasn't really my idea. She bugged the living shit out of me. I don't know why she picked on me. I guess it's because my ex, Lillie, is her friend."

"Oh, I don't know. Alma speaks well of you, Mike." Buchanan let his sarcasm show.

"Now listen, Buck, don't believe everything…" He stopped.

Mike looked away at the light indicating the floors as the elevator moved slowly down. He fidgeted slightly. The silence obviously bothered him.

"I saw your piece in the Sunday paper about that mystery writer. I've told everyone at the club to look out for it."

The elevator stopped and Mike hurried out without another word.

In the lobby Buchanan found a phone and called Cammie.

"I'm sorry, she's out," Mae told him.

"Tell her I'll call again from somewhere down the road." He felt strangely relieved. He really didn't want to face Cammie again so soon.

His lie about Penny was a chasm between them now.

He was halfway to Martinsville before the reality of Penny's death descended over him like a pall. He pulled off the highway and collapsed over the steering wheel in an uncontrollable paroxysm of soul-wrenching sobs.

Chapter Seventy-seven

DOC WINCED AS MACK JONES spit in a milkshake cup he'd brought along. "So this Buchanan Forbes has quite a way with the ladies, huh? Fast talker, an artiste, draws pretty pictures of the ladies, writes for magazines, likes to play around?"

Chief Lew "Snoopy" Dowdy thought a moment before he spoke. "Don't know I'd say it quite like that. He's a clean-cut sort. Minds his own business, pays his bills on time. Everybody seems to take to him. I kinda like the guy, myself."

Snoopy was getting a trifle agitated. His reputation was at stake. If Buchanan Forbes was mixed up in a wrongful death, maybe an abortion ring, right under his nose, he'd never live it down.

"Tell me more about this Sugarshack. Movie starlets, airline stewardesses, nurses, secretaries and schoolteachers. Local doctors, pharmacists, traveling men, attorneys—most of 'em married, I'd bet on that. For an old-timey family beach, sounds like you're running a regular little Melrose Place."

With obvious effort, Snoopy Dowdy controlled himself. The Chief was a man who took care of things. People in the highest places returned his calls, no matter what the party in power.

Over the years, Dowdy had accumulated an incredible wealth of favor in the rarefied sanctums on both sides. The Chief had rescued the sons and daughters of countless generations of governors, legislators and the wealthiest powerbrokers around the South. If he ever called all his markers in, half the well-known figures in the most recent issue of *Town and Country* would come to him on bended knee.

"Cut me some slack, Mack. I've never had a moment's trouble at that address. And, as a matter of fact, by God, this *is* a 'family' beach. Just call the governor, ask half the legislature or the Reynoldses, the Hanes, the Stephens, the Springs, almost anybody who is somebody, far away as Washington and New York. They all bring their wives and children here. And by God, we don't have any rundown boardwalks and sleazy carny shows to attract the riffraff." Snoopy couldn't resist slipping in a gentle reminder that some of the beaches south of the Cape Fear were in Mack Jones' jurisdiction and attracted a rather seedy clientele.

Wrightsville Beach numbered among its permanent year-round residents a small cadre of commercial fishermen and quiet, mostly local-born blue-collar types. Some were loners, but there was a scattering of solid family men. Snoopy's reputation for showing an unfriendly face to mainside grifters and drifters was known far and wide, and Wrightsville Beach was usually given a clear berth by local ne'er-do-wells trolling for the lower exercises of social life.

"Well, all right, tell me all about this fancy little social club. I'm told the mortgage is held jointly by a Ted Harper, Henry Long and this here Dr. Eugene Lindamood?"

"There's not a lot to tell. The property was originally built by an executive of the old Coast Line Railroad. The railroad moved their general offices to Jacksonville back in the sixties. The property was left to a granddaughter who lived out west. Harper got his buddies interested and they picked that cottage up for a song. Long's mother-in-law owns a medical supply outfit in Raleigh and he operates the local branch. Lindamood came down to the hospital last July as resident specializing in obstetrics. He's married to a rather snooty type—word is her old man's in real estate—has a wad of dough somewhere up in Virginia. I'm sure the hospital has a file on both Harper and Lindamood. Want me to call Norma Jean in hospital personnel?"

"Sure, ask her if I can stop and see his file on the way out of town…"

Snoopy pushed the intercom, "Effie, call Norma Jean at the hospital personnel office and ask if it's OK for Sheriff Jones and Doc Lyon to come by to look at the Ted Harper and Dr. Lindamood's files."

"Thanks, Chief. Now, tell me more about this Sugarshack. Word is it's a place to pick up local women. Any drugs? Cards, gambling, stuff like that?" Mack persisted.

Doc cringed as Mack drooled spit in the nasty cup.

"I don't allow no flagrant drug use on this island. Somebody fires up an occasional joint now and then, and maybe take a dex or barb or two here and there. But no crack. No real dope, and no deals. That cottage on Lagoon is strictly a private residence where very respectable locals get away from home, relax. I told you…I've never had a moment's trouble from that address."

"Does this Forbes hang out, pick up women there?" Mack persisted.

"Forbes almost never shows up there. The regulars are mostly…get out your pad and write down these names…"

Doc sat back and listened in amazement for the next half hour as Snoopy ran down an exhaustive list and personal history of twenty or thirty well-recognized local men and women who more or less hung out regularly at the Sugarshack. Mostly names the sheriff would want to think twice about before risking upsetting them.

"I hear that Forbes had a thing for a local named Maggie O'Brien. She's got a little history of IUD-connected death all her own." The sheriff told Dowdy about Maggie discovering Zoni Corbett's body, pausing to drool more brownish sputum into the cup.

Doc struggled to keep from gagging.

"Maggie, an abortionist? That's pure bullshit! Her finding Corbett was just a bizarre coincidence, bad luck. I've known Maggie Oaks—Maggie O'Brien—for over thirty years, since she was on her mama's breast." Snoopy began to recite the woman's history as Doc listened in wide-eyed fascination to the details and dates that supported the man's information.

"By the way, Maggie and Forbes split a few weeks back," Dowdy added.

Mack Jones sniffed. "Seems like we have a wealth of coincidences here. When O'Brien and Forbes split up, were there any other women Forbes was seeing, even just now and then?"

"Well, just one. Her name's not germane here."

"I think I should be the judge of that, don't you?" Mack snapped and spit again and wiped his chin. "Who is she?"

"Sorry, my people know I look after them. Their comings and goings are their private business. If that name should ever become relevant to this case, then of course, I'd clue you in, but it won't! Trust me, this woman's not involved." Anger flashed in Snoopy's eyes.

Mack caught the look. He knew better than to overstep his welcome, but there were a lot of questions still unanswered here.

"Well, we can always ask Forbes," the sheriff shot back. He resented Snoopy's reluctance to trust him.

The Chief stood and walked across and opened the door to signal the interview was at an end.

Standing at the counter, Effie, the town clerk, picked up a notepad and said, "I called the hospital, but it's late. Norma Jean said to call back any time tomorrow after eight A.M."

"Thanks," the sheriff said and started out again.

Across the counter, a strikingly pretty woman had been passing the time of day with Effie.

"Hi, Maggie, how was Daytona? By the way, the remodeling on the house looks great." Dowdy spoke to the woman as she turned to leave the anteroom of the small town offices complex which also served as office of the clerk.

"Thanks, Snoops." The Chief winced visibly at the use of the rather undignified nickname. It was widely joked about that only a favored few of the long-standing permanent denizens were permitted that unprofessional familiarity in public, and even then, it was not a thing the Chief enjoyed. "It's good to be back. Daytona's OK, but the kids and I miss this place. See you around," Maggie nodded at the sheriff and Doc. "Sheriff Jones, Dr. Lyon, long time no see."

They both nodded politely.

Maggie smiled and waved as she went out the door.

"That Maggie O'Brien's a piece of work," Dowdy reflected paternally as they watched the pair of white shorts and the overburdened bandanna halter top jump into the old VW bug and back out onto Lumina and head back down the strand.

"Me-oh-my," Mack Jones let out a breath, his eyes glued on Maggie's pert behind as she'd walked across the parking lot.

"I don't know what his wife looks like but, if you ask me, this guy Forbes doesn't do too bad for himself," Doc whispered in quiet admiration.

"Well, he's going to have time to think a lot about that one when he's behind bars. C'mon Amos, we still gotta drive fifty miles before suppertime." Mack Jones spit into the cup again as he headed out the door.

SNOOPY DOWDY stood in the hot, late afternoon sun and watched the rustic pair get in the official Brunswick County Sheriff's car and drive north along the Banks Channel toward the bridge. He shook his head in wonder and turned and walked back inside and told Effie to go on home and waited while she collected her things. When he'd bid her a friendly goodnight and locked up, he pulled the blinds behind her. Then he walked back into his office and dialed an outside number.

"Mae, this is Lew Dowdy at Wrightsville Beach. Get your boss on the phone." His voice conveyed a no-nonsense tone.

"I'm sorry, she's in conference, Chief...not to be disturbed..."

"Just buzz her, Mae, and tell her I'm on the line. I'm sure she'd be upset if she knew she missed this call."

"But..."

"Don't argue. Mae, I don't believe you'd want me to tell her that you wouldn't call her to the phone?"

He waited. In less than a minute, a woman came on the line.

"Lew, what can I do for you?"

"I'm sorry to interrupt your meeting, but something's happened that you should know…" He quickly told Cammie everything concerning the suspicion of Buchanan's involvement.

"I see. Thanks Lew, for your, discretion. I hate that Mr. Forbes' name has been unnecessarily brought into this. I hope they won't make things difficult for him. You know he couldn't possibly be involved. He was with me. But, I'll have to protect myself. The party's good image is at stake. Mae will put you through any time you have further word. I know you have to cooperate with your fellows in Brunswick and Myrtle Beach, but I hope you'll be as helpful to Mr. Forbes as you can. Thanks again, goodnight."

CAMMIE PUT DOWN THE PHONE.

"Has Mr. Forbes called again?" she asked Mae on the intercom.

"Yes, ma'am. I told him you were out and he said that he was on the road and would call back."

"Oh, yes, well thanks, and thanks for staying late. You can lock up at six o'clock. I'll see you tomorrow. Have a nice evening, Mae," she said and closed the door and turned to look out the window.

God, what had she gotten herself into?

What were her options here? She needed time to think.

She was sorry that they were going to have to question Buchanan, but it really served him right. He'd lied about the girl. She'd never forgive him for that.

Her face burned with shame thinking that he had compared her to that nineteen-year-old.

As ye sow, so shall you reap. Buchanan Forbes had only himself to blame.

Still, he was innocent. After all, she was his alibi.

But surely it would never get that far. Snoopy would do his best to keep her out of it.

McCain himself had called her this very afternoon. The party needed her. There could be no turning back.

She picked up the phone and pushed the intercom. "Mae, if Mr. Forbes calls back, tell him I'll be tied up all afternoon."

Chapter Seventy-eight

BUCHANAN PULLED INTO A RESTAURANT in Hillsborough and found a phone and dialed Cammie's number again.

"She said to tell you she was sorry, Mr. Forbes, but not to bother to call her back. She'll be tied up quite late." Mae's voice had a final ring.

In his present state, he truly didn't know if it made him happy or sad.

The sun was getting lower in the sky when he dialed the number at The Wit.

"Jimbo, this is Buchanan Forbes. I have some cleaning that needs picking up. Is Tory or Goose or Isis, or anybody there who can walk down the street and pick it up and keep it there for me? I'll be coming in quite late."

"Maggie just walked in…would you like to ask her?"

Before he could tell Jimbo no, Maggie came on the line.

"Buck, where are you? The police are asking questions. What's it all about?"

He caught his breath. Mallone or Inger had spilled their guts. He'd been afraid it would come to that.

" I'm not sure," he lied. "How'd you find out, anyway? Were they asking you?"

"I was at city hall to pay my water bill and I heard Snoopy Dowdy talking to the Brunswick County law in the back room."

"What did they want to know?" His throat was dry.

"Something to do with all those abortion deaths. The latest one was that coed in Myrtle Beach. What could they possibly want from you?"

"I knew that girl, but I know nothing about her death. Tell me what you heard…"

Listening to Maggie, Buchanan's mind raced ahead.

HE HAD KNOWN THAT THE COPS *might eventually want to talk to him about Penny's death. But, what did he know? He'd simply tell them the truth and that would be the end of it.*

But if his name leaked out on this, Wickline would surely have his job.

And Alma's accusations of adultery. The thought left him weak.

The Roanoke paper said there were those other deaths involved. Did knowing Penny link him to a major case?

Things were clearly getting out of hand.

Maggie was his alibi for the night the body in Brunswick was found. The two of them had read about it the next day. He remembered that quite well. And Penny? He hadn't seen or heard from her in over two months. Best of all, he'd been with Cammie at Pawley's.

Absolutely nothing to connect him. He had nothing to hide. He'd call and simply talk to the Brunswick law.

Easy enough.

Just explain. Both nights he had an ironclad alibi.

Once they saw his innocence, the truth about his intimacies with Penny was a secret he saw no need to come to light.

There'd be no reason to bring his name into the rest of it.

He had a totally impeccable alibi. A bona fide senatorial candidate. Screw 'em, let 'em deal with that.

Sweetjeezus!

If that got out, the scandal would make headlines everywhere.

It would devastate Cammie's career.

His mouth went dry and his legs were suddenly wobbly.

Of course, if it came down to his future, Cammie wouldn't let him down.

He thought again about Alma's mention of divorce.

Maggie and Cammie.

In court his alibis were like taking a front page ad that he'd cheated on his wife.

She'd fix it so that he'd never see his kids again.

His job, his kids, his life hung in the balance here.

He shivered against the sudden chill.

"WHERE ARE YOU NOW?" Maggie's question brought him back to reality.

He told her and where he'd been and why. "I'm on my way back there right now."

"I'm sorry about your wife, but listen, I'm sure the local cops have your place staked out. They're going to pick you up, so don't be too surprised. By the way, I overheard Snoopy stall the Brunswick law. He managed to keep your snooty friend in Raleigh out of it, for the present at least." Maggie got in her dig.

"She's not involved," Buchanan said. "There's no reason to compromise her with this."

"Oh, sure, and it doesn't matter about me. My reputation's ruined anyway, is that what you're trying to say? Well, what will Lewis Warrant have to say about my working for his company if he finds out? Or my kids? I guess you don't really give a shit." Her words hit a nerve.

"You know that's not what I meant. None of us should be involved, but how could I have known? I only met that girl casually. I was with Sharkey Mallone." It wasn't a lie. "I'm sorry. This has turned into a mess. But thanks for looking out for me."

"OK. All right, I'm sorry, no need to come down on you. As far as we were concerned, it took two to tango. I guess we both knew that. I plan to be around. I'll keep my ears open. Get back to me when you're closer home, before you come back out here. I'll see what else I can learn."

"Thanks. I'll be coming back late tonight. I'll try to reach you before I cross the bridge."

"I'll be at home after nine. Before that you could try me here at The Wit."

"I'll owe you one." Buchanan breathed a word of thanks.

"Just hold that thought," Maggie murmured as he hung up the phone.

BUCHANAN FOUND A PAPER RACK and carried the paper inside the restaurant and ordered coffee and skimmed Joe Jordan's piece.

Three previous deaths: Greenville, Rockingham and the body dumped in the Brunswick County swamp. Penny in Myrtle Beach made four.

Hospital records of IUD-related abortion cases in Fayetteville, Wilmington, Florence—the list had risen to ten in all. Some additional reports from hemorrhages treated in the offices of physicians and emergency room complaints. The list was growing daily, as reports kept trickling in. There were also recent cases—not yet confirmed—as far away as Monck's Corner down Charleston way and an isolated instance six months ago in Virginia, near Lynchburg. The hunt was on. The papers were screaming for the perpetrator's hide and a full Food and Drug investigation was just getting underway on G/uL Technologies Lab's T3 IUD. A warning was out to all physicians and hospitals to carefully rule out early pregnancy before inserting the device in any patient regardless of marital status and previous history of pregnancy. And it was hinted that even a total recall of the product was a suggested possiblity.

Good old Joe Jordan.

Incredible. For three months, since those holy-rollers in the White House closed down the abortion clinics—and the centuries before *Roe vs. Wade*—every day, dozens of dirty sticks and rusty coat hangers were maliciously poked into pregnant uteri. Countless infections and deaths over the millennia and suddenly the national media had reinvented abortion, as if it only started since the legalization of the IUD. Now, G/uL Technologies threatened to replace Jack the Ripper as the "Criminal of the Ages."

Jordan should be writing for the *Enquirer* or the purple paperbacks.

Buchanan paid his check, carefully folded the paper beneath his arm and left.

As he drove numbly eastward, ideas skittered around inside his skull like water on a hot skillet. Frantically, he considered and discarded scenarios of how to go about getting off the hook.

He couldn't just walk right in. The press was surely camping out.

He had to have a plan.

He got off I-40 in Raleigh and felt a wistful pang as he drove down Western Boulevard and passed the park where he and Cammie always took the kids. At a service station on the outskirts of the city, he stopped again and called the Realtor who was handling his house. The agent wasn't in but the receptionist said she thought they might have someone interested in his "property."

He'd heard that song before.

He bought gas and a six-pack of Corona and popped off a top as he started rolling east again. Driving along, he lost all track of time as he tried to sort things out.

Finally, he got off I-40 again near Clinton, his arbitrary halfway point, and stopped and called Maggie's house. Melly said to try her at The Wit.

Luck was on his side. Jimbo put her on the line.

"Nothing new. Snoopy's deputy's been hanging around. And they're watching your place like a hawk. This is serious, I think. I don't know what else I can do."

"Thanks," he said. "I know you don't owe me anything, but you might help me out on this. I think I've got a plan." He told her what he had in mind.

When he'd finished, she laughed out loud and said, "You've been reading too much Sharkey Mallone, but count me in. I'd kind of like to see the show."

OUT OF CLINTON HE TOOK OLD 421. The lights of houses showed fewer and far between as the road ran through a sparsely-populated section of country. Twenty minutes passed before a small sign warned Harrell's Crossroads was just ahead.

Slowing at Harrell's, Buchanan pulled off into a weedy, once-graveled parking lot of a long-abandoned country store. The crumbling brick ruin loomed, a ghostly shadow against the star-filled night.

With his window down, toward the east there was an almost-imagined rumble of distant thunder and the occasional peach-glows of heat lightning revealed the line of an approaching summer storm.

Tree frogs and crickets serenaded a raucous cacophony. If the moon was up, it was behind the clouds.

A car whooshed by. Buchanan waited until the red taillights disappeared into the blackness.

Cutting his lights, he took a leak in the weeds before he found his flashlight and retrieved a plastic camping tarp from his toolbox in the trunk. Then he checked both ways for traffic before he spread the tarp and rolled underneath the car.

In less than a twinkling he slid out again and killed the flashlight before he turned and sent the tiny metal box sailing off through the night to crash deep into the underbrush behind the abandoned store.

Buchanan was humming softly when he put the car back on the road again.

"Rainy days and Sundays always get me down…" Erotic images of Maggie came flooding back as he improvised new lyrics to a familiar song.

MACK JONES WAS HOME eating a TV dinner when he took Maggie's call. When she hung up, he dialed Doc Amos and told him what she'd said.

"Well, if that don't beat all hell. Sounds like some damn movie on cable TV." Doc still couldn't quite believe his ears. "What'cha think he's got in mind?"

"He's coming in, I guess…said to make damn sure we're all sitting in my office when he calls tomorrow morning at nine."

Chapter Seventy-nine

AT 8:55 A.M., MAGGIE STOOD at the ferry slip and watched the gulls gliding and dipping in the wake of the Southport Ferry as it made its ethereal approach out of the river mists from the Fort Fisher side.

She waited until the boat had nosed into the slip and docked. As the cars began rolling off, she went to the phone and made the call.

"Sheriff Jones, I'm calling for Buchanan Forbes," she began and briefly detailed Buchanan's instructions.

When she replaced the phone, Maggie retraced her steps to her car just as the line of waiting vehicles ahead started to move aboard the ferry for its return trip. When the crewman had guided her into place up near the front, she got out and walked back along the rail, watching the last of the cars come aboard. In a moment, the Brunswick County sheriff's car came careening down the street and pulled into line and moved warily aboard. The doors opened and three men got out and started to look around as if they were lost.

"What the hell, this is a frigging wild goose chase. We're being jerked around. I don't like this at all," Puckett Crump complained loudly to the sheriff.

"Well, go ahead. You can still get off. Go on home. I'll call you later after Forbes has played his hand." Mack Jones wasn't any happier to be part of this than Puckett was, but he added grudgingly, "As much as I hate to admit it, right now it's the only game in town."

"Well, I ain't about to leave, but I want to know what the fuck's going on. Is Forbes going to meet us on the Fort Fisher side? I still don't understand." He turned to Amos Lyon, looking for an ally in his frustration.

"Don't look at me," Doc Lyon shrugged.

The sheriff moved to the rail and spit. Both of his companions stepped quickly back out of the wind to avoid being sprayed with the foul-smelling tobacco juice which was instantly atomized by the wind. Mack ignored them and wiped his chin with his bandanna. "Well, I don't like all this cloak and dagger shit, but I sure'n hell want to clear this up."

"He's just trying to clear himself. Can't blame a man for that," Doc Lyon said, cringing at the tobacco spit.

Now the boat was already moving away, headed back across the Cape Fear shipping channel.

MAGGIE LOOKED UP TOP where Buchanan stood at the rail looking down at the three of them. He looked down at her and gave her a little wave. He had his fingers crossed.

"Hey! Up here!" Buchanan's shrill whistle startled them, and the trio looked up as he waved and motioned for them to join him topside at the observation rail. "Down this way," he pointed to the stairs at the forward end of the salon.

"Well, I'll be damned, c'mon." Doc laughed and shook his head in appreciation. He led them past the entrance to the main salon and lifted the chain bearing a little card: UPPER DECK CLOSED and motioned the others up the companionway. "Can't say he ain't the dramatic one…"

"Ahhh, shitfire, whooeee, I'm too goddamn old for this!" Mack Jones wheezed as he neared the top of the narrow stairwell. He looked up at Forbes waiting at the top. "I don't like being jerked around like we was a bunch of hick Keystone Kops."

"This better be goddamn good," Puckett Crump mumbled from the rear.

"Well, I guess you're Forbes." Mack reached the top first and growled at Buchanan who was standing against the bright morning sky waiting with a half-smile on his face. "As far as I'm concerned, you can just consider your ass under arrest."

"What's the charge?" Buchanan knew the mustachioed man was serious enough but found it hard not to laugh.

"Material witness, at the very least. Probably negligent homicide… criminal manslaughter…wrongful death." Jones tried to catch his breath as he blurted out the words.

"Before you put the cuffs on me, I thought you gentlemen might want to hear what I have to say. But, if you insist on being unfriendly, I'll just enjoy the ride and you can meet my attorney on the other side."

"Humph, as long as we're here, might as well let him say his piece." Mack Jones turned to Puckett Crump for approval.

"OK, but that don't mean I'll promise anything. The jury's still out on you," Puckett grunted, bringing up the rear.

"Fair enough," Buchanan said and moved back to a bench along the rail where he'd left a plaid stadium bag with a thermos and a sleeve of paper cups. "There's coffee. Please, help yourself, and have a seat. This may take a while." He indicated the bench facing him.

Buchanan Forbes sat down and told his story, leaving out only the identity of his weekend companion and their final destination. "So-o-o, I was in Virginia at the hospital Monday when I saw the story about Penny Wagner's death." He finished his recitation before the ferry had crossed halfway. "What else do you need to know? I'll answer any questions, best I can."

"So, you admit it was you who was the father...the one what caused the Wagner woman's pregnancy?" Chief Crump jumped right in.

"I could have been. I certainly don't deny it, but I hadn't heard a word from her since March. I've saved her letters. I can show you later. And, I talked with her on the phone from Utica, after she got back to school. That's all I know. I had absolutely no inkling she was pregnant. But the question is moot. My blood type is O-positive, in case you've had the fetus genotyped. The point is, I had nothing to do with her death, and furthermore, I'm completely in the dark about any of these other abortions. As a matter of fact, until yesterday when I read *The Raleigh News and Observer*, I was barely aware that this thing had become so widespread."

"Don't give me that," Puckett Crump snorted his disbelief. "We got you tied to this airtight."

"Trust me, I told you I have an ironclad alibi for both nights in question, and if you still need proof, we can probably verify my whereabouts in every one of the other cases. My life's an open book, but not one a married man with four sons would care to have his wife and children read."

"Three women, one of 'em dead and the other two are your alibis. Besides, what's the good of an alibi if we're not free to check it out?" Mack Jones said and shifted the bitter lump of Beechnut chewing tobacco in his jaw with his tongue.

"Well, you're free talk to Maggie O'Brien about my whereabouts on the ninth of May. As for Friday night, the airline stub and the car rental clerk should be proof enough. I just can't bring my companion into this. There's no reason to jeopardize an innocent person's hard won career and reputation. Besides, there's really no need for that. You're barking up the wrong tree. I think your man may be this Gene Lindamood. Maggie O'Brien's down below. You can call her up here right now. You'll see I couldn't possibly have been involved in that case when they dumped the body down your way." Buchanan spoke directly to Sheriff Jones.

"O'Brien? She's aboard this boat?" The sheriff shot Doc Lyon a meaningful glance.

"Right there, standing by the rail." He pointed to where Maggie stood on the fantail, letting the gulls swoop down and take stale bread from her hand.

"Well, OK, but you first. We won't need to bother her right now. As far as the airline ticket and rental car, if you wanted to argue the point, that merely tends to prove our case. After all, that puts you in Myrtle Beach on Friday night."

"But I told you I was with someone. I can prove I rented the car and drove on down south. Bought gas in Litchfield Beach."

"A mysterious highly-positioned witness whose identity you can't reveal? What a crock of shit!" Puckett Crump snorted with disgust.

"Well, she's real enough. But listen, let's go back to the other cases first. Call Maggie up, let's get them clear."

"Look, she's in your harem. She'd lie. We have witnesses that you cleaned blood stains off your car seat the afternoon after we found that body in the Town Creek swamp." A tiny trickle of tobacco juice ran out the side of Mack Jones' mouth as he extracted a paper cup from the stack Buchanan had provided and used it as a cuspidor.

"I don't know where you got your information, but that is true. When Lindamood returned my car, it was a mess. There was a stain on the back seat covers and mud and underbrush caught all underneath. I was pretty pissed. At the time I thought that Lindamood and Jaynie Lockfaw had used the back seat to do a little sport fucking in the woods somewhere."

"Now you think otherwise?" the sheriff asked.

"Hell yes, don't you? I already told you, I checked the liquor closet. That story about needing Scotch was just an excuse to use my car. Lindamood's married. They work together at the hospital. At the time, I thought they were merely trying to slip away for a steamy little interlude without attracting undue attention to themselves. But now it's perfectly obvious. They used my car to get rid of that poor woman's body."

"Don't you think it's pretty suspicious that you claim to have an alibi, yet, both nights it was your car that left the beach..."

"Not this past Friday. I took the plane!" Buchanan reminded him emphatically. "I have witnesses that Lindamood gave me a ride to the airport, remember? I left my car at home. I carefully parked it off the street."

"I don't care where you parked it. That vehicle went across the draw-bridge early Friday night, headed south on U.S. Seventeen."

"Oh, come on. No way! Who told you that? There's some mistake. A lot of cars look like mine."

"No mistake. Our informant says that car was yours. When it was returned, sometime after two A.M. Saturday morning, the odometer had turned up two hundred fifty-two miles." Puckett Crump was referring to a page of notes scrawled on a sheet taken from a legal pad. "How do you explain that?"

"Are you sure? Can you prove that? How'd you get the odometer reading? Who followed me? My car, I mean?" Buchanan was completely flabbergasted to learn someone had used his car.

Now a hundred desperate questions rattled around inside his head.

Thinking back to Sunday night when he'd started the long drive to Virginia, he remembered the puzzlement he'd felt when he'd noticed the discrepancy in his mileage reading.

Of course! Lindamood had used his car. He wasn't at all surprised that the car had been tailed. After all, just last night he'd thrown that god-damned tracking device a hundred yards in the underbrush at Harrell's Crossroads. Let the frigging Feds put a tail on that.

"Just take our word. We have impeccable testimony that will support the case that your car was used." Puckett bluffed. He was well aware their source had to remain anonymous.

"I must admit, all that starts to make sense to me right now." Buchanan explained the confusion he'd felt Sunday night on his way to Virginia when he'd noticed the discrepancy in the recorded odometer reading. "And Lindamood knew I'd be gone."

"You seem to have a convenient memory, Mr. Forbes," Puckett sniffed.

"It's the truth. I have no reason to lie. That's why I asked you here."

"I guess we'll see. Don't you have to report your daily mileage to your company on an expense report…keep careful records on the car?" Crump didn't wait for an answer. "Didn't you check your reports to see how you could have made such a mistake? Don't you have to reimburse the company for non-business miles?"

"Yes, I do, but no, I didn't check my reports right then. And I've dri-ven too many miles since Sunday night to check 'em now, of course. I made a mental note to check my reports that night, but my wife was hav-ing cancer surgery…I had other things to think about. I average over one hundred miles a day. How the hell was I to know all the bullshit in the whole goddamn world was about to come raining down on me? I told you I didn't even know about Penny's death until my friend called me at my father's Monday night."

"Is this friend your mysterious alibi?"

"Look, it doesn't matter who gave me the news, and I can't, I positively won't, reveal the name of my companion. Even if I have to go to jail on this. I'm innocent. You're wasting time. Gene Lindamood's the key."

"Do you remember how many miles your car was driven that other time, the night you loaned the car to the doctor for the liquor run?"

"Not exactly. Quite a few, as I recall. I was upset, but I was more concerned about the sad condition they had left it in. It really messed up the new seat cover on the rear seat, and there was all that mud and minor scratches."

"But the mileage, that's the question now, Mr. Forbes." Mack Jones drooled in the paper cup again. The sickening odor of the tobacco juice mingled heavily with the wet salt air.

"I don't remember, exactly, more than a hundred, I think. Maybe two?" Buchanan wondered if the sheriff was asking him for information or if his inquisitors already knew and were just checking to see how truthful he had been.

"What would you say to three hundred fifty-nine miles, Mr. Forbes? Does that ring a bell?"

"That's more than I remembered, but I tried to explain…"

"Right. You were upset about the condition of the car."

"Yes, and besides, how do you know all that?"

Someone had been tailing him, tapped his phone, most likely. These hayseeds had been handed an uncanny amount of detail about his private life.

FDA?

IRS?

"Well it seems simple enough to check. Didn't you report that mileage as personal mileage on the company swindle sheet?" Crump made the question sound like he was stealing from the poor.

"No, I didn't report all of it as personal mileage. I probably buried most of it in with my business miles later in the week."

Had they already contacted Wickline?

"Isn't that the same as stealing?"

"Come on, I'd loaned the car to a doctor and a nurse. My job is trying to create goodwill with the medical profession, build personal entrè, create credibility. A lot of my success has been on the golf course and at cocktail parties at the country club. I just kiss the right asses and my company's glad to pick up the tab. Things like letting Lindamood use that car go with the job description. I certainly don't have to put that on my personal tab."

"Seems to me you have a convenient explanation for everything. It's all too pat. With you everything seems to come out just right."

"Hey, didn't I call and volunteer to meet you? I'm doing the best I can to help. I'm trying to answer your questions as honestly as I can. I simply don't know anything about this case."

"You admit you're mostly likely the cause of the Wagner woman's pregnancy, and your car's involved. That's quite a lot, I'd say," Puckett Crump sneered.

"If Lindamood, or anyone, took my car Friday night, that's one thing, but to jump to the conclusion that it was involved in Penny Wagner's death is something else again."

Who tailed his car? He was afraid to ask.

"What about your keys? Where did you leave 'em?"

"I had my keys with me. My house key's on the same ring," Buchanan said.

"You didn't leave your car unlocked, did you?"

"No, I'm sure of that."

"And Sunday night when you started out to Virginia, was there any evidence that the door locks or the wiring had been tampered with? "

"No, nothing like that."

"How about the key you say you let Lindamood have that night he took the car on the liquor run?" Puckett Crump butted in.

"It wasn't Lindamood who eventually returned my key. As I recall, it was over a week later that Nurse Jaynie Lockfaw finally left it with Jimbo at The Wit—The Wit's End, it's a place I go to eat a hamburger and grab a beer now and then."

"What do you make of that, Mack? Mr. Forbes is trying to make us believe that, with no evidence of tampering, his carefully locked new Buick automobile just mysteriously up and drove itself across that bridge Friday night and went south for a round trip of two hundred fifty-two miles and came back and parked itself again." Crump's voice dripped sarcasm.

"Not hardly. What do you think, Forbes? Where do you keep the extra set of keys? Is there another set of keys you haven't told us about?"

"No, not at all. There's only one extra set. I keep it in my top bureau drawer at home."

"You sure of that?"

"Well, yeah. It was there the last time I looked. I've been meaning to have an extra made to keep with me on the road, just in case. But I've never gotten around to it."

"Does anyone have an extra key to your apartment?"

"I leave one in a big conch shell under the camellia bush by my door...and my landlady has one. She sometimes lets the delivery man in to unload my company sales supplies."

"So you don't have an explanation of how that car was taken without your knowledge or permission?"

"Not a clue. I still find it hard to believe."

"There's a lot about this whole damn thing I find hard to believe. And most of it has to do with your story," Puckett said.

"Haven't you heard a word I said? I told you I was with someone—someone I shouldn't have been with, it's true. I flew to Myrtle Beach and rented a car. I have the receipt at home, along with my plane ticket and those letters Penny Wagner wrote me in Utica. You're welcome to look at them. As soon as I get home I can check to make sure the car key's in place. Maggie O'Brien's right down there. Why don't you talk to her? She'll verify my story about the night that Lindamood used my car. What else do you need? I don't know a damn thing about my car being used Friday night. I was a long way from there."

"Yeah, Myrtle Beach. We can prove that at least."

"But I didn't stay there. I rented a car and drove somewhere else. Remember, I have the receipts and, worst case scenario, I have an alibi."

Had Roxy Guest seen him deplane with Cammie in Myrtle Beach?

"Yeah, someone you refuse to let us talk to! If someone was helping you in this, then they could have validated that ticket and picked up the car. After all, you'd already prepaid the damn thing by credit card at the airport here. Then you could have doubled back and taken your own car easy enough. For an abortionist trying to cover his tracks, pretty clever if you ask me," Crump fired back. He'd obviously been giving the matter thought.

"Oh give me a break! Talk about a fairy tale...that's right out of *Strangers on a Train*...or some corny old Hitchcock flick."

"Yeah, just like something you might dream up. Anyone who thinks he's clever enough to have set up this hokey scenario where we wait for a call and come running out to board a frigging ferryboat, for chrissake. Don't talk about movie plots to me."

"Look Chief, don't you see how preposterous this whole thing is? Whoever you're looking for is a doctor, or a nurse, certainly someone who has a medical background. What would I know about inserting an IUD?" Buchanan looked from man to man. Finally, he turned to the old doc and pleaded. "For godsake, doctor, can't you tell 'em? This abortionist is someone who's had competent medical training. The IUD is highly specialized technology. Whoever's been doing this knew exactly what he or she was doing."

"A good point." Clearly gloating, Crump referred to his notes again. "Weren't you an Army medical officer during Desert Storm? Ah, yes, your official Career Management Field was Ninety-one—Operating Room Specialist?"

"That was just a fancy name for a largely administrative function. I was a soldier, mechanized artillery. I wasn't a doctor by any stretch of the imagination." Buchanan waved his hand in dismissal of the ridiculous suggestion. "How'd you dig up all this shit, anyway?"

"Well, the sheriff here's had a month, remember? He already had your file," Crump said.

"My file from where?"

"Military record's in the public domain, Freedom of Information Act. If any of this ain't correct, just speak right up," Crump snapped.

Buchanan shrugged.

"Your record says you got a commendation...Silver Star for performing an operation in combat under enemy fire, an inverse something. What'd ya' call it, Doc?"

"An inverted cone amputation of the arm, above the elbow," Doc Lyon spoke up. He gave Buchanan an admiring smile. "Quite a feat. You deserved a medal. Glad I never had to do one myself."

"That was a freak of combat. We were trained for things like that. But that has nothing to do with abortions or IUDs. That's an entirely different ball game." He looked anxiously from face to face. Incredible as it seemed, he could see they were far from convinced.

"Well, the G/uL Technologies labs' medical director says the insertion procedure is really simple enough. In his view almost anybody who's been around operating rooms could learn to do it. This medical equipment guy, Hank Long, went up to Richmond and learned to do it. Before he married the daughter of the owner of that Physician's Supply house, he was a technician... repairing x-ray equipment. So much for your theory about complicated procedures and advanced medical training."

Hank Long?

Of course...why hadn't he thought of Long?

Hank was always around, and he'd been trained by IUD experts.

"Have you checked out Long? He and Lindamood are buddies."

Doc looked at the Sheriff. Mack Jones shrugged and spit into the cup again.

Crump looked at his notes. "Ellis Henry Long, III..."

"The intial 'E' again!" The old doc raised his eyebrows.

The Sheriff shot him a warning look.

What was this about the initial "E?"

"You guys are so hellbent on railroading me you haven't bothered to check out the most likely suspect."

"No, that's not true. It's also beside the point," Crump said belligerently.

"It's very much to the point. What the hell's wrong with you, anyway? I have an airtight alibi. I'm giving you Lindamood and Long, two prime suspects. What else do you need? You're wasting your time on me." Buchanan stopped as he saw the sheriff digging around in his pocket.

"Ever seen one of these little slide rule calculator things? This Hank Long's medical supply house gives 'em away?" The sheriff pulled the ruler out and held it up for Buchanan to see.

"Oh, sure. I think I may have one or two at home. I meant to send one in to our promotion department. I was impressed with the idea. What about it?" Buchanan eyed the lawman suspiciously. He had a sinking feeling. This wasn't turning out at all like he'd expected.

"How do you explain your fingerprints on the identical slide ruler we found under the body in the swamp?"

"Come on, I know you're bullshitting now. Let's keep this serious, OK?"

"Serious as a heart attack, I'd say." Mack looked at Crump and the chief looked back and nodded.

Buchanan tried to clear his head. None of this was making sense. "No way my prints could be on anything that had anything to do with her, whoever she was. Besides, it's Long's gizmo, anyway."

"Well, there were fingerprint fragments on that rule. Washington says one of 'em is yours. Let's hear you weasel out of that." Crump smirked.

The implications hit him like a fist.

"Those gadgets were being passed around at the Sugarshack that night. I looked at one then. And once before, Henry Long gave me several when I was being interviewed for the Stribol job in March. I can't remember who had 'em at the Shack that night, but I think it was Lindamood. Besides, you said one of the prints was mine. Everybody handled 'em, even my landlady, Rochelle Guest. Who do the other prints belong to?"

"We haven't gotten another match."

"Have you checked out Lindamood? And while you're at it, check Long."

"There are no prints of Long or Lindamood on file."

"Why don't you just ask them both for their frigging prints? Or is that too goddamn complicated? And the others, Jaynie Lockfaw, how 'bout her?"

"We will, all in good time."

Chapter Eighty

CAMMIE WAS GROWING TIRED of the rat-faced little jerk's insulting questions about her personal life. "I've told you, my life has been rather dull to say the least. I've told you everything."

"I'm sorry. We have to be sure there's nothing that we've overlooked. No surprises." During the past several hours, the abrasive little PR pipsqueak from the New York agency had asked the same questions for the hundredth time at least.

The party bigwigs had been giving her the third degree since before eight A.M.

"Now, let's go back…you were at Duke and later up north at school… Harvard…Yale, too, I see. And some summer courses at Columbia Law. We know you have no record of arrests. Did you participate in any demonstrations, on campus or otherwise?"

"Nothing, not officially, anyway. If you mean was I a member of any radical groups? Or carried any signs? And while we're on that subject, I never burned the flag…or my bra…"

"Good. How about drinking, ever had a problem? Gotten smashed, made a public display? Got your picture in the campus paper? Anything like that?"

"No, but I've been pleasantly high a time or two." Her thoughts drifted off, momentarily remembering the champagne breakfast she and Buchanan had shared naked in the bed at Wrightsville Beach and again, just three days ago, at Pawley's Island.

Her reverie vanished as the obnoxious pipsqueak cleared his throat and persisted, "High? Nothing more?"

"No. I've never gotten really drunk in my life. I was always the one who had to drive the others home and clean up their mess and tuck their silly butts in bed. I saw enough of that to know that I didn't need to try it—one of the rare things I never had to learn the hard way."

"Good. That's something most of us can't say. And, for someone whose life is going to be in the public eye, that'll be a plus. When the shooting actually starts, knowing that you're as pure as a nun will cut us all a little slack…widen up our comfort zone. Listen, I hope you appreciate the fact that the holy-roller President is scared shitless, afraid McCain is going to eat his lunch. Powers knows he has to win this North Carolina senate seat to truly have a chance down here. Christian Coalition or not, Aaron Claiborne Powers is a no-holds-barred, knockdown, drag out, kick-em-in-the-nuts street fighter. The man is ruthless. He'd sell his ugly wife and those homely daughters into white slavery, cut your heart out and drink your blood for breakfast if he had to, to win another term in the White House."

"I think I get the point. You've nothing to worry about. I have no secret past." Cammie looked ceilingward and sighed.

She wondered what they'd have to say if the press found out she was the primary alibi for a man being questioned in an abortion death. The thought brought an involuntary shiver.

"What about drugs?"

"Never, nothing. Hardly an aspirin."

If the police were giving Buchanan a bad time, it couldn't really amount to much. He was innocent. If they really gave him a hard time, if it actually came down to truth or dare, she'd come forward, of course. But she didn't foresee a need for that.

And, after all, it served Buchanan right to sweat a little. He'd brought it on himself.

Cammie's resentment rose, remembering Buchanan's rather uninspired performance in the bedroom at Pawley's. She blushed with shame, thinking how she must have looked to him after he'd been in bed with that nineteen-year-old. And her? Whispering starry-eyed bon mots of undying love.

She examined her nails, to hide her secret pain.

The PR creep shot her a slanted look. "This may be tedious, but I assure you it's serious and very necessary. We can't be too careful here."

"I've nothing to hide."

"OK, let's move on to your personality profile and lifestyle parameters for a while. We can come back to this later." He backed off a bit.

"Personality profile? Lifestyle parameters? Will you speak English for a change?"

"Well, you're going to be living in a goldfish bowl. We can't take any chances on likes and dislikes, prejudices, where you go, what you do, who you're seen with, that sort of thing. You understand…"

"I'm not exactly sure that I do. For instance, I assume I can still take my children to the public park to play."

"Well, sure. A lot of good press potential there. Sounds like just the setting for a media shoot. Get the mothers out in force. Mothers constitute a major segment of the vote."

"I'm serious. Surely I'll have some time alone? I'm not running for the office of Sideshow Freak."

"Well, not that, of course, but no more slipping away for a weekend alone again, like you did when we got back from DC Friday. We can't take any chances. I tried to call you all weekend. Where'd you go?"

"I just decided to get out of town for a day or so. After going through this inquisition, I'm certainly glad I did while I still had the chance."

"But where did you slip off to? You have to be careful where you're seen."

"That's none of your goddamn business…" The indignation came rushing out of her.

"But that's just the point, you see. We're getting ready to announce your candidacy for one of the most prestigious public offices of our country. You're everybody's business now."

Chapter Eighty-one

"UNRELATED CIRCUMSTANCES?" Puckett Crump fairly screamed at Buchanan. "That was your baby that poor dead girl was trying to get rid of, right?"

"Probably, I don't deny it." Buchanan didn't flinch. Their constant barrage of accusations had numbed any residual sense of grief he was feeling over Penny's death.

"Your car was mysteriously absent both nights in question, right?"

"I'll have to take your word about Friday. I certainly wasn't driving it either time."

Crump bore down. "That's what you say! But unless you let us talk to your witness you can't prove that."

"Look, one witness is right down there. If you clowns will check out the likely suspects, there's no reason to keep going back to that." He was getting very frustrated now.

"We got your fingerprint on the slide rule thing? We could charge you as an accessory on that alone, hold you as a material witness at least. And your tire prints too, we left that out."

"Come on, Lindamood had my car. Why won't you go down and talk to Maggie? Or let me call her up here?"

"No, not yet. We aren't through with you."

"But she was witness to the whole thing about Lindamood's taking my car for the liquor run…"

"So you keep saying," Puckett Crump mumbled and checked his notes again.

"Look, just let me call Maggie up here. She's my alibi for the night you found that fingerprint, and that's the only real piece of evidence I can't explain. You're wasting your time with me. You need to check out Lindamood and Long."

"Oh, we had our eye on Lindamood, but it's your prints that showed up on that slide rule thing. Tell me more about the stain you found on the seat of your car." Mack was leaning closer now. "You cleaned the seat covers?"

"Yes, I did. Say, maybe you can match that stain, it looked a lot like blood. I loaned that car to Lindamood and Lockfaw, the nurse. I thought she might have been on the rag that night. But now it's clear, they put that dead girl's body back there. You've got to check the blood stains out..."

As the sheriff leaned closer, Buchanan got a whiff of his tobacco breath. Suddenly, his cold coffee looked too much like tobacco juice. It brought on a vagrant twinge of nausea, a tangible symptom of fear?

"Yeah you already told me. How well did you know this Lindamood, anyway?"

"Not at all actually. Until that night, I'd met him in the coffee shop at the hospital with Ted Harper, the chief pharmacist, and in the hospital clinic, when I was detailing the house staff on our new antibiotics, but I'm sure he's the one you ought to be questioning now."

"You're mighty anxious to point the finger to Lindamood."

"Well, don't overlook Long entirely. He's just as good a suspect as anyone. Get both their fingerprints."

"You better hope we do. We already matched you up with the prints in Penny Wagner's motel room." The Chief shot Buchanan a hateful look.

"Motel room? Come on, you shittin' me? What're you Mickey Mouse clowns gonna come up with next?" Buchanan looked in disbelief.

"Would I shit him? Ain't that right, Mack?" Crump rubbed his hands with anticipation.

The sheriff nodded, then asked, "What you mean? Mickey Mouse?"

"Mickey Mouse, you redneck Barney Fife. I stay in that motel on my business trips. She was found in one twenty-five, right?"

"How'd you know that?"

"That's the same room I had in March—the two nights when I...when we were together. There must be some scientific way to establish that those prints weren't fresh. I read about dust overlays, Carbon-14 dating process, or some such lab thing?"

"Well, maybe, but that's not all. We found a T3 insertion tube in the room where she died. What would you say if I told you we found your print on that? This looks pretty cut and dried, I'm telling you right now, even if your alibi proved you were on national TV with Billy Graham

[380]

Friday night." Crump leaned forward. His breath smelled of rotten fish. "We got you nailed to that room that night."

Another fingerprint? On the tube? Impossible!

Jeezus, this had frame-up written all over it!

"No way, there's got to be an rational explanation." He was suddenly weak with fear.

"You better hope so."

"No way. I'm telling you, there's some mistake."

"Tell it to the Grand Jury."

"No way my print was on the tube, no goddamn way. This is pretty heavy stuff, it's just frigging impossible." Buchanan was sweating now, completely at a loss for words.

That tube had to be some sort of plant.

Or, maybe? Were they just baiting him to get his reaction?

Sure.

"You're trying to bullshit me. How'd you get a match so soon?"

"Mack here already had your file, remember? Let's see you talk your way out of this?"

"I'm telling you, no-frigging-way. Just let me make a call as soon as this boat docks. I told you I have an airtight alibi."

Buchanan squinted against the morning mist, trying to locate the Fort Fisher terminal. He remembered seeing a red-paneled phone booth at the end of the dock when he'd come down crabbing on the historic Fort Fisher rocks with Maggie and her kids.

No getting out of it. He'd have to call Cammie now.

"Look, this is all too goddamn fantastic to be real. I came down here three months ago to take a new job. And start a new career and now it's raining heavy-duty shit everywhere I turn. I just can't believe that's my fingerprint. You're sure?"

"It's yours, right enough," Crump never blinked his eyes. "No mistaking that."

"Well…it doesn't change anything. There must be a perfectly reasonable explanation."

"That's the damnedest thing I ever heard in my life. We've got this guy's fingerprint on the instrument of death and he says it doesn't change anything?" Mack Jones exploded. "I can hardly wait to hear this perfectly reasonable explanation."

Replaying a kaleidoscope of images, Buchanan tried to mentally retrace his steps.

"The first time I met him, Hank Long showed me a handful of the G/uL TechnologiesT3 IUDs. He told me he was going to be a distributor and offered me a job. That was the same day he showed me the little slide rule things. Those IUDs would've had my prints on 'em. Penny's abortionist obviously used one of those same tubes."

"Long again. To hear you tell it, the poor SOB was working overtime making sure you put your fingerprints on all our future evidence! Is that the best you can come up with?"

"I'm sure there was one other time at least that I handled some of the T3 tubes."

Silence as Buchanan feverishly racked his brain.

"Sure! Friday heading for the airport. Lindamood had a box of T3s in his car!" It came back in a flash.

"Lindamood, again. Why am I not surprised?" Crump looked at Mack Jones and shrugged derisively.

Buchanan felt his anger rise.

"Last Friday when we were going to the airport, when I put my duffel in Lindamood's car, he had a box of T3s in his trunk. I picked it up, took several out of the box and looked at them real close. And Lindamood could have had a key made to my car. He kept that key almost a week. That's it, by God. Lindamood's your man."

Crump laughed a hollow laugh. "And if he handled those same T3 tubes, how come his prints aren't on 'em, too?"

Buchanan scratched his head. "Lindamood was wearing those little nylon driving gloves. I watched him put 'em on when I was handling those tubes. That explains everything."

"Oh, now it's nylon driving gloves in the summertime. That's really convenient."

"I don't know why you refuse to believe me," Buchanan's voice cracked. *To tell the truth, he was scared to death.*

The Fort Fisher ferry slip loomed in the near distance. To the north the sky was graying and the river was beginning to show a frothy chop. Through the haze, he thought he could see the little red panels of the phone booth.

What if Cammie wasn't available by phone?

His stomach cramped and his sphincter tightened. Proudly, he remembered he'd never shit his pants in combat under fire.

Careful. There was always a first time for everything.

"Look, I haven't seen or heard from Penny Wagner since I got those letters and talked to her on the phone at the Hotel Utica. But, you win, I want this over with. I'll try to call my witness as soon as we hit the ferry slip."

Under his shirt, a cold bead of sweat trickled down Buchanan's spine and slid into the crack of his ass. Panic gripped his chest.

"Cuff him. I don't wanna take no chances," Crump said.

"No, wait. Come on, no need to lock me up. Just let me make one call. There's a phone booth right there." Buchanan pointed as they neared the dock.

"One call. It better be good, or else I'm going to have to officially detain you." Crump's hand moved to his gun.

The ferry was making way now carefully between the pilings of the slip. The crew was already standing by.

"OK, go with him, Puckett, and let him make his call." Mack Jones turned back to Buchanan. "By the way, where's your car? I'll get on the radio and call Dowdy and have him get his kit and take samples from those seat cover stains. OK?"

They had started down the stairwell in the companionway.

"If I can get my party I can clear this whole thing up then I'll get my car myself and take it to Dowdy. After that we can just all go our separate ways."

"I wouldn't count on that," Crump said as he hit the bottom step and stepped out in the light.

"Let him make his call, then we'll see. Doc and me'll bring the car," Mack said. "Take him over there, Puckett." He pointed to the phone booth.

As soon as the retaining chain went down, Crump followed as Buchanan walked nervously across the dock and slipped into the airless old-fashioned booth. Closing the door, he dialed in Cammie's private number and then his credit card and waited for the connection.

Mae picked up on the second ring. "Sorry, Mr. Forbes, Mrs. Brawley can't be disturbed."

"But I have to reach her. This is life or death. I gotta talk to her right now, Mae."

Sweat was rolling off his forehead now. The back of his shirt was wringing wet.

Idly, Buchanan watched an albino spider already trying to rebuild its web in the corner where he'd knocked it loose when he closed the door.

Life ain't always easy, he mused telepathically to the spider.

He watched Maggie drive her car slowly off the ferry and move it to the side of the pavement out of the line of cars. She rolled her window down and waved.

Mae came back on. "Mrs. Brawley said to tell you she'd be tied up all day. She was sorry, but not to waste your time."

"Mae, did you tell Mrs. Brawley this is life or death? I'm not kidding."

"I'm sorry, Mr. Forbes. I'm just telling you what she said." She softly broke the connection.

Buchanan went completely numb. Slowly he replaced the phone back on the cradle and slumped forward with his head on his forearm. Then he opened the folding door and stepped out into the fading sunshine.

"She's in conference, but I left word..." His voice cracked. His head was spinning.

"I wonder why I ain't surprised." Crump was obviously overjoyed.

"I'll try again later, and she knows to call me at home. Just trust me on this. Please. Please just let me go unrestricted this afternoon. I need to go to work. I've got to keep my job...I can get Maggie to drop me across the river at Leland where I left my car. I'll save Snoopy the trouble and drive it by the station, I swear..."

BAAAANNNNGGGALANG!

Buchanan flinched at the loud clattering behind him. He turned to see the sheriff had kicked an empty beer can and sent it skittering down the dock.

"Shit-fire! Now we've got a mess on our hands, for real."

"Whassamatta?" Puckett Crump asked.

"I just called Snoopy Dowdy on the two-way. He's gone. Just up and disappeared."

"Gone? Dowdy's gone? I don't understand." Crump said, confused.

"No, goddamnit, not Dowdy. I said I just talked to Dowdy," the sheriff growled.

"Who's gone?" Crump began again and gasped. "Not Lindamood?"

"Yeah, Lindamood. What the fuck you make of that?" Mack Jones kicked at another empty can and missed. "The Lockfaw woman's missing too. She didn't show up for work."

Buchanan grabbed the sheriff's arm and spun him round. "I'll tell you what I make of it. They're both guilty as homemade sin. I been trying to tell you that. Did you put a bulletin out on them..."

"Of course, what'cha think I am?"

"Don't tempt me, sheriff," Buchanan smiled and winked at Doc, smelling victory now.

Doc shook his head and laughed out loud.

The sheriff gave them both a scathing look and turned back to Crump. "There's another thing. Dowdy said that Rivenbark woman that Dr. Martin treated for bleeding at the hospital finally talked. She told him that it was a doctor did her in a motel room up north of Scott's Hill, Hampstead Lodge, the first Friday night in March..."

"See, I told you," Buchanan counted up the days inside his head.

[384]

"That was the sixth. I didn't even have my job interview until the ninth, that following Monday afternoon."

Buchanan was jubilant now.

"Oh, shut up, I can count. Besides, that doesn't prove a thing!" he snapped, and turned his back on Buchanan. "But listen to this, she told Doc Martin that this guy had his initials embroidered on his cuff...want to take a guess what the letters were?"

"'E'...for sure?" Buchanan spoke right up.

Crump shot him a warning look.

"No, better'n that. This time you're really in luck. An 'L' too..." The sheriff begrudged Buchanan. "Said they were in some sort of a fancy little diamond shape..."

Buchanan stopped, looked heavenward and breathed a fervent prayer. "EL...bet your sweet ass...Eugene Lindamood. Thank you, Jesus, free at last!"

Chapter Eighty-two

WHEN OGDEN BRANCH CAME INTO THE ROOM he held the clipboard with Alma's chart.

Alma was already packed and waiting in the chair.

"Well, you're looking fit. Blooming like a rose. I hear you've been walking all around, challenged the orderlies to a race."

"Not quite, but I'm ready to get out of here." She managed a small laugh and held her side to ease the tenderness.

"I'm going to let you go, but first we need to have a chat." He turned the clipboard over and looked down at her chart.

"What's wrong?" She involuntarily reached down and touched her abdomen.

"Well, nothing, don't jump to conclusions now. It's just that the pathology report shows there were other nodes involved, six in all, not just the two suspicious ones, as we first believed."

"Oh, my God, you didn't get it all..." She gasped and clutched the chair. "Do I have to go back to surgery? Am I going to die?"

"No, not that. I don't think we need to operate. Nothing else showed up in any of the surrounding tissue. I still think you're looking good, but we want to be sure, maximize our odds."

"What's all this mean? What are you trying to tell me? You want me to have cobalt, right?"

"Well, that too, but I was wondering if you'd consider letting me send you down to Duke? They're doing some miraculous new chemotherapy there."

"Oh, I don't know. This takes me by surprise. If you think it's best. I'll have to find a way, of course. You know I will. How long will it take? My sister could drive me down."

"That's just the point. You'd have to go there once or twice a week. Maybe overnight…for several months at the very least, maybe longer. It's not going to be the most pleasant thing, and it's expensive. But, ironically, Buck's insurance with his former company is still in force and is going to take care of most of that. I already checked it out. I know you've made it clear you don't want to move back down that way, but it would be to your advantage. If it were me, I would leave no stone unturned. I'd move mountains to go down there. I thought with Buchanan working in Raleigh, well, of course, I don't know the circumstance…"

"Well, Buchanan's moved down to Wrightsville Beach. That's quite a way from Raleigh, but we still have the Raleigh house."

"Good. Well, think about it. See if you could work something out. I'd like to refer you right away. I wouldn't want to delay."

"Duke, huh? OK, if that's it, I'll give Buck a call and try to work things out."

"Call me Monday and let's talk again. I could start you right away if you have someone to drive you down." He touched her hand. "Take it easy now, and don't look for things to worry about, OK?"

"OK…and Ogden, thanks." She squeezed his hand. "Now, tell Jan to come bring the kids in here. I'm ready to have her bring the car around."

Alma looked at the vase of flowers the young candy striper had just brought in, hoping that the card would be signed with Michael's name.

The Women of the St. James Church.

Well, so much for that, she mused.

Michael had stuck his head in the door late Tuesday and said, "Hi! You're looking good. I'm in a rush. I'll stop by again."

Just that once.

Three days now and no other sign of him.

Plain enough, she guessed.

"Mommy, Aunt Jan's going to take us home." Garrett rushed into the room and almost tackled her when he hugged her legs. "And Daddy said we could have a dog."

Alma laughed and brushed away a wayward tear.

Chapter Eighty-three

IT WAS EARLY SUNDAY EVENING when Maggie walked into The Wit. Through the shadows and the smoke, she spotted Buchanan sitting at the far end of the bar.

"Hi. I kinda hoped I'd hear from you. Did you have any trouble from your boss-man?" She waved to Jimbo for a beer.

"Well, no. No sign of him. Everything's back to normal again, I hope. And, say, I did try to call, you know, more'n once or twice. Once a day at least since we took the famous ferry ride. I couldn't track you down."

"Last few days I've been decorating a big restoration over near Burgaw."

Jimbo brought her beer. Thirstily, she gulped half of it. "Well, I heard that Hank Long's in the clear. What do you hear about Lindamood? Has he turned up yet?"

"I talked to Snoopy this afternoon; nobody's heard a word. Apparently, Lockfaw drove to Miami. They located her car at the airport there. That's about all I know. I went by the hospital Friday to see Ted Harper, but he'd gone out of town. Vacation, his assistant said."

"Lockfaw, Miami. I'll be damned! You think she left the country? I'll just bet Lindamood's with her wherever she's gone. Him and those fancy monograms on the cuffs of his shirts."

"Yeah. Looks like they got him dead to rights. But I understand they're still having trouble checking out the dates and times. I just don't know…the whole thing's so damned incredible. To tell the truth, I kinda liked Gene." Buchanan shook his head.

"Not even my grandbabies will believe this one. I still can't believe it happened myself. Truth is stranger than fiction, so they say."

"For a while I thought I was a goner for sure. There for a moment at the end, I had this crazy urge to dive over the top rail of that ferry." Buchanan leaned the stool back and laughed over the buzz of background conversation, ever-rising as the early evening crowd drifted in.

"What do you hear from your wife? Her surgery? She going to be all right, you think?"

"Well, she's coming down to take some chemotherapy at Duke, supposed to be moving the boys back in the house in Raleigh next week if she's able. Her sister's going to drive them and stay a while until Alma's strong enough to get back on her feet."

"Well, I guess I knew you'd always go back to her."

"Don't jump to conclusions. She's coming to be close to Duke

Hospital. Her sister Jan is going to care for her, drive her around. Chemo's no piece of cake. But, I'm staying right where I am. I like it here, and the job looks like it might start paying off."

"Then you're not going to go back to her?"

"I have no plans. Certainly I'll be going back to Raleigh on weekends. I truly miss those boys."

"I hope it all works out...I really do."

"Thanks." Buchanan didn't look her in the eye.

"Buck, you know something? You're just so goddamn dumb." Maggie snorted and drank the rest of the beer.

"What do ya mean?"

"You'll go back to her. Spending every weekend in that house with her, old habits die hard. The pun is intended."

"Don't be so sure." He tried to sound convincing. "By the way, thanks again for everything. You saved my life, you know? I owe you a big one. I'll find a way to make it up."

"So you keep telling me."

"I guess I'd better get on back. I have some paperwork to catch up."

"OK, coward," She gave him a wilting look. "See ya."

"Sure..."

"WELL, SHIT!" BUCHANAN PARKED THE CAR off in the grass and cursed under his breath when he saw the light beside his apartment door had burned out. He groped his way through the velvet gloom, around the side of the house.

Fumbling in the darkness he finally opened the door and reached in to turn on the light.

"Don't turn that on!" The voice was a rough whisper coming from the tall oleander shrub behind him.

Buchanan's heart jumped into his mouth. Instinctively, he groped for the thick handle of the crab net that usually leaned against the wall outside the door.

He couldn't find it in the dark.

His senses quickened with an adrenaline rush as he jerked around, squinting into the shadows, trying to protect himself from attack.

"It's just me, Buck! Gene Lindamood."

"Lindamood, what the hell?" Buchanan moved his hands frantically again, still searching for the crab net handle, anything to protect himself.

"They think I butchered those girls, but I swear they've got me wrong. I can prove it, man."

"OK, but why come here?" Buchanan's mind was racing.

"I need to trust somebody. I thought I could talk to you. Leave off the light 'til we get inside...just wait'll you hear what I found out. Just hear me out. I need you to help me clear my name." The dim figure emerged from the flat blackness beside the oleander bush. Buchanan could see Lindamood gradually taking form as he was outlined against the stars, his facial features contrasted above the collar of his plain white dress shirt.

Watching warily, he thought of making a dash for the car but quickly dismissed the idea. The car doors were locked. He'd never get them unlocked in time.

"I don't know what you think I can do, Gene. You better call the cops, get it straight with them."

"All right, I'll call the cops, OK? I promise, but first I want you to hear me out. Come on and get inside and let me close the door. Standing here in the darkness is giving me the creeps." Lindamood moved toward the door.

Inside, Buchanan closed the door and fumbled for the switch.

He could smell Lindamood's sweat. A breath of onion mixed with alcohol trailed in the air, as the shadowy form brushed past him through the narrow doorway.

Shielding his eyes, he blinked hard against the sudden light.

The young doctor's clothes had seen better days and his hair was uncombed and badly needed a trim. With a heavy stubble of beard, Lindamood reminded Buchanan of Brad Pitt in a gangster role. He was wearing a wrinkled pair of khakis and a white shirt with the familiar monogram on the sleeve.

Lindamood's hands shook slightly as he reached across and pulled down the shade covering the window in the door.

"You look like death warmed over. Where the hell you been?" Buchanan's voice betrayed his nervousness.

Adrenaline subsiding now, Buchanan was struggling to conceal a tremor of his own.

"I took off when Norma Jean in personnel told me that redneck Southport cop had asked to see my file. I suspected all along who dumped that body in the swamp but I needed proof, a chance to clear myself. First I drove to Atlanta and I just got in from Charlotte about an hour ago. I've been waiting out there in the dark. The goddamn no-see-ums about ate me alive." He rubbed his arms and his hand went to the back of his neck.

"Proof? Proof of what? They've got enough on you to..." Buchanan didn't finish. He didn't want to panic the man.

"Yeah. I know. It looks bad all right, but I've got all the proof I need now to clear my name."

"I don't see how. It was you who used my car that night, and they've matched the bloodstains, everything, you'll never get out of that. And where's Jaynie Lockfaw gone? They found her car down there."

"Lockfaw, how the hell would I know about Lockfaw? Found her car? Down where?"

"Miami, at the airport."

"I'm not surprised. She was the brains, set the whole thing up. They've been together quite a while."

"Been together? Who? Come on, man, the Rivenbark woman identified you by the monograms."

"Monograms?"

"Yeah. On your shirts, EHL"

"Not me, it was Ted."

"Ted? Ted Harper?"

"Harper's the one. When the Rivenbark girl gets a look at me, she'll clear my name. I'm sure of that at least. Harper and I don't look anything at all alike."

"But what about the car? You had my car the night that woman's body was dumped in the swamp. They've matched the bloodstains and seat cover fibers. They have tire prints too."

"That's just it. I gave Harper the car key that night at the hospital. I had an emergency. Harper said he was coming back here with Lockfaw to complete the liquor run. Remember, it was Lockfaw that finally returned your key. Don't you get it now?"

"But the monogram? Are you telling me he borrowed one of your shirts to set you up? I have a lot of trouble with that."

"No, goddamn it, he's always worn a monogram on his shirts, a lot like mine…"

"But his initials aren't the same. His name is Ted…T…H…" Buchanan said.

"But his name's not Ted, that's for Edward. Don't you see? And his middle name is Leonard…"

"Edward…by God, I never thought of that. But, still…" Buchanan scratched his head. "That's ELH. Are you saying the Rivenbark woman got the initials out of sequence? Is that it?

"No, not out of sequence. Not that at all. Think about it. His monogram is E-L-H, but the way he has it done it's…"

Lindamood stopped speaking and moved to the desk and turned on the lamp. He found a pencil and drew a little diagram on a memo pad:

He held up the characters for Buchanan to see. "See how the smaller 'E' and 'L' bracket the larger 'H'? Don't you get it, now?"

"I'll be damned. I never thought of that. But Ted Harper? He's a pharmacist. Where'd he get the medical know-how to do something like this?"

"He was kicked out of med school in Georgia. That's why I went to Atlanta. Guess why the med school gave him the boot?"

Buchanan shook his head and considered him more thoughtfully now.

"He was suspected of botching an abortion on a girlfriend. He'd stolen a speculum and some gynecological instruments from the hospital. The girl hemorrhaged badly and almost died, but in the end they hushed the whole thing up. After that, Harper's family hustled him up to Augusta, and he transferred to pharmacy school."

"Why didn't she prosecute?"

"She was just a poor, scared, cotton mill girl. Ted's family are all doctors, practically gods down there. The Harpers have money, a lot of pull."

"Say, I just remembered something. You don't smoke do you?"

"No, sorry." Lindamood thought Buchanan was asking for a smoke.

"I'm not asking for a cigarette. I just remembered there was a cigarette butt in my car when I got back last Sunday night. The cops said it had a fingerprint. Someone took my car for a joyride, the night Penny Wagner bled to death in Myrtle Beach. Doesn't Ted Harper smoke?"

"Sure, I'll bet my life that fingerprint is his."

"But, what about Lockfaw? How does she fit in?" Buchanan was confused. "I always thought you and Lockfaw had something going…"

"We had a steamy moment or two when I first got here. My wife and I don't have much between us and Jaynie's a swinger. She was Harper's sometimes-mistress back in his traveling days in Charlotte. Nursed at Baptist there. She followed him when he left the Aster pharmaceutical job and came down here. They both like to party, and you know how Ted is for chasing women. If you cut his head open, a million little pussies would fly right out. He probably got started by aborting himself out of trouble and one thing sort of led to another. And, I imagine he had a sweet thing going. If you're careful and have good instruments, mostly all you need to do is violate the os, and nature does its work. A thousand clams a shot. It's easy money. I know he's been spending money like it was going out of style." Lindamood stopped to take a breath.

Buchanan nodded, remembering about the houses Ted told him he'd bought.

Lindamood went right on. "My guess is that he got in over his head buying local real estate. Since the movie people followed Dennis Hopper here, he was buying everything in sight. He was buddies with Hank Long and probably got the idea of using the IUD from him. I talked to some of my old profs up at Charlottesville. Using the IUD as an abortive device would ordinarily be almost foolproof, but the G/uL TechnologiesT3 has some inherent structural anomaly that raises more hell in a pregnant uterus than anyone can explain. The whole technology is too new to theorize right now. Anyway, I know the cops tried to hang this thing on you. I want you to go with me when I go down to tell 'em what I know."

Buchanan was still hesitant. He'd had enough of cops.

"If your story's true, when the Rivenbark woman gets back from Tennessee, her ID of a mug shot of Ted is probably all it'll take to convince the cops."

"Aw, come on, Buck, you know how cops are. They'll want to fuck me over, take my prints, lock me up 'til she gets back. I'm a doctor. Can't you just imagine what that'll do to me? It's bad enough as it is. I may have to start over somewhere else, anyhow. My reputation's suffered enough already with the rumors about the wild parties at the Sugarshack flying around. I heard that Snoopy quietly closed it down."

"Yeah. Snoopy Dowdy had a friendly talk Wednesday night with Ted and Hank, I hear."

"Well, I'm glad. Come on, Buck. You've got to help me. I heard about what you went through, trying to convince those bastards. Please, man. After all, you're the one who sicced 'em on me in the first place. You owe me. Now everyone's looking to burn my tail." Lindamood gripped him by the shoulders. "Come on, man, help me. You should know better than anyone how it is when you don't have a friend and your ass is hanging in the breeze." He earnestly searched Buchanan's face for a spark of support.

The phone call to Cammie crossed Buchanan's mind.

"I guess I do, at that. OK, but first, let's make a plan."

Buchanan stepped back and pried Lindamood's fingers from his arm.

"All right, I'm so tired I can hardly think. Just tell me where to start." Lindamood collapsed on the sofa.

"First, calm down. Right now, I think we could both use a drink. We have to think this through. The last time I went off half-cocked, I damn near wound up diving over the top rail of the Southport ferry."

Chapter Eighty-four

TRY AS HE MIGHT TO REMAIN CALM, Buchanan's heart leapt up when he saw Cammie in the distance as he turned Alma's new Tahoe into the parking lot off Western Boulevard.

"Look guys, they're here," he said.

The boys all started to shout before Buchanan finished parking the car.

"There's Amy, Daddy, see? Tyler, too, Way up there, by the swings and sliding board. Come on, let's hurry up."

"Hey, Tyler, Amy, we're moving back." Garrett got out, waved and bounded across the pavement. His stubby legs started up the path.

His older brothers were grinning and waving too, slightly embarrassed by Garrett's childish enthusiasm.

Finally, Grayson could stand it no longer. He gave in and followed Garrett at a trot. The others stepped up their pace with manly Granger bringing up the rear trying his best to act nonchalant.

Buchanan knew Granger didn't want to let on to Tyler how much he'd missed her. They'd been writing back and forth.

"What a nice surprise," Cammie said, a bit ill-at-ease and turned her head to look at the children all talking at once in wild confusion. "When did they get back in town? Tyler told me Granger wrote to say that his mother will be going to Duke. It's not bad, I hope?"

"Bad enough. They found more positive nodes than they originally thought. Still, they think they got it all. She's started with cobalt. They're going to give her chemo at Duke, not a pleasant thing, I've heard."

"I'm sorry she's faced with that, but we should be grateful when we consider the alternative."

He shrugged and looked away, afraid to look at her again. Being close like this took the heart right out of him.

"Well, like old times," she murmured, uncomfortably.

"Yeah." He kicked at a stick and missed.

"I'm sorry I haven't been in touch, but you can imagine how it's been with me."

Buchanan nodded and took a deep breath and started in, "I'm sorry I lied to you about the girl. Sorrier than you'll ever know. I hated it. I'll always have to live with that."

"Well, it's over now. I'm sure you're even sorrier for the rest of it."

He remembered his less than convincing performance as a lover at

[393]

Pawley's. Pretty obvious. What more could he say of that?

In the distance an auto horn. Closer by, a mockingbird.

"I actually didn't expect to see you here. I told the kids that you were much too busy now, what with the political campaign and everything. I tried to call, you know."

"I know. The way things happened, I just thought it best that I didn't call. I was crazy to think it would have ever worked anyway. I want you to know that Lew Dowdy called me from the beach. I told him I could vouch for you the weekend they found the girl. He told me he would keep my name out of it if he could. High level politics, I hope you understand."

"Sure. I'm sorry you decided not to run. I can't help but ask. Was my being mixed up in that mess the cause of your dropping out? I'd hate to think I'd cost you your chance. I thought you'd win. You'd have made a great senator, would have gotten my vote, anyway."

"No, it's nothing to do with you. It was strictly hard-nosed politics. To tell the truth I'm just as glad. After I got through that inquisition by the little asshole from the Madison Avenue PR firm, I was having second thoughts anyway. All's well that ends, they say."

"Sometimes our tragedies turn out to be our blessings in disguise."

"Aren't you the philosophic one?" It was good to hear her laugh again. "By the way, whatever happened to the *Esquire* piece?"

"Believe it or not, they took it. It'll run when Mallone's new Stalker MacKnight is released in September. I'm doing another piece on IUDs and abortion for Hersh Roberts at SNS." He looked anxiously to see her reaction.

"Why not? Sooner or later someone will do it. You can bet on that."

"I guess. They always do."

"I'm taking the girls down to Pawley's for our annual summer trek the weekend after the Fourth. Seems like it gets shorter and shorter every year."

"Time...it runs out. Keeps foreshortening everything," he said.

"My, you are running deep today. Well, it's getting late for me. I have to go," she said and called the girls.

They made small talk for another few minutes, then Cammie turned to take the girls.

The boys followed the girls down the hill, grumbling.

"It was good seeing you. I'm glad we had the chance to talk."

"Me too. My girls really missed the boys. Maybe we'll be seeing you again, now that Alma's here?" Cammie stopped at the car door.

"Sure. Lunch some Friday?"

"Almost like old times?" She put her things in the car.

"Almost. Nothing ever stays the same. Take care."

"I will. And you keep well."

As they pulled out, the radio in Cammie's car was playing Gordon Lightfoot. "*That's what you get for loving me.*" The lyrics drifted on the summer air.

Dedicated from who to whom, Buchanan wondered now.

Chapter Eighty-five

MAGGIE WAS AT THE WIT.

"The usual," she told Jimbo. She'd suddenly switched from Chevas to beer again.

"Heard you just got back from the Caymans? A little visit to see your social security?" Buchanan said as he climbed aboard the adjoining stool.

"News travels fast."

Buchanan signaled Jimbo for a beer and said, "Guess you heard the news?"

"You mean about your visit from Lindamood and the Ted Harper thing. Craziest thing I've ever heard. I still can't believe any of it, but I wish we coulda put that ferry ride on film. Shades of the Spanish Inquisition. Should make a great piece for the magazines."

"Maybe even a book. And now that *Esquire's* about to discover me, I need to get back to the writing while I'm hot, put some money in the bank. My boys will be ready for college before I can turn around."

"Yeah. Mine are practically grown already."

"I was with the kids last weekend. Can't believe how much they've grown. We're going to have a big July Fourth weekend…going up tomorrow, leaving at the crack of dawn."

"You're going back again tomorrow? I told you, you'll soon be back living with her."

"That's on the rocks. But I still have the weekends with my sons. And Saturday's the Fourth, fireworks and a band concert, everything. They're looking forward to that. I really miss those guys."

"What I'll never understand is why you've let it go on this long. Why did you marry that bitch in the first place?"

"In high school, I was the quarterback and she was the cheerleader. Right out of the movies. Afterwards, I traveled a lot. It worked because I was always gone. Anyway, it's over. She's got a hard row with the chemo, but the marriage is just a formality now. I told her that."

"Then why don't you bring the boys down here with you? You said they love the beach. Time's a'wastin.' Summer's almost gone."

"I don't have room. With Alma's medical bills, the season rent here would break me up."

"They could stay with me."

"Thanks, but that would really put you out."

"Not at all. I'd be glad to have the company. Ryan and Melly are in Blowing Rock with their granddad for a while. Besides, I'm living in the new house now. I've got the room. You can keep your distance, keep it on the up and up."

"Maybe I'll think it over. That would be very nice of you."

"Don't wait until the summer's gone. I'd love to have 'em, be more fun for me than them, I bet."

"Knowing you, I bet it would."

"So why not do it? Take a day or two off. We could go fly a kite again, like you did with Melly and Ryan that time we rescued the turtle eggs."

"Sounds tempting, but Alma would probably smell a rat."

"So what? I thought I heard you say it was on the rocks."

"Well, yeah."

"How's that fancy lawyer woman doing nowadays? I heard she's not running for that senate seat."

"That's true, but I'm sure she'll do just fine." He pushed his stool back and sat down his empty glass. "How was Lewis?"

"He hasn't called in two weeks. We're not lovers anymore. He wasn't in the Caymans when I went down, if that's what you're driving at. I still do some work for him. I'm decorating a new place down there. Flash and Filigree. I have a business of my own, you know?"

"Which reminds me. Have you ever heard Lewis talk about the off-shore banks?"

"Some. I know he does some banking down there. After all, he owns the Moon Bay Lodge, and he's building Flash and Filigree outside of Georgetown. A lot of money comes in and out of there. Why'd'ja ask?"

"Oh, I just remembered you told me that you'd taken your child support and squirreled away a nest egg for your kids. I mean, I see all the things in the paper and novels about the Mafia laundering money in the islands. It's away from Uncle Sam's prying eyes. Just curious."

"I do have some money stashed. Lewis put me on to the idea. The Cayman banks are more discreet than the Swiss."

"When you fly down there, how long does it take? Are the connections good?"

"Not as bad as you might think. I take the redeye to Atlanta and go to Miami. Leave here at seven and I usually have time for a swim and cocktails before dinner."

"And you flew down and back over the weekend…"

"Takes all day just getting there. A trip like that actually isn't any fun. Spent most of the time in airports and on the plane. After you take off from Miami, it's still puddle jumping from island to island down there. Why? You thinking of making the trip?"

"Just curious about those banks, really. I wondered how it works… international financiers, movie stars and gangsters and celebrities…"

"Say, how much does *Esquire* pay, anyway?"

"Oh, hardly that much, I'm afraid."

"You're not planning on robbing a bank or anything? I mean after the ferry ride, haven't you had enough of dealing with the cops? Just count me out next time."

"Relax. I'm thinking about writing a novel. My hero has to get some cash out of the way of prying eyes." He smiled. "Don't worry. No more cops for this old boy. By the way, I'll never forget, you saved my life. I'll find a way to show you how grateful I am."

"You keep promising." She blew him a kiss and laughed.

"Well, you never know…"

"We could always sneak in a rainy day or a Sunday, Buck…"

"Lewis wouldn't like that at all," he said.

"Lewis is history. I'm young. There's got to be more in life for me…"

"No doubt. Well, take care," he said.

She saw him glance over at the sketch he'd done of her, hanging on the wall.

She smiled. "I knew the artist well."

"Best thing he ever did. We're talking art here, of course." He suppressed a self-conscious laugh.

"Yeah, he had the touch. Art, I mean."

"Well, keep well. Again…"

"You too." She watched him start to leave and then jumped down and caught him at the door.

"Wait up, Buck. You're so dumb, you know it?" She grabbed his arm and spun him around.

"Huh?…"

"To think you'd choose that stuck-up lawyer bitch. You gave up the best thing we both almost never had."

She watched his color rise. He had a helpless look.

"Don't look so scared. I won't bite…"

"So what? Maybe I am scared. Not of you, of myself. Look, if we started up again, sooner or later you'd just start talking all that marriage stuff. After what Alma put me through, I've had enough of taking prisoners to last the rest of my life. As for Cammie, what I found with you was making me too vulnerable. I liked it far too much. Cammie represented a way to insulate myself from you...from us. Cammie was my way out. I certainly didn't love her, wasn't in love, I mean. I like her. I respected her a lot. She was my best friend. And, Cammie was safe, she already has a husband. Just for the record, Maggie I really do care. But I'm not ready for strong feelings, yet. And I don't trust myself. I don't think I could just go back to sleeping with you and not..."

"Buck, what I'm saying is...well...I...maybe, I've learned my lesson. I realize I pushed too hard. What the hell. I really do love you. Quite a lot. If that scares you...too bad for you...." She gave him a pixie grin. "But the next time, if you'll give it a chance, it will be different. Why can't we just enjoy each other? No promises asked, none given? OK?"

"Where have I heard that before?" He looked down at her and laughed. "You really do know how to push my buttons. I'm just plain scared."

"I can't believe you're going to pass up the best offer you're going to ever have. Remember the *Captain's Paradise?*"

"Huh? Oh, your movie thing again. Yeah, I remember. I can have my cake and eat it too, huh?" He had to laugh.

"Sure, why not? You can trust me..."

"Yeah? Sure I can, but you still don't get it—can I trust myself?" He turned to leave and then stopped and faced her again. "Besides, having too much cake almost did me in. I'll be seeing you. After all, I'm not leaving town...."

He started to turn away.

"Damn it! Wait up, Buck. You know you really ought to take me up on the offer to keep your sons. Think about the boys. We could take 'em to Southport on the ferry, feed the gulls. I'll behave if you want me too—well, maybe. After all, I seem to remember you're a grown man. Why don't you just quit playing like you're the flipping victim? That act is getting old. Did it ever occur to you if you want to get laid, you're responsible for your own relationships with women? That's what this free-loving twenty-first century is all about."

Buchanan stopped and looked down at her. His heart was in his eyes.

"We had some moments you and me. Rainy days and Sundays, remember?" Her voice softened.

"Yeah, you're right. We did."

He looked back at his sketch of her hanging on the wall.

"What the hell? Let's do it. I'll bring 'em back with me Sunday, after the fireworks on the Fourth." He shrugged, then laughed and shook his head.

Why fight it?

There was something magic about freckles and beestung lips.